Rosalie Ham is the author of four previous novels, including her sensational number one bestseller *The Dressmaker*, now an award-winning film starring Kate Winslet, Liam Hemsworth, Judy Davis and Hugo Weaving. Rosalie was born and raised in Jerilderie, New South Wales, where her family still farm, and now lives in Melbourne, Australia. She holds a master of arts in ive writing and teaches literature.

Also by Rosalie Ham

*The Dressmaker*
*Summer at Mount Hope*
*There Should Be More Dancing*
*The Year of the Farmer*

# THE Dressmaker's Secret

## Rosalie Ham

PICADOR
Pan Macmillan Australia

Pan Macmillan acknowledges the Traditional Custodians of country throughout Australia and their connections to lands, waters and communities. We pay our respect to Elders past and present and extend that respect to all Aboriginal and Torres Strait Islander peoples today. We honour more than sixty thousand years of storytelling, art and culture.

First published 2020 in Picador by Pan Macmillan Australia Pty Ltd
This Picador edition published 2021 by Pan Macmillan Australia Pty Ltd
1 Market Street, Sydney, New South Wales, Australia, 2000

A catalogue record for this
book is available from the
National Library of Australia

Typeset in Adobe Garamond by Post Pre-press Group
Printed by IVE

MIX
Paper from
responsible sources
FSC® C018183

The paper in this book is FSC® certified.
FSC® promotes environmentally responsible,
socially beneficial and economically viable
management of the world's forests.

*For Dorothy*

# Chapter 1

**January 1953**

THE SEAMSTRESSES WERE reading an article on the coming coronation of Princess Elizabeth, the newspaper spread on the cutting table. Hartnell was indeed the right chap to create the gown for the queen-in-waiting on her big day, or so the royal expert said. They traced fingers over the sketches of her ancestors – Queens Anne and Victoria – at their coronations, their gowns signalling majestic tradition, stability and predictability.

'I walk past Hartnell's every morning,' Shirley said, 'and all I ever see in the window are those heavy boxy things.'

'But he's a royal couturier,' said another seamstress. 'The princesses always look lovely.'

'Well, we all know what Melbourne's fashion houses and couture salons will present for their winter coronation collections,' said Shirley. Some of the summer collections had been daring, perceptive and visionary, but of Salon Mystique's collection, the very same expert they were reading had declared that 'the mannequins had galumphed around in lumpy English imitations made of war-ration fabrics, hip-length fitted jackets and single-breasted buttons, and that most efficient of sleeves, the insert. Very 1947. The collection, as a whole, will satisfy Salon Mystique's usual clients, the respectable and traditionalists, but though there was no evidence of her in the summer collection, word has it there is new talent at Salon Mystique.

Shall we dare to anticipate a livelier contribution in the winter coronation collection?'

The new talent had in fact been working quietly at Salon Mystique for a couple of years now and was at that moment using a shaft of morning window light to illuminate the dull weave of a tweed afternoon suit and warm her chilly fingers. It was January, but the workroom – or *atelier*, as Mrs Flock had renamed it – had thick walls and small windows. The Salon Mystique staff were excited to be creating the suit, for a client sailing to England to attend the coronation. The new girl finished the bound button-hole and reached over to rummage through a bureau drawer, the thread whorls, dressmakers' hooks, buttons, bobbins and tins of sequins shuffling together as she searched for a better needle.

'Shhh!' Valda glanced over to the landing, where Mrs Flock's artificially cultured voice drifted up the stairwell. Valda's auburn hair was permanently waved and her features gathered in the lower half of her face, as if they had slipped. Her title was Head of Workroom but Mrs Flock had recently returned from Europe, and suddenly insisted on using French terms, taken from the small French–English translation dictionary she carried in the pocket of her white dustcoat. Valda's name tag now read *Atelier Première and Directrice Technique*, though Valda could not pronounce those words.

The new girl adjusted the tweed jacket over her knees. It was impossible, really, to do good work without her table, but every table was stacked with second-rate fabrics that Mrs Flock – or rather, *Madame* Flock – had shipped back from Europe to make the winter collection. Madame informed her staff that she'd attended dozens of the European spring collection shows and had returned 'with many new ideas for our winter coronation parade in April'. Madame's 'new ideas' were Europe's last season's fash-ions, and they were currently secured inside the steamer chests, solid leather and timber suitcases, tall as a man, their brass hinges locked. Soon, an army of outworkers would arrive to unpick them, make up toiles and patterns, and flog the resulting frocks as 'new winter coronation fashions'.

In her time at Salon Mystique, Tilly had detected no change in Mrs Flock's designs, no new silhouettes or fabrics; Mrs Flock had nothing to express. And despite Tilly's best efforts, at Salon Mystique the female form remained defined by rounded shoulders and constrictive corsets that thrust nipples chinward and strangled internal organs and their processes. On this day, the new girl was trying to create a buttonhole that didn't draw attention to itself. She had worked with precision – the rectangle and the lips centred and symmetrical, the tension consistent – but the tweed Mrs Flock had purchased was of inferior quality and it was not quite as discreet as she'd hoped. Over near her office, Valda was hammering a lace ruche with a thick needle, attaching it to a white poplin collar on a sateen blouse. She was using double thread, which meant the tension wasn't consistent, but Valda was Head of Workroom and so Valda did what Valda wanted.

When the light in the stairwell dimmed a little, the newspaper vanished and the seamstresses skipped lightly to their positions around the workroom and turned their backs. Mrs Flock appeared at the top of the stairs. Shirley once described her as 'a giant bodkin wearing a sewing machine cover'. It was assumed Mrs Flock covered her painfully thin body in large plain attire to affect a stylish and refined elegance.

She circled the workroom, pausing beside Shirley, the Head Cutter, or *Coupeuse de Tête*, who was staring at the fabric on the table in front of her. 'You cannot waste any more time over that,' Mrs Flock declared. 'Get on with it.'

She moved to one end of the workroom and composed herself to make one of her announcements. Unlike Valda's, Mrs Flock's features sat high in her face beneath a narrow forehead and a low widow's peak. Her chin was long, her upper lip short and her nose fled skywards shortly after leaving its bridge. The new girl was staring at her. Mrs Flock looked unwaveringly back at the new girl sitting beyond the steamer chests. Mrs Flock knew she disapproved of appropriating designs for commercial gain, but then she was just a country girl who'd arrived begging for a job. She was talented, granted, but she'd still be on that desolate hill above the rubbish tip in a small town if it weren't for Mrs Flock's misguided pause in central nowhere a few years prior. A gruelling, rattly train trip through the outback from Sydney had exhausted Mrs Flock's politesse, and so she'd disembarked, depleted, seeking revival in what she assumed was a quaint rural village in a vast peacefulness. Dungatar proved nothing but unsettling: a limbo of sparse khaki bush and unpleasant frumps prancing between dusty, understocked shops wearing exquisite couture. All sizes, shapes and classes strolled about the wasteland dressed to the standard of Marie Antoinette. Finding the seamstress responsible was not difficult, and now she was raising her Parisian-shaped eyebrows at everything Madame Flock produced and silently undermining the seamstresses around her. In her first week at Salon Mystique, the new girl had shown – wordlessly, effortlessly, precociously – that she possessed talent. It had to do with the architectural structure of a raglan sleeve which would not settle. She had seized the garment while Valda was downstairs, adjusted the bicep line so that it was parallel to the floor, then draped and pinned the inset, making the sleeve perfect. Valda was far from grateful and said it was a cruel act, and so the new girl retreated, the weary, frayed thread between her heart and her work finally snapped.

'I am a zipper,' she'd said to Shirley. 'A clever, functional accoutrement with infinite potential but only if given the right circumstance.' She contented herself with skirts, seams and hems, her heart and imagination burning for the new future and the home she was working towards.

Mrs Flock placed her long hands over her heart. 'Marvellous news: we have a new client, an important one.' She paused. 'Miss Post Office Picnic! We are to make a gown for her Miss Moomba quest. I see it as a pathway to Miss Australia, and on to Gown of the Year.'

The seamstresses clapped dutifully. Valda cried, 'Congratulations!' As Head of Workroom it would be her duty to attend to Miss Post Office Picnic.

Mrs Flock took the sateen blouse with its grubby poplin collar from Valda. The ruche was not sitting right and the décolleté was warped. She thrust it to the new girl, who was not clapping. 'Fix this then be downstairs in fifteen minutes to meet Miss Post Office.'

Someone gasped, and the other seamstresses looked to the new girl who had just been elected over Valda.

Mrs Flock then handed the tweed jacket to Valda, who was clearly stunned. 'It turns out this suit is just for the governess. It won't be seen at Princess Elizabeth's coronation after all. Finish it. But don't ruin it.'

Tilly's stomach tightened as if someone behind her had tugged her belt. Mrs Flock had delivered to her the dubious glory of outfitting Miss Post Office Picnic.

'Well, lah-di-dah,' Shirley said, not unkindly.

And the new girl replied, 'Obviously Miss Post Office Picnic hasn't read the summer collection reviews.'

The newly crowned Miss Post Office Picnic arrived at Salon Mystique wearing something from Olive Ferris – postwar surplus mosquito netting and tulle – and a brand-new pair of DeLiso Debs.

Tilly took notes while Valda measured and explained to Miss Post Office Picnic that at Salon Mystique they worked as a team.

'I am *Atelier Première* and *Directrice Technique*' – her pronunciation dreadful – 'so the seamstresses will make up your dress under my guidance.'

Miss Post Office Picnic explained her new life as a mannequin. 'Me mum said, "Jesus will arrive by train before you ever bloody win anythink," and, bugger me, I win the bloody Miss Bulleen competition. How's that?'

'Unbelievable,' said Tilly, checking that Miss Post Office's biceps were in fact eight inches in circumference.

After lunch, Tilly sat looking at the square of white sketching paper in front of her. Shirley, too, remained perplexed by a toile arranged on silk organza before her, though she was a natural dressmaker with the hands of an artist. Shirley checked the scrap of paper pinned to the corner again but could not reconcile the measurements with the design. Client number 114 had chosen vermilion, an unusual colour for a world darkened by parading royalists still mourning the death of King George VI. Shirley scratched her scalp through masses of dark brunette curls and positioned the scissors in her hand above the gaudy fabric. She put the scissors down. 'I'm glad this isn't in the winter coronation parade, it's going to look awful.'

It was a garment Tilly was curious about. The fabric was good, though the cloth was dyed rather than the yarn itself, but it didn't need cutting.

Shirley shook her head. 'It just won't do for that sort of figure.'

Valda went to her small office, which was basically a broom cupboard, and found the client's file. Her mouth turned down. 'I know that customer, she's theatrical, but I see what you mean – she's forty-four, forty-five, forty-four.'

The needle slipped in Tilly's fingers and a dot of blood swelled from her fingertip. She stuck it in her mouth, flinging the blouse aside.

'I'll tell on you if you ruin that,' Valda said, but Tilly was already winding the edge of her white coat tight around her finger, willing her pounding heart to cease. It was the measurements; forty-four, forty-five, forty-four. An image came to her of Sergeant Farrat one hot afternoon, drinking tea on a country verandah, a damp orchid in a lovingly recreated Rita Hayworth ensemble, the fine sleeve seams straining to contain his shoulders and the brim of his hat drooping with crepe-paper roses caught in netting, like dead budgies. Before she could stop them, her thoughts went to Dungatar and the handsome, curly-haired man standing in her little house appraising her wraparound magenta gown. 'Dangerous,' he'd said, and pulled her to him.

Tilly shut down those thoughts, pulling tighter on the cloth around her stinging finger. The past that Sergeant Farrat and Tilly Dunnage shared was one that needed distance, and so they had agreed to go their separate ways, get on with life – unless it was necessary, or worse. Why was he seeking her out now? What had happened?

Shirley crossed her arms. 'I'm not doing that to a nice piece of silk, even if it is the colour of a bonfire. You cut it, Valda. You're the *Prem-ee-air*.'

'Exactly, and you are the *cutter*,' shot back Valda. 'You're the one who did the *diploma* course.'

Shirley sighed and picked up the scissors. 'Here goes.'

'Don't!'

The two women stared at the new girl.

'It needs only one seam.' Tilly pointed her bleeding finger at a Stockman, a toile pinned in place. 'Use that toile on the Stockman, just drape a length of fabric onto it.'

'We don't do that kind of draping here,' Valda said, turning her back to them. The lesser, two-year trade course had not taught

Valda the art of self-expression through draping, and so she remained unable to solve a technical problem with her fingers. It was the diploma-course seamstresses who made toiles.

Tilly went to the first aid tin, bandaged her finger and unfurled a long piece of calico. It was possible, she thought, that there were others with barrel-shaped figures who were bold enough to demand an obscure Dior-inspired design.

'Is there an ostrich feather?' she asked.

They looked at her, confused.

'I can't see one,' said Valda.

'Are we doing accessories?'

'Yes.'

The three seamstresses all turned, startled, for Mrs Flock was there, as if she had been lowered by thread. 'The client has suggested that you will know what to do with the ostrich feather.'

Tilly felt the resentment in the room thicken, then Mrs Flock added, 'But she said nothing about draping.'

For the benefit of the other apprentices and seamstresses, Tilly met Mrs Flock's gaze. 'I will drape the material to divert the eye downwards and the seam at the back will have a further mini-mising effect. But the fabric will reveal its hidden talents and secrets when I confront the three-dimensional step of the design process, that is, sculpting on the form.'

Mrs Flock crossed her arms. 'Drape,' she dared, and watched the seamstress fearlessly drag the biggest of the two dressmaker's stands to the meagre window light. She held the calico in front of her like a towel and embraced the Stockman. Deftly, she pinned and draped the material around the thick form, letting it fall, shaping it around the bulky curves. She circled, carefully pinning fabric to the toile, rolling it up and under, letting it slip so that it clung in even creases to drop in warm symmetrical folds, the other seamstresses mesmerised by the way her fingers worked – no one else pinned so visually, it was as if the image travelled from her imagination down her arms to infuse the fabric with life. As the miracle continued, the bodice took shape, like Aphrodite emerging from marble. Even Tilly felt a little inspired.

Valda said, 'Dorothy Lamour wore a sarong dress like that in *The Jungle Princess*.'

Mrs Flock added, 'And Dior had one in his spring-summer collection of 1948.'

'Yes,' Tilly said, 'but it's how the simplest of lines work, the art of draping and the personality of the dress.'

'Just make one up in the vermilion silk.' And with that, Mrs Flock turned and wafted down the stairs.

Shirley shuddered. 'She doesn't even make the boards creak when she walks over them.'

'She can probably walk through walls too,' Tilly replied, and Shirley laughed.

Valda did not. 'You'll hide the buttons in that seam, won't you?'

Tilly shook her head. 'A zipper.'

A zipper. In couture. Shirley was fascinated, but Valda was dismissive. 'Only an outworker would do a thing like that.'

At Salon Mystique, the flair and natural ability of the outworkers went unacknowledged for the sake of profit. The clever seamstresses – mostly women – toiled in cramped rooms in stifling houses, unpicking the bargain couture Madame brought back from Europe. Patterns were made and European imitations pumped out for the plump, skinny, short, tall, long-waisted, big-hipped, bow-legged, shallow-bottomed and beautifully proportioned hoi polloi of suburban Melbourne.

'I'm making this garment for an individual, a particular client, and the dress will support a zipper,' Tilly declared, and then said, thoughtfully, 'This gown is not to impress or to change or disguise, it's actually to make someone more themselves. He, I mean *she*, will be happy with a zipper.'

'We'll see what Madame Flock's got to say,' Valda said.

Shirley speared Valda with her big green eyes. 'You do that, Valda. Can't have anyone being better than they're meant to be around here, can we?' She turned to Tilly. 'Where'd you learn to drape like that?'

'Paris,' she said, proudly. 'I learned from Madame Vionnet at her salon on Avenue Montaigne, way back in 1937. In her hands, fabric was like music.' Tilly didn't go on to say that her time with Madame Vionnet was sabotaged by war or that she was sent to Spain to source fabric for Madame Vionnet's friend, Balenciaga. It was difficult – consumption was cut to 50 percent – but she had contacts in London and fine dresses were still made and sold, mostly to actresses and women who held a 'couture card'. Some houses even sold to profiteers, the wives or mistresses of German officers, or black marketeers who had made money from stolen Jewish property. Tilly liked to imagine those clients against a wall, facing their fate dressed in Balenciaga.

The form in front of her would become a fat red-orange thing, but it would be a beautifully balanced, *well-constructed* thing. The seamstresses standing around her and Shirley were numb with awe.

Valda said, 'Where would you put a feather on such a flash towel?'

'Looking at this creation, Valda, tells me that the client does not possess the delicate décolletage required to *explain* such a gown, so I would suggest the feather distract from that.' She found a feather and placed it across the bodice, and Shirley said, 'Gee whiz, that's perfect.'

Shirley glanced at Tilly, looking chic in her red silk cheongsam collar, which peeped out from her white dustcoat. If she hadn't been certain before, Shirley was positive now that the country girl would not be contained by the thick walls of Salon Mystique.

\*

At the end of the day, the seamstresses hung up their white coats and rolled their scissors, tape measures, pins and threads and thimbles and chalks into their chamois purses. As the seamstresses from the back room filed through to the stairs, they stopped to look at the silk gown in the middle of the workroom: a swollen Dorothy Lamour, a ludicrous superstar standing in a puddle of light, and Tilly was again taken back to Dungatar and the ugly gawping women. Tumbling along behind came the sergeant and her smiling mad mother and then her boyfriend and his grief-stricken family. But she couldn't blame them for her pain. She'd gone home anticipating a short stay with Molly, but her needle-point skills had kept her there, saved her, then betrayed her. Now here she was, the sad mess of her life enduring and another past from which to flee. And today that past was calling her, and her world was about to shift again, seismically. First, Miss Post Office Picnic had arrived, bringing with her a chance to rise, but at the same time, the vermilion silk organza rip-off was burning in front of her like a witch on a pyre, lighting the way for the past to collide with the present, and determine her future. She'd worn that dress the night her true love died.

Mrs Flock saw the girls off the premises, standing at the front door repeating '*Au revoir*' and '*Merci, mademoiselles*' as they filed past. Her Australian accent made no accommodation for French inflections.

From the Regent Theatre opposite, the paperboy watched. Clare, the glamorously aloof hostess and receptionist, held her compact up to catch the light and scraped the corners of her mouth with her fingernail. The seamstresses gathered around her. As usual, the girl he was most interested in stood just beyond the group, the drizzle around her catching the lamplight. On this day, she seemed particularly alert, glancing up and down Collins Street as she adjusted her hat and sank into her trench coat. She hurried east up the Collins Street hill, a furtive Marlene Dietrich figure between the soft glow of the streetlamps and the bright boutique windows of Le Louvre, La Petite, Georges, Oggs and the notorious photography studios. She ducked into the doorway of Number 9 Collins Street, a haven to artists, poets, musicians and people of literature, but no one was following, the paperboy could see, so she slunk quickly along, turned onto Spring Street and vanished.

From the front window of the house near the corner of Nicholson and Gertrude streets, Mr Short peered out. 'Spying,' he said.

'What?'

'That woman who came, the spy, standing out there in the drizzle dressed like Princess Margaret at the races.'

In the park opposite the boarding house, a thick woman in a bottle green A-line ensemble with a matching gold swing coat and a brimless, pudding-bowl hat stepped back behind the fig tree.

'You should go over to her,' said Mrs Short, a bulbous woman pressed between the armrests of a large verandah chair. 'Tell her to come back Sundays and follow Tilly Dunnage. See where she goes and then come and tell us.'

Mr Short, a small unshaven man in high-waisted trousers, said, 'If she does meet a man every Sunday then that would be his wife over there behind the tree. I can see why her husband would take a mistress: she needs every bit of that giant fig to hide behind.'

'Terrible. Some women just let themselves go,' said Mrs Short, whose knees had gone some years prior under the pressure of her weight.

Mr Short let the curtain drop and turned excitedly to his wife. 'We'll be hauled up before the judge as witnesses for some sordid ménage à trois case, you can bet your bottom on that one, dear.'

He bent down in front of his wife, hands on his knees like a Sumo wrestler peering under a cow, and, adjusting his legs, he flung his arms under his wife's fat arms. She locked her podgy hands together at the wrist, around his neck.

'After three,' he said. 'One, two, three . . .' Then he leaned back, gritting his teeth, his face red with strain, and lifted his wife from the chair. They balanced, knees and foreheads pressed together, bound by their arms, and inched around until Mrs Short's bottom hung above the bed. Mr Short relaxed his grip and his wife fell back, pulling him with her. He lay on top of her, panting.

'Thanks, Shorty dear,' she said, and they kissed.

She could see no one sitting in the cars along the kerb or loitering in the park opposite, but that didn't mean there wasn't someone hiding behind a tree. But she was chilly in the light summer rain so she skipped down the street, slipped into the foyer and made a dash for the stairs. Mr Short had left his wheezing, beached wife and was waiting.

'No mail today,' he said as she brushed past him.

She took the stairs two at a time.

'You never get mail from anyone.'

'I never write to anyone,' she mumbled, hanging her trench coat behind the door. The room was sparse and airy and her foot-fall on the floorboards sharp. Apart from a bed, a wardrobe and a small table supporting her sewing machine, there was an electric hot plate, toaster and a tin of ground coffee beans arranged neatly on a packing crate. A large west-facing window gave her plenty of light and an excellent view of Nicholson Street and the park opposite, and of any stalkers. She lifted the window and reached out to the branch wedged discreetly behind the neighbour's chimney. The galah said, 'Hello, cocky,' and shifted sideways on his perch, dragging his thin chain towards her. She unclipped it and scratched his knobbly scalp, and the galah dipped into her handbag, his tail feathers stabbing upwards, and brought out an apple core. He carried it up her arm in his beak, clawed his way to her hat and spread his wings for the ride to the wardrobe, where his birdseed waited with a tin filled with fresh water.

'Lucky cocky.'

She threw her hat onto the narrow bed, took a bottle from the wardrobe, poured herself a glass of wine and prepared a light dinner of dry biscuits, tasteless cheese and sliced ham. 'Oh, for a baguette and an olive.' She sat on her bed, her dinner on her lap. Beside her a picture of a grey-haired woman scowled from within the silver frame – Molly, tea-cosy on her head, sitting in a wheel-chair that dripped with wool threads, ribbons of torn material and necklaces of cotton reels. Tilly stayed perfectly still, her eyes on the photo, the definite line of her jaw gilded in fuzzy, reflected light, the planes of her face dark.

'Molly,' she said, and smiled.

Then she rolled a cigarette and climbed out to sit behind the chimney, where she smoked, gazing up at the dulled stars peeping through the clouds. In the park opposite, the Exhibition Building glowed in the lamplight and workers under their umbrellas headed home. A squat person wearing a pudding-bowl hat oozed out from behind the tree and moved away into the gloom. She pointed and said to the galah, 'My past has arrived.'


A little later, at the rear of an old milliner's shop in Darling Street, East Melbourne, client number 114 glanced up and down the lane and slipped quietly through the gate. She unlocked the back door, lowered all the blinds and, as she moved through the kitchen and workroom to the old shop at the front, turned the lights on. Again, she checked that the curtain was pulled tight before removing her hat and placing it carefully on an old milliner's block. She removed her coat, brushed the damp from it and hung it in the cupboard under the stairs. She went up to her bedroom where she unzipped her skirt, unbuttoned her blouse and kicked her shoes into the corner. Hoisting up her petticoat and rolling her step-ins down, she peeled off her stockings and kicked the warm, soft mass into the corner with her shoes. Then she luxuriated in scratching her hairy stomach. Later, comfortable in her cushioned armchair, wearing harem pants and Ali Baba slippers, she knitted, her thick hands working away in the light of the standard lamp. She sipped her gin and tonic and sighed, whistling a little.

Suddenly, she dropped her knitting and bolted down the stairs to the front door, her slippers scraping across the old English tiles. A plain envelope waited in the wire letterbox attached to the back of the door. She gently picked it up and turned it over in her big soft hands. On the back, printed in elegant type, were two words: *Salon Mystique*. Breathless, she went to the writing desk, took a pearl-handled pocketknife and sliced open the envelope. Then she carefully extracted the letter and, with one hand on her beating heart, read:

An appointment has been allocated for your first fitting.
Please telephone to confirm.
Thank you,
Madame Flock, Directrice de Ventes
Telephone: 861231

'Oh, my pretty hat,' she said, fanning herself with the envelope.

# Chapter 2

As always, Tilly's rest was filled with dreams, pictures and flashes from the past, those shrill women coming at her in ill-fitting couture, the corrugated lines on their faces gathered around squinting green eyes and protruding yellow teeth. And, always, the handsome face of a football hero: a beautiful man, open-mouthed, shedding a coat of brown grain, the tiny slippery seeds falling on her skin, tingling across her face. She'd wake in the night brushing her cheeks, crying, then force herself to think of her future, and her baby. Sometimes, she would doze again.

In the morning she looked at the cocky, his head still tucked under his wing, and said, 'Sunday tomorrow.'

The galah lifted his head, looked at her with one small black eye and tucked his head straight back under his wing.

She dressed, put the galah out behind the chimney with his bread crust and tin of water, slung her small rucksack over her shoulder and left the house, pausing at the gate to adjust her hatpin and scrutinise the passengers waiting at the tram stop. Then she studied the park opposite and the cars parked along Gertrude Street. Soon, she knew, the stalkers would step out in front of her. She pulled her hat low, shoved her hands in her pockets and set off to the work she no longer liked and the people she dreaded, eyes on the paving beneath her espadrilles.

Mid-morning, as the girls drank tea and looked resentfully at their daily biscuit – plain, sweet, one each – Clare stepped into the tiny kitchen and held up a large black dress. 'It's Mrs Drum.'

Shirley looked at Valda. 'I'm not doing it. I've tried. It's someone else's turn.'

Valda pointed at Tilly. 'She can do it.'

Tilly shook her head. 'I had Mrs Marten this morning.' Mrs Marten was a short-legged, long-waisted woman with the teeth of a carnivore. 'Mrs Marten wants a dress with bon-bon sleeves, a tall picture collar and a fan-fold pleated skirt with a train.'

'Well, you're so clever . . .'

'Mrs Drum's got that shoulder,' Shirley said, and Tilly's eyebrow rose.

Shirley explained: Mrs Drum was an heiress to a chain of butcher shops and had one shoulder bigger than the other from chopping meat.

'She says her new dress is the wrong size.'

Tilly put down her cup of tea, took the dress from Clare and inspected the bodice; the right armhole was bigger than the left, the bodice was lopsided and the seams split. It had been altered twice, at least.

Mrs Drum stood in the middle of the salon, and Lois Pickett came to Tilly's mind, a grimy bollard of a woman whose appearance at the Dungatar street stall guaranteed a fall in sales. But this woman, true to her name, was more bass drum than bollard. Tilly thought she should smile at Mrs Drum and her man-sized right arm, but found she couldn't. 'Good morning, Mrs Dumb.'

'Mrs *Drum*. What you people have done to me is –'

'I suggest,' Tilly interrupted, 'that we make something suitable for your actual shape.'

'I will not pay for shoddy dressmaking.'

'The dress looks shoddy because it isn't the right size or design for you.'

'It's the latest fashion, you silly girl.'

She had been called worse, but Tilly took the tape measure

from around her neck and said loudly, 'Let me check your measurements.'

Mrs Drum handed Clare her handbag. 'I'm size SW. Sometimes I'm a W, but not very often.' She stepped onto the small stool and spread her arms. The stool groaned, her feet strained the white straps of her sandals and her toes jutted rudely. Tilly found that Mrs Drum was also fermenting a little in her black frock, which explained why Clare, the receptionist, was standing as far away as she reasonably could in the small fitting room. Tilly reached around her bosom; Clare raised her notepad and pencil.

'Bust eighty-eight inches, waist ninety-eight, hips ninety.'

'That's a lie!'

Clare lowered her notepad.

Tilly replied, loudly, that Mrs Drum was in fact an XXW.

'Well, in that case you should have noticed that my size had altered when you measured me.'

'The dress has been altered, *expanded*, at least once, and I believe Mrs Flock measured you last time. Shall I fetch her?'

Mrs Drum fidgeted with her sparkling ruby necklace – entirely inappropriate for daywear. 'I paid forty-five pounds for that dress. That is a lot of money and I buy at least three dresses a season.'

Tilly folded her arms and raised an eyebrow. 'The dress fitted you last time you left the salon. It no longer fits you. That can only mean –'

'You can either do something or I will simply buy everything from Le Salon from now on. That is my final word.'

'We are happy to make you a new dress . . . for forty-five pounds.'

Mrs Drum drew a handkerchief from her brassiere and dabbed her eyes. 'I bought this dress specially to mourn the death of our monarch, dear King George.'

'He's been dead a year.'

'Queen Mary is unwell, I might need a black dress.'

'Mary might get better, and we're about to get a nice new queen. You could buy a new dress, perhaps royal blue?'

Mrs Drum began to weep and Mrs Flock swept through the curtains clucking and 'there-there'-ing, and stroked Mrs Drum like an old cat, and Tilly, to her great relief, was dismissed back to her plain sweet biscuit and cold tea, her thin patience thinner and pendulous Lois Pickett and Dungatar stuck at the forefront of her mind. She had been fitting awful people for far too long.

Mrs Flock slid into the tearoom. 'What were you thinking?'

'I was trying to save you forty-five pounds and forty hours' labour. The coronation collection looms and there are three chests of Europe's second-best upstairs that we'll have to remake.'

'It is not your place to be concerned about those things,' she said haughtily.

'Perhaps if someone was concerned, then this place would be a proper salon.'

Mrs Flock recoiled. 'Just do what you are employed to do.' She dropped Mrs Drum's dress on Tilly's lap. It was another sign, like the sarong dress: Tilly would use the same technique she'd used on the sergeant's matador suit three years before, though she'd use satin inserts to 'expand' Mrs *Dumb*'s costume and no tassels would be requested. She tossed the dress into a corner, ignoring her stunned co-workers.

'Thanks for trying,' Shirley said, and Valda sipped her tea.

That afternoon, when Clare arrived on the landing and directed Tilly to go downstairs immediately, Tilly replied, 'I'm fixing Mrs Drum's dress. Valda should go, she's Head of Workroom.'

'It's the sarong dress.'

Tilly felt the knot in the pit of her stomach pull again.

Valda asked, 'Is the client displeased?'

'On the contrary,' Clare said. 'Though it's obvious something plain and black would have served her better.'

What they didn't know was that the client also believed she looked good in a checked gingham cowgirl skirt. Tilly gathered her tools, squared her shoulders and followed Clare's slender mannequin's physique, the dressmakers' stands and machines passing dreamily, then alongside Valda's office they went and down the narrow staircase lined with photographs of models in unremarkable garments. They passed Mrs Flock's bureau and entered the main salon, skirting the gilded imitation chaise longue and the receptionist's desk, where Clare turned slowly, smiled and pulled the curtain aside. There, on a small stool in the middle of the fitting room, against a backdrop of creamy draped curtains, stood the pale, cylindrical form of Sergeant Farrat, his stomach straining against the parakeet-coloured dress and the thick brassiere-corset straps pinching down on his furry bare shoulders. His makeup was immaculate and his wig understated; he was beaming. Then his expression fell, taking the joy with it. 'Your hair,' he said. He had not seen her for nearly two years and Myrtle Dunnage no longer appeared fragile. Her chin was squarer, she was leaner, harder, beautiful, but still without the glow of joie de vivre.

She ran her fingers through her short dark crop. 'Much easier, but my hats are all too big now.'

'But it's so *un*becoming.'

'I'll grow it for you,' she said. She knew her short crop marked her as odd in a city full of stiff brown curls and neat buns, and she also knew that her cover was probably about to be blown. The thread holding her to her bloody past was unbreakable.

She circled the sergeant, scrutinising the drape. 'What do you think of your gown?'

'It's perfect!' she cried.

'You look like a Christmas bon-bon.'

Clare said, 'Oh!' and Mrs Flock said, 'I do apologise –'

'Oh, shoosh!' Client number 114 spread her arms. 'You remembered my shape so well! Do you think we should add little cap sleeves?'

'Yes.' Tilly smiled and stepped towards the sergeant. 'And we'll do some sculpting to give the illusion that you have a waist.'

'Oh!' gushed Farrat, touching his false bust. 'You could give me a waist! Truly?'

In the sparkling asylum office in a small town in far-flung rural Victoria, Marigold Pettyman and Beula Harridene were attentively watching the superintendent read a report. He closed one file and reached for the other and Marigold's fingers tightened around her handbag. Inside it was a letter addressed to Marigold's dead husband, Evan Pettyman. It was from the convent for the homeless and wayward and appealed to Marigold's late husband, 'a long-established patron', for money. But Marigold wanted the money. It was hers.

Finally, the superintendent stopped reading, put Marigold's yellow file on top of Beula's and squared up the sides. Marigold watched him go to the window, but Beula was focused on a vague shape in the corner, a globe on top of a filing cabinet.

'Most unusual,' he said, gazing into the sky. Beula started jerking about in her chair so Marigold pressed her foot on Beula's, and Beula settled.

'I feel better than I ever have,' Marigold declared, a little shrilly.

'You've made good progress,' the superintendent said. 'Both of you, so I have nothing against granting you supervised leave, it's just that Miss Harridene isn't an entirely suitable chaperone given she's eighty percent blind and somewhat deaf.'

'I can see a bit,' Beula said, addressing the globe. 'And I've got hearing aids.'

'We've known each other for thirty years. Beula's volunteered to be my companion and I will care for her as if she belonged to me.'

'And so will I. Out of the goodness of our hearts,' Beula cried, her voice thick and snotty through her crushed nasal bones.

The superintendent looked at the quivering, whippet-like woman with the startled bearing and nervous rash on her neck. Her friend, Beula, sported a dent in her forehead, a broken nose, a pink fleshy cavity in the middle of her face, and an undershot chin beneath a downturned mouth and two brown stumps where her eye teeth had snapped off at the gums. She'd been hit by a flying radiogram while attempting to visit a grieving friend at night, according to her file, though the superintendent was also informed that Miss Harridene was the town stickybeak. 'But,' he said, 'what's the point of attending the coronation celebrations and fashion shows if you can't see them?'

'We'll help each other,' Marigold begged.

'You'll stay at the Kew Lunatic Asylum, but you'll have day passes –'

'But my friend, Caroline Hawker,' Marigold continued, 'who happens to be my financial guardian's wife, has given me tickets for the Smalls Charity Coronation Ball, it's *the* ball to go to. We won't ever see a coronation again.'

'Unless the new queen dies in the next couple of years,' Beula suggested.

'Your guardian, you say?'

'Yes. Mr Hawker.'

The superintendent sat down at his desk. 'You say there are fashion shows?'

'Every day,' said Beula, and Marigold said they had three parades a day at Myer.

'My wife's keen on frocks.' The superintendent could do with a week alone with his hobbies, the gramophone on loud and as much whisky as he wanted.

'You will take a nurse.'

'A nurse?'

When they had gone, the asylum's resident psychiatrist came into the office and said, 'You're not seriously letting them go, are you?'

He shrugged. 'What harm can two impaired old hags from Dungatar do?'

'Stab someone? Burn a town down? Sell hashish cakes?'

'Yes,' said the superintendent, 'but think of the hysterics and bawling if we don't let them go, and with a bit of luck they might walk under a tram.'


As Tilly left at the end of the day, Mrs Flock stopped her. 'There will be dozens of coronation balls in every suburb – an epidemic of fundraisers, dances, fashion shows and street parties. Salon Mystique has a chance to be seen so we must make an impression at the Smalls Ball. From now on, your full attention will be on Miss Post Office. You will also consider some designs for the winter coronation collection. The others will focus on gowns for the rabble at the Commercial Travellers Association Ball and the Grand Charity Ball and the Lord Mayor's Ball and the like.'

It was an opportunity for an underpaid junior seamstress, and a responsibility.

'Your reputation will soar,' Mrs Flock added.

What Mrs Flock hoped was that *her* reputation would soar, but given the standard of dresses Salon Mystique ordinarily pumped out, the exercise might prove to be neither rewarding nor lucrative. Was it time for Tilly to soar? She'd been hiding in plain sight and now she was found, but Sergeant Farrat wasn't the only hovering spectre. Before her was an opportunity. Why not make a winning dress for Miss Post Office Picnic? Why not face up and cry, 'Here I am'? It might just bring her closer to a more satisfying future in dressmaking, to her own home and a brighter life.

'Mrs Flock, if I am to focus on the coronation collection *and* new clients, then you must allow me to design the signature pieces.'

Mrs Flock raised her chin. 'With the approval of myself and Valda.' She looked out the window. 'And if we don't attract new customers, *decent* customers, you'll be back doing seams and hems.'

By 'decent', Mrs Flock meant wealthy establishment clients – better than Le Louvre's clientele, more chic than La Petite's – and that's exactly what Mrs Flock deserved, for 'decent' customers were notorious for their rudeness with the seamstresses and their late payments, if they even bothered to pay at all.

On Collins Street, Tilly headed east. Sergeant Farrat stepped from the shadows and took her elbow so firmly that she asked if he was taking her to be arrested.

'Arrested? What on earth for?'

'The fire . . .'

'Oh, that.' He waved a hand dismissively. 'Well, they asked for it. And anyway, the District Inspector's report didn't even mention you.'

'I was very much enjoying a quiet life.'

Across the street, the *Herald* boy spruiked.

'Me too.' Client number 114 drew her close. 'This reunion of ours will be longer than our previous associations. And this time we must start off with complete honesty.'

At a previous reunion, she had asked about her mother and the sergeant had hidden his neglect of Molly by saying simply, 'Molly doesn't get out much these days.'

The sergeant directed her to a red 1936 Fiat Balilla – a four-seater with a soft ceiling that folded away – just the sort of car to turn heads in a crowded street. 'This is Mother's car. One of the things she brought back from one of her trips away. Now hop in, quickly, or me and my frock will be the ones arrested.'

'And I am in no position to post bail, Sergeant Farrat,' Tilly said, though he was very convincing in his dress.

'You can call me Horatio . . . as in Hamlet's fearless, trusted friend.'

Across the street, the paper boy called, 'HERALD!'

Tilly settled into the front seat. 'I need a trusted friend; I'm sure people keep *following* me.'

'The past is prologue,' the sergeant quoted, starting up his little car. 'It was possibly me, though my greatest attribute is discretion.'

She raised an eyebrow at his conspicuous maroon crepe coat and floral felt hat. 'Why did you choose the magenta sarong dress?'

'It was a memorably beautiful gown.'

'That very gown got me thrown out of the Dungatar ball and I ended up at the silo.'

'I'm sorry, and no one can change that night, but if I had asked for a tweed ensemble you'd never have been summoned, *warned*. I did show up at your place but your landlord told me that he disapproved of adultery, never permitted visitors, and then shut the door in my face.'

They drove to the end of Collins Street and turned right into Spring Street. 'You're not going to actually wear that red thing out, are you?'

'It'll make quite an impression at my club. You could get lots of customers, all sorts of unique people.'

'Madame Flock thinks Salon Mystique will make an impression at the Coronation Ball.'

The sergeant looked pained. 'Salon Mystique is the poor man's Le Louvre – it featured box pleats in its summer collection. No wonder it got terrible reviews.'

They pulled up at a small venue in Toorak, a single-fronted, two-storey terrace house sitting inconsequentially between two insignificant houses. A light burned on the first floor, but otherwise the house was shuttered and dark. The sergeant knocked, two kohl-rimmed eyes peered through a high letterbox slit and the door opened just enough for them to press through into a dim vestibule. The eyes belonged to a small woman wearing net stockings, running shoes and a sequined swimsuit with a shark fin attached to the back.

'Welcome to the Hippocampus Club,' she said, unlocking the door to the main venue. She seated them at a table against the wall. 'Your usual, Horatio?'

'Yes, please. This is Myrtle,' said the sergeant. 'Myrtle, I'd like you to meet Serenity, our hostess, emcee and judo black belt.'

'Myrtle? The priestess Myrrha?' From deep between thick eyeliner and long, long lashes, Serenity's eyes twinkled. 'Greek legend tells that you were ill treated by your father but a favourite of Venus and so she transformed you into a fragrant evergreen to keep you safe from ardent suitors.'

'It didn't entirely work,' said the sergeant.

Serenity lit a candle, shoved it into the neck of a bottle and left.

The sergeant removed his maroon crepe coat to reveal a sea-green linen shift. Tilly looked around for the cloakroom. 'Keep your coat with you,' the sergeant said, 'in case the police surprise us and we have to run for it.' He hung his coat over the back of the chair. 'For paid-up members the first drink is on the house then we use our own. The club is private, invitation only. It's hippocampus as in seahorse, not the brain.'

Serenity put two glasses of punch on the table.

Tilly sighed and lit a cigarette, relaxing into her chair and taking in the surrounds. The patrons in the tiny venue appeared to be faded showgirls, retired vaudevillians and eccentric maidens, handsome, baubled women and pretty youths. Most wore running shoes, and most would have benefited from wardrobe advice, but Tilly felt at home, submerged in the oceanic hue, with brightly painted fake coral bulging from the walls and paper seaweed hanging from above. She was sitting in an open clam, reflections of shifting water glancing across the walls. The hull of a boat curved from the dark blue ceiling alongside fishing lines with dead fish attached, and seagull legs. A male's torso swam across the ceiling, and seahorses dangled, like chandeliers, with their tiny babies around them. Mermen and mermaids reclined on the backs of floating papier-mâché groupers and octopi, and lurking in the shadows was a shark, dressed as the Police Commissioner. The menu offered sardine entree and fish patties with 'sand-coloured rice salad' or seashell pasta.

'Why did you introduce me as Myrtle?'

'No one's who they're meant to be in this place, everyone's being who they really are.'

'But you don't have another name for when you're dressed?'

'No. I'm still me, I just dress the way I want. It's complicated.'

'It is.'

'The famous actress Miss Nita Orland comes here to feel ordinary.'

A huge sea turtle stepped onto the stage wearing a piano accordion, while a woman wearing a pink suit of fish scales sat at a drum kit. At the piano, a large whale rolled her dark pectoral fins back over her thick arms and played the opening lines of 'God Save the King' with gusto, the grey fronds from her blowhole-hat waving. No one stood for the anthem; most people ignored the musicians until the sea turtle kicked in on the piano accordion and the perch brought the drums to life. The bartender, a tall sinewy woman wearing a glittering sequined skirt, led the clapping, her cut-glass earrings swinging in her hairy earlobes. In a bawdy baritone, the bartender joined the band to sing, 'Our happy King is dead, died in his royal bed, poor man is dead, he wasn't trained at all, couldn't even speak at all, now he's mute once and for all, oh-oh happy days.' When the performance ended the dim room applauded and rumbled, and candles flickered. Sergeant Farrat removed a bottle of sparkling wine from his handbag, uncorked it and filled Tilly's glass to the top while a group called Beautiful Losers sang a song about 'blowing up the natives'.

'It's an allegory,' the sergeant explained. 'It's about our Prime Minister bombing the desert to oblivion.'

'Radiation.'

'Some nights it's cocktails and recitals or political discussion, sometimes lessons on dressmaking, makeup and grooming. We read poetry, and of course there's bridge night for those fanatics. And there's nude night, weather permitting: a string quartet likes to perform naked. Tonight is irony night, and the Razettes perform.'

Tilly drank, the whale played some gentle music and the Razettes took to the stage. They were three older women, possibly in their fifties, slightly worse for wear, but nothing a good costume wouldn't fix. Razette number one placed a plank on her head and stood very still, smiling, while Razettes two and three poured champagne into flutes and placed them at either end of Razette one's plank. The plank tipped to the left dangerously, the drinks wobbled. Numbers two and three drank from the flutes to even the tides.

The sergeant arranged his hem across his knees. 'Do you visit the convent?'

'Every Sunday. I'm a volunteer, though they don't reduce the fees I pay.'

Razettes two and three replaced the champagne flutes on Razette one's plank and it tilted a little, again. They removed the flutes and added a splash to one of the other flutes.

'When will you be able to stop paying fees?'

Razettes two and three placed more champagne flutes on Razette one's plank and it steadied, perfectly balanced.

'When a rich maiden aunt I know nothing about dies and leaves me a fortune so that I can buy a house and retire, or at least work from home.'

Razette one raised her arms, and two and three placed hoops on her wrists, which she started twirling. The hoops sparkled. The music escalated, and two and three danced seductively. The drinks wobbled.

'Failing that, a frightfully rich husband?' he asked.

'Well, that's tempting tragedy, isn't it?'

'If he's rich it won't be such a tragedy.' He looked at her. 'I'm sorry, it's a bit soon for black humour. Are they kind at the convent?'

'They don't come bothering me, largely.'

Razette one raised a leg, hoops twirling, and the champagne flutes shifted and the sergeant turned to watch. Tilly wondered why he'd brought her to this place; why had he contacted her?

The plank tilted again, the crowd gasped, but Razette one remained, her leg raised, arms and hoops twirling, the glasses holding. Razette one lowered her foot and stood still, numbers two and three removed the hoops from her wrists. The crowd clapped politely. Above, a slight girl descended from the rafters on a pink ribbon, doing the splits in a diaphanous costume with strategically placed sequins. Razette two reached to retrieve the champagne flutes and the plank fell, splashing champagne all over the patrons on table four. The crowd went mad with happiness, and while the Razettes bowed and cleaned up their mess, the acrobat overhead turned somersaults and tied herself in pretty pink knots on her ribbon.

'I love your slacks,' the sergeant said. 'Are they mousseline?'

'Yes.' She held his gaze.

'I'm living at Mummy's. She's dead, dear Mummy, went in her

sleep, thank God. Oh dear!' He touched her arm. 'I didn't mean to imply anything –'

'People die, Sergeant Farrat,' said Tilly, leaning forward. 'Some of them senselessly.'

The air between them grew tense as thoughts of Teddy McSwiney arrived and faded.

'Look,' said Tilly, sitting forward, 'I know that in going back to Dungatar I became like them. I was responsible for Teddy –'

'Nonsense.' The sergeant slapped the table. 'I won't have it. We've been through this: don't let fear send you back into that mire. You have a responsibility now to be positive and nurture a new life.' He smoothed the fabric across his knees. 'Like I have.'

'You really have forgiven me for your losses?'

'As I said two years ago when we went our separate ways, it was high time I moved on from Dungatar, and as you can see, my new community is friendly, like-minded.'

They drank, and Tilly thought of the sergeant's lonely life in Dungatar, with Molly as his only friend, and even that was dangerous. She remembered walking to her mother's casket, which lay darkly in the meat safe behind Pratts, a shadow in a sad place, as Molly's presence had always been, and declaring, 'Pain will no longer be our curse, Molly. It will be our revenge and our reason. I have made it my catalyst and my propeller.' Then she howled from the top of The Hill, wailing like a banshee because she would not abandon the sour people of Dungatar.

'I should have cared for Molly better but it's the living we have to care about now,' the sergeant interrupted. 'And our future. We have sacrificed a lot for our future.'

'Yes.' Sergeant Farrat had allowed her a chance at a future; he had lied for her, lost his job and home. 'But I am sorry you lost everything.'

He shrugged. 'I have a surprise for you, it will cheer you up.' The sergeant reached into his large green handbag. He extracted a brown paper–wrapped object, cleared his throat and with great authority announced, 'Tilly Dunnage, it gives me very great pleasure to present to you, on behalf of the Dungatar Social Club, the inaugural eisteddfod first prize for best costume for your brilliant work on the astounding seventeenth-century baroque costumes for the early sixteenth-century Shakespeare play, *Macbeth*, a play about regicide, ambition, hierarchy, murder, violence and life's meaninglessness.'

When she peeled away the paper she found an ornate silver cup inscribed, 'Best Costume, Winyerp Dramatic Society, 1950'.

Tilly threw her head back and hooted. Everyone in the room turned to stare. 'But you didn't find me just to give me this cup, did you?'

The sergeant turned his pale eyes to her and put his hand over hers. 'Young Charles McSwiney is the paperboy at the Regent.'

She remained perfectly still. The Regent . . . opposite Salon Mystique. Charles McSwiney was the loud paperboy.

'Charles studied you from afar for quite some time before he was sure, and then, wisely, he came to me. He has not mentioned any of this to his mother.' The sergeant took his hand from Tilly's. 'But he wants the galah back, for Barney.'

The air was suddenly thinner, the din further away. 'Barney?'

'No one wants to upset you in any way, but they'd be pleased if they had their bird back. You see, that bird belonged to –'

'I know, yes . . . of course.'

She brushed cigarette ash from her lap. The last time she had seen Barney he had laboured up The Hill with the galah on his shoulder, the cow at his heels and the chooks pecking along behind him. He stood in front of her with his hat in his hands, but couldn't get his eyes to meet hers. She wished Barney would hurt her, or embrace her, but he just choked and lurched away, leaving the animals. His parents, Mae and Edward, took their remaining children and left the town, and those animals kept Tilly and Molly alive. Her past was arriving now, Mae and Edward, the big girls and Barney and the small McSwineys coming bit by bit. They deserved to know everything, needed to know; it was their right. But how was she to live it all again?

'It's not fair for Charlie to keep such a big secret, Tilly.'

'But it will hurt them –'

'And it's not fair for you to keep your secret.'

Tilly felt an urgent need to see Barney, but would he want to see her? 'I'm afraid.'

'I doubt there's any reason to be. It's been three years, and they've moved into a house in Collingwood. The big girls have jobs in the city. It's very risky, so rather than just bumping into them or Charlie bringing them for a confrontation, you should make the effort.' The sergeant poured more wine. 'Once they see you and know the truth they'll have hope in their lives. Mae and Edward deserve some joy.'

She could never give their son back to them, but she could give them *something*. When she had a home perhaps they would all spend Christmas together, maybe a whole lifetime. If she had a home, she could have everything again . . . though nothing she hadn't already lost. But if she gave life one more go she would *know*, she wouldn't go mad *not* knowing, waiting and hoping, as Molly had.

The piano player launched into a tune and invited the crowd to sing along. Tilly said, 'I hate singalongs,' but apparently so did the crowd, who either made their way to the bar or turned away to talk to each other.

Finally, she asked, 'You will tell them about Joe?'

It was better that way.

# Chapter 3

IN THE MONTHS after the death of their star full-forward, the bitter folk of Dungatar watched the little house on The Hill. Below it, the rubbish tip burned, ash iced the house and putrid smoke eked up to lick the eaves. Tilly and her mad mother hid there and occasionally the people of Dungatar saw faint fire glow through the window. Only under the cover of moonless nights would Sergeant Farrat take food to Tilly and Molly Dunnage. Otherwise, nothing moved up on The Hill. It remained that Teddy McSwiney, Dungatar's star footballer, was gone, and that his father, Edward McSwiney, night cart collector, fresh fish and rabbit supplier, spare parts and contraband provider to all, had folded his sad wife and children together and abandoned the town. And that Tilly Dunnage was held entirely responsible.

Inside the dull house, the murderess and her mad mother, Molly, locked the door to the nasty town and the hard world and cuddled their desolation. Each evening, Molly Dunnage rose first. She stoked the stove, fed her shattered daughter and waited with her: Tilly's scarred heart trudging on and on, Molly's bitterness eating what was left of her soul, the sad lines on her aged face etching deeper. Mother and daughter remained as one in their smoky cottage, the walls around them leaning and all sounds loud in the small hours. When she could, Tilly left her mother to roam the plains and creek bank for firewood, and on one of those dark nights, she bent to pick up a log and was caught by a dull, bone-bending cramp. She walked carefully home, stopping from time to time to accommodate the waves of pain. She dropped the wood at the back step and lit a kerosene lamp which she hung on the clothes line. Then she prepared her bed and the room.

The sergeant was on alert so it wasn't long before he saw the dull orange light burning. He drove immediately to The Hill. 'Now, Tilly, I have read all there is to read, I know exactly what to do.'

'We all do,' she said. After all, Tilly had done this before, as had Molly.

Had Beula Harridene not been recovering in a nearby asylum, had she indeed been able to see at all, she would have witnessed Sergeant Farrat's car drive up The Hill that December night and drive home again a few hours later, for it had proved true: Molly, Tilly, Sergeant Farrat and baby Joel knew what had to be achieved.

Beula also missed Sergeant Farrat's car a few weeks later, when it ascended The Hill in the dead of night and then drove carefully away towards Winyerp. Tilly Dunnage was gone from Dungatar one week, but of course no one noticed. And when she returned, the weeks rolled to months and more months, a slow-drip torture for Tilly and her frail, old-before-her-time mother. Another baby was lost and the women were held captive on The Hill and rendered inert by the town and its poison. Myrtle's beautiful face was a picture of pain and longing, like Molly's own. She could endure no more. Only more loss would unite the new mother and her child. This time, Molly would leave.

She watched her daughter fill the kettle and put it on the stove, cut some lemon grass and drop it into the teapot. 'Good morning, Myrtle.' Her daughter's face showed shock. In all the time Myrtle had been back, Molly had not said her name.

'I had a dream last night,' Molly said, 'about a baby. A bonny, round baby with dimples in his knees and elbows, and two perfect teeth.' The old lady looked closely at Tilly. 'It was your baby.'

Tilly turned away.

'I lost a baby too,' said Molly, 'I lost my little girl.'

That was the day that Molly fell, and died.

# Chapter 4

THE SERGEANT DELIVERED her home from the Hippocampus Club and she crawled into her bed, emotionally wrung and a little drunk. When she woke she knew it was a new day, the start of a future spoiled by the past, but the past was with her anyway. Sleep brought flashes of women dancing in ill-fitting haute couture circled by flames, and Stewart Pettyman running towards her, behind him a posse of screaming kids, and Molly, peaceful and cold in a butcher's cool room, around her beef shoulders and lamb forequarters and pig hocks hanging. Often she did not sleep again because she feared Pablo might come, and some nights she could bear no more pain.

Tilly dressed quickly, put an apple in her small rucksack and pulled her hat low. Below, Mr and Mrs Short listened to her footfall. During the week it was a sluggish barn dance, but on Sundays the ceiling of Shorty's small apartment played a happy ballet that bounded downstairs, took a left turn at the bottom, and headed through the kitchen and out into the day. The sun had not yet hit the backyard. In the wood shed, where once she'd lived, her bicycle waited. She drew protective gloves over her fine seamstress hands, waved at the peeping Shorts and rode out the back gate towards Gertrude Street. The asphalt was damp, the bluestones lumpy and the tram tracks slippery. As she set off, she only half scrutinised the cars at the kerb and the passengers waiting at the Smith Street tram stop. The last Mr Short saw of her she was freewheeling through the

39

backstreets, in the golden rays of the Fitzroy morning, towards Hoddle Street.


There weren't many passengers on the Melbourne to Itheca via Winyerp train, so Arlen O'Connor had a compartment to himself. As the train left the crowded, gritty backyards of Melbourne, Arlen settled into his comfortable leather coach chair and watched, like a seven-year-old boy, until there were no more houses, and then the small towns dotted amid the hills disappeared and the landscape subsided into undulating plains. He opened his newspaper. The government announced a royal commission into the proposed introduction of television to the nation, the trial of twenty-five ex-SS men had started in Bordeaux, eighteen-year-old Ken Rosewall had won the men's singles, and in New Zealand Godfrey Bowen shore 456 sheep in nine hours. When Arlen looked up, the landscape was just one vast plain sliding past. Stray grey sheep darted occasionally from the scrub, kangaroos bounded alongside the carriages, crows watched from telegraph wires and great blankets of cockies rose and swirled away. As they travelled further into wasteland – just red and grey dirt supporting sparse stands of trees all the way to the horizon – he found his way to the refreshment carriage and ate a stale corned beef sandwich.

At last the train slowed and warped around a great curve past a singed sign announcing Dungatar. Someone had painted the word 'New', but there was nothing to support that New Dungatar was an actual place, just a long platform, the charred remains of a few buildings and a massive corrugated-iron grain silo. No one else in the carriage was preparing to disembark. A husband, wife and daughter leaned forward to watch him, and as the end of the platform loomed, the husband said, 'You have to jump.'

'Jump?' He realised that the train wasn't going to actually stop.

The husband opened the door and shoved Arlen out into thin air.

He found himself on the ground, the steam and ash and grit evaporating, then felt a sharp pain in his torso, like he'd been speared. The next sensation Arlen felt was of small prickly things crawling all over him, which he assumed were Lilliputians. He stood and wobbled about, brushing ants from his suit and scraping them from beneath his collar. He was not Lemuel Gulliver, but his head thumped and his ribs bit when he breathed. The culprit – his suitcase – lay on the ground at his feet, its contents waving in the slight breeze and the lid some distance away. Flies buzzed and galahs trilled and the faint sound of an engine pattered across the plain to him. The breeze brought the stench of burnt timber, wood smoke and rotten ash.

As far as he could see, the landscape was soot, burnt trees and fences, the charred timber remains of houses, their corrugated-iron roofs heaped in the grey ash, and, through it all, the worn brown grooves of township traffic. On top of a lone hill one chimney remained erect, supported by the remains of a scorched vine. He followed a vague road that led him to what was obviously once a town, his suitcase under his arms, the lid held in place with his spare tie, and the sound of the engine getting louder. Someone had painted white lines all over the black ground, like tailor's chalk on dark felt, which depicted boundaries of build-ings. But there was one building: Pratts General Store, locked and deserted, and out the back a loud generator banged away. The petrol pumps outside were padlocked to the bowsers. He peered through the chicken wire nailed to the shop window. Nothing, just black. Then a face popped up in front of him and he yelled, arching back. As he picked himself up off the ground for the second time that day, the door opened. A soft, brown-eyed woman with thick curly hair was looking at him. 'What do you want?' she called, over the noise of the generator.

She was dressed in a wide, three-tiered skirt, green satin tumbling from panniers that extended three feet beyond her hips. The outer skirt was trimmed with gold fringes and tassels, like parted curtains. Her bodice was tight, low-cut across the breasts, and featured yards of grubby torn lace. She looked like a walking church altar, the blood dried on her bodice like spilled wine.

He started picking up his underwear, shirts and toiletries, shoving them back in his suitcase. 'Well, anything really, since I haven't seen a milk bar, a hotel, or any sort of accommodation . . . perhaps a drink, some food?'

She went back through the doorway – sideways to accommodate the satin panniers – and he followed her, securing his suitcase with the necktie again. It was a simple shop divided in two by a central wall; the rear obviously functioned as living quarters, and the front boasted a small counter and cash box. The produce was displayed high on dusty shelves behind the woman, who opened the cash box with a key tied to one of her golden tassels.

The generator cut out and the silence felt like a cool sea breeze.

'It runs out of petrol,' she said. 'I have tinned food, one loaf of bread, cheese, and some fresh vegetables.'

'I'll have some bread and cheese, please. I don't suppose you've got any beer?'

She smiled, transforming from a humourless woman to someone actually quite pleasant to look at. 'The generator's been on so it'll be cold.'

He paid – it was all very expensive – smiled and thanked her. 'I'm not from around here.'

'I'd have most certainly noticed you,' she said, eagerly, for he was a stylish man, his suit three-piece, double-breasted, the waistcoat single-breasted. His trousers were narrow with no turn-ups – very modern – and his trilby was the same grey as his slip-on shoes.

Arlen felt entirely scrutinised by the intense, slightly manic woman. He turned away to look out into the void. 'What happened?'

'There was a fire.' She shrugged, and leaned on her counter, close to him. Then Arlen made a mistake.

'I was actually looking for someone,' he said. 'She lived here as a child, then she was a dressmaker.'

The woman stiffened and recoiled, and he continued, warily, 'Perhaps you knew her, Myrtle –'

'I know her!' Her face contorted and turned a puce colour, sweat beads popped across her forehead and her hair stood on end. She screamed, possessed by fury and incoherent rage, swearing like a water-starved sailor and swinging her fists at him across the counter. He fled the spitting creature and his suitcase landed on the ground at the base of the bowsers, the shop door slamming shut and the noise inside wailing on. Once he'd gathered himself and picked up the contents of his suitcase (again), he strolled to the top of The Hill and ate his cheese and bread sitting on a hearth, his only company a gutted, charred dressmaker's stand and what was once a wheelchair. A melted sewing machine served as a footrest. 'Well,' he said, 'it seems you were here, but where are you now?'

He looked out beyond the defoliated trees and black destruction of the town to a red roof, shimmering and knee deep in acres of square green paddocks. He drained his bottle of war beer, gathered his case and set off down The Hill. Walking through what remained of the town he skirted the general store but drew close to the razed pub, avoiding the hole that led to the cellar, and kept on between the white lines on the black ground towards the house. It was quite a walk, but the wheat crops either side of the road were plump and leafy, the sun was shining and the air fresh. Finally, he walked under the elaborate gate arch declaring 'Windswept Crest' and his hopes rose even further. The house sat on a rise just high enough to catch every passing breeze, the croquet lawn was a brown waste but looked as if it could be restored and the house itself was well maintained, though the dusty winds had shredded the paintwork and the rain had rotted the windowsills. But there were people. Most stopped to look at him, then went back to their work – some in the vegetable garden on the bank of the creek, one was fishing, others were playing tennis on courts that had seen better days, and they were all of them dressed in shabby baroque costumes. The men wore skirts with petticoats, yards of lace dripping from their frilled and ruffled extremities. One big chap wore chain mail and a metal chest plate. Their below-knee pantaloons, godet bell-bottoms and deep flounces above high-heeled Cromwell slippers were oversized, their hats heavily plumed so that their brims drooped. But the most poignant were the women. They were trying to go about their everyday life, at the clothes line or washing by hand, encumbered by full-tiered skirts with ruffled bustles, elaborate multistoreyed, architect-designed fontanges, torn jackets with shredded jabots and revers. None of their dresses accommodated their bodies, the zippers were burst and their bodices wide and gaping from their torsos. Their hems and shoes, like his own, were dusted black with soot. On the verandah, several people were reciting Shakespeare. Albany addressed Goneril, 'Shut your mouth, dame, or with this paper shall I stop it. Hold, sir, thou worse than any name, read thine own evil. Nay, no tearing, lady. I perceive you know it.' Albany handed Goneril a piece of paper and Goneril addressed her much shorter husband, Edmund, 'Say, if I do? The laws are mine, not thine. Who can harass me for it?'

Edmund replied that she had recited the wrong line, and Albany cried, 'How many times do we have to tell you – the word is *arraign*.'

'Doesn't make sense. "Who can arrange me for it"? *Harass* sounds better.'

Arlen turned away.

Then a little girl's voice said, 'It's *King Lear*, but the costumes are left over from *Macbeth*. They're rehearsing for the eisteddfod. Again.'

He looked up. The little girl, possibly five, or a mature four-year-old, was sitting on the edge of the verandah roof holding a pair of binoculars. She was dressed in a small, sheared playsuit.

'They did *Macbeth* the first two times but this year they're trying something new because they think it'll help them win.'

'I see.'

'I saw Mummy throw you out of her shop.'

'Yes, I upset her.'

'They call her Gertrude the Terrible. What's your name?'

'Arlen, what's yours?'

'You're tall, dark and handsome, aren't you?'

'Thank you. Others might not agree.' He looked towards the machinery shed.

'My name's Flick. It's short for Felicity Joy but Grandmother says Flick's a name that's appropriate to my temperament. Grandmother's in the pantry counting the tinned food but Daddy's in the machinery shed.'

'Thanks,' he said, and set out for the shed. Then he stopped. 'Can you try to answer a question for me, though I suspect it might be the wrong thing . . .'

She nodded knowingly. 'Give it a go.'

'I'm here to find a woman called Myrtle Dunnage.'

She thought for a moment, looking at the binoculars in her small hands. 'I'd ask Daddy, he's nice all the time but the others get upset, especially about her.'

'Thank you, you are most gracious.'

'Someone has to be.'

William Beaumont was dressed in contemporary costume and turned out to be a genial sort of chap who carried an air of resignation about him, but there was yearning in his eyes. He was leaning into the engine of an ancient Triumph Gloria. Parts of it sat around the benches in the shed. He didn't pay Arlen much attention after the initial shock of seeing him standing at the shed door.

'What is it?'

'Spark plugs, fan belt, cracked cylinder head. What can I do for you?'

Arlen whispered that he wanted to find Tilly.

William wiped his hands on an old rag. 'You're not the first to come looking.'

'Oh?'

'There was another chap from the arson department.'

'Oh, yes,' said Arlen, pretending he knew all about the arson department.

'She isn't here. No one knows exactly where she is.'

'Her mother? Father?'

William shook his head. 'Mother dead, father dead and step-mother in the local asylum.'

'The asylum?'

He resumed tinkering with the car. 'As I say, no one knows where Tilly Dunnage is and you can't get to Winyerp to the asylum because our bus needs petrol.' He nodded at the old footballers' bus parked under a peppercorn. It was the only functioning vehicle they had and had survived the fire because they'd used it to attend the eisteddfod in Winyerp that day. 'You'd have to go to town and buy petrol. Lots of it, from Gertrude.'

'Gertrude the Terrible?'

He grinned. 'I gather you've met my estranged wife?'

'Oh, God, I didn't mean, or rather, I didn't think, but yes, I have met her, she's quite –'

'She's not really "terrible". Unworldly. Emotional, but quite soft, really.'

Arlen apologised, adding, 'I'm willing to try for petrol, especially if I can get a bed for the night.'

'There are no spare beds but you can have the couch.'

He shrugged. 'It's just for a night or two.'

'Oh, no,' said William, 'the train only comes through once a week. I'll telephone Winyerp and get them to make a trunk call to Melbourne so the train will slow down to collect you when it comes through next Sunday.' He glanced at the case under Arlen's arm, his torn coat and grazed cheek. 'Don't send your suitcase to the guard's van next time, keep it with you in the carriage.'

'Is there a passenger bus back to Melbourne?'

William nodded, 'A Greyhound, but it won't stop either, in fact, it speeds up through Dungatar.'

The dining room, like the Windswept Crest homestead, was well proportioned and stuffed with Victorian décor. The chairs and lounge furniture needed reupholstering, the crockery was mismatched and the cutlery patchy. Lois and Bobby Pickett slaved over a four-ovened wood stove. Some people headed outside to eat but most stayed, curious about the new man. William's mother, Elsbeth, a small, sharp, razor-thin woman with a long nose and an imperious expression, insisted that Arlen dine next to her at the head table. She dismissed Scotty Pullit, still inhabiting his role as Donalbain, prince and heir, and sat the new man to her left. Scotty put his crown back on in defiance of the 'No Hats at the Table' rule, and went to sit at table number three. To the right of Elsbeth was William. Felicity Joy sat opposite.

Arlen studied the cast of Dungatar. A woman called Muriel, whose wire-framed collar swung from the top of her fontange to her armpits and had lost its fabric, announced they had won Best Costume twice and pointed to a silver cup on the mantelpiece. 'The 1950 cup's been stolen.'

'Ours are clearly the best costumes, though the judges say they're wrong for 1606,' Elsbeth said. 'That's the costume maker's fault.'

A small pale man called Fred pointed to his voluminous knee-length breeches, torn and mended, and said, 'We won't win this year.'

Elsbeth said, 'So this year we *must* win Best Play, Best Director *and* Best Actress!'

Purl, dressed only in a cotton shift, stays, petticoat and pockets, explained that the first time they'd taken their play, *Macbeth*, to the Winyerp and Itheca Drama Club Eisteddfod, it was an unseasonably hot, extremely windy day and the play had not gone well. For a start, Banquo – Sergeant Farrat – was missing and the replacement Lady Macbeth made a spectacle of herself, thrashing about on the mock bed and rummaging through her underskirts.

'We swapped to *King Lear*. *Macbeth* is cursed,' Elsbeth declared, fiddling with the sadly insubstantial betrothal rings on her aged, sun-splotched hand. 'I am the director and the producer, and I play Cordelia.'

'You play Cordelia?'

The women opposite Arlen nodded, rolling their eyes.

Felicity explained, 'She's got a costume and makeup, don't you, *Grandma*?'

William glanced at Arlen and said, tentatively, 'May I suggest, Mother, that *Macbeth* is not cursed. It was *us*. The first act ran an hour over time.'

Felicity said, '*H.M.S. Pinafore* won. The cast could sing *and* act.'

'It was cursed,' Purl explained. 'Tilly Dunnage cursed it, and when we got home the town was burnt to the ground.'

'To the ground,' said Septimus, everyone reflecting on that terrible day, standing in the wafting smoke, hankies to their noses, coming to terms with the fact that they were burnt out of existence. Only the lone chimney on The Hill remained, and they all stood in the hot charred clumps on top of The Hill, looking down to where their homes once stood. The local sergeant – the missing Banquo – singed and soot-smudged, sat on the chimney hearth, slapping a blackened, withered branch up and down between his blistered patent leather shoes.

At the time, the District Inspector was lodging with the sergeant for the purpose of investigating a recent spate of suspicious tragedies: Teddy McSwiney's fall, then Molly Dunnage's fall, Beula Harridene's blinding mishap, Mr Almanac's shuffle into the creek, and Evan Pettyman's gruesome end. But it was his role as third witch in *Macbeth* that kept the District Inspector in Dungatar.

'We were homeless,' said Purl, concluding her intriguing story, 'but the fire didn't burn all the way out to Windswept Crest, so here we are, safe and sound.'

'They're all leaving the second the town is rebuilt,' said Elsbeth, through clenched teeth.

'We'd tell you where she was if we knew,' William said, unconvincingly, and Elsbeth added, 'We said the same to your predecessor from the arson department.'

'He wasn't as nice as you,' Flick said.

Arlen wondered if he should deny he was from the arson squad, but he did need to find her. He wanted to pay her back.

'She had no reason to burn down the town,' said Elsbeth.

Lois said, gravely, 'She's cursed, that girl.'

'Trouble wherever she goes,' someone declared and someone else echoed, '*Bad* trouble.'

Irma Almanac, a sleepy arthritic woman in a wheelchair, joked that if Arlen found Tilly perhaps he could ask her if she'd like to make the costumes again? She slapped the armrest of her chair and laughed.

'Yes, tell her we'll pay her double,' Elsbeth said. 'Then we'll tie her to the railway line on Monday and leave her until the train comes Sunday.' She smiled at the new man, who was staring at her, dumbfounded. 'I imagine there's lots of coronation excitement in Melbourne. Are you looking forward to the season?'

Arlen gathered himself. 'The season?'

'The coronation festivities. A marvellous spectacle, don't you think? We'll have something here too. A ball!' She put her hand on Arlen's. 'William is the mayor. He'll build the hall for the dance.'

Arlen slid his hand free from Elsbeth's cold spidery claw and went to the cool breeze on the crumbling verandah, trying to come to terms with the things he was learning, while inside, the locals argued that housing was more important than a ball, or perhaps medical facilities, or even a fire station.

# Chapter 5

ON MONDAY, TILLY woke in her bright, bare room, vanquished her nightly terrors of ugly women and the beautiful hero and replaced them with thoughts of yesterday – Sunday, the day that made the following days possible.

'Kiss cocky,' she said, and the galah lifted his wing, looked at her with one small black eye and lowered it again. 'No,' she said. 'You have to get up and eat breakfast, we're going out.' She poured a handful of seeds at his feet and scratched his head. He deposited a small black and white shit into his drink tin.

While she readied herself to face Salon Mystique, Tilly forced her thoughts to the winter coronation collection, the Smalls Ball and Miss Post Office Picnic, but nothing inspiring came, so she turned back to her friend the galah. She gave him a dry biscuit, packed his seed in her bag along with yesterday's apple core, buttoned an old cardigan around his cage and carried him towards the city – the paperboys yelling from every corner, trading mid-traffic, at tram stops, small islands in the river of commuters. In Collins Street she stopped under an elm and looked across to the Regent and the curly-haired boy wearing woollen shorts and substantial boots, calling, ''ERALD!' He handed out papers and took money and issued change in the swift, practised movements of a paperboy in full command of his enterprise. Tilly crossed Collins Street and put the galah down beside his newspaper stack.

Charles McSwiney looked at her with eyes like Teddy's

and said, 'Thanks, missus,' his attention back on the workers streaming past and the rapid exchange of coins and newspapers. She unbuttoned the cardigan and poked the apple core through the wire to the galah. From a few paces away, Tilly looked at the bird, standing on his perch looking at the apple. She hoped she would see him again. He turned one small black eye to her and his crest rose.

Mrs Flock appeared in the doorway of Salon Mystique. 'You're late.'

'*Bonjour, Madame Flock, vous êtes une menteuse et une voleuse laide et sans talent, et je vous souhaite de percuter un lampadaire et de vous casser le nez.*'

'*Oui. Merci,*' Mrs Flock replied, nonplussed.

Madame Flock's skilled in-house seamstresses had found their upstairs atelier littered with tissue-paper scraps and thread, pins and calico offcuts, and knew that the inadequate fluorescent lights had burned all Sunday above outworkers unpicking the bounty from the steamer closets. In unstitching the European couture, they would have gained much knowledge of its intricate techniques. And now, in suburban kitchens across Melbourne, more outworkers were creating toiles and patterns and using the jolly fabrics Mrs Flock had brought back to construct frocks to suit the quaint urban department stores and rural boutiques of the far-flung colony of Melbourne. The careful seamstresses would skimp on the seams and hemlines, the collars and pockets of their allocated fabrics to make an extra dress or two for their friends and neighbours. In this way, the hard, treeless streets of Collingwood, Preston and Frankston were made pretty with European imitations.

They heard Valda burst in downstairs. 'I just saw Miss Victoria!'

Upstairs, the seamstresses rushed to the landing to see.

'I've heard she's quite pretty,' sniffed Clare, 'but there's no need to be hysterical.'

'But she was headed to Le Louvre.' Valda pointed east, the sweat stain under her arm reaching the darts on her frock bodice.

Madame Flock assumed her version of French composure. 'We have Miss Post Office Picnic and she will wear a gown to the Smalls Charity Ball, and soon the right people, society people, will rush to us.' In this way Mrs Flock would realise her dreams: after hours some nights, she danced with her dresses, tears in her eyes, and bowed to the adoring crowds – flashbulbs bursting, applause deafening – while next to her Miss Australia wore Salon Mystique's Gown of the Year and the models of the day – Bambi and June, Elly and Maggie, Ann and Janet – circled in their Salon Mystique gowns and Helmut Newton and Athol Smith fought over who would photograph her next collection. Madame's days of need, raiding provincial European towns to snap up low-end couture, would be over.

'We'll need new staff to cope,' Valda said, and the seamstresses moved quietly back to their tables and resumed their quiet stitching.

'Yes,' Madame agreed, 'new staff.' Valda was an adequate *Atelier Première* and *Directrice Technique* in terms of garment construction and discipline for the timely outcome of a collection, but she knew little of conveying to the seamstresses the inspirations behind Madame's sketches. Valda's idea of translating Madame Flock's ideas was to hand over one of her sketches, sometimes with an accompanying photo from *L'Officiel*, and instruct, 'Make one like that.'

But Madame did not know that her sketches did not say anything. That members of the meagre audiences who attended her collections dribbled away afterwards feeling there was something missing. Madame did not see that the difficulty she had merchandising her dresses was because there was no 'essence' to spruik. When she read the newspaper reviews or overheard *Premières* and Head of Sales people from other salons talking of motifs and identity and 'the intensity of their defining expressions', she wondered what making nice frocks for society ladies had to do with 'recontextualising the past for the future'.

What Madame did know was that in the past, Tilly Dunnage from Dungatar had made and sent to her lovely dresses. The outworkers had copied them and they'd walked out of the dress shops and into the streets in their dozens. And once, Tilly Dunnage had instructed everyone in the workroom that the purpose of a toile went well beyond a mere cost-saving procedure. 'They are a blueprint to create designs that communicate and are not mere mimicry,' she had said, very boldly. But Madame had to admit Tilly Dunnage had a point. And now, it was coronation season and Madame would take a gamble that would disrupt the hierarchical harmony in her workrooms, but the boastful country girl would rise to the test with Miss Post Office Picnic, she was certain. Then Madame would bluff, pretend she had capital to finance stock to make scores of frocks; she would open accounts, buy more fabric, put on a momentous parade . . . sell herself as someone with backing, resources, credibility, substance. It was all about timing, and Madame had been waiting for just this moment. Tilly Dunnage would create remarkable gowns, they would win Gown of the Year and go on to fill Melbourne with perfect gowns for stunning people and Madame would move her salon further up the Collins Street hill to the Paris end. She would rise.

'You will make sure our seamstresses work harder, Valda. Tell them they'll be rewarded. And you will visit the outworkers to do the same, that is your job.'

'But the collection . . . I am *Direct-treece Tech-neek*, I need to oversee –'

'I will oversee, you will focus on being an *Atelier Première*.'

Valda was not often stuck for words, but she had been relegated to manager, administrator, the guard on horseback cracking the whip at the captives, and she was entirely numb.

Mrs Flock took from the steamer a crushed evening gown. She turned to the mirror, embracing the dress, and pressed the fabric to her body and ran her hand down the embroidered silk satin skirt. 'Summon the seamstresses for the morning meeting.' She looked dreamily at her reflection. 'We need a mannequin that will give this dress the necessary *empoigner* and *enlever*,' she whispered, her accent appalling. For the winter coronation parade she would use older mannequins (they were cheaper), or girls from Bambi's or Elly's modelling schools (who were free), but next time . . .

The seamstresses arrived to see Madame standing proudly beside the creased evening gown on a Stockman. She composed herself to make one of her announcements, gathered her high features in a serious moue and placed her hand on the Stockman's shoulder. 'This is our centrepiece for my coronation collection.'

It was a Victor Stiebel creation, most likely his 1947–48 collection, obviously purchased second-hand. The strapless bodice featured silver and pearlised beads as well as rhinestones. The only flair, as far as Tilly was concerned, was a pleated, draped cowl waistband that was caught at the hip to fall to the hem, adding even more fabric volume to the Dior full circle skirt. Elegant, unstartling, perfect for a Melbourne red carpet photo. It was not a complicated dress and would require the standard fittings but also, and more importantly, fabric that would give it meaning. Tilly recalled no such fabric in the bolts Mrs Flock had brought home from Europe.

'I have kept the cream of the European samples for you girls, my première couturiers. They represent the future for us.'

Tilly raised an eyebrow. It was not the same future Tilly had in mind.

Madame allocated Shirley some very lovely pleated linens by an unknown Irish designer, Sybil Connolly. 'My friend at *Harper's Bazaar* gave them to me. They'll never go beyond the Dublin department stores.'

But they were exquisite, and Tilly suspected Mrs Flock had been sold them by an opportunistic sales girl out to make some extra cash. Sybil Connolly's designs would most likely appear in European fashion magazines the following year, though no one would recognise Mrs Flock's ill-gotten, inferior copies.

To the other seamstresses, Madame doled out the rest of the frocks – prêt à porter from less reputable European salon and fashion shows – telling them they were 'the best of their kind she had found'.

Valda shrugged. 'You could have just bought patterns from a *Vogue* catalogue.'

Madame ignored her. 'Tilly Dunnage from Dungatar feels she is capable of producing the signature pieces, therefore she is obviously capable of recreating the centrepiece.' She turned to the Victor Stiebel but all eyes in the room were on Tilly, the shame filling her. She had just been affirmed, endorsed, but the reward was the unethical and troubling task of copying someone else's creation for retail profits to further Mrs Flock's ambitions and standing in the fashion world. Mrs Flock had also deepened any divides among the seamstresses, pitting them against 'the new girl', forcing them to apply their dressmaking skills in the pursuit of one-upmanship.

Valda started, 'But Madame –'

'I know what you're going to say, Valda.' Mrs Flock pointed at Tilly. 'There is no need to unpick a signature gown just to make a toile when I know *she* can just copy it.'

Tilly said she thought Valda, as Head of Workroom, should be in charge of signature copies.

'Valda will have her hands full supervising outworkers and the couturiers. You will recreate the Stiebel. As for copying, we are not doing anything that everyone from Sydney to Dungatar isn't doing.'

'But you will make it your première piece and claim it as your own design, and it's not.'

Madame's great moment introducing her coronation parade ideas was not going as smoothly as she'd imagined. 'According to the story you tell, Tilly Dunnage from Dungatar, you have worked in the fashion industry for a long time. Everyone knows that everything is a copy to some degree – for example, the sarong dress for client number 114. So, you might as well preserve Victor Stiebel's talents and just copy the bloody thing, as I know you can. You can find some adequate fabric, surely.'

The penny dropped. Mrs Flock wanted to keep the original dress . . . for herself. Mrs Flock could claim the Stiebel as her own, but Tilly would make her mark in the winter coronation collection, with originals. She would seize the opportunity to make an impression as Tilly Dunnage, Designer, and from there she would create a small enterprise and a secure future.

'Right,' Mrs Flock sighed. 'And now to Miss Post Office Picnic's dress.'

But Clare rushed from her desk, breathless. 'A woman just telephoned, she's on her way to see about a gown. I've heard of her, Nita Moreland.'

'Bloody hell.' Madame's refined accent dropped away. 'Did you say Nita Orland?'

'I think so.'

'She's an actress,' Valda said, and Shirley added, 'Always in the social pages.'

Clare looked at her wristwatch. 'She'll be here at ten.'

Everyone tried to remember the scandal attached to Nita Orland.

Valda cried, 'She's divorced!'

Shirley whispered to Tilly, 'That's why she's coming to Salon Mystique – she's hit hard times.'

'She's photographed everywhere she goes,' Madame gushed. 'What does she want? What did she say?'

Valda, trembling, said, 'Ten o'clock? That's very soon.'

Mrs Flock was suddenly more alive than anyone had ever seen her, walking in circles and hopping on the spot. Valda was sent to dust, sweep and polish. Shirley was told to wipe down the walls of the fitting room and Tilly was dispatched to find fabric samples, but did not bother because they had nothing suitable for someone as widely photographed as Nita Orland apparently was. So she re-dressed the front window while Mrs Flock flapped about, searching for her very best gown, which she gave to Clare to model.

At ten-fifteen Valda and Madame Flock were despondent, crushed. They decided it was all a ruse, a cruel joke organised by Le Louvre, and slumped behind Madame's designing board. Upstairs the seamstresses flicked through old magazines, gazing at their phantom customer: Nita and the glamorous cast on the opening night of *The Cocktail Party*; Nita smiling, her arm looped through the elbow of her handsome leading man; Nita, on the occasion of her engagement, wearing a gown from Paris. 'That cluster on her finger is the same size as the bloke's coat button,' Shirley declared. There were snaps of Nita opening a theatre, Nita getting married, Nita boarding an aeroplane for her honeymoon, Nita visiting sick children, Nita hosting a garden party, then, finally, Nita outside a courthouse, her hand raised to shield her face, the headline tall and fat: 'Divorce.'

'Anyway,' said Valda, rallying, 'they say she's a half-caste.'

Clare said she heard she was Indian, *Nanditha*, though she appeared quite fair. 'There are ways to make yourself pale.'

Then there was a movement downstairs. They dashed to the landing and crowded together on the top step just as Tilly Dunnage fled the front window and ran to hide in a change room.

Valda clattered back down the stairs while from the small space between the curtains, Tilly watched the window where she had placed one of her own creations. A figure made ghostly by the front netting hovered like a hanging scarf. Then the divorced actress stepped into the salon, shoved the door behind her closed with one foot while removing her sunglasses and sliding her free hand from her glove using her teeth, the gem on her finger glinting. Tilly Dunnage loved her immediately. Her demeanour was forthright but unassuming and charming and the black chemise dress she was wearing – a Balenciaga – was exquisite. Nita Orland's skin would be best expressed in either the blackest of black or the purest white, but she was a woman who could carry anything off. Her hair was shiny black and cut in a sharp fringe across her high aristocratic forehead and gathered in a natural bun at her nape, but generally, the gaze was drawn to her generous mouth, painted red. It was the only makeup she wore. Nita Orland was delicate yet strong-featured, a flawless girl with olive skin, like chamois, and dark almond-shaped eyes, thickly lashed. But she was odd, a *jolie laide*, a woman with unusual features that together were beautiful. The most striking thing about Nita Orland was her prepossessing smile. It burst into the air and made those around her smile, even Mrs Flock.

Madame Flock announced she had 'just the thing' for Nita Orland to wear and would 'personally service her every need' to ensure she stood out at every coronation ball. She snapped her fingers and Tilly's heart sank: Clare, in her role as *demoiselle du magasin*, stepped into the salon wearing a sleeveless satin gown that featured a faux sash. Balanced on top of her Barbara Stanwyck fringe was a coronet of glistening glass chips.

Nita just smiled her sunny smile and ventured around the salon, peeking into Madame's office and lifting the skirts on show dresses, while Valda boasted that Salon Mystique was designing a ball gown for Miss Post Office Picnic and name-dropped their clients, mostly brides-to-be. Tilly decided that if she could, she would dress Nita Orland in attire that did not advertise her breasts or enhance her body for the male gaze. Rather, she would show her sketches for Nita, for *her* body, dresses that would work to create a frisson, perhaps a flesh-tone lining beneath Chantilly?

At Madame's nod, Clare walked slow circles while Madame explained that the gown she was modelling was very popular. Nita Orland moved aside a fitting-room curtain and found what she was searching for: the slender woman with the short undisciplined hair, the 35-year-old with enviable cheekbones. The bloom of youth had been replaced by a worldliness and sharp scrutinising gaze and her skin was without the sun blemishes found on most of her peers. She was wearing mousseline trousers under her white coat.

'Tilly.'

'Yes.'

'I admired the lovely green paletot a mutual friend was wearing and she told me where to find you. She also showed me some sketches of a sarong dress you are making at her request. I need something special for the Smalls Charity Coronation Ball.'

Tilly smiled. The sparkling ring on Nita's finger was a walnut-sized, diamond-crusted skull, its eyes black holes.

Madame said, 'We aim to please. I will first show you some more of our special gowns and then we can create a design from there.'

Clare vanished and Valda presented the next assault – pictures of Indian women in saris.

'Why are you showing me these?'

Tilly interrupted. 'Mrs Flock has made some assumptions regarding your name.'

'Nanditha,' Madame said proudly.

Nita glanced scornfully at the women, grasping the full weight of what they were implying.

She smiled, though it wasn't her dazzling smile. 'Nita is short for Anita, the diminutive of Ana. It's Spanish, though just as exotic and culturally rich as India. At a stretch you could conclude the sari is a little Vionnet, a hint of the toga too, but I'm not certain my Spanish ancestors, the Infante Alfonso, Duke of Calabria and Infanta Alicia, Duchess of Calabria, would approve. My surname, Orland, is a derivative of Orlando, from my noble Calabrian ancestors.' She turned her back on the tiresome women. 'I am here *only* for the skills of this very smart, well-informed and talented dressmaker. I take it you are Australian, Tilly Dunnage?'

'As Australian as a platypus eating a lamington,' she replied, 'but I lived a long time in Europe.'

'In Australia,' Madame interrupted, 'for this delicate occasion convention and tradition would be the guiding rules.' On cue, Clare arrived wearing another square, clunking creation made from satin and lace, the strapless Elizabeth gown in her arms like a dead princess.

'Delicate? It is a ball, Madame.'

'And your re-entry into society after your misfortune.'

Nita threw her lovely head back, laughing. 'I have had no misfortune. I have, in fact, triumphed over prejudice and oppression. And anyway, I do not dress for anyone else, I dress for me.' Again, she turned her back on Clare, Valda and Mrs Flock, who stood together like the ugly sisters at Cinderella's wedding. 'Now, Tilly, I think you know a little of my personality, but we should know each other more. Shall we begin?'

'Please,' Tilly said, leading her to a sofa at the back of the salon. 'When I hear you, I hear Hecate, Greek goddess, luminously beautiful and powerful. Hecate, a "virgin" goddess, liked solitude and was unwilling to sacrifice her independent nature for the sake of marriage.'

'A widely revered and influential goddess too. Go on.'

'But when I see you, I also see Jeanne Paquin, and Erté, of course, and perhaps the principles of the Japanese –'

'Of course. The use of shadow?' Miss Nita Orland took Tilly's hand and spoke quietly. 'I am told, Tilly, that you are a seed waiting for the sunshine. I am your sun.'

Still, they could not rid themselves of Mrs Flock, who insisted on recording Nita's measurements in Tilly's little black book, then, when they were finished, she showed Nita to the door. 'We will make up some drawings –'

'No need.' Nita handed Tilly her card. 'Tilly will telephone me when she has some sketches.'

They watched Miss Orland pause at the door, put on her dark glasses and gloves and step out into the afternoon shoppers. For the second time in as many weeks, Tilly felt a small sense of anticipation, even excitement. Miss Nita Orland was a woman who could bring a dress to life and who would feel alive in a dress made for her. She was concerned with wearing a dress that was herself, her best self.

Mrs Flock turned to her and said, 'You need to make her look better than everyone else.' With that, Marigold Pettyman's imploration, 'I want to look better than Elsbeth,' rushed front and centre in her thoughts, and all those treacherous Dungatar gerbils followed, bringing all the efforts of her wasted art. And the night of the footballers' ball and its tragedy.

She went shakily to her spot by the window. Outside, Union Jacks fluttered from the lampposts above large red, blue and white corsages. The Victor Stiebel dress hung, stiff and queenly. She took it from its hanger, unbuttoned the bodice and looked for the tag. There was none, nor was there a secret seamstress tag hiding in the seams. It was a copy – a very good copy, but a copy nonetheless. She felt better, and wasn't swayed even when Valda appeared and announced haughtily that Mrs Drum was waiting. She gathered her sewing kit – scissors, pins, thread, needle, quick-unpick – flung her tape measure around her neck and went cheerfully to Mrs Drum, who was waiting in her corsetry, like one of those bacon-wrapped oysters that were all the rage at cocktail parties.

As she saw Mrs Drum off, workmen were hanging royal sashes from one traffic light to the next on Collins Street. Miss Post Office arrived, eyed the retreating Mrs Drum and said, 'Cripes, I need ta look better than her.'

'We'll try,' said Tilly, dryly.

Miss Post Office Picnic was not the sort of girl to please the judges. For a start, she would need small inflatable breasts to buoy the contestant's already stuffed bra. She would need every enhancement possible in the evening gown section of the competition to carry the judges through the swimsuit section. Tilly took up her pencil and paper and drew an empire-line dress, a loose bodice, pleated, like feathers – a feather fan! And falling from the bodice – possibly silk chine? Make it a soft pattern: floral with a deep backline dipping almost as far as the waist. Soft, graceful and very, very pretty. And a small train – not bridal, but fetching – and some exposure of pale flesh.

So, with Miss Post Office under way, she turned the page of her sketchbook and smiled. Now for Nita Orland.

Mae McSwiney was in her kitchen running a warm iron over a dark blue school shirt, a basket of clean, sun-crumpled school uniforms on the table and the James Farrington Band playing on the wireless. A breeze moved lightly through the back door, all the way down the hall and out the front door of the small worker's cottage. He was a breeze today, rather than a draught or a shadow. In the evenings, and when it was quiet, she felt her eldest son stand behind her, as he used to, watching her cook, or sew, or do the ironing, but just then she felt the breeze swell and lift the bottom of her muu-muu, and Teddy was taken. The street noises, the cheery sounds of kids playing kick-to-kick, ceased. She folded the warm, smooth shirt, placed it neatly in the laundry basket and moved cautiously down the hall.

From behind the screen door she watched a red Fiat Balilla convertible puttering steadily towards her, the driver watchful. The vision prompted a dreadful apprehension and she recalled the night the moon suddenly vanished behind clouds and the stars stopped twinkling in the deep, velvet universe. Her son, her fine young rascal, her pride, her joy, her firstborn, was dead. And here was the sergeant coming again, and she felt the familiar tugging in her chest, though this time he was not in uniform. He arrived at her door smiling, a plate balanced in one hand and his hat in the crook of his arm. The kids had resumed their footy game.

'What?' Mae suspected the visit had something to do with the return of the galah.

'I have brought a teacake.' He opened the screen door and stepped into Mae's hall.

She put the kettle on and the sergeant sat, placed his hat on his knee, and continued smiling at her over the top of the crumpled uniforms in her laundry basket.

'Well?' she said.

'Your galah?'

'Happy to be home.' She looked out to the yard, where the cocky sat on the clothes line. 'Barney's out with Ed, be home soon.'

'How are you?' The question he was asking was: *how are you coping with the loss of your boy now that you know Tilly Dunnage is close by?*

Mae shrugged.

'Where are your big girls?'

'Margaret's at work, Mary's with her boyfriend. He's got an automobile, which could mean trouble.'

'Yes . . . secluded, private.'

'Not that my girls are like that!'

'No . . . indeed.'

'Elizabeth's got a fiancé. She's working at Patches. You know, "Beautiful is the bride".'

'Oh, yes, Patches.' Hail spot and Chantilly lace. 'Who's the young man?'

'Nice lad, a bit posh. She wants to be a seamstress at Georges, in their workshop. Not much point if she's going to get married.'

'Things might change,' Sergeant Farrat said, and thought about the big McSwiney girls, their rouged cheeks, stocking tops and petticoat lace showing beneath their hems, blue roses in their hair, giggling and smoking cigarettes at the Station Hotel in Dungatar. He cleared his throat to tell her what he had come to say but his courage failed, so instead he told the story, again, about Mae's robust, straightforward girl, how he'd had to arrest her for punching a Winyerp wingman at the pub. 'He made the mistake of pinching her bottom. Never did it again.' The sergeant slapped his thigh.

Mae sighed. 'They're good girls but I can't stop them doing what they think they want to do.' She had never been able to stop her oldest boy's wild ways. She put a cup of hot water in front of the sergeant.

'And the others?'

'They're busy with pets, doing what kids do. How are things at Mrs Farrat's Hat Shop?'

'Peaceful.' The sergeant admired Mae's vegetable garden through the back door.

She put her iron down and her hands on her hips. 'All right, niceties over. Why are you here?'

'It's nothing sinister. I'll explain.'

She flicked the iron off at the switch on the skirting board with her toe and sat opposite him with her cup of hot water.

'Water's just right,' said the sergeant.

Mae nodded, and something in the air eased. They were the only two people they knew who enjoyed a cup of hot water. She gave him a knife and he cut two slices of cake, but they didn't eat. Instead they sipped their water, gazing at the floor. Then the sergeant put his cup carefully in its saucer and looked her fair in the eye. 'I need to explain something to you about Tilly.'

She reached with her foot and flicked the electricity back on, stood up and attacked the next school uniform, thumping the iron. The sergeant let her finish the back of the uniform before he said, 'You need to know.'

She didn't say anything, just stood the iron on the end of the board and walked down the hall and out into the street. Immediately the noisy kids fell silent. Mae bellowed, 'Get off that car, 's'not yours! Henry! Go and see if the big girls are coming. Now! Not you, Lotte, you won't come back. Charlotte! Get back here.'

Mae came back, muttering, 'Defiant little so-and-so . . .' She walked straight to the back door and looked out at the Hills Hoist.

'Mae, I want you to sit down.'

She picked up the iron. 'I can't take any more bad news sitting *or* standing, Sarge.'

'This isn't bad news.'

But there was something in his eyes that told her it would still hurt.

He took a pure-white precisely ironed hanky from his pocket and put it on the table. 'It's time you knew . . . and Tilly wants you to know.'

'Ed and I are thankful you helped us get the kids back from the convent. We're very happy in this house and we've thanked you for being guarantor, but we agreed that girl wouldn't try and see us, I thought you made that clear to her.'

'I did, but –'

'I got nothing against her, it wasn't her fault, but if it hadn't been for her –'

'You don't have to see her if you don't want to.'

Mae looked at Sergeant Farrat's posture and the delicate hands draped casually across his knees. Nothing about him suggested he was about to deliver death or tragedy. She sat down.

'But you'll want to see the baby.'

Mae just blinked at him.

'You have a grandson. His name is Joel Edward Dunnage and he is two and a bit years old.'

She held his gaze long enough to see that it was not a joke, that the sergeant was telling the truth. His pale eyes looked earnestly into hers, his mouth didn't twitch and he did not slap his knee and cry, 'Joke!' The breeze swirled around her again and it was warm, like a cardigan. Out in the backyard, the galah, a brilliant pink and grey, bobbed on her clothes line, his crest rising – 'Kiss cocky,' – and the sunlight twinkled through the leaves onto the dirt, suddenly magical, and the colours of the yard were extreme, the light sharp and clear, and though she couldn't fathom why, she was filled with amazement at how beautiful it all was.

'Joey?' said Mae.

'Joel.'

And while her heart shuddered about her sore breast, more words fell solidly into the warm air around her.

'I call him Joel, but others call him Joe. Tilly gave birth to him thirty-nine weeks after Teddy –'

'Yes, yes!'

'The baby was born in Dungatar, late December. At the end of January, I drove them to Winyerp, they caught the train to Melbourne. We didn't know where you were.'

Mae walked to the screen door and looked at the clothes line, which still looked magical. 'We'll have to deal with the Welfare Department again?'

The sergeant nodded. 'Children's Services.' They had seized Mae's children when she first got to Melbourne, and the sergeant had written a letter for her.

'We want to get him out of the convent, we just need a home for him, good care for him, while Tilly works for their income.'

Mae put her hand out and the sergeant placed the hanky in it. She buried her face in it and her shoulders shook.

When she drew her face from Sergeant Farrat's limp hanky, she was almost composed. Businesslike, she strode to the front door, yelled at the kids, 'Go'n getcha fartha,' and then came back, running a comb through her hair. She took the iron to the sink, emptied the water, removed her apron and straightened her muu-muu. 'I'll just get my purse.'

'We can't visit until Sunday.'

'Sunday is . . . it's six days away?'

'Tomorrow it'll only be five, four sleeps.' He wanted her to be calm when they united, a woman with a sensible plan and her wits about her.

Mae was defiant. 'I'll get the house ready for him anyway, set up another cot, get the gates fixed.'

'Keep yourself busy, time will fly.'

But they knew it would drag: the minutes would seem like hours, the days weeks, and the week a decade.

She looked again at the brilliant blue sky, the rich green trees over the back fences. They would find a way to make this work, but could they, *would* they, bear the burgeoning weight of Tilly Dunnage and her tale of woe?

'Joe,' she said.

# Chapter 6

OVER DINNER AT Windswept Crest, William introduced the topic of his exciting plans for expansion and productivity on the property. 'After harvest –'

'Harvest?' Suddenly, Elsbeth remembered the significance of all those green paddocks. 'We have a crop cheque due?'

'All going well, and then I will put into place a new crop-cycling regime and expand to lentils. I'm putting all my university education to use, Mother.'

'About time,' she said, and looked to Arlen. 'He squandered his opportunities when he married the grocer's daughter.' Elsbeth went on to remind everyone that William would build a hall for the community. Purl backed her up, saying they needed a space to rehearse *King Lear*, the eisteddfod was only a few months away, and Faith O'Brien mentioned she'd like to get the band back together. Septimus removed his hard hat and spread the town plans across the dinner table. His head was very strange: flat on top, with watery deltas of thinning hair spreading across it before dripping over its square edges.

William said they should build the fire station on the creek bank, near water, and Felicity Joy volunteered to clear the dinner plates and Arlen left the table. This time, he took himself all the way to the creek, the blood-orange sun blaring at him from between the dry gums, their slim branches rattling as birds settled for the night. He counted up the hours before the train returned.

On Arlen's third day, the people of Dungatar rose, crawled

into their impractical costumes, lined up for the bathroom (or the water tank in some cases; others went to the creek) then queued for breakfast – porridge, arduously prepared by Irma Almanac, who glided about the kitchen in her ancient wheelchair. Some set to work, sweeping the verandahs and washing the windows, trimming paths or digging in the vegetable garden. Some set off fishing or hunting rabbits; others rehearsed Act 1 Scene 2. Elsbeth Beaumont handed Arlen the play and announced he would be their prompt for the day.

Septimus chanted, 'This is the excellent foppery of the world – when we are sick in fortune, we blame the sun, the moon, and the stars for our disasters because we are villains, fools by heavenly compulsion, thieves, and treacherers, drunkards, liars, and adulterers –'

'Those words are an approximation of Shakespeare,' said Arlen.

Edmund shrugged. 'He's dead.'

Arlen began to consider escape even if it meant throwing himself in front of the speeding bus. Then William appeared, bounced on his toes and said, 'It's a good time to go for petrol. Gertrude will have calmed down by now and Mother's preoccupied: she's counting the chickens again, then she'll do the sheep.'

On their drive to Dungatar, William grappled with something. Eventually he said, 'People think little Myrtle Dunnage burned the whole town down, but it was an unseasonably hot day. It could have been a piece of glass on dry grass, or the rubbish tip – it had been smouldering for almost a year. And, as you know, the arson department have the report from the sergeant at the time, Sergeant Farrat, and the District Inspector.'

'Yes,' said Arlen, convincingly, and mentioned he had some personal ideas on the matter. He said he was 'on the trail of Tilly Dunnage' in order to reveal the actual truth.

'I wouldn't imagine you'd get much out of the stepmother,'

William offered. 'But you blokes are trained, you'll probably glean a lot from an encounter with her.'

They pulled up at the petrol pump. 'So,' William went on, 'use that training to get the key for the bowser from Gertrude and you can drive this bus to Winyerp to see Marigold Pettyman tomorrow.'

Gertrude the Terrible was standing brightly behind her counter; her hair was tidy, her lips red and the dress under her cardigan was contemporary, a big swishy thing.

'Hello again,' she purred, blinking rapidly, her painted blue eyelids like a busy wren.

'Good morning. I'd like some petrol, please.'

'Of course,' she said and, tottering out from behind her counter in high heels, she vanished behind the shop. The generator engine filled the air with noise and fumes then Gertrude brushed past, leaving a trace of Moonlight Mist. She unlocked the bowser and lingered, knowing her estranged husband waited behind the steering wheel. Gertrude was a girl who had been told by her father that she had the charisma of a canvas water bag. But she had shown him. She'd shown everyone. Gertrude had married the most eligible bachelor in town and she would win him back. She just needed an opportunity. And her opportunity was before her, a tall sinewy chap with straight black hair and lovely brown eyes, like her own. She could make William jealous by having an affair.

'You know,' she shouted over the generator, 'Tilly and I went to school together.'

Arlen said nothing, just watched the shillings and pence click over in the bowser meter, wondering what she was after.

Gertrude removed the nozzle from the bus. 'She makes lovely frocks.'

So, it was frocks. 'Did she make that dress?'

'Yes,' she lied, and Arlen produced the first of many jerry cans that needed to be filled. He concluded the dress must have been lovely once, and it would have fitted her.

She stepped close to him. 'I could come with you, help you look for her.'

'What about the shop?'

Her face changed and she lowered her voice. 'They can just go to bloody Winyerp, plenty of petrol there. You know, I was cast as Lady Macbeth for the Winyerp and Itheca Drama Society Eisteddfod.'

'I imagine you were believable in that role.' He put the full jerry can in the bus and took an empty one from William.

'I've been married,' she purred, 'and there are things about married life that I miss.' Gertrude fluttered her blue eyelids again.

Arlen said he knew very little about marriage, then regretted it when she offered to show him. He said he had no time, that he had to go back to Melbourne, then regretted that too.

She glanced up at William, ran her fingers over Arlen's cheek and yelled above the generator din, 'The train will be here Sunday. I'm happy to go with you. There's nothing for me here anymore.'

He screwed the lid on the last can. 'Thank you, Gertrude, and if I need help I'll let you know.'

William started the bus and Arlen said, 'Tick it up.'

'No credit allowed, cash only!'

'We haven't got any cash, dear,' called William.

Gertrude watched the bus lurch down the black dusty road, low and slow, jerry cans lashed to every seat, thrilled because William had seen her flirting, heard her say that she missed the joys of marriage. Now all she needed was Tilly Dunnage. She had made Gertrude look wonderful for the Dungatar dance, when Gertrude had captured William, so all she needed was to look wonderful again. And this man, Arlen, could lead her to Tilly.

*

Tilly Dunnage's stepmother was tremulous, like a small jelly mould, not quite set. A rash on her throat smarted when he spoke to her, yet there was something relentless about her. The other one, the blind one with the hole in her face, was withered and skinny, turtle-headed and toothless beneath the huge dark glasses. She had a fraught, desperate air about her, which was understandable given she depended on others for everything her senses once provided.

Marigold said, 'Who are you?'

'I'm an old friend of Tilly's.'

'*Friend?* Ha!'

'Liar,' snarled the turtle.

He was startled that she was so venomous. 'I knew her once but she sailed away.'

'Well, she came back by bus,' Beula said.

'And left again by train, the people at Fart Hill tell me.' Arlen sat down opposite the two women in the surgically clean asylum common room, all around them people conversing with no one, knitting, conducting an invisible orchestra, dancing to the orchestra, weaving baskets or, in one case, pissing into the fish tank, scattering the pretty little fish and dislodging the aquarium weeds. 'The question is, where is she now?'

'Melbourne.'

'Why do you say that, Mrs Pettyman?'

'I know everything you want to know.' She grabbed his hand, leaned up to him and whispered, 'I could take you straight to her, if you get me out of here.'

'*Us*,' said Beula, 'if you take *us*. We know everything, we've got the letter.'

'It's from the convent,' said Marigold. 'To my late husband.'

Arlen was struggling to fathom the two women. 'I'm sorry about your husband.'

'No need,' said Turtle-head.

With her free hand, Marigold clasped Arlen's lapel. 'The letter asks if Evan will donate money since he is "a long-established patron". They'll post me Myrtle Dunnage's file, if I want. They had the nerve to tell me to send a stamped self-addressed envelope.'

'You might know more than us?' Turtle-head suggested, excited.

Marigold continued, 'I can take you straight to the convent and I can ask the nuns for her address. And you wouldn't have to worry about me in Melbourne.' She put her hands to her throat where her rash pulsed. 'I have plans, and accommodation. In Toorak.'

'Have we? In Toorak?' Beula was even more excited.

Marigold had not yet made reservations at the Country Women's Association Hostel but she stood confidently and offered her hand to Arlen. 'When you confirm with the superintendent, have him phone to organise the train to stop to collect us.'

'Well, I'm not sure –'

'You'll be perfectly safe. We won't poison you.'

He laughed, then realised they possibly weren't joking.


Gertrude's plans to travel to Melbourne were scuttled when Faith mentioned, a little too gleefully, that Marigold and Beula were off to Melbourne on the Sunday train.

'The last time I went to Melbourne it was just grey, smelly and noisy,' sniffed Gertrude.

'I'd say it'd be all dressed up for the coronation these days, and they'll be getting lovely new frocks for Elsbeth's ball.'

'Ball?' Her chance to recapture William!

Faith was thrilled to convey to the failed Lady Macbeth and grocer's daughter that it was a special coronation ball.

'William's building the hall,' Lois chimed in.

'So I'm getting the band back together,' Faith said, as noncha-
lantly as she could.

'I won't be going to Elsbeth's silly old ball so I don't need a new
frock, and if I did, I'd just order something from Georges.'

Lois added, 'The rehearsals are comin' along, too. Elsbef's
doin' a good job of Amelia.'

Faith corrected her. 'Cordelia.'

Faith and Lois picked up their bread and sugar and left
Gertrude, mighty rips of glee and jealousy tearing beneath her
calm surface.

On Sunday, the superintendent drove Marigold, Beula, Arlen
and their nurse-chaperone to the Winyerp railway station. As
nurse-chaperone, the superintendent's wife proudly wore the
white nurse's uniform from her life before marriage, motherhood
and housework. The superintendent gave his wife a peck on the
cheek, shook Arlen's hand, wished him luck and went straight
to the pub. Marigold sat opposite Arlen so that she could gaze
at his dark, endearing eyes, the clickety-clack of steel wheels on
rail calming her as the bossy nurse chatted pleasantly about her
housework and the exorbitant prices since the war. 'Thank God
rationing has ceased, the price of sugar was far too high and I do
love baking.'

Passing Dungatar, Arlen again reflected on the grey-black
dirt and rubble, the broken goalposts at the footy ground, the
willows along the creek, big, dead and curled, the hulking silo
matched only by The Hill, and the one lone building in the main
street, the general store, where Gertrude the Terrible tyrannised
the locals. And all of it smack in the middle of those bountiful,
ripening crops.

Marigold shuddered. 'All that soot and ash.'

As the train drew away from the razed township Arlen

pondered; Tilly Dunnage was capable of burning a town down, he believed, so what could she have achieved in the years she'd been missing?

At Itheca, the train paused to take on freight, mail and passengers. Marigold announced, 'I'm parched,' and made for the tearooms. The nurse was compelled to accompany her gelatinous charge and her impaired friend. Beula climbed carefully from the train and followed the smoky shape of Marigold's blue frock and the loud voice coming from the nurse's hazy white form. Arlen happily declined the trek to the tearooms and opened his newspaper, glad of the quiet. Marilyn Monroe was America's foremost pin-up girl, Josip Tito was President of Yugoslavia and the USA was buying huge amounts of Australian uranium. 'Christ,' he said, 'the world will end up like Dungatar.'

Marigold sat her blind, deaf friend at the table with the nurse, who continued to fill the air with pointless words, though she had moved from shopping to the best use of washing powders. Marigold purchased a plate of sandwiches and pot of tea each, making sure the nurse got the plate containing the tinned tuna sandwich. Beula ate only the cakes on her saucer and Marigold nibbled at a plain sweet biscuit like a caterpillar with a leaf. When they left the cafeteria, the nurse stayed dozing, her chin on her chest, fingers through the cup handle and a half-chewed tuna and rice sandwich hanging from her lolling tongue. Beula followed Marigold's blue shape back onto the train and when it departed, Arlen looked up from his newspaper and smiled. 'Feeling better?'

'Much.'

'Where's the nurse?'

Marigold smiled. 'Resting. I brought you tea.' Arlen assumed the nurse was in the rest room. The tea was sour, so he went back to reading about the 1956 Olympic Games.

He woke at Spencer Street railway station, the big shed humming with fumes and steam. He found Marigold standing on the platform with a hanky pressed to her mouth and, beside her, Beula, disoriented in the draught and noise.

'Where's the nurse?'

'I have no idea,' Marigold said, clearly uncomfortable in the smelly, gritty railway station. She patted his arm. 'You go and organise a luggage trolley.'

'I don't need one,' he said, holding up his small shattered suitcase. 'What did you put in my tea?'

'I don't know what you're talking about.'

'You're trying to get rid of me, but I won't let you out of my sight until you honour your obligation to me in this Tilly Dunnage conspiracy, whatever it is. I can quite easily make a phone call and have you committed again.'

Beula blurted, 'She'll steal our money.'

'Why would she do that?'

'She's my next of kin. Everyone thinks I'm mad so naturally she'll want to claim my money,' said Marigold triumphantly.

'I can help you get your money.' He handed her his business card.

He watched the emotions play out on her face. First, she was intimidated, threatened, then cautious, then her face lit up. 'Certainly not. You'll just take my money too.'


That evening, the asylum superintendent had poured his second whisky, put aside his wartime magazine on the Battle of Passchendaele and was about to change the gramophone record when the telephone rang. It was the refreshment rooms at the Itheca railway station asking him to collect his wife, who had been sleeping soundly in one of their booths all afternoon. The superintendent rolled his eyes, looked at his watch and said, 'It can't be my wife, she's in Melbourne.'

'Her driver's licence matches her library card, it's your wife.'

'Well, just make her comfortable, I'll be there in the morning.' He hung up, turned the gramophone up and settled back with his whisky. The phone rang again. On his way to wrench it from the wall, he had another idea. 'I'm sending someone,' he told the canteen lady, and then phoned the asylum. When he had spoken to the ambulance driver he asked to be transferred to the night nurse in the emergency admissions ward.

# Chapter 7

AT THE THICK timber doors, she removed her gloves and rang the brass ship's bell. You could never hear them coming and they never hurried to the gate unless they were expecting the Monsignor, so she removed her hat and coat and waited, steadying her bike.

They used to see the nuns dawdle towards those doors – Sister Maria was particularly slow – every kid in the place watching from behind the tomato bushes or peeping from the cloisters, hoping. At first little Myrtle imagined her mother would come for her, but when she made a friend there, he advised, 'If you give up it doesn't hurt so much.'

But how could you give up when occasionally someone's mum or gran or father came and took them home, and at night the office phone rang and rang and rang while in their bunks they wept? Years later, twenty years in fact, Myrtle learned that her mother rang every Sunday and that Ruth, the Dungatar telephonist, never put the call through. Poor Molly was left in the phone box outside the post office, nothingness ringing in her ears, sending her mad.

A face, framed in a stiff white coif, appeared in the small square grate. It was Sister Patricia's soft pink face, smiling at her. This meant Tilly would not have to work in the laundry; she would be in the nursery today, surely?

The small timber door within the carriage door opened and Tilly said good morning and the sister said bless you. Tilly let her bike fall against the wall and bolted in case Sister Maria arrived to send her to the dungeon of industrial washing machines and forlorn unwed mothers. She ran past the chapel and the schoolrooms, past the midwifery building and the padlocked house and high-wire 'exercise yard' for wayward kids, and past the orphanage to the nursery.

The high chairs and low chairs bustled with round, chirping infants, while chubby babies wriggled, worm-like, on the floor, their short legs kicking. The toddlers stood at their playpen bars, eyes on her. Some bellowed, others whimpered or gurgled, and some were diverted by the pretty colours dancing through the high leadlight windows. The aspirants, postulants, novices, visiting mothers and volunteers glanced at her and then continued tending the infants. As she tied her apron, she saw her boy, standing perfectly still, beaming at her from the corner like a bonny child in a Vegemite advertisement. He ran, fat-legged, to her, arms flapping, his glorious blue eyes vivid in his chubby face, and she hurried, reaching for him, when suddenly a dark boulder blocked her. The precipitous Sister Maria, her robes blacking out Tilly's son. She had been there all along and she would be there next time to pounce and snatch up Joe. 'You haven't washed your hands yet.'

'I was just about –'

'You take Robin this morning.' She moved away like a giant manta ray, her black robes flapping, Tilly's son in her arms. Joe's face showed surprise, his eyes filling with tears and bottom lip turning down. Tilly smiled and waved, and he suddenly looked resigned, opening and closing his little fist, waving back. His small spirit was already crushed, his sense of protest quashed, and he wasn't yet three years old.

Banished from the perdition of Dungatar, little Myrtle Dunnage had found herself in the pitiless custody of the convent. Then she found Sister Patricia, and it was to Sister Patricia that she handed her son. It was to be a temporary hiding place: affordable, orderly, constant, with regular meals and a sense of security, the walls forbidding danger from outside. In her time there she had found most of the nuns kind, enlightened, well intentioned and hard-working, and Tilly was comforted that for those who were not, revenge belonged to the children from time to time. She'd occasionally left a pin in the bloomers she made for the nuns, and the kids on kitchen duty bragged that not everything in Sister Maria's soup was from the vegetable garden. In gangs, they gathered at the belltower with their slingshots. It was a perfect vantage point for a fair go at Sister Maria's ample bottom. It was that camaraderie with her fellow wards that had saved her, but Joe was young, vulnerable, so Tilly nurtured the relationship she'd had as a child with the kindly Sister Patricia. She would shield Joe as she'd shielded Tilly, allowing her to work towards a future. Soon, Tilly would be Joe's walls, his safe place, and every cell in her body told her this was coming to them both.

The ginger-haired baby was wailing, his little fists clenched and his face scrunched around his big wet mouth. 'Robin,' she cooed, and scooped him into her arms, snuggling his sad, pale body into hers. Immediately he eased and she took him to the kitchen for a bottle. Joe was there in a high chair, scooping food in the general direction of his face. Cradling Robin, she sat next to him and he offered her his gooey white dinner.

'Thanks, but I've eaten,' she said, and whispered, 'Today, you will meet your grandparents, and then soon, hopefully, I can take you home.' Joe smiled and touched her head with his spoon. The sergeant was confident they would like Joe, and Tilly was hopeful they would want him as part of their family, but she was wary. The apprehension of seeing them all again after what had happened made her nauseous. Would they repel her, or would they claim Joe, take him as their own?

\*

They watched her walking to them through the garden, rudely alive. Her hair was short, dark and messy and she wore a plain pinafore over a black sweater. She was sure-footed but graceful on the grass in her red ankle boots, more angular than they remembered, holding the boy to her hip, as one.

The waiting group stood, Sergeant Farrat wearing a navy double-breasted suit and Mae McSwiney wearing her best hat, the same best hat she'd always worn, and a blue muu-muu with a frill at the bottom. Behind her, Edward McSwiney, smart in one of Sergeant Farrat's casual jackets, held his hat in his scrubbed hands. They did not look at her, their gaze and beatific smiles only for the small boy she put on the grass before them. Mae picked Joe up. He leaned back from her, looked to his mother, who smiled and nodded, so the boy touched the tears sliding down Mae's cheeks. He looked at Edward as if he'd seen him before but wasn't sure where, then studied all the other people, carefully, his expression grave. They all stared, wordlessly, noting his arms, fingers, his ears and nose, his curls. Finally, Mae looked at Tilly. 'You got any money?'

'I save what I can after rent and Joe's care, but I haven't quite got enough for a home –'

'He can live with us,' Edward said.

'Why did you put him here?'

'No one can come and take him away. He's voluntary so I can take him home, as soon as I have one.'

'They're not all kind, here.' Mae moved the boy, a heavy two-year-old, to her other hip.

'No, but Sister Patricia was always kind to me. She told me that what happened to Stewart Pettyman that day wasn't my fault.'

'We knew that, but we didn't know about Joe.' Mae continued to glare at her.

'When he was born we didn't know where you all went. No one knew where you were.'

Edward said again, 'Leave him with us, just until you're on your feet. You can take him of a weekend.'

She had dreamed of waking with him, being alone with him for an entire weekend, but the Shorts wouldn't let her have her baby in her room, even for one day. 'No children,' they'd said, and suddenly Tilly was afraid and feeling apart from everyone, and vulnerable. 'If I did that you could only keep him until I found somewhere that would have children. I do want him with me, he's mine.'

'We would never take him from you,' Edward said, and Mae added, 'We know what it's like to lose a child too,' the sword of Mae's grief cutting her heart.

The sergeant said, 'And Tilly would never take him from you, would you?'

'Never,' she said, and meant it.

Then Sister Maria was gliding towards them, her arms tucked up into her outer sleeves, veil floating and the cross on the end of her rosary beads swinging. 'Put the child down now, he will expect to be held all day.' Mae did not let the baby go, and Sister Maria slid her hands from her sleeves, readying for a fight. 'And you, Mae and Edward McSwiney, itinerants who secrete umpteen children into poverty, a camp on a river bank, you're not thinking of taking this child, are you?'

'We are his grandparents,' Edward said.

'That is my point. I doubt the Welfare Department thinks you're suitable.'

How foolish Tilly had been to think things would end well.

'How do you do?' The sergeant stepped forward. 'I am Senior Sergeant Horatio Farrat.'

'I don't care who you are.'

'I am Joel Edward's godfather, and an old friend of the family. The McSwiney family camped by the river as a temporary measure. It was easy for Edward to earn an income and search for a home. The home they have now is far more suitable than this sparse and draughty institution. Joe will have the undivided love of his family, plenty of people to care for him and, most importantly, his mother.'

'So we'll be taking Joe with us today,' Mae announced.

'That's not possible,' Sister Maria said. 'He is an illegitimate child of an illegitimate mother, and you, Myrtle Dunnage, are not married, you have no home, and the child should be speaking by now and he isn't. There's something wrong with him.'

'There's nothing wrong with him,' Mae said.

'I suppose you think there's nothing wrong with that middle boy of yours, either.'

'Barney's perfect the way he is,' Tilly said.

'Nonsense. He needs special care and you can't even see that.'

'Joe is mine,' Tilly said firmly. 'He's a voluntary ward, and now that I have found care for him with his grandparents I am taking him with me.'

'You cannot take a child like that and just hand him to someone who is not suitable.' She grabbed Joe's arm. 'Speak, child. Say something.'

Joe looked at the ground, clearly afraid.

Mae said, 'This is wrong.'

Sister Maria hauled up her rosary beads and pointed the cross at Mae. 'We don't consider any of you fit to have any child, let alone this one. You need to take it up with the Monsignor and the Welfare Department.'

She turned and marched back across the lawn, a black fluttering thing dragging a toddler by the arm. Stumbling, Joe turned back and waved.

They retreated to the McSwineys' homely dwelling in Collingwood, where they sat in the hot kitchen despondently drinking tea, Ella Fitzgerald on the radio singing 'Someone to Watch Over Me'. The tears continued to slide down Mae's face.

Barney clutched the teddy bear. 'But I wanted to meet him.'

Tilly held her midriff as though it were haemorrhaging, her confused situation scraping like barbed wire in her mind. That very morning she had been standing alone and upright, but now . . . The past was indeed prologue and somehow, in doing the right thing, she had lost her child and her ability to cope, to maintain things. And her tragedy was once again the McSwineys' pain.

'There is a way to fix this,' Edward said, though he had no idea what that way was. Still, the McSwineys were grateful that he spoke. His words gave them hope.

Around him all the women were weeping and the sergeant felt he should take command, but in what way? How could he stop this torment? Then an idea came to him. It would fix everything, but he needed to think through the implications. It was his duty to help them get Joel Edward back, he owed them that. But that meant he would come under the close scrutiny of the Welfare Department. They would surely visit his home. What if they followed him to the Hippocampus Club? Sergeant Farrat started to feel sick. If he acted on his idea to save them all then he would not be able to *dress* again. Ever. To be discovered was to be harassed, charged with corrupting the moral order, wrongly accused of homosexuality and hauled up in court, *exposed* . . . jailed. Only four years ago he might have hanged.

A vision came to him of many police tearing shoes, hats, frocks from his wardrobe and throwing them from the balcony into the street. But . . . if Tilly and Joel were there with him, if they lived in his house, it would legitimise every item in every wardrobe. Tilly wore dresses, though not as often as she once had.

The sergeant stood, straightened his tie and stepped towards Tilly. He sank to one knee. 'Myrtle Dunnage,' he said, taking her hand, tear-drenched hanky and all, 'you would do me the greatest honour if you would marry me.'

Mae and Edward and their children remained mute, incredulous. The McSwineys looked at each other. It was an idea, a way to fix things.

'It's possibly worth a try,' said Edward.

And Mae said, 'It's perfect.'

Tilly was turning this startling notion over in her mind. A wedding meant attention, they would have to appear married, be a couple, their lives scrutinised. But in an instant she would have a home, a future with Joe. They would live as a family. The Welfare Department, Children's Services, would raid them, surely? Sister Maria would see to that. Though it was simple, really – one wardrobe for women's clothing, one for men's. Normal. Legal.

She thought of Nita Orland throwing her lovely head back, laughing. 'I have had no misfortune. I have, in fact, triumphed over prejudice and oppression.'

She leaned across to the sergeant and for one horrible moment he thought she was going to kiss him, but she just said, 'I'll make you something special to wear to the wedding.'

He smiled. 'Good, I look like a flaming gatepost in the vermilion sarong dress.'

# Chapter 8

TILLY NOTICED THE man lingering by Charlie's newsstand. It was his suit – three-piece, double-breasted, the waistcoat single-breasted. The trousers were narrow with no turn-ups and his trilby was the same colour as his slip-on shoes. Very modern. The man was tall with the familiar, prepossessing posture of stylish men. A faint reassurance placed its arms around her shoulders and with it came a sense of previous times, pleasant times. There had been days of sweet security in her past . . . then her mind started heading back to Teddy McSwiney so she barged into the salon, filling it with Melbourne morning air – a dash of garbage bin, exhaust fumes and tram dust.

The staff were assembled for the morning meeting. Salon Mystique had more new clients than anyone was equipped for, the Smalls Ball was looming and Mrs Flock's final designs for the winter coronation collection were on their way. Tilly found the outworkers and their supervisors standing patiently amid the strange new forest of half-dressed Stockmans. Some seamstresses moved around them like maypole dancers; some gathered like moths, in circular huddles, around squares of windowlight, stitching. Enclosing them, the walls were a showroom of sketches and samples and the air was warm with the smell of fabric; velvet, jersey, gabardine, melange cottons, poplin, silk, satin and faille, wool blends and houndstooth, herringbone jacquards and brocades.

Valda said, 'You're late. You are unreliable and far too selfish to work in a team.'

'I know.' Tilly sighed. 'I tried to change once, but it didn't work.'

'Fair enough,' said Shirley, and Mrs Flock said there was no place for insolence at Salon Mystique.

'Not much place for anything, even the customers,' said Shirley, her gaze moving around the crowded salon.

A mannequin arrived, half-naked, wearing a half-constructed toile and said, 'I can't raise my arms, I can't even bend my elbows.'

'Tilly will fix it,' Mrs Flock called.

'It's not my design.'

'Well, make it yours.'

Mrs Flock seemed quite happy with most of what passed before her on the mannequins, or Clare; even some of the seam-stresses modelled. Tilly, on the other hand, considered some of the workmanship all too obvious. Occasionally, a toile appeared on a Stockman or a model and it was refreshing to see that the diploma-course seamstresses who made the toile had brought something new to Madame's design, but some toiles emerged inappropriate to the sketch and others simply appeared as calico garments that in no way met their potential, like the one currently before her, on the mannequin. Usually, trying the toile on another mannequin might work, but in the interests of saving time and of good craftsmanship, Tilly was happy to cull . . . which is what she would do to the toile with the unusual sleeves that the manne-quin was trapped in. It had missed the basic point, which was that it needed to be able to be worn. Tilly asked the mannequin to please remove the toile and bring it to her.

Shirley showed Tilly her punctured, sore fingertips. 'I swear my fingers are shorter than they were a month ago.'

'That's because you're good at your job. All these extra clients might turn into decent wages and a good reputation that will take you to a better salon, and you can erase this place from your memory.'

Madame Flock gestured at her salon, at present a working atelier, and raised her upturned nose. 'Today, I will present the final remaining sketches for the winter coronation collection. You will take direction regarding these designs from Tilly Dunnage.'

Valda blurted, 'She's the head designer now, is she?'

The entire room turned to look at Tilly.

Tilly shrugged. 'I'll never be head designer, I'm unreliable and far too selfish.'

'And you don't work well in a team,' Valda agreed.

'Which means she's better off in a room of her own,' Madame Flock said. 'Valda will take over the utility room and Tilly will use Valda's room.' This meant Valda would work from what was basically the cleaner's cupboard.

'But that's full of –'

'You will remain *Atelier Première*. Tilly Dunnage will be *Directrice Technique*. She is making the signature pieces and over-seeing the collection.'

It became clear that resentment was moving from Valda through the ranks of the outworkers, those supervisors who tirelessly toiled at home, in neighbourhood factories, anywhere, waiting for a chance to show Madame their designs, hoping to work in the atelier. Tilly was accustomed to hatred, but preferred the mutual respect she'd enjoyed during her years working abroad, talent working with talent and everyone working with pride, towards beauty.

'I cannot be expected to design and make costumes for beauty queens and dowagers, create signature pieces as well as oversee the coronation collection for forty-nine shillings a week. It's illegal.' She held her arms out, embracing her colleagues. 'We are all working very hard for you, what will you do for us?'

The room was silent.

Madame crossed her thin arms, pressing her sack-like dress against her inadequate torso. Her voice was low. 'You are all here because you want to make couture, or at least that's what you told me when you came for the job. Your duties are more satisfying than they've ever been, surely?' She pointed to Valda. 'Any complaints should be directed to the *Atelier Première*; it is her job to satisfactorily coordinate activities in the workrooms.'

Tilly knew she was venturing into risky territory but was unable to stop. 'We are complaining now.'

'Actually,' said Valda, haughtily, 'most are not complaining, most just want to work. It's only you, our new technical director, who is unhappy.' Around her, the workers shuffled in agreement and doubt.

'I'm not happy,' called Shirley, and the crowd turned to her. 'I want to be treated fairly even if no one else does.'

'Then leave, find employment elsewhere,' said Mrs Flock. 'There are plenty more cutters out there.'

Shirley demurred; she would stick with Tilly Dunnage from Dungatar. It seemed to Shirley that the new Director of Technique was going places, and Shirley was determined to go with her.

Tilly smiled reassuringly at Shirley while the rest of the room was static with indecision, thrown by the prospect of the new supervisor. But Tilly's only concern was that her pieces would be noticed, what she had drawn interpreted correctly, the cut, its shape, living line and movement perfect.

Madame started distributing the final sketches to the supervisors. 'The supervisors know to choose toiles and patternmakers to suit each design, and of course, the right seamstress. Your input and hard work will see results in sales and you will all be rewarded appropriately in good time.'

Madame Flock raised her chin, turned on her heel, and left, Valda scuttling along behind her.

Tilly felt the eyes of the resentful women around her, the tireless home workers who dreamed of a real job in a real salon, who had just been usurped by a Tilly Dunnage from Dungatar.

She needed those seamstresses onside, so she raised her hands in surrender. 'Please, just stay and listen to me, that's all I ask.'

The women in the room stood still, but most chose not to look at her.

'Mrs Flock is right. You know the particular individual talents of your co-workers, so you are best placed to find the right person for the right design among yourselves, and you know how to work with your friends. I don't doubt that every seamstress will work tirelessly. I will support you in any way I can. All you have to do is ask, but I appreciate that you are all talented and have initiative.'

Their sour expressions faded but nonetheless, they turned away.

'I'd like to feel we're all working together towards a collection you can be proud of, a collection that shows your skills as seamstresses . . .' Even if the designs were terrible, the work needed to avow the women who had built them. The supervisors were moving to the door to go back to their sweatshops and the workroom seamstresses returned to their quiet, precise stitching, to their Stockmans, cutting tables and sketchpads. But the fact remained that the actual production of everything was the responsibility of the upstart, and she did not have her colleagues onside. Yet.

That evening, Tilly joined her fiancé at the Windsor. She sashayed up the stairs, looking very pleased with herself, ordered champagne and settled into the plush lounge next to him. Sergeant Farrat was dressed impeccably in a lovely striped two-piece suit made of fine-spun wool, and a silk shirt, baroque, with ruffled cuffs and shirtfront. 'Hello, dear.'

'Dearest,' she said affectionately, and lit a cigarette.

'You look as if you've been naughty.' Her fiancé's socks had ruffled trims.

'I've been promoted.'

'Do tell.'

'I am assistant designer to Mrs Flock.'

'No!'

'I even have an office, a *bureau de rêveries*, a home for my imagination, my creativity.'

'Tilly, such news!'

'I can't escape the resentment from some of the girls in my daydream room, but I have managed to implant notions of mutiny.'

'I guessed that somewhere there'd be trouble. You will, of course, leave when it erupts?'

'Of course. But I cause trouble only for truth and justice, and those mutineers are artists, so visionary couture will rally them.'

The sergeant looked amused. 'Or vengeance?'

'Out of it I hope to create a sense of pride in the seamstresses, and gratitude, and a good name for their skills, but most particularly, my skills.' Tilly sat forward. 'Now, where do I have to go and what do I have to do to make your big day perfect?'

The barman arrived, bringing champagne. He picked up a list from the table and glanced at it. 'Is this our guest list?' he asked, archly.

'Our guest list?' One of Tilly's eyebrows shot up. 'We are having guests?'

'Tilly, this is Elmer, an old friend, you might remember him from the Hippocampus Club.'

'The whale,' he said.

The sergeant snatched the list back. 'It's one of the lists required to create a wedding, why?'

'Oh, no reason, just being supportive as I always have been these past years. These past many, many years.'

The sergeant rolled his eyes. 'Elmer, just because we were in the force together doesn't mean you have any sway in my wedding.'

'We graduated together.' Elmer explained to Tilly that he had retired honourably some time ago.

'It's not really a wedding, Elmer, it's more of a practical arrangement,' Tilly said.

'Obviously,' he snapped, eyeing the list, 'but it's still an occasion.' He sniffed. 'Now, Horatio, how many attendants are you having?'

'None,' cried Tilly.

'Horatio should have attendants, it's not as if he'll ever get married again.'

Tilly pointed out that she had no friends she could ask.

'You have us now,' said Elmer. 'Perhaps wear something that marks your presence against ours?'

'Thank you, Elmer, I will.'

'Tell me the colour so we don't clash,' he said.

'You're not wearing white?' Sergeant Farrat asked.

'You can try to be funny, Sergeant, but you never will be,' Tilly said.

# Chapter 9

THE FOLLOWING DAY, she walked home from work in the muted dusk carrying the sense of her new beginning, and as she pushed opened the gate, Mr Short jumped out in front of her. 'You have to get rid of them.'

'Who?'

'Your visitors. We turned a blind eye to that bird you had hidden up there but you know visitors are strictly forbidden – children and adults, even if they have travelled from the country.' He pointed to the front door of the house.

Dread pulled on the knot in her stomach. She felt hot, breathless. 'Please tell them I won't see them.'

'I'm not your butler,' he called, his voice shrill.

'You once said to me, "I make the rules, I enforce them".' She heard noises swelling in the vestibule. She felt an impulse to bolt, to run to the maze of bluestone lanes.

'They'll only come back again,' said Mr Short, hitching his high grubby trousers higher. 'There've been others.'

'Others?'

'A woman in a gold coat.'

Tilly wiped her sweating palms on her trousers and squared her handsome shoulders, readying herself to face whoever it was. At the sight of the two women standing at the bottom of the stairs, bile rose. Marigold, still nervous and whippet-like, was holding a hanky to her throat, and beside her, wearing thick glasses, was Beula Harridene. Beula was facing the wrong way and clutching a long white cane. A luggage tag was pinned to her cardigan between her shoulders. It said, 'I am blind, my name is Beula Harridene, my address is Winyerp Asylum.'

Here it was, her past come for her. And she was afraid.

These two women before her were devoid of the jewels of life: compassion, generosity and intelligence. She knew their flaws, she'd covered the likes of them in expensive cloth and beautiful lines; she'd made them even more vain, more competitive and greedy, and they had self-destructed over a cursed play about ambition, treachery and reprisal. But they had not heeded her reprisal. And here they were again, resurrected. Marigold was wearing a dress Tilly had made from pale pink Belgian linen. It had a wide stand-away collar of white cotton, very pretty, and as Tilly had attached the small bow to the side of the straw pillbox hat, which Sergeant Farrat had built from a gardening hat purchased at Pratts General Store, Molly had wheeled up to her and spat, 'I don't know why you bother, they'll never like you.'

She was suddenly enraged. 'How did you find me? You had me followed, didn't you?'

'Wrong!' cried Beula, as if it were a quiz.

'It was the nuns, then. They had no business telling you my address.'

Marigold screeched, 'We know about the boy . . . my step-grandson. You hid him from us in Dungatar.'

Tilly pointed at the front door. 'Get out.'

Mr Short opened his apartment door so that his beached wife could hear more clearly.

'We know things about you,' Beula said. 'We can tell the nuns that people have died because of you.'

Mr and Mrs Short gasped, and Marigold turned blind Beula so that she faced Tilly rather than the coat stand.

'It was self-defence,' Tilly said softly. 'And anyway, she didn't really like him, did you, Marigold?'

Marigold shrugged. 'Stewart *was* very much like his father.'

'Who you killed,' Tilly reminded her, herding Marigold towards the front door.

'You've killed more people than me.'

Behind them, Mr Short turned pale.

Tilly leaned close to Marigold. '*I* didn't kill anyone on *purpose.*'

Beula nudged Marigold. She pressed the hanky into her reddening throat. 'If you don't help me I'll go straight to the convent and tell them everything about you.'

Tilly saw her reflection, fierce but not quite convincing, in Beula's dark glasses, so she stepped closer and spoke to the dried, frothy saliva gathered in the corners of her unfortunate mouth. 'What is the real reason you're here? You want a gown? Just make an appointment, you know where I work.'

'We can't afford new frocks since you made us homeless. We have nothing.'

Mr Short said, 'Jesus Christ Almighty.'

Beula pointed away from Tilly towards Mr Short's voice. 'But if we get Marigold's money back –'

'So, it's money.' Tilly turned and ascended the stairs, two at a time. 'And the authorities won't give you your money, Marigold, because you're insane?'

'You wouldn't really expect them to, if that's the case,' said Mr Short, heading up the stairs behind Marigold and Beula, bashing along.

Marigold called, 'I need a new guardian.'

At the top landing, Tilly barred them. 'I will kill you if you try to take my child.'

'As it turns out, you, Tilly Dunnage, are my only remaining next of kin.'

Tilly looked at Marigold, so pitiful. It was wrong, but it was also the law. As a woman, Marigold had no voice in the matter.

She had been abused and exploited by her husband, as had Tilly's mother. They were almost comrades.

'We're women, and we have "pasts", so the law won't favour us in anything. It's your money, Marigold. *Yours*. Get a lawyer.'

'Be my guardian.'

Tilly laughed. 'That will ruin your case entirely. It's been interesting, this little encounter, but I never want to see you ever again.' Tilly grabbed Beula's hand and put it on the balustrade. 'There are ten steps and one small landing and then another ten to the bottom.'

'Thank you.'

'A year ago, I would have told you to turn sharply to the left after ten steps and watched you splatter onto the tiles.'

Marigold started wailing, 'Please. My lawyer won't even see me. We were turned away.'

Tilly shrugged and lit a cigarette.

'And she relapsed.' Beula pointed in the general direction of Marigold. 'Took some sleeping potion and passed out for two days.'

'The bottle slipped as I poured, that's all.'

'Just appoint another guardian. Why don't you appoint Beula?'

'Yes!' Beula said to a dress hanging behind Tilly's door. 'I'm the only one here who hasn't killed anyone.'

Marigold grabbed Tilly's arm. 'My guardian must be a person of sound health, she must have *vision*, someone who is worldly, with financial savvy, perhaps someone who has run a business. And she needs to be someone who is compelled to act *only* in my best interests rather than her own.'

Tilly retrieved her arm from Marigold's grip. 'I see. You need a guardian you can blackmail.' She blew cigarette smoke in Beula's direction. 'So, I'll have to do what you want or else you'll tell on me and I'll lose Joe.'

'Exactly,' said Beula. 'Clever, isn't it?'

'But as your guardian, I can have you sent to the asylum. You'd never get your money. I'll take it.'

Marigold steeled herself. 'Your baby will go back into custody and we'll also tell welfare about the clothes Sergeant Farrat wears and his collusion with the District Inspector over the fire.'

They heard Mr Short gasp outside the door.

Tilly was not fazed. She had endured worse. Then Beula snarled, 'Those tip-livers, the McSwineys, we can tell the Welfare Department much more about them.'

'Your father, my husband, stipulates in his will that in the event of his untimely and unfortunate death, all money is to go to me but only if I'm deemed to be completely healthy by the relevant medical professionals. Failing that, it's to go to Stewart, the next of kin. But Stewart isn't here –'

'Because of you, Myrtle Dunnage!' Beula pointed her stick at the dress.

Outside, they heard a noise, as if someone had dropped a puppy. Mr Short had fallen to the floor. 'My God . . . you women.'

Marigold stamped her foot and Beula snarled, 'We'll tell the convent that you killed a footballer, blinded me, and that you're a pyromaniac and you burned the town down.'

Marigold pulled her gloves on. 'You could at least come with me to see my lawyer, Mr Hawker. Oh, and by the way, I want a coronation gown.'

Tilly was almost speechless. 'Outrageous!'

'No, just do your usual – make something simple, stylish, timeless.' Marigold handed Tilly Mr Hawker's card. 'Telephone me at the CWA, in Toorak, when you have made an appointment.'

'We can make sure you don't get your son, ever,' said Beula.

As Tilly watched the two women cross Nicholson Street against the traffic lights, a tram missing them by an inch, she knew that even with the safety of marriage, they could still destroy her, and others.

# Chapter 10

EVERY DAY, MAE fronted up at the convent, a cane basket over her arm filled with soft toys, balls, clothes and puzzles, but she was never allowed to see Joe, her first and only grandchild. Eventually, she left the gifts for the children and hoped they were passed on. When Sunday came around Mae could not see any of her gifts in the nursery playroom, but Joe was happy to see his mother and new friends again and went easily to the garden to play with them. They brought him a sandwich and a cupcake, a spade and bucket, and he set to work with a pile of dirt. When he got bored he sat on everyone's knee before going back to his quiet ways with his new tools.

Tilly felt the McSwiney family's reserve and knew the thing that lurked. They would always wonder why, how, what had actually happened that night. As her mother had carried shame for a lifetime, it was her penance to carry the death of Teddy, but the void in their life might be somewhat filled with Teddy's son.

As they were all leaving, they found Sister Maria waiting, standing as still as a gatepost in her black robes.

'You will not get this child,' she said. 'There is someone suitable to oversee this boy's care, an agreeable type of person with social standing and a secure financial situation.'

Tilly was rendered speechless, but suspected who it was.

Mae took a step towards the old nun. 'Who?'

'We are in contact with his step-grandmother.' For a full three seconds, no one could think or speak until Mae cried incredulously, 'Marigold Pettyman?'

'She's the one who needs care!' cried Edward. 'She's mad as a box of hot frogs.'

'She is not long released from the asylum,' said Tilly, coolly.

'She's cured,' Sister Maria said. 'I have paperwork that proves it.'

'A letter only proves that someone wrote that Marigold isn't nuts,' Edward said. 'You should ask who wrote it and why.'

'We'll get to the bottom of this,' Mae said.

Sister Maria said, 'We see that she will be a stable, respectable influence, and she has a home.' Sister Maria walked away, calling over her shoulder, 'We have sought advice on the matter . . . from the Welfare Department.'

Tilly knew not to mention that Marigold's home was just ash; it would provoke questions, and in the face of Mae and Edward's injury, fury and disillusion, she could only turn away.

On Monday, just as everyone was about to start peeling spuds and running the bath for their youngsters, the children up and down the Collingwood street fled, gates crashing shut and front doors slamming. A dark, coat-clad figure appeared on the footpath at the end of the block, growing larger as he progressed. He kicked aside abandoned hopscotch taws, cricket bats and footballs. Eyes peeped through lace curtains and from behind foliage. Where was the Child Welfare Department officer heading? Whose house? What reports and files were in that briefcase, light in his big hand?

Someone shouted, 'Watch out,' but it was too late. The welfare officer was already at the vacant block on the corner. He studied the large piebald half-draughthorse dozing under a fruit tree, a galah perched between his ears. Standing on its back, reaching up into the tree and stuffing apricots into their pockets, socks, shirts, hats and skirts, were several children. McSwiney sprogs. A stone flew past his ear from behind and hit the ground near the horse, who opened its eyes and gently turned its head in the direction of the officer. The welfare officer took a file from his case: George, Victoria, Charles, Henry and Charlotte. He looked up. That would be the imbecile child, Barney, standing beside the horse, holding the hand of the youngest, Rex.

'You're stealing,' he called. 'And the horse is not safe.'

The children raised the fruit to fling it at the man in the suit but Barney said, 'Welfare,' and the small thieves looked for an escape. The officer was standing in the gateway. They sat down on Graham and dropped the fruit to the ground, the horse gathering the apricots with his fat lips and squashing them sweetly with his tongue.

The hulking man, big and square with a small head and deep-set eyes, proceeded onwards to the McSwineys' house, the curtains along the street falling back into place as he passed. In Mae's warm, cluttered kitchen, he said, 'In my capacity as Welfare Officer of Children's Services, I have been asked to gauge your living conditions. It is my duty to make sure the children are released into a secure and suitable situation –'

'I know.' Mae stirred the stew simmering on the stove and went back to her ironing. 'You keep telling me that and I keep telling you they are secure and we are suitable parents and we live in a house and we have jobs. The kids go to school.'

'When you decamped the banks of the Yarra River for this . . . dwelling, your spawn were discharged back into your care. You have provided shelter, but not care. Those minors are unsupervised infidel miscreants.'

'Isn't that the same thing? Miscreants and infidels?' She turned the shirt and ran the iron over the sleeve, front and back.

'The menaces of the world should be supervised lest their dangerous actions harm others.'

'Well, why are you loose in the world?'

She saw the shock on his face at the same time he tried to defeat it. 'You, Mrs McSwiney, are insolent and disrespectful.'

She flipped the shirt on the ironing board. 'Those two words mean the same thing too, insolent and disrespectful.'

The welfare officer stamped his foot.

'Now see here,' said Mae, gesturing with her iron. 'It's dangerous getting kids to stir huge pots of boiling soup, to send them out to tables with trays full of scalding porridge, making them work like grown criminals in your ruddy reformatory, not to mention the emotional torture and cane whippings. I take care of my kids. You harm them, for life!' She ironed the cuffs of the shirt and slipped it onto a hanger in front of the officer, blocking her view of him.

'The horse is an animal, it can't be trusted.' He reached to brush the shirt aside but she slapped his hand away and inspected the garment for grimy marks.

'Graham was born into this family twenty-seven years ago. Like his mother before him and her mother, he would sooner front up at the glue factory than see any of those kids hurt. He's been known to stand over them to keep them dry on a rainy-day picnic.'

'I am writing that he is a horse, and horses are not safe.'

'He'd dispute that if he could read,' Mae said, and removed his briefcase from the table near her ironing. 'Leave my house – you are making my laundry grubby and your presence is preventing my children from coming in to eat their dinner.'

The welfare officer opened the small kerosene fridge and cupboards to see if there was sufficient food. Mae pointed to the fecund vegetable garden in the backyard and got on with her ironing. At the chook shed, the officer turned up his nose, and put a hanky over his face when he came to the ferrets. He sneezed when he got to the rabbits and, fortunately, missed the pet mice entirely. He returned to inspect every small crowded room of the McSwiney home, pulling back blankets, scrutinising sheets for infestations and opening cupboards to check on clothing.

'You have pets and a chicken coop, you will attract disease and rodents.'

'Obviously.'

The welfare officer missed her sarcasm and informed her that she could expect another inspection at any time, by any number of officers.

'Well, the sooner you're gone the sooner you can come back.' She closed the door firmly behind him and gathered her worried brood from the back lane, where they were hiding. 'Hands up who thinks Graham's a safe horse.'

Everyone put their hands up, except Barney. 'He's not safe from the officers.'

And neither were the McSwineys, now that Tilly Dunnage was back.

It was poetry night at the Hippocampus Club, and Sergeant Farrat arrived early, intending to choose the judge as a discussion partner. He joined the Supreme Court judge at the bar and handed him Shakespeare's sonnets, knowing he was a fan, though the judge had come dressed as Dorothea Mackellar, expensively wrapped in a short mink-trimmed cape, with glacé-kid lace-ups and matching handbag. The sergeant had come dressed as himself. While the judge read Sonnet Two, Elmer poured his favourite drink.

'When forty winters shall besiege thy brow
And dig deep trenches in thy beauty's field,
Thy youth's proud livery, so gazed on now,
Will be a tattered weed, of small worth held . . .'

The judge finished the poem and they mused that if it was the sixteenth century, they'd be long dead, but still beautiful because they would have died before their brows were besieged, yet these days there was no shame or lack of pride in old age given a good frock could make you feel like a queen before her 5 pm gin and tonic; and how, actually, for them it was a bit of a toss-up when it came to old age versus dying young and beautiful. The judge then pointed out that his beauty was preserved since he had several offspring and many grandchildren, and thus the sergeant was able to boast that he was about to become a father.

'So I hear,' the Supreme Court judge said, then reminded Horatio that marriage licences were outside his field and drew his cape closed.

'Well, I'd never want to impose,' the sergeant said, 'but I do like your shoes – where did you get them?'

'Flattery won't work, Horatio, I mean really . . . what's your poor defrauded fiancée going to do when she finds your frocks?'

'She makes them for me, she's a seamstress.'

The sergeant had his full attention now.

'I knew it! You always said you made them yourself but you have some dresses that are clearly made by someone who knows couture. Well, then, congratulations, lucky man.'

Elmer, dressed as Emily Dickinson in a severe 1880s crinoline and velvet throat ribbon, his hair parted down the middle, quickly filled the judge's glass.

'Thank you.' The judge looked down at his silk and velvet hip-length wrapover dress with its bias-cut waterfall side panel. He'd had it made in 1929. 'Look, I do know someone, and a marriage licence won't be a problem, but I want a coronation gown, all right?'

Elmer filled Sergeant Farrat's glass, and one for himself.

'Naturally.' At the very least, Tilly would measure, consult and design, but where to find the time to make the gown?

The judge took a packet of cigarettes from his bag. 'And am I invited to the wedding?'

'We all are,' said Elmer, and the sergeant went on to say that they hadn't finalised the guest list. 'We have great plans to decorate the club.'

'I hate weddings, *normally*,' said the judge. 'But I'm looking forward to yours.' He looked at Elmer. 'I'd be careful not to celebrate here, though. In fact, I'd be careful for the next few weeks.' If the judge said not to have the wedding here, if he said to be careful, then Elmer knew to close up for a while, or at least to warn the regulars not to *dress*.

Tilly put aside thoughts of Marigold and Beula and set about transforming Miss Post Office Picnic into a beauty queen while keeping an eye on the largely dated and uninteresting collection for the coronation parade. She ignored Mrs Flock's Victor Stiebel gown, instead conjuring four signature pieces for the collection and a glorious gown for Nita Orland. And all the while she dreamed of Joe, her arms heavy with the need to hold him, every stitch bringing her closer to independence.

Her thoughts drifted, as they always did, towards her other lost son, Pablo, and that's where her mind was the morning Nita Orland emerged from a long black car, floated straight in wearing a hat as wide as the doorway, and took possession of the salon. The actress removed her hat and placed it on a table, the only surface large enough to support it, and smiled. The room seemed lighter. She passed her small, handgun-shaped purse to Mrs Flock. 'Tilly, I just know you have something wonderful for me!'

She followed Tilly to the *Directrice Technique*'s office and, leaving Mrs Flock and Valda outside, viewed Tilly's drawings as if they were a basket of puppies. Which one to hold first? There was discussion about the fabrics, with Tilly suggesting a dress featuring the lace and satin train, a folie à deux of texture. Ultimately, they decided the folie à deux was perhaps 'a little too Hollywood costume' and picked the dress they thought would best serve Nita's purpose at the Smalls Ball.

Then Nita smiled her glorious smile, kissed Tilly on both cheeks and said they really should have cocktails soon, then left to attend a luncheon with friends. Within the hour, Clare had taken three more bookings. Two more actresses phoned after lunch. All asked for an appointment with Tilly Dunnage from Dungatar.

The sergeant never imagined he'd get to plan a wedding, let alone his own. It was the first occasion he had organised with himself celebrated at its centre. There was his marching-out, of course, but he had been just one figure amid a hundred other police graduates, some well-groomed horses, and a very fine (and loud) brass band.

This time, he would source advice from his sophisticated circle regarding flowers, catering, decorations and, most importantly, what to wear.

'I'll be honest,' Elmer said. 'What's most important for you is to be able to look at your wedding photograph in twenty years' time and not cringe.'

'It's important, yes,' the sergeant agreed.

The evening after his consultation with the judge, Sergeant Farrat dressed in his best brogues (leather and linen uppers, very stylish), his tartan waistcoat and navy trousers, white shirt and polka-dot cravat and arrived at the Regent at 6 pm, bearing a huge bunch of flowers. Charles McSwiney was in his usual spot, taking coins, delivering change and distributing newspapers.

'Those flowers for me, Sarge?'

The sergeant broke one stem from the bunch and handed it to Charles, who slid it into his buttonhole.

He nodded towards Salon Mystique. 'I see a lot more ladies go there these days, good lookers, some of them. Here's one of them now.'

It was Tilly. The sergeant smoothed his hair and put on his best smile. His fiancée, sporting aviator sunglasses, cuffed trousers and a striped bateau blouse, her short dark hair flattened with Brylcreem, walked towards him, dodging a tram and a couple of brand-new FJ Holdens. She smiled at Charles and asked the sergeant why he was so dressed up.

'Looks real dapper,' said Charles, and went back to spruiking. ''Erald, git your 'Erald!'

The sergeant thrust the flowers at her, took her hand and slid his mother's large diamond engagement ring on her finger. It was too big so they slipped it onto her middle finger. Then he kissed her cheek. Charles shook the sergeant's hand and congratulated Tilly.

'It's a beautiful ring.'

'It is,' the sergeant said. 'I could have had it altered to fit my finger, but diamonds aren't really me.'

Tilly and Sergeant Farrat retired to Hotel Australia for cocktails. Charles declined their invitation, citing his needy public and the fact that he was only fourteen, and a beer man anyway.

# Chapter 11

GLADSTON, AN EARNEST-LOOKING man in a grey woollen jacket, bow tie and corduroy trousers, was typing invoices when Marigold and Tilly arrived.

'Hello, Gladston. How nice to see you.'

'And you, Mrs Pettyman. Father is busy, take a seat.'

The ladies sat.

'This is Tilly.'

Gladston smiled at the unconventional-looking woman, and Marigold said, 'She is my stepdaughter,' and the stepdaughter flinched but then looked him in the eye and grinned slowly.

Marigold asked after his mother.

'Mother is very well, thank you, Mrs Pettyman.'

'Do thank her for organising the tickets to the Smalls Charity Ball.'

'My parents are looking forward to it. Father won't be long.' He tore an invoice from the typewriter and fed another into the carriage and typed rapidly with two fingers.

Tilly took the opportunity to scrutinise the office. She had never been inside a real solicitor's office but it was as she imagined – leather couches, brown décor, a statuesque hatstand and, contrary to what she'd imagined, this solicitor's office was home to a lush green fern. A small spray bottle of water sat next to it on Gladston's desk.

The phone buzzed. Gladston rose, opened his father's door and said, 'You can go in now.' As they passed, Tilly glanced down at his typewriter. Some poor criminal or victim was about to receive an invoice for £125. She hoped Marigold would retrieve a substantial amount.

They sat in front of Mr Hawker, the light from the window behind him blinding them and creating a swirling halo of pipe smoke. The office smelled of ashtrays and whisky, the decanter and glass on the sideboard. There was nothing apart from a pen and ink well set on Mr Hawker's solid, overly ornamental desk. Gladston hovered. Without any conversation, Tilly knew that neither charm nor combat would be an effective weapon to get Marigold a fair hearing. Tenacity was the order of the day.

Mr Hawker grinned at the two outwardly composed women. He noted that Marigold's rather good-looking friend was particularly well dressed. He'd tell Gladston to get the name of the lass who ran up their dresses. That might please the little woman at home, since she seemed more strident of late. 'Well, ladies?'

'Firstly, please thank your lovely wife for organising the tickets to the Charity Ball.'

Mr Hawker looked even more pleased with himself and glanced at Gladston: *You must remember to tell her.* 'You women get excited about these things.'

'Not all of us,' said Tilly. 'We're not all the same.'

Marigold cleared her throat and placed her hand gently on Mr Hawker's desk. 'Now, as you know, when I married Evan, you transferred all my money to him.'

'Correct.'

'Well, he's dead now, so you have to give it back.'

'As I said in my letter to you, Marigold, you're unwell.'

'I'm better now and so –'

'It's all quite safe, believe me,' Mr Hawker said. 'And Evan was good enough to provide for you. You'll receive a healthier allowance once you can show evidence that you are completely well.'

'I'm cured.'

'We would arrange to seek proof if we felt it reasonable. In the meantime, we will continue to manage all of your costs, as we have always done, but good of you to drop in – Gladston will see you out.'

'I have a right to that money. It's mine, it's in the will. Myrtle Dunnage here, my stepdaughter and therefore next of kin, has a son, and they need me.' She reached out and took Tilly's hand. 'And I need them. I want her to be my guardian.'

Mr Hawker studied Tilly for a full three seconds, his memory dredging up the details of the matter of the illegitimate child and her needy, bedraggled mother. They were quite cheap to run, he remembered, and he could see that the bastard daughter in front of him was more like her mother than his friend Evan.

'Paternity was never proven, though Evan was kind enough to contribute to the child's upbringing.' He glanced again at Gladston – *You will find me the relevant files* – then leaned forward and smiled indulgently. 'Your request is neither rational nor possible.'

'You can make it possible,' Tilly said.

'And it's perfectly rational,' Marigold added, stopping herself from shouting that without her husband she was more rational than she'd ever been allowed to be.

Mr Hawker just kept looking at them, from one to the other, smiling. 'You don't seem to understand –'

'I understand perfectly. That money was mine. You and Evan took it, then you spent it –'

'Not all of it. I turned most of it into a healthy sum.'

'Which Evan didn't share with me, choosing instead to spend it on his mistresses and the great many pornographic films he kept at his office.'

Marigold was outwardly maintaining a forthright level of composure, but Tilly's blood was starting to boil. 'That money is rightfully Marigold's.'

'And I want it.' Marigold's grip on Tilly's hand tightened.

Solicitor Hawker leaned back in his chair and checked his watch. 'Your stepdaughter just wants your money – why do you think she showed up after all these years?'

'I found her, and further to that she doesn't lie, swindle or steal. Through her I saw the truth about Stewart and about my husband.' Tilly had arrived at her door in Dungatar one evening, bearing flowers – marigolds. She told Marigold a story of an innocent young girl swept off her feet by an ambitious, deceitful man, a charming liar. The girl's parents believed he was good, and they let her go on a walk with him. The charming man was very persuasive, forceful; he took advantage of her and she found herself in trouble. 'It's my mother's story,' Tilly had said. 'That is what happened to Molly.'

Marigold realised it was her story too. Her parents had made Marigold marry the man, and she was deeply unhappy.

Mr Hawker blustered, 'This is truly preposterous. Neither of you is capable of living a responsible, respectable, law-abiding life. Marigold, you killed your husband, *her* father, and she is illegitimate and now has her own child, probably illegitimate too. And what of the child's father? Where is he?'

Again, Gladston saw the stunning stepdaughter flinch.

Tilly's blood reached boiling point. 'The man who fathered me was an abusive bully who kept his wife, Marigold, drugged for decades. He neglected my poor mother and his illegitimate child, me. It was his own fault that he died. There might be more of Evan's children out there, given his serial lechery and adultery. I suppose we should check with some of the others?'

'Like Una Pleasance!' Marigold said.

It was Mr Hawker's turn to flinch.

'Miss Una Pleasance?' Gladston blurted. A couple of years prior Una had arrived, penniless, from the country. Apparently, she'd fallen out with a cousin. At first she attended the theatre with his parents, but these days it was only his father who saw Miss Pleasance . . . every Friday morning before going to his club.

'I see her out of the kindness of my heart,' Mr Hawker had explained. 'She's a spinster, and lonely. No need to mention it to your mother, we can't have her getting jealous.' It also explained the cheque butts, ten quid every Friday for 'expenses'.

Mr Hawker attempted to stand but his weight kept him merely craning forward, red with exertion. 'I remember you! I see it all now. You're the one who killed little what's-his-name.'

'Stewart,' Marigold prompted, and Tilly flinched, again.

'And you, Mrs Pettyman, what you did to your husband –'

'He was having an affair,' Marigold said. He'd always had affairs. He'd never loved her. And his son, the fat, freckled, rude and smelly little bully who elbowed her when he passed, spied on her in the shower and assaulted little girls . . . if it weren't for him she wouldn't have had to marry Evan.

But she remembered what she was trying to achieve. 'Anyway, I *said* I was sorry.'

Gladston looked around for a chair to sit on and, finding none, gained support from the heat bank beneath the window.

Tilly retrieved her hand from Marigold's grasp. It was beginning to throb.

Marigold tapped the table with her tiny gloved fist. 'It's *my* money. And you knew what Evan was like and you watched me marry him, and then you accommodated his trysts here in Melbourne. I bet you've got a hussy somewhere yourself and she probably self-medicates before she has to endure you.'

Mr Hawker pointed his finger at Tilly. 'You can't be anyone's guardian. You just want money. I will fight this application, so you will need more money than even I've got for legal fees.'

'You should spend some of your legal fees on a dentist,' Tilly said. 'Your mouth's like a guano pit.'

The solicitor looked at his watch again. 'Get out, the pair of you. I'll be late for lunch with the Archdeacon.'

'You'll be hearing from our lawyer,' Marigold declared.

Mr Hawker laughed at the women, who swanned out of his office triumphantly, belying the fury and humiliation in their bellies.

Gladston helped him out of his chair and handed him his hat, and Mr Hawker declared he'd be out for the rest of the day. 'Tell your mother I won't be home for dinner, I'll stay at the club.'

Gladston closed the door behind his father and stood for a moment, taking in all he had heard. Then he went to the filing cabinet.

Out on Bourke Street, the trams rattling and dinging, the cars tooting past, the women paced. 'Pickled old scrotum,' said Tilly.

'My whole life I've had to scrape around at the damp, smelly feet of men,' Marigold said softly. 'Bad men, faithless and duplicitous. And there's not one sound reason why it has to be that way.'

'It's the way it is.' Tilly held out her hand to shake goodbye. 'Sorry I couldn't help. All the very best with the rest of your life.'

'It's sickening. I could easily slice his hamstrings.' Marigold smiled, again picturing Evan on the floor, writhing in agony, his flaccid feet smearing neat rainbows of blood on her shiny linoleum.

Just then, the sound of metal on metal and breaking glass shattered the city din, sending pedestrians scampering and ducking from screeching tyres. A rogue car careened across the intersection of Queen and Bourke streets and plunged into a lamppost, to avoid hitting two other cars that were rammed together, headlight to headlight. From the centre of the tragedy came Beula, following her white cane, her face waving like a leech sniffing blood. Someone took hold of her elbow but she shoved the Samaritan away, her nose to the trace of Marigold's English

Lavender perfume and the dull, colourful forms of Tilly and Marigold. Behind her, drivers got out of their dented vehicles and shook their fists at her.

Gertrude was watching her husband erect new Dungatar. His farmer's trousers needed a good wash and every time he bent down his pencil fell out of his top pocket, but he was giving directions and being a leader, a mayor, and she found it mightily attractive. Her father, dressed as a lord from *Macbeth*, stood beside William as he hammered in the stakes. Then Alvin stretched string between the stakes, Septimus following with the sports club boundary marker, a powdery white line in his wake.

They heard the bus approaching and Gertrude watched them dash to where the footpaths would be, letting it zoom past, dust and twigs flying. Then the men met in the middle of the road to consult the town plans.

Alvin asked, 'What's next?'

'The post office.'

'We've got no one to run the post office.' Septimus dusted off his breeches.

'Good point.'

'Put the post office in the general store,' said Alvin, and William agreed that was a capital idea.

Septimus said, 'You're monopolising essential services – horizontal integration.'

'Well,' said William, 'let's just mark it out and discuss it tonight. We must keep moving, get the walls up and floors down.'

Gertrude turned to the bundle of newspapers and settled at her counter to catch up on Melbourne society. For a few pages the news was all quite predictable: a dance at the Trocadero; a coronation party in Canterbury; photographs of a debutante ball, the debutantes wearing crowns and sashes; a beauty contest whose winner looked remarkably like Princess Elizabeth. But then she turned the page and there was Mr Horatio Farrat making public his engagement to a dressmaker, Miss Tilly Dunnage. They were attending the opening of the National Theatre's production of *Swan Lake*. The sergeant's white socks and spats were rather uncalled for, but Myrtle Dunnage looked amazing. Her blouse was thick creamy linen, with fat ping-pong-sized circles embroidered all over it, each side counter-stitched so that the effect was more or less relief. It was sleeveless, but the armholes were slightly capped, an inverted triangle–shaped top that accentuated the wide shoulders and narrow waist. Her skirt was mid-calf, also cream-coloured but thick, lustrous satin. The waisted design enhanced the female form and the insouciant, enormously wide linen bow at her hip suggested a party, or a gift. But why? He was older, thickset, with no prospects, and in her strappy stilettos his fiancée towered over him. The paper described the pair as 'uniquely chic and causing much envy', which made the unusual combination the perfect subject for the weekend gossip pages: 'clearly members of Melbourne's new emerging bohemian class of refugee artists and displaced elites from war-ravaged Europe. Apparently, the bride-to-be is a Paris-trained couturier and is making her name in some quarters.'

'The seamstress and the sergeant,' said Gertrude, intrigued. The arson department would surely find her now. But Gertrude was more concerned about organising a new frock before anyone else, like Elsbeth, saw the article and drove to Melbourne. It was a mere day's drive – two if you stuck to the speed limit.

For a new dress, Elsbeth was capable of anything. She had accompanied Gertrude and William on their honeymoon, sat in the front seat next to William, all the way to Melbourne and back, and forced them to attend her daily shopping expeditions. It was Elsbeth who ended up with the most bargains.

Gertrude glared at her shabby frocks, hanging from nails

along the picture rail – a few Dior copies that no longer fitted, her Lady Macbeth costume and two miserable mail order frocks that were far too small – they'd changed the entire sizing guidelines while she was in the asylum, and nothing in her size fitted anymore. It was thievery and trickery, a cruel conspiracy by the entire fashion industry, who were out to exploit and humiliate her. She reached for her scissors and spent the afternoon carefully removing the social pages from every newspaper in the bundle.

# Chapter 12

Wednesday, Tilly arrived at work and was admonished for being late. 'Again!'

The receptionist at Salon Mystique pointed a pencil at her messy, crowded appointment book. 'And the phone just keeps ringing, it's all your fault. I didn't even get time for a cup of tea yesterday.'

The phone rang. Clare yelped, picked up the handset and let it drop onto her offensive appointment book, the hard black thing like a mummified foot.

Tilly continued on and settled into her small office, turned to her gowns for Miss Post Office Picnic and Nita Orland and, while she stitched, pondered the signature pieces: day wear, evening wear, cocktail frock and bridal gown – clearly the work of the 'new talent at Salon Mystique' which, she hoped, would gain her the trust and respect of the other seamstresses before the show. And she would soon have her boy. Her arms warmed, feeling Joe in them. Elated, she rubbed her hands together and went in search of a free Stockman.

Some hours later, the light in the stairwell dulled and Mrs Flock appeared on the landing, Valda behind her. The quiet industry of the workroom continued while they circled, glancing at pattern-making, bead selections, belt buckles and fabrics, and finally arriving at Tilly's tiny quarters and her signature pieces. They said nothing but it was clear Mrs Flock was pleased with what she saw.

Then she took up her position by the landing, her hand on

the balustrade post, and the seamstresses put down their work and turned to her. Her face was almost beaming as she prepared to make one of her announcements.

'This coronation season, Salon Mystique will not only be the best, but we will also be the first . . . Salon Mystique will host an *aperçu*, a *l'avant-première*. We need as many clients as possible before the coronation in June because there will be many occasions, many celebrations, and Salon Mystique must be represented at each of them. Now it is up to you to make my *aperçu* happen.'

'So,' said Shirley, crossing her arms. 'How long have we got, exactly, to get this early preview show ready?'

'We will show as soon as possible in April.' She smiled at Tilly, or rather, parted her meagre lips, displaying her small teeth. 'An early show will get everyone talking. They'll come like flies to a cow pat.'

'Six weeks,' Tilly said.

'Six?' Shirley's eyes filled with tears.

'Six weeks until the start of April. Six days a week. Thirty-six days.'

A murmur washed through the atelier all the way to the very rear of the workroom. Madame said that, naturally, there would be some overtime, as there always is before a show.

'Whacko,' said Tilly. 'All that extra cash in our pay packets.'

'Something to anticipate,' said Mrs Flock, and went on to say that Valda, as *Atelier Première*, would be responsible for making sure the collection was made quickly, in plenty of time for April, then she slipped silently down the stairs and Valda turned to the seamstresses.

'Very well, get a wriggle on.' She clapped her hands. 'Stitch, stitch and sew!'

She handed Tilly a shrug she'd just finished for Mrs Piggot. 'The welt.'

Tilly waited.

'The fabric won't support the opening with just a welt. You need a tab or flap – at the very least a button.'

'It's not necessary on bouclé.'

'It's not your design, it's Madame's.'

'It's not, it's stolen. Mrs Flock has simply added the false pocket to give what she considers to be flair. A welt is unnecessary.'

Valda's small face at the bottom of her skull puckered disapprovingly. Why was it that these pin-pushers thought they could speak to her as if she was beneath them! 'You have come so far,' she said haughtily. 'Surely now is not the time to lose your job?'

'You'd be lost then, wouldn't you?' Tilly turned back to her Stockman, leaving Valda holding Mrs Piggot's shrug.

That evening, she flopped down in the sergeant's kitchen and told him about her day.

'Mrs Flock could have used a better metaphor,' the sergeant replied, though flies and cow pats were a valid comparison.

She shrugged. 'I can cope with Valda, but an early show!'

'I can hardly wait.' The sergeant was clearly genuinely thrilled. 'It will be wonderful.'

Then she looked troubled. 'I won't get to see Joe nearly as much as I want to.'

'Joe will not be neglected. Let Mae have him for a while. You'll demonstrate your skills at the preview parade and be a success and then Joel Edward Dunnage can be all yours, all day every day.'

For a moment Tilly was returned to her *atelier Parisien* and the child care Madame Vionnet had provided, Pablo so happy with all the other babies and children. She, too, had thrived within Vionnet's steady ethic, of quality over haste, and her superior team of artists and craftspeople. If everyone was happy, then the design was superior, the pleats sharp, the feathers startling; the artificial flowers looked alive, the leather was lustrous and handsome, the costume jewellery dazzlingly complementary; the embroidery, lace and weaving became breathtaking, and the passementerie subtle but vital. Unlike Salon Mystique, where there was no understanding of finesse, no appreciation or love for the vision, and where she felt slightly irritated by her seamstressing life. In her new life, Tilly would have a home, her son, a large family with all its eruptions and its predictabilities – she might even have friends. She would be content, but realised she wouldn't be content dealing with the same clientele, the competition, the jealousy and vanity. But what else could she do?

When she got home from her day, Mr Short rushed to her across the vestibule, an envelope in his hand. 'You got a letter.'

He stood waiting for her to open it, but she skipped up the stairs.

'It's from the welfare.'

She smiled at him. 'So I see.' Dread, fear and anger rising.

Tilly, dressed as a respectable young mother, attended the meeting with the Head of Welfare and the representatives from the convent with her fiancé. She carried with her all the necessary paperwork, and proof of betrothal.

The sergeant was directed to a chair in the corner but they did not ask Tilly to sit down so, feeling hollow and sick, she stood before the Head of the Welfare Department, Mother Superior and the Monsignor on watery legs. Sister Maria waited behind them all, staring at her while the officials shuffled papers between themselves, making small, disgruntled noises through down-turned mouths.

The Head of the Welfare Department, an affable-looking man wearing a slightly crushed suit, glared sideways at the nuns and the welfare officer. 'I was informed that you have no husband,

Miss Dunnage, no home or structure, no support for the infant who cannot speak.'

'He's like his uncle,' said Sister Maria. 'Retarded.'

Tilly looked at the people behind their impressive desk and said calmly, 'He simply has not been able to speak, he has been silenced.'

The Head of the Welfare Department nodded. 'The information I've been given from Children's Services tells me you can't provide the child with the special care he needs, a safe home and a secure future, whereas your stepmother can. It's been suggested this matter could become a custody dispute, but I do not see an application for custody.' He looked questioningly to Mother Superior who looked to Sister Maria.

Tilly said, 'My son is a temporary voluntary placement, and I am to be married soon' – the sergeant coughed, but they didn't look at him – 'and so I have a home and suitable care for him.'

'Her child is illegitimate, as she herself is, and so she will go to Hell, as did her mother before her,' Sister Maria said.

Though she wanted to punch Sister Maria's teeth to the back of her throat, Tilly shoved her hands deep into her respectable dress pockets and looked to Mother Superior. Tilly remembered her as a harmless presence, though aloof.

The Head of Welfare mumbled something about the over-zealous Children's Service's Department, and then Mother Superior spoke, finally, her fleshy chin dripping over her tight coif. 'We shepherded this girl for five years. Myrtle visits her child every Sunday and does good work with the children. She has benefited greatly from our guidance.'

The Head of the Welfare Department threw his pen onto the pages in front of him and pointed out that the department could not detain a voluntary placement, especially given all fees were up to date. Then he resumed his affable countenance. 'A child is usually best off with its family, a mother and a father.'

From her post at the wall behind them Sister Maria said, 'But you can take him from them any time, isn't that so?'

'It is often necessary,' the Monsignor said.

Mother Superior then said, 'Sister Maria, you will bring us tea in my office,' and they gathered their notes and files and departed, leaving a newspaper clipping of Mr Horatio Farrat and his fiancée making their small, forgettable-to-most official debut into Melbourne's decent society. Tilly slumped into the nearest chair and the sergeant rushed to soothe her.

Horatio Farrat's reflection showed a pale, squat, middle-aged man in white trousers and a navy double-breasted blazer, his boater sitting jauntily on his head. Satisfied that he looked like a genuine father, he made his way to the nearest toy shop. As he stepped inside, the bell clanged above him and he found himself in an impenetrable but colourful enigma. He could not remember his busy mother ever taking him to a toy shop, or providing him with boyish playthings, and felt if he took a few more steps he might never return. Just then a rotund man wearing shorts and a propeller hat smiled at him. 'Can I help you?'

'I'd like a toy, please.'

'Boy or girl?'

'Boy.'

'Age?'

'Two and a bit.'

'A boat?'

'Isn't water dangerous for toddlers?'

The shopkeeper looked at the sergeant's nautical attire and shrugged. 'Take swimming togs just in case. How do you feel about sand?'

'At a beach?' The sergeant was horrified at the thought of all that glare and grit.

'Sandpit.'

'Perfect,' said the sergeant. He needn't even leave home.

The salesman led him to a back corner, the propeller on his hat turning. 'You'll find something here.'

He faced the shelves. There were many different coloured shovels and buckets, small tin graders, more buckets and spades and miniature tractors, a front-end loader and then . . . there was a big, strong tip truck. His inner boy reached out and snatched it up. He glanced about the shop and then lowered his nose to the toy and inhaled the bright red paint. He rolled it along the floor on four firm rubber wheels, and he pressed the lever. The tray rose noiselessly and he saw how the sand would indeed tip out. He took three – no, four – spades from the shelf and a bucket just in case, and clutching them to his blazer, searched across the top of the shelves for the propeller hat.

Tilly's day at Salon Mystique passed in a painless blur. As the seamstresses wearily put on their hats and buttoned their jackets, preparing to leave, Valda handed them their pay packets. There was, of course, no extra money in anyone's envelope.

Tilly shoved her chamois purse of implements into her bag. 'I won't be in tomorrow,' she said. 'I'm getting married.' She pushed past Valda and out into the cool Friday evening, which smelled of the future and freedom.

Shirley followed. 'You coming back to work?'

'I will, but I can't stay there forever.' She buttoned her trench coat and put on her hat.

'Where will you go?'

Tilly shrugged. 'Someplace that doesn't exploit me and treat me like a second-class citizen.' She watched the peak-hour crowds, men, mostly, bankers, clerks and technicians, lawyers and managers, waiters and maintenance crews, and said far too loudly, 'Someplace where I'm held in the same regard as a man!'

Shirley tied a scarf over her springy curls. 'Let me know where that place is and I'll join you.'

Tilly remembered that she didn't have to hide anymore so pulled off her hat and shoved it in her pocket. 'You know, Shirley, we put up with our place in the hierarchy out of fear, but we don't need to. The world can't do much without us.'

'Madame Flock can't do anything without us.'

'As you know, our co-workers don't really listen to me, but just so you know, I think your cornelli work is superb and you're very good at Chantilly –'

Shirley stepped close, her face eager. 'I don't like too much decoration, I'm better at cutting. But sometimes I see a pleat and my hands want to bead it; sometimes I fancy embroidering a pocket. And I reckon cuffs are neglected, a wasted opportunity, what I'm saying is, I will do anything.'

Tilly put her dark glasses on. 'I'd suggest a drink but I have to go home and soak in platypus milk, sleep for eight hours in freshly shorn Merino fleece and iron my pure white bridal gown.'

''Course,' Shirley laughed. '"Biggest day of a girl's life".'

Tilly looked Shirley dead in the eyes and said, 'We will talk again.'

# Chapter 13

ON SATURDAY MORNING, earlier than usual, Tilly Dunnage's footfalls danced across the Shorts' ceiling. They heard her thump down the stairs and out the door, letting it slam behind her. Mr Short watched her skip across Nicholson Street, where she was absorbed into the gardens of the Exhibition Building opposite. Ten minutes later she returned, her dressing-gown leaving a trail through the dew, and a bunch of freshly cut flowers in her hands. She put the flowers in a jar of water while she bathed, speaking to the photograph on her dresser. 'I'm getting married today, Molly. It'll be a good marriage, just a partnership in parenthood.'

At this point, the bride sat on her bed and caught the tears brimming from her eyes in a handkerchief. 'My life's been a mess, ever since I started school, torturous for the best part of thirty years. But we don't want my life to proceed like that, do we? From now on, my life will be the way it should be. A safe life, with Joe.'

She reached for her dress.

Graham was lovingly shampooed and brushed, his fringe and mane trimmed and his hooves polished. An ostrich plume sprouted from the crown of his shiny bridle. Barney washed the cart, George painted the wheel spokes and Charlie hung streamers from the tray while Edward created seating from hay bales for Elizabeth, Margaret and Mary – blue roses in their hair and smiles as wide as their faces – Barney, George, Victoria, Charles, Henry, Charlotte and little Rex, all smiling. It was a happy thing to see. Even the small brown and white dogs found a spot between the bales.

The McSwiney family, an understated but well-turned-out wedding party, arrived at Tilly's early. She heard Graham's footfalls and thumped down the stairs and out the front door, wearing a grey mid-calf silk jersey dress, boat-cut across the shoulders with a pleated bodice plunging to a low back, the pleats culminating in a bustle beneath her bottom. It was a Balenciaga prototype from long ago that had never made it to the catwalk, but it would work very well for the town hall registry office in Melbourne, 1953.

As Edward helped Tilly up onto the cart, Elizabeth said, 'I love your dress, Tilly.'

And Margaret asked, 'Would you have worn it to marry Teddy?'

'I'd have worn magenta,' Tilly said, and smiled away the swelling tears.

She sat up the front between Mae and Edward, her composure fragile knowing the McSwineys' thoughts were with their lost hero, their devoted eldest boy, the comet, the bright handsome man and talented footballer, the adventurous and mischievous brother. She would have married him, and what a wedding it would have been. Instead they were gathered to see her married safely to someone not too dissimilar; a man who knew what was important, and valued it, a friend, true and courageous, a talented man who loved beauty and upheld freedom. It was all for Joe, their phoenix.

Graham moved steadily, his plumes pert, clopping through the royally themed streets of Melbourne. British and Australian flags draped over balconies and fences, and Princess Elizabeth and her dead father, George VI, gazed at them from shop windows and rattly green trams. Pedestrians on Swanston Street turned at the sound of horse hooves on asphalt and saw the McSwineys and their festooned horse, who flattened his ears a little and dug his shoes into the slippery bluestone incline to drag the McSwiney family up and around the unnecessarily grand driveway of the town hall. The groomsman and groom waited on a red carpet that stretched from the driveway up the stairs and across the grand marbled foyer into the ballroom. Elmer wore a top hat and tails – bright green, though his shirt was pink – and Tilly's fiancé looked splendid in formal black tie of the Scottish Highlands – McLay, from his mother's side – kilt, sporran, Prince Charlie jacket, waistcoat, white lace jabot, white hose, evening dress brogues and dirk. He'd abandoned the highland bonnet when Elmer had said, 'It makes you look like you should be doing something with bagpipes.'

Edward helped his wife down from the cart. She smiled at the sergeant, who told her she looked lovely, though lovely possibly wasn't an accurate description.

Mae sneezed into her flowers and Edward led them towards the door. 'Joe's waiting,' he said, and they carried their thoughts of the past and the future up the red carpet while Graham turned his nose towards the manicured lawn.

The celebrant looked at the short, square Scotsman with translucent skin and his tall, luminous bride. 'Ah,' he thought, 'a rush job,' though the bride did not look pregnant. Perhaps a money match? Revenge? Behind them, a wrong-headed youth wept quietly. The bridesmaid, Mae, had seen better days, obviously those days when her dress fitted, but he had seen worse. Like a ringmaster who'd lost his freak show, the best man made up the quartet. The service was brisk and pleasant, the wrong-headed youth stepped awkwardly up, and said confidently, 'I DO!' in unison with the bride, who threw the bouquet over her head and the robust, curly-haired girls yelped and recoiled from it, knocking the lectern over. The best man grabbed it and buried his face in its perfumed petals and then the stout bridesmaid ushered them out. They froze on the steps while Margaret took a photograph and then ran like blazes to the waiting horse and cart and were gone less than three minutes after the celebrant declared, 'I now pronounce you . . .' The bride and groom didn't even kiss.

Graham travelled as fast as he could through the crowded Saturday morning streets of inner Melbourne towards Joe.

The grass on the convent lawn wasn't as sweet as the lawn outside the town hall but Graham made do as his family vanished through the tall brown doors, where he sensed the grass was better. The McSwiney and Farrat family assembled at the office, bearing the marriage certificate, the necessary forms complete and duplicates made and, just in case, a letter from the bank manager declaring that Horatio Farrat was a man of property and independent means, and one from a judge supporting that Myrtle and Horatio Farrat were fully entitled to their child. Tilly had brought along Joe's birth certificate. They waited patiently with their gifts: soft fruit, a bunny rug Mae had crocheted, a sunhat, cardigan, spare nappies. They waited and waited. After what seemed like hours in the dull and chilly cloisters, it was the amiable and compassionate Sister Patricia who finally came rushing towards them carrying the boy.

Joe saw them and beamed. He reached for his mother and she folded him into her arms and put her face against his smooth, fat little neck.

Mae and Edward embraced Tilly and Joe and the others wrapped around them like peony petals. Rex presented Joe with the family teddy bear, passed down from Teddy to Elizabeth, then Margaret, Mary, Barney, George, Victoria, Charles, Henry, Charlotte and Rex.

Sister Patricia ushered them to the big brown doors, whispering, 'The days a child is returned to his mother are too rare and wonderful and God's will. Bless you all, now quickly, off you go.'

The aunts and uncles, reverent disciples, fussed and cooed as they bore Joe through Sergeant Farrat's beautifully decorated house, his new home adorned with flowers and ribbons and canapés and buckets of champagne. Joe's room was stacked full of toys, and had a warm, safe bed and he was able to look directly at his mother in her own bedroom opposite. But it was the sandpit with the bucket and spades he wanted most. There were things to climb on outside, and a tree hut carefully constructed by Edward and the boys for when he was older, and Joe was played with, fed and nursed, bathed and dressed for bed, played with again, and sung and read to. Barney told him his version of his favourite story, *The Turtle and the Hare*. The sergeant said the version he'd read had the hare racing a tortoise, and Barney said he didn't care what his name was, he couldn't help being slow and anyway, he won the race.

Then Joe was tucked in and they all sat and watched the boy close his eyes and go to sleep surrounded, as he had been always, by other people.

Mae and Edward stayed, sitting either side of him, while the others headed downstairs to champagne and canapés and, later, a seafood banquet with about thirty of the sergeant's dearest friends from the Hippocampus Club.

Mary's young man, her beau, a soft-jawed young man who loved to wear a bow tie, arrived with flowers, and then Elizabeth's well-to-do fiancé plonked a box of fine wine on the kitchen table. Tilly grabbed a German beer stein and said, 'Fill it up, please.'

Nita Orland, dressed in a fine tuxedo and patent leather brogues, the skull with its black eyes sparkling on her middle finger, toasted her new friend Tilly and immersed herself in the joyous crowd. When Tilly's stein was half empty, Elizabeth sidled up and asked for a job.

'A job?'

'I'm happy to start off picking up pins, maintaining the bobbins, sweeping and re-threading.'

'She won't let you down,' said Mary, and Tilly asked them what on earth they were talking about.

'When you set up your business.'

'They'll sack me when I get married,' Elizabeth reminded her.

'Very well,' Tilly shrugged. 'Bring me some samples.'

Elizabeth grabbed her fiancé's hand and dragged him to the dancers in the front room.

Margaret came and stood next to Tilly. 'So, you going to set up shop?'

'It seems the time has come.'

They perused the crowd of well-dressed cross-dressers and theatrical types and Margaret said, 'I'm not going to find a husband in this lot, am I?'

'No,' said Tilly, and they laughed.

Next door, Miss Peachy looked at the common wall and tried to imagine what was happening next door; dancing in the shop-front? A buffet dinner in the millinery? Drinks in the upstairs sitting room? A birthday celebration, or an early coronation occasion? She wished the wall was thicker, though she was pleased it was the first party her neighbour had held, as far as she could remember. And he could have at least told her it would be a noisy weekend.

The groom noticed his bride was somewhat downcast and came to her from across the kitchen. 'My dear, what's up?'

'Nothing. On the contrary . . .' She pointed to the floor. 'The shoes.'

The sergeant followed her gaze footward. Almost everyone was wearing fantastically wonderful shoes. 'Good grief.' He turned. 'Elmer!'

Elmer came, his tray stacked with drinks.

'The shoes?' the newlyweds asked.

'Our treasured new shoemaker,' he said, then pointed to a big-boned, handsome woman standing next to the judge.

Tilly made straight for her and grabbed her hand. The woman possessed a firm handshake and a sincere twinkle in her lovely eyes.

'I'm Tilly, you're the cordwainer?'

'I am.'

'Do you make shoes for couture houses?'

'Opinionated haberdashers,' the judge said.

The shoemaker shook her head. 'I am a lover of glorious art so I just make custom shoes these days, for my regulars. Sometimes I do the hoi polloi, but I'm discerning.'

The sergeant studied the woman's shoes: a classic shoe, blue suede, with a low stiletto, but the sole covering the shank of the heel was dark, the two tones giving the impression that the heel was actually quite slim, which made the particularly large foot it was housing seem almost dainty. Further to that, the outer sole beneath the ball of the foot was thick, though the sole of the shank remained slim, so the shoes gave the impression of *fine* footwear, a delicate glove for a substantial foot. My God, how clever! The sergeant's eye rose to the ankles – slim – the calves – sturdy – and the knees. The knees! Lovely knees, toned but not sporty: female knees. Knees so often gave a 'girl' away. Her face was round and sweetly strong, though the tyranny of oncoming age was stealing her defined jawline and baby-skin throat. The sergeant's gaze darted to her shoes again just to make sure he wasn't imagining all of this, then straight back up to her hair – wavy, light brown, loose about her strong shoulders. Finally, her hands. Worker's hands, but not indelicate, and her fingers were pliable and fit.

Tilly was talking, gesticulating, and the two women were earnest in their conversation. The sergeant's gaze lingered on the shoemaker's face. She was utterly lovely, and then she turned and smiled at him before turning her attention again to Tilly, and something happened, something shifted. Horatio Farrat experienced a strange sensation. Tinsel glittered around the periphery of his gaze, lighting the perfect form of the woman wearing the sublime shoes, and every detail of her features became vivid to him – more real than real, amazingly alive and oddly familiar. He felt at one with the stranger. Somewhere music played and the crowd seemed to dull and fade and she, whoever she was, was standing alone, glorious and wonderful. And then someone called, 'Julie,' and she turned, waved her remarkable hand, and walked lightly across the room in slow motion.

'So there you are,' he whispered. 'And your name is Julie. What a pretty name.'

The sergeant's solid breast filled with hope and warm, thick love, and relief – oh, such relief. Finally. Here she was, she'd arrived, she was found, and then his new wife cupped his new love's elbow in her hand and the sergeant stopped himself from rushing to push his wife aside, to hold Julie's shimmering skin over her perfect elbow with its firm, ivory bones. But then Tilly was steering her towards him. His heart was a choir. All around him the air was warm and he had an acute sensation in his person that he'd only ever felt this once before, when he'd encountered Burmese lotus flower silk (and on occasion, avocado flesh). Then a voice on the exterior of his tingling world said, 'Sergeant Farrat, this is Julie. Julie is the best cordwainer in the world,' and the sergeant was looking into Julie's eyes, and Tilly pointed to Julie's shoes. 'Lovely, aren't they?'

'Yes,' the sergeant said. 'Blue,' and he was looking down at the vamp of her shoe, which featured tiny diamantes.

Tilly fell quiet. The gaze between Julie and her husband was locked.

The sergeant saw that Julie possessed a faint downy moustache, as some women did, and straight white teeth that were cocooned in the moist lips of a very kissable mouth. Sergeant Farrat was feeling something he had not felt in decades.

Julie looked down to the sergeant's shoes: evening dress

brogues. She noted that he was wearing foundation, and the impact of his kilt, sporran, Prince Charlie jacket and waistcoat was enhanced, Julie knew, by a corset. And then it dawned on her that a bee hummingbird was nesting in her heart and, at the same time, she was falling, like Alice, into something unfamiliar. Yet she knew what it was, and she felt it was safe. Julie had read about moments like this, had seen them in motion pictures, though she'd never dared to hope that she'd find someone who would love her broad shoulders and strong calves. Boys in the past had objected to her trade and her love of brewing superior beer, her weekend birdwatching, hiking, polo and archery. Hope suddenly took Julie's breath away. Was this smiling person, Sergeant Farrat, 'the one'? Was this uncurling frisson indeed what she suspected? Dare she hope?

Despite feeling she'd been somehow dismissed to the periphery of the room, that her presence was not necessary, Tilly asked, 'You've not met Horatio before?'

'We have mutual friends.' She gestured to everyone else in the room. Then Julie said, tremulously, 'Congratulations on your marriage,' and the sergeant looked stricken.

Tilly cried, 'No!' The room turned to look. 'Horatio is my husband,' she whispered, 'but in name only. He is my friend, my dear friend, and he is free to do as he pleases, as am I. We want only for each other to be happy.'

Julie tore her eyes away from Horatio just long enough to gauge if his wife was sincere. She was.

Though his mouth was suddenly dry, the sergeant managed to say, 'I love your shoes . . . Julie,' and she asked if he'd like to try them on. The heavenly music faded and the noise of the room returned and the sergeant took Julie by her adorable elbow and escorted her to the staircase near the front door, where they exchanged footwear, their feet sliding into the warmth of each other's soft shoes.

Tilly went to Margaret McSwiney and said, 'It's funny how the world works.'

And Margaret said, 'Hilarious.'


As the sun rose, the window behind them went from black to pink then blue, and a rooster crowed somewhere. Around them, party-goers slept, and Julie and Horatio's chatter slowed, and ceased.

Julie finally said, 'I'm busting for a wee but I don't want to go in case you're not here when I get back.'

'We'll go together.' Horatio took her fit cordwainer's hand in his and they walked together, Julie towering in the sergeant's black brogues and Horatio at ease in her blue suede stilettos.


On Sunday morning, Joel Edward Dunnage woke in his new home at 27 Darling Street, East Melbourne, stretched his arms and legs and looked through a window to an unfamiliar sky. The room was strange and he was not in his usual bed. He stood at the bedside waiting for someone to come and tell him what to do. When no one came, he went to the room opposite and watched his mother.

When Tilly Dunnage opened her eyes, she looked directly into the considered gaze of her boy, his new teddy bear under his arm. 'Joel, my son.' He smiled. She sat bolt upright, flung back the covers and gathered him into her arms. The thing that was missing was now found – hers – and the world around her full and warm, her soul content.

She kissed him and took him downstairs to the toilet, according to the routine of the convent. Then he sat patiently, as he knew he had to, until food was placed in front of him. He watched her search the messy kitchen, party detritus crowding the benches, streamers dangling and three white balloons staring at him from beside a half-eaten white cake. His mother made toast and egg, not porridge. And she gave him a second slice of toast with sweet red butter. 'Jam,' she said, when he touched it with his tongue.

'You live here now,' she said to Joe. 'This is your new home. You will spend time with your grandparents, aunts and uncles, but you will live with me from now on.'

She carried Joe back into her bed and she pressed her nose into his short white neck and inhaled. He still smelled a little like convent soap, but this would change. While he brutally flicked through a picture book she studied his lips and teeth, his hair, ears and nose, and ran her hands along his smooth arms, fat thighs and feet and blew raspberries on his tummy. He smiled up at her and she memorised his perfect crown, how his hair curled up and folded over in circles. She wrapped him in her arms, trying not to squeeze him too tight, and indulged for the first time their oneness. 'I will try not to smother you, but I want you to know that you, above all else, are important to me. I will do anything it takes to provide you with a safe and full life of wonder and excitement.'

There was a sound on the stairs, like a herd of tiptoeing elephants, and Joe frowned at the twelve other people who came through the door to stand around the bed. They stared at him. Mae said, 'I'm your grandmother and this is your grandfather, as you know. The others are Elizabeth, Margaret and Mary, Barney, George, Victoria, Charles, Henry, Charlotte and Rex. All good solid royal names, except for Barney, because when he was born his big brother Teddy said he looked like he'd had a bit of a barney.' She looked sideways at Tilly. 'There are no royals called Joe.'

'Joe is better than Phil,' Tilly said. 'And Joe, this man is your new father, and his name is Horatio.'

The man wearing the floral brunch coat stepped forward and presented Joe with a big, strong tip truck. 'Welcome, son.' Joe had eyes only for the truck and pointed one small finger at it but was too afraid to hold it. He slowly raised his arms, unsure that anyone would pick him up, but hopeful. His grandmother leaned in and scooped him out, putting him on her hip. He knew he'd been there before and liked it; all he needed was the truck. Again he reached, and his new father handed him the truck and all was well.

'You can talk to any of these people here whenever you like, and they'll only ever say nice things back to you,' Mae said, 'not like those nuns.'

'Sister Patricia was all right,' Tilly protested.

'We brought fresh eggs. Anyone wants breakfast, Tilly will cook.' The McSwineys again closed around their new family member.

Tilly looked at her new husband. 'How are you today, dear?'

'My first night of marriage surpassed every other hour I've been alive.'

'I'll try to make sure you have many more.'

On Sunday afternoon, Edward McSwiney, Sergeant Farrat and the younger McSwiney boys drove to Mr and Mrs Short's abode. As they carried Tilly's suitcases down to Graham, Mr Short protested that Tilly 'had not given notice' and so must pay rent until the room was rented again. He followed them to the horse and cart while the little boys, George, Charles and Henry, wandered into the Shorts' apartment and stared at his huge, startled wife. 'No visitors,' she cried. 'No children!'

Barney plopped down on the end of her bed, twirling his hat on his finger, and told her in great detail about his horse, what he ate, the usefulness of his poo, and his fine work carting furniture and dry goods to people's homes. Then he explained the general state of the Yarra River for fishing and, all the while, Henry and Charles crawled under the furniture, searching for threepence George said he'd dropped.

Out on the stoop, the cart loaded with Tilly's meagre possessions, Edward spoke. 'Mr Short, for years you made kids from the convent pay to sleep in your shed. They were freezing and terrified of your threats about the authorities and you refused to let them move inside.'

'They didn't pay full rent.'

'They were naive and afraid and they had nowhere else to go, and you took advantage of that.'

Mr Short looked to his apartment door, hoping his wife would call out her support. 'You're very rude, you people, she can't have her key money.'

'Tilly never imagined she'd get it back,' the sergeant said, and slammed the front door so hard the glass shattered and the doorjamb cracked.

That night, when Mr Short put his obese wife to bed and climbed in beside her, his side of the bed collapsed and his wife rolled, landing face first on top of her small husband, trapping him.

# Chapter 14

SOME OF SERGEANT Farrat's East Melbourne neighbours were appalled at the visiting horse, but Graham tidied up the fruit trees drooping over the back-lane fences and donated manure for Miss Peachy's vegetables. Miss Peachy found herself enjoying the music over that weekend, and the floor thumping rhythmically with dancing; she heard wine glasses clinking and smelled sweet cigarette smoke. From the window of her defunct grocery store Miss Peachy watched many people come and go. The people who owned the horse, of course, and others who appeared distinctly bohemian. And there was a man, a watcher, who parked his dark car opposite and employed binoculars. The celebration noises through the common wall never went late because, of all things, there seemed to be a child living with Horatio Farrat. A toddler, actually, a sweet boy with blond curls and big blue eyes.

On Monday, Miss Peachy intercepted the rather beautiful brunette who also seemed to have moved in. She was rolling her cuffs up, preparing to ride away on her bicycle, the child clinging to her stylish pants, when Miss Peachy arrived with an armful of silverbeet, tomatoes and beans.

'Good morning, I am Miss Peachy.'

'Good morning, I am Mrs Farrat, but please call me Tilly. And this is Joe.'

Miss Peachy was small and old. She wore her grey hair in a sensible bun and was dressed in an ankle-length skirt and lacy blouse with a clerical collar. When she finally spoke, she said,

'I waved little Horatio off when he walked down this street to his first day of school. I watched him play with the neighbourhood kiddies, I went to his march-out when he joined the police force, and I gave him tomato seedlings when he was transferred to the country. I never in a million years thought he'd marry, let alone have a child.'

'Joe's father died.' She said it in such a way that the woman's hand shot out and touched Tilly's arm.

'That's terrible dear, if there's anything I can do?'

'Thank you, the sergeant has saved us.'

'You call him the sergeant?'

'Yes. He's always been Sergeant Farrat to all of us. We all still call him that even though he's left the police force. Funny, aren't we?'

'Yes,' said the neighbour, not unkindly, and Tilly smiled again and picked up Joe. 'I must go, I can't be late for work.'

'Work?'

'Yes, I'm a dressmaker and tailor.'

'Oh, my dear,' she said, 'I don't want to intrude –'

Tilly bristled. 'Then don't.'

'Look, I just want you to know, Tilly, that I understand that Horatio has always preferred a guarded life, but I have only ever known him as a kind and lovely person. He was very considerate of his mother's reputation, rest her soul, and her hat-making business . . . moving far away, as he did, to pursue his interests.' She paused, searching Tilly's face for any kind of sign, but Tilly gave nothing away.

'You see, when Horatio was a little boy his favourite game was dress-ups.'

Horatio's new wife still did not indicate anything, she just strapped Joe into the bicycle seat on the handlebars, so Miss Peachy moved a little closer to continue her story. 'I sometimes gave him old dresses because, as you can see, they made clothes to last back then so I'm still wearing my mother's frocks. These days things are so expensive.'

Tilly stopped, put her hands on her hips and said, 'Spit it out, Miss Peachy.'

She held the vegetables in her arms tighter, alarmed. 'My dear, as I say, I'm not intruding.'

Tilly nodded and Miss Peachy continued, quietly, 'I have also known for a very long time that some people on Darling Street are not "worldly", or trustworthy, but I want you to know that I am.' She smiled, and searched Tilly's impassive face for some sort of invitation, a way of signalling neighbourliness.

Though she would remain wary of Miss Peachy until she discovered exactly what her intentions were, Tilly softened. 'I'm grateful, Miss Peachy, thank you. Now I must get going.'

Miss Peachy smiled at Joe and to her delight he smiled back. He had lovely new little teeth and his mouth was very wet and there was some sort of cereal stuck in his fringe. Miss Peachy watched them roll north, towards Collingwood, cuddling the vegetables, breathless in admiration of Mrs Farrat, compassionate friend of Horatio, career woman and breadwinner, like Miss Peachy herself. Next time they met, she would be sure to ask Mrs Farrat about the man who watched from the car. She left the vegetables on Mrs Farrat's hat shop stoop.


Barney, George, Victoria, Henry, Charlotte and Rex waited at the fence. Soon Charlotte ran inside, calling, 'They're coming,' and Mae put the guard in front of the wood stove and packed away her ironing and pushed the high chair up to the table and straightened the cushion in the pusher. When Tilly put her white-haired boy down, he looked from Tilly to Mae and Edward and his new friends – Elizabeth, Margaret, Charles and Mary – and did not know what to do. Tilly picked him up again and kissed him and cuddled him. He put his arms around her neck and she said, 'You will stay here each day. Barney will play with you and Mae will look after you and Rex will let you hug his chook, and then you will come home with me and your new truck will be waiting.'

He looked again at the people, who he knew to be kind.

'I will come and get you at the end of the day.'

Mae nodded. 'She'll come and get you later,' and the others nodded, and Joe was reassured. In his short life, Tilly had always come, so he reached for Mae, waved at his mother, turned and smiled at Barney. Then Joe's life proceeded much as it always had, toddling about and discovering what things were, playing with other children, eating what he was given and doing what he was asked. At this place, though, everyone spoke nicely to him and there were no high walls or nuns, just family and plenty of love and warmth, and he began to express his opinions by pointing, smiling or frowning, though he was yet to master the art of words. One day he would learn to request things.


When Tilly arrived at Salon Mystique on Monday, Mrs Flock was poring over the accounts. Clare stood fearfully beside the telephone and Valda stood sentry at the door. Tilly had parked her bicycle and untucked her trousers from her socks and when she came through the door, Valda looked pointedly at her watch. 'Every morning you are late.'

'Yes, I know.' But you cannot hurry an infant if he doesn't want to be hurried, she thought, particularly one who is experiencing something new and strange every day.

In the workroom Shirley and several new girls toiled, their garments on the tables before them and their eyes to their stitching. Nita Orland's Coronation Ball gown waited like a goddess emerging from a cloud and Miss Post Office Picnic's neat little dress sparkled on its hanger. Tilly took Nita's dress and laid it flat on her table before sensing Valda behind her.

'You must leave those,' she said, gesturing to Nita's dress. 'This week you're to give priority to the dresses the outworkers have delivered.'

'I've just the finishing to do –'

'Then you'll have to work late.' Valda sighed. 'You will be paid after the show. Just work, like you're *employed* to.'

But she wouldn't work late even if Mrs Flock paid them all accordingly, plus back pay, and she worked only on the evening dress for Miss Post Office and Nita's Orland's ball gown, consoling herself that the people at Smalls Ball would notice these gowns. She was also working on a top-stitched mikado silk dress that most of the special guests viewing the press preview would not care for. But this dress, too, would get her noticed – at Myer. She hoped to place it there for their consideration, so she constructed a toile from patterns, moulage and draping, matched it with some grey silk and started cutting the calico, her yearning for her son stealing the small pleasure from her task. Their future together drew her on, though, and as she draped the toile onto the Stockman, Valda circled, like Sister Maria at the convent. Tilly ignored her.

Just as they were preparing to pack up for the day, Shirley came to her, sheepishly, and said, 'I don't know what's happened, Tilly, but the seams are all wrong.'

It was the straightforward gown, well cut but meaningless because it lacked suitable fabric – it was the Victor Stiebel copy, structured and precisely sculpted for a mannequin called Mercy, who was capable of showing a far superior garment. But the lines of the gown were not as Tilly had intended. She had made a toile that was pure, created the pieces of the gown and sewn the *fil de sens*, or threads, accurately, but on the constructed gown, the balance was wrong. The Victor Stiebel was a well-cut dress because it contained minimal cuts, and so the *fil de sens* were of the utmost importance. One thread followed the warp of the grain, the other thread was placed at right angles to it, following the weft, showing the true bias that lay between them. In this way, the threads exposed the faults in the cut and balance of the piece. The dress Shirley was holding looked correct – the *fil de sens* said the grain was accurate from a distance – but because they had been moved before the dress was constructed, the garment was, in fact, lopsided. It looked as if it needed darts and the seams were odd. The bodice was crooked, but the *fil de sens* suggested otherwise.

Then Valda said, 'You must have put the threads in wrong. Someone's made it all skew-whiff.'

'Valda, that is absurd.'

As Tilly stepped towards the gown, Valda stepped back. She looked at her watch. 'Better get a wriggle on, you haven't even looked at what the other seamstresses are up to.'

Tilly looked closely at the fabric and then turned on Valda. 'You moved them, didn't you, Valda? You spent hours sabotaging that dress, didn't you? How? What did you do, move the threads then have some poor apprentice make it up?'

Valda's ploy was not going to plan. She said weakly, 'Very shoddy work, yet you expect to be paid more.'

Tilly would not be destroyed because of her dressmaking skills. She would not be ruined by other people's jealousy of her talent, again. If Tilly Dunnage traded in vanity, then she would use that vanity, employing the power of her talent. It was what people wanted, so she would give them what they wanted, once again. This time, though, she would do it on her own terms and then leave them to themselves. She stepped very closely to poor, cowering Valda and spoke very clearly. 'What you fail to understand, Valda, is that I will not stay back and remake that gown. I don't care if Mrs Flock is upset when she sees it tomorrow. I don't even care if it goes out onto the runway the way it is, because my signature pieces will show who the artist is in this establishment, and my signature pieces will show that you and Mrs Flock are as creative as mule scavengers. I will advise Mrs Flock to remove the gown from the show.' Tilly removed her white coat, snatched the Victor Stiebel from Shirley and threw it at Valda. 'And I will tell Mrs Flock why the dress has been removed.'

Under the Victor Stiebel, Valda's face suddenly drained of colour.

Shirley stepped close to Valda, a statue covered by a lush dust sheet, 'Better get a wriggle on if you're staying to fix it; it's nearly six o'clock, and you're not likely to be paid overtime.'

Out on Collins Street, in the soft evening breeze, Tilly tucked her trousers into her socks, proud of her new-found self, and rode away on her bicycle towards her son, the everyday workers around her moving like a gentle creek and the streetlamps flickering to life.

About this time, over at the Shorts' place on Nicholson Street, Marigold Pettyman and Beula Harridene knocked on the front door. It creaked open. The doorjamb was splintered and in the empty foyer dry leaves from the garden swirled in a small happy circle. There was no sign of Mr Short.

'Yoo-hoo.'

There was no answer, just a terrible smell coming from the Shorts' rooms. Beula waved her head, sniffing, and followed her cane towards their door. Marigold knocked and heard faint moaning inside. At first, she was startled – appalled! – then she realised it was the moaning of pain rather than passion and, wishing to avoid being further appalled, Marigold sent Beula in.

Beula, wielding her cane, clacked her way in and called, 'Come out or I'll scream.'

It occurred to Marigold that she really should carry a knife; it was sensible for a vulnerable woman in a large city to pop one in her handbag, just in case.

Mrs Short said, 'We can't come out. We're stuck.'

Marigold entered and saw only Mrs Short, wedged against the wall like a pig in a vice. The side of the bed had collapsed against the wall and somewhere under Mrs Short was her husband. Marigold leaned over them and said, 'Where is Tilly Dunnage?'

'Gone.'

'Gone where?'

'We're stuck, get us out.'

'I will, just tell me her new address.'

'I don't know where she's gone.'

If Marigold had a knife, she thought, she might have threatened them for an answer. Then Mrs Short said, 'She works at Salon Mystique.'

'Oh. That's no good, is it, Beula? We'd have to wait for an appointment there.'

'*We* discovered her,' Beula said.

A noise came from beneath Mrs Short, and she extended her fat arm. 'Help.'

Marigold stopped a passer-by, suggested they telephone the police, and then left.

It was established that the nuts and bolts holding the bed together had finally succumbed to Mrs Short's weight. Mr Short was lucky to survive the days beneath his wife and the hospital staff were amazed that he had cared for his non-ambulant, elephantine wife for so long. It was agreed that they deserved to stay together, but the permanent damage to Mr Short's pelvis meant they were admitted to a war repatriation nursing home way out in Caulfield. Their respective wards housed approximately thirty patients each, fifteen along each side, and so Mr and Mrs Short's days were filled with other people's visitors, children and grandchildren, who even brought along their pets from time to time. And, of course, the overworked nurses were bustling and cheery, the cleaners industrious and the catering staff loud and friendly. There were also bothersome dementia sufferers and traumatised war survivors. It was quite a change for them, but happily, twice a week they were wheeled out to sit together at the edge of the breezy, covered walkways – wind tunnels, the staff declared – to watch life pass them by.

An Australian flag drooped listlessly from a pole shoved into the ground outside the rising town hall, its wall frames erect and half the floor laid. Rehearsals for *King Lear* were in full swing on those carefully constructed floorboards, the remaining beams and joists acting as temporary seating. Gertrude, her suitcase packed, headed off through the half-built town towards the railway platform to catch the train to Melbourne, her generator secretly sabotaged, her shop made secure and her hopes high.

Then she saw William Beaumont standing on the platform, looking back at New Dungatar, his great work. Felicity Joy was standing on the edge of the platform looking for an approaching train, and Gertrude was displeased to see her daughter had chosen a short playsuit and gumboots for the day. But she didn't want them to find out so soon that the shop was unguarded, that she'd gone to Melbourne. She scuttled back to her shop and soon the air quaked with the noise of the generator again.

William's crop cheque was in the bank. Happily, no weather, plague, flood or drought had ruined that fat green sheet of grain and it had turned golden bang on time and was duly harvested, dispatched to the silo, shipped off and sold for a good price. And now, most of the town's white lines and stakes were gone and the foundation stumps in, and even some fence posts. More timber was sent for and about to arrive. William felt manly and purposeful, though he wished Gertrude could stand here with him. Despite everyone else saying that Gertrude was a cow and deserved a few more months in the asylum, the fact was she was better than no one – for there was no one else – and she was mother to his only child, and he was lonely for her.

'Here comes the train,' Flick said, and William turned to the faint whistle and the tiny black line in the far distance. As the steam cloud grew on the horizon, Septimus and the others hitched up their pantaloons and waved their large frilly arms at the train, which slowed, groaned and stopped a kilometre from the station beside the giant grain silo. The driver climbed down, pulled a lever on the side of the track and then the train veered slowly to a wayside, where the driver uncoupled a goods truck. He had been told to collect a passenger, but saw no one on the railway platform, so he chuffed away.

William went to his tractor and started the engine, his jubilant daughter on his knee, pulled the flatbed trailer to the carriage and parked close. The men opened up the truck. Inside, stacked neatly, were the palely pulsing timber joists and girders, rafters and posts, beams and purlins, and weatherboards. There were also boxes of nails, saws, and a lot of corrugated iron, guttering and fascia, rain heads and bits no one recognised.

New Dungatar: a new future for all.

# Chapter 15

The week continued, quietly and arduously. Valda kept her distance and Tilly continued to ignore her. The Smalls Ball loomed. Each morning the seamstresses arrived, sewed, draped, unpicked, stitched, grabbed a quick mid-morning cup of tea, worked some more and, somewhere along the way, scoffed lunch. The mannequins modelled, the seamstresses adjusted, ripped, pinned, tacked and sewed into the early evening, the phone ringing downstairs and Clare screening desperate clients, all asking for Tilly Dunnage of Dungatar. Daughters, dowagers and debutantes arrived and were delivered of their gowns by Madame and Valda, and as they toiled in their atelier, focused – the only sound the slice of scissors through fabric, thread drawn through cloth, the flick of a tape measure and the nuanced rhythms of stitching and draping, and chalk on fabric – the seamstresses could only assume the ladies of Melbourne were happy with the product.

Occasionally Mrs Flock appeared on the landing, as if lowered by a thread, to look, to hear Valda's lies – 'Their work practices are shoddy, there is a lack of cultivation and form in the design that emanates directly from the backward society Tilly Dunnage was formed in and the "slum childhoods" of the seamstresses, and Tilly Dunnage has a complete inability to convey to the workers your beauty and perfection, Madame' – and all the while Clare's telephone rang and rang and armfuls of frocks from outworkers arrived and were left in a pile on Tilly's table for her scrutiny, and Madame Flock looked at what was being fitted on bored mannequins and glowing on Stockmans. Mrs Flock grew more and more confident. She began to haunt the Collins Street hill, specifically, the block between Exhibition and Spring streets, the quintessential Paris end of Collins Street.

Of a night, Tilly slept as she hadn't in years. On this morning, she woke at dawn, Joe beside her and soreness in her shoulders. Her forearms ached and fingertips were tender, but the rodent-featured nightmare women and their bad clothes had been vanquished, and Teddy McSwiney had visited, smiling and happy. He winked at her, then faded, and she realised that he no longer lingered through the day. She would hold on to his image, but in time it would fade, like the others she'd lost, the part they'd all played remaining. The memory of Teddy was being replaced by his son, more vivid before her every day.

Joe liked his routine, and was happy with his new life for there was love and toys and much company. So midway through the week, when she put him in his chair at the table with the McSwineys, he peered at his porridge and apple and watched his mother drinking strong coffee and chewing on jam toast. He turned his two blue eyes to Mae, porridge across his face and apple squashed in his fingers, and pointed to Tilly. 'Debdendoan.'

Tilly stopped chewing. Edward lowered his paper. Mae said, 'He said toast.'

Edward said he didn't say a word at all; it was a noise.

'But he's telling us he wants red toast,' Tilly protested.

'He didn't say words.'

Mae put her hands on her hips. 'He's made a request. That's a first.'

And it was. Joe's life of sitting quietly in a big room with high windows, waiting his turn, watching for an indication of what was to happen next – going outside onto the grass or to the playroom with the others – had ceased. Now he had asked for something, and he asked because he felt the people were good, gentle and loving. And they were. They gave him a slice of toast with jam.

On Friday, it was hot and sunny, the atelier stuffy, and Tilly's fingers were slippery on the needle and too damp for silk. She expected no extra money in her pay packet, but still thought there might have been, and when there wasn't she slipped out early, excusing herself to Shirley, saying she was off to search for gold chain and cherry-blossom buttons for the grey mikado silk dress.

She found herself on the corner of Flinders Lane, which rang with the busy business of the *schmatte* trade up and down the bluestones. The footpaths were narrow, the window ledges wide and entablatures over doorways grand. Men in dustcoats ferrying clothes racks – the clothes carefully shielded beneath a sheet – dodged trucks and vans, like metal orbs in a pinball machine. Workers with great bundles of clothes on their shoulders rolled from warehouse to factory to shop, and women moved purposefully in and out of the buildings or sat on steps eating sandwiches. Hawkers plied their wares, and pulleys lifted huge fabric bolts and crates up to platforms above. The people were made differently and moving energetically, their gestures and animations those of survivors, like little Myrtle Dunnage.

She had arrived at this corner as a fourteen-year-old, paralysed with hope and fear and holding a letter from Sister Patricia and a bag with samples – convent bloomers, a towel and a handmade shirt. Her friend at the time helped her find the right warehouse and climbed with her to the second-floor manufacturing business. Myrtle emerged from the warehouse and told her friend, 'You are looking at a maker-upper,' and her hope turned to faith and her days became wonderful. She made many, many frocks and blouses for Mr Belman and she loved being a *schmatte* girl. The people took her under their collective wing and shared their hearts and their humour. She was devoted to Mr Belman: he'd made her part of the whole big manufacturing and fabric family and then, one day, he came to her carrying a gown she'd made. 'Tilly Dunnage,' he'd said, 'this is not my design.' She was about to apologise when he said, 'It's perfect.'

She could not speak.

'You wanna be a designer? I gotta find another seamstress but once I do, you can be a designer.' It was as if someone had pricked her with a pin and she'd shot off in whistling circles all the way to the ceiling. 'That's the feeling of joy,' her friend said, and went with her to trawl the fabric sellers along the lane and select materials for her designs. Each day she set off to work and searched for fabrics when she could, then skipped home at night to the wood shed at the Shorts' or to her second job as a theatre usher. When Tilly was eighteen years old, she boarded a ship for Europe carrying a letter from Mr Belman. 'It's getting dangerous over there,' he warned. 'So if you don't like it over there, you come straight back here to us.' That was in early 1933. She would come to learn that even solid, true friends would let her down. Others would open a door and welcome her into a whole new world, would nurture and care for her.

And standing here on Flinders Lane, all these years later, she saw that her favourite passementerie and costume jewellery warehouse remained, though she recognised none of the staff. The quality of the artificial flowers, beads, feathers, leather trims, buckles, belts, sequins, fans, lace and weaving materials were unchanged and she found her gold chain and cherry-blossom buttons. As she wandered back towards Salon Mystique through the bustling lane where it had all begun, she arrived at a decision.

She found the sergeant sitting on a director's chair beside the sandpit, his legs crossed and sandshoes on his feet. He wore his mother's silk bathing cape, circa 1918. The design was thick vertical stripes of black and white, with three giant tasselled buttons linking it loosely across his chest. His sunhat sported a wide polka-dot band and he was holding a pink umbrella over Joe, who was coated in sand and twigs, his chest washed clean with drool.

'You're home early.'

'I am.'

The pale-skinned, pale-eyed sergeant said, 'I am concerned for Joel's complexion, the sun is so harsh.'

'Of course.' She looked up at the tree house carefully constructed by Edward, but they were not brave enough to lower the ladder to the small boy just yet. She was thoughtful as she set up a fabric tipi over the sandpit, while Joe watched, clutching his truck. 'This is a cubby for you to play in, Joel, my boy. You can keep your trucks here . . . out of the sun.'

The sergeant told her about the tram ride home: Joe standing at the window watching Collingwood pass, then holding the sergeant's finger all the way up Darling Street to the shopfront and home at number 27. They read *Incy Wincy Spider* while he sat on the potty. 'Mae says he asks to go now.'

'That's spectacular.'

The sergeant thought she should have been more impressed. 'What's up?'

As she perfected the bedsheet tipi she explained that she was tired of being taken for granted, underpaid, and that she had arrived at a decision. 'I need to know more about award wages and working conditions,' she said. 'I'm going to phone the union.'

The sergeant leapt up. 'NO! You can't.'

'Why? Is the phone bugged?'

'Julie might ring.'

'Why don't you just ring her?'

'She said she'd phone at six.'

'It's only five.'

The sergeant gnawed on his thumbnail.

Tilly sighed. 'I'll phone on Monday.'

He dashed inside, swift in his sandshoes, to sit beside the telephone. Julie phoned at exactly 6 pm.

# Chapter 16

As THE CORONATION neared, magazines became thicker and the social sections of newspapers expanded for feature articles, photos and competitions for such prizes as royal postcards, coronation cups and monarchy dinner sets. On the streets, the lampposts fluttered with notices of royal street parties, and Princess Elizabeth lookalike competitions were held at Saturday night dances. Recipes for Union Jack icing and edible crowns circulated through the heart of suburbia and a stroll through any shop meant tripping over bins of coronets and sashes, British flags, royal tablecloths and dishcloths, and exclusive tea towels, allowing housewives to dry crockery with Princess Elizabeth's face. There were cake tins and bread bins shaped like royal carriages and sheepskin slippers encrusted with strings of pearls or fat sapphire and diamond brooches. Red and royal blue velvet had made a comeback and one fabric shop had the salesgirls wear paper tiaras. Special coronation hats, gloves and stockings were for sale, as were British coronation linen, insignia cutlery and crockery, and special edition coins, and it seemed every school assignment each child completed featured a crown, sceptre, orb and cross, or some element of royal history. Advertising campaigns cashed in with royal soap powder and nappies and motor cars, and the blockbuster sales flogged last season's fashions with a special royal embroidered badge. This year, the fashionable crowd was spread thin. The coronation extended the royal frisson to pretenders, which meant even Madame Flock could get on some list for some fashion event somewhere; certain city salons hosted couture parades four times a day. For months, all over Melbourne, men had come home at the end of the working day and heard only the loud sound of the Kelvinator signalling an egg and ham salad waiting on the middle shelf. And now the biggest event had arrived, the spectacle to kick off the season, the Smalls Charity Coronation Ball, and those men came home to a princess in the kitchen and took them dancing.

At the tram stop on Toorak Road, a short walk from the CWA hostel, Marigold Pettyman waited. She was wrapped in a pale shawl which protected her blue silk crepe gown. The close-cut bias featured a saucy short train, and a high, fine net cowl caressed her delicate throat. Tilly had made it for the Dungatar Social Club Ball, and while Tilly had sat under the stars on top of the silo with her new love, Marigold had been awarded Belle.

Beside her, Beula stared down the tracks in entirely the wrong direction. 'Here's the tram,' she cried, and Marigold grabbed her arm as a lorry rumbled past, coating them with city grit. When they arrived in the heart of Melbourne they climbed down from the tram, expectant and a little lost, and were drawn along with the well-dressed people towards the lush, swelling melody of an orchestra, floating from the town hall.

Nita waited in her car with Daisy Lou, her driver. Timing was essential for maximum impact. When Mr Guston Small, his charming wife and son – who had discarded her – were basking in the glory of their own magnanimity, Nita made her entrance. Daisy Lou dashed around to open the door and stood proudly in her smart black slacks while Nita emerged, foot first, her ankle encircled by gold straps. She stood in her black velvet stilettos with golden heels while the flashbulbs burst, her legs shimmering with gold dust. She placed one hand on her hip, the diamond-crusted skull glittering on her finger, to present her gown. It was black, slim-fitting and one-shouldered; a thick collar of gold chains circled her throat and joined her left shoulder strap before continuing, draping her upper arm and sweeping around the asymmetric neckline. The gold was real, though only nine carats, and the skirt trailed a substantial train which culminated in a golden tassel, which Miss Orland picked up and hung over her sleeveless arm, like a curtain tassel, and walked up the stairs. On the fifth step she paused on the red carpet for more flash bursts, the golden trims on her dark silhouette twinkling. For her next photo opportunity, Nita hung the curtain tassel around her throat, which pulled the gown above her glittering knees and revealed its golden silk lining. Her third *pause dramatique* was to then drop the train again and let the tassel follow her elegant form into the din of bosomy, flower-shaped matrons – bunches rather than single stem – and Princess Elizabeth lookalikes.

At the top of the stairs, two unfortunate women shot from the crowd. The blind one cried, 'We discovered Tilly Dunnage!' and Nita tucked them away in her memory to use for characters in a play one day. Her chaperone for the evening, a tall, lean man, stepped forward and more camera bulbs burst before her handsome companion ushered her towards the music and lights – passing, but not acknowledging, the Small family. Mrs Small asked her son, 'Is there no way we will ever be rid of your ex-wife?'

'No,' he said, as his wife danced off into the crowd, her eyes only for her smouldering matinee-idol partner. He wished he'd thought to bring one of his young mistresses.


At home, Tilly tucked her boy into his cot, read *The Tortoise and the Hare* and left Joe with his truck, a small furry koala and a knitted zebra. Then she addressed the matter of the sergeant, who was standing at the front door, trying to muster the courage to open it and go to collect Julie. 'Would you like me to telephone and say you're sick?'

'God, no! I'll go, I just need a little more time.' It was going to be a very long tram trip to Hawthorn, too long to be nervous.

She poured him a shot of whisky. 'Joe and I could walk you to the tram stop.'

'No, thank you,' he said, and took a step towards the door.

'You do look very lovely,' Tilly said, and reached out to embrace him.

He cried, 'No! You'll squash my tie.' But still he couldn't bring himself to open the door and go through it.

'She wouldn't have said yes if she didn't want to go out with you.'

The sergeant's hand went to his heart. 'I once had a lady friend, you know. She dropped in one day, unannounced. I was doing housework, floor day, I'd put all the chairs up. I tried to tell her I was my own aunt, but she knew it was me under the chiffon apron. I've been wary of rejection ever since.'

'Julie was happy to swap shoes with you the night you met.'

The sergeant looked doubtful, pained, tilting his head this way then that, and declared, 'You're right. I'll go.' Once more he checked he had change for the tram and once more he smoothed his hair. Finally he saluted and marched out the front door. She waited, then went to the front fence. 'Keep walking,' she cried, for he had stopped, frozen, outside Miss Peachy's.

He arrived at the Hawthorn tram stop with half an hour to spare but walked the twenty yards to the clinker-brick flats with the neat lawn anyway, though he continued on past. At the corner, he stopped, took a deep breath, raised his chin and said, 'Horatio, you are an upright officer who has encountered, and survived, much danger in both your lives. Just do it. Now.'

He turned, a policeman's toe-heel turn, saluted no one, and marched directly back to Julie's building, where he stopped, stamped his foot and executed another toe-heel turn before going straight up the front steps. It took a very long time for the door to open but he kept his chin high and his eyes direct. Suddenly he was cast in hall light, then darkness as a form in the doorway blocked the light. The sergeant looked up into a brilliantly backlit silhouette.

'You're early,' Julie said, and clapped her hands.

The sergeant was speechless.

'Come in and have a drink,' she said and the sergeant saluted, but quickly lowered his hand. He followed, stopping in the passage on the busy floral carpet to remove his policeman's cap only to realise he was not wearing one. He followed her to the lounge room, where she stood beside the drink trolley, a big empire-line shape, her gown blue, like her lovely eyes. He remembered her firm and lovely calves and knew they were there under her long skirt, and then he caught a glimpse of her shoes! Of course, the wonderful blue suede she'd worn the night they met. Her smile remained and he noticed for the first time that she had dimples.

'I like your suit.'

The sergeant was dressed in a black velvet suit with a velvet bow tie.

Julie handed him a tumbler containing a huge amount of whisky and he took it, his hand shaking. 'I'll drive,' she said. 'I've got Dad's old car.'

Sergeant Farrat saw that Julie wore sparkly blue shadow on her eyelids, just a hint of pink lipstick and a mere smudge of rouge on her cheeks. She was just a little taller than him.

He sank his whisky in one gulp. 'You are absolutely beautiful, like the clouds parting in the sky.'

It was an awkward metaphor and she blushed. 'Thank you. The dress is my design, but I had it made.'

'That colour is your colour, Julie.' Her name was like two notes in birdsong.

She put her drink down. 'I've had other suitors, you know.'

The sergeant's heart sank. Was she going to tell him she liked them better?

'They all stood there, exactly where you're standing now.'

The sergeant looked at his shoes on the carpet and moved from the big pink flower to a large leaf.

'I think you're interested in *me*, Horatio. I hope you don't just see me as sport.'

'Yes. I mean no. I mean not sport. I very much appreciate you, but I hate sport, well, most sport. And I'm here, for you, at last – not that it's bad that I took so long to get here, I wish I'd been here sooner but I was posted to the country, but here I am. And I'll be back. Back I'll come, and I'm very lucky no one else . . . stuck . . . because you're there and I'm here . . . babbling.'

'I know this is very early in our friendship but I never want you to lie to me, or hide things from me, and I won't do it to you.'

'I am an honourable man and I like you very much,' he said, 'and I hope our friendship lasts for the rest of our lives.'

'Oh,' she said, breathily. Then she leaned a little and placed her hand on the wall to steady herself, fanning herself with her free hand. 'I'd like another drink, would you?'

'No, thank you. I don't want to fall over on our first outing together.'

'Me neither, but let's have one anyway.'

Julie expertly reversed the car down the long drive and out into the traffic, chucked the stem shift into first gear and planted her foot, and they roared off towards the city, the speed pressing the sergeant back in his seat. He felt the thrill of the gay, free night air and the suburbs rushing past and the ball waiting and the glorious woman by his side.

At the town hall, Julie parked in one deft manoeuvre, an arm across the back of the seat and her gloved palm winding the steering wheel. She turned off the lights and looked at Sergeant Farrat, shyly. 'I bet you looked wonderful in uniform.'

'I was always happy as a mere sergeant. A lower rank meant I could manage the subtleties of my life without much . . . scrutiny.'

They were nearing the town hall stairs when he saw Beula Harridene and Marigold Pettyman. They were gawking at everyone, blocking the flow of the crowd. Marigold looked nice, Beula wore something a whirling dervish had discarded. He took Julie's gloved arm and was steering her away when Marigold called, 'Yoo-hoo,' and walked towards him. 'I see your wife didn't make you a new frock?'

'Obviously, she didn't make you one either.' He led Julie away.

Marigold, smarting from his comment, watched the sergeant ascend the stairs, a striking man in luxurious black velvet, and his friend an impressive blue presence at his side, her handbag glittering on her firm arm, and felt slight resentment at their togetherness, and she suspected they might even look better than her.

Because they weren't quite sure what to do next, Beula and Marigold found a spot to the side of the door to listen and observe. A matron with a sapphire resting in the small crepe nest of her cleavage said, 'That's different,' and her companion, a woman held erect by foundation corsetry, exclaimed, 'Gracious me, that's Miss Post Office Picnic,' and flashbulbs exploded. A man with a notepad and pencil started to sketch, adding to the bottleneck, and the critics from various fashion pages tittered, 'Miss Post Office Picnic is wearing something aspirational.'

'Yet contextual.'

'And it has a strong narrative.'

'Coherent.'

'Not dull, not common.'

'Quite specific.'

'A piece of art.'

'It is fashion.'

'Fashion couture.'

'From Salon Mystique.'

'You're kidding?'

'I'm not.'

'They have a new designer.'

'Tilly Dunnage,' said the blind woman wearing what she regarded as mere clothing. 'She was ours first,' she blurted, and her friend in the angel-sleeved dress said, 'She's my stepdaughter.'

Just then, the band played 'God Save the King' and everyone stopped, hands on hearts, chins up and eyes to the far middle distance.

Beula Harridene pondered the large blurry shape standing as one with the dark shape she recognised to be the sergeant. 'Who is that person?'

'That is Julie, of Miss Julie's Shoe Shop. Julie is the best shoe-maker in Melbourne. She's made my feet happy for many years.'

Beula had no idea who answered her, but she was happy with the information.

While Nita Orland dazzled, Miss Post Office Picnic shone and Melbourne danced, Tilly Dunnage slept in the front room of the McSwineys' cosy house with her son, curled together like puppies in a slipper.

On Saturday morning, Nita Orland, wearing Tilly's virtuoso of black, solo-shouldered silk satin, smiled at Melbourne from the social pages. The photograph was large – the largest – and it was bang in the middle of the special feature page. Around Nita, the establishment appeared as lost ladies-in-waiting – to Queen Victoria. She was a triumph, and beneath her, a bigger triumph. An article, small and thin but extremely well placed, reported that the Tailoresses' Association and the Clothing and Allied Trades

Union of Australia were to lobby the government to inquire into working conditions for seamstresses and tailors of Victoria, who had asked for better pay and, rather boldly, child care for working women. And this was what Madame and Valda were reading when Edward stopped the horse and cart outside the salon and helped Tilly and her bike down. Barney held the door for her and as she wheeled past Mrs Flock said, 'Thankfully, it is very early and no one has seen you arrive! If you must travel by horse and cart, have these people park that agent of disease somewhere further away!'

Barney had inspected the door quite closely and informed Mrs Flock and Valda that he was a doorman but his door had less glass in it.

'Move,' said Mrs Flock, and Valda nudged him away.

Edward removed his hat and stepped a little closer. 'You probably don't remember me from Dungatar, Mrs Flock, but I drove you from the station the day you arrived for your short holiday, in that very horse and cart.'

Barney detected her confusion so helpfully reminded her that she 'sat up in the back with the mail bags and some chickens'.

'Small world, eh?' Edward put his hat on and left, Barney limping behind. Valda arrived with the vacuum cleaner to suck the chaff from the carpet.

The telephone rang. Clare cried, 'Make it stop.'

Tilly presented Mrs Flock with the tally of overtime hours. 'I should get to it, I suppose, given the winter coronation parade's so close, or perhaps I won't?'

'Please,' said Mrs Flock. 'We will see to your pay.'

When she was sure Tilly was in her workroom, Mrs Flock phoned her real estate agent and asked him to find her a shop further up on Collins Street. 'I am happy to pay a higher rent should premises become vacant sooner rather than later,' she said, sweetly.

*

That evening, Julie came for dinner.

The sergeant opened the door as Tilly was putting Joe to bed. He was bawling because she had removed him from his soft, murky cubby and his new tip truck was left abandoned in the sand with his favourite sticks and twigs. The small boy looked to the sergeant, his eyes pleading, desperate, fat tears spilling down his red cheeks.

'Who owns the baby?' asked Julie.

'Quite a few people, actually, but he is mostly ours. Tilly's his mother.'

Julie's face fell and the sergeant reached out to her. 'No! I'm not the father. He has no father, but he does have grandparents, aunts and uncles. I just helped the boy out, they were in a tight spot.'

She looked questioningly at the sergeant as Joe wailed on.

'It's a very long story,' said the sergeant.

'It's just that . . . well, I quite like babies, in their place, but I'm not very good at them,' Julie said.

'Neither is Joe's stepfather but we're not asking him to be,' Tilly said.

'I gave him a truck and he's been torn away from it,' the sergeant said, poignantly. 'There's so much to tell you, but we will share it, when I'm feeling brave enough.'

Julie nodded. 'No good comes from secrets.'

Tilly continued out to the sandpit and retrieved the tip truck, a toy crane, a small metal bucket and shovel and the precious sticks and placed them all in Joe's bed. He stopped crying, and when he was asleep, the Farrats and Julie enjoyed a quiet meal of Cornish pasties, the vegetables from Miss Peachy's garden. Two bottles of wine were consumed and then Tilly served chocolate cake and stewed cherries with cream, all the while talking of shoes and fashion and Paris and life and cultural events, all of which happened before Tilly returned to Dungatar. The rest of the story would be told next time because, after coffee and a liqueur, Tilly excused herself and went up to bed. Joe slept soundly in his cradle of toys and sticks and Tilly slept soundly across the hall. The sergeant stayed at the table with Julie, the pair smiling like teenagers, their hands touching across the table, and it seemed that finally, everything in the world looked well.

Around 3.30 am, the sergeant saw Julie to her car and kissed her cheek and she said, 'I haven't felt so happy since I conquered my first size twelve and a half, extra-slim fit, standard last.'

'Splendid,' said the sergeant, and marvelled that Julie could make a 'last', whatever it was.

# Chapter 17

SUNDAY MORNING, JOE was in his high chair; in front of him, a banana. He was frowning at it, but the sergeant said, 'Look, son, I'll show you.' He held the tip of a banana, steadying the curve against a plate, and slit it down the centre, then dissected it at one-inch intervals. He put his knife down and carefully peeled back the skin and picked up a dainty dessert fork. He smiled at Joe. 'Now the good bit.' And then he popped a small half-moon into his mouth and chewed quickly. Joe reached into the banana and picked up a half-moon. It slipped from his fingers onto the floor so he picked up another piece, squashing it with a firmer grip, and smeared it in the general area of his mouth.

'Remember, Joel, that yesterday we discussed manners?'

Joe picked up another piece of banana and pressed it into the top of his tray.

'Perhaps we will start again when you are three.'

'I'd wait until he's four,' said Tilly, and started washing wine glasses and leaving them to drain. She reached for a plate and the doorbell rang. It was Sunday morning, so Tilly didn't bother looking through the net window curtains or the peephole. She would never again fail to check. It was the welfare officer.

'Just a routine follow-up after your recent consultation.'

'Really? On a Sunday morning?'

'A most convenient time,' he said, and pushed past her. 'Most people are at home, some are not, most are still sleeping.'

'You've got no right to be here. Joe was a voluntary placement.

I paid for his keep with the nuns because I thought it was safe from predators. I was wrong.'

'Joe was discharged from the convent because he has a home now and I am his father.' Sergeant Farrat stood in his Sunday morning galligaskins and Aladdin slippers, henna reviving what was left of his hair and sliding into his face mask, which was fermenting and drooling onto a towel wrapped tightly about his torso. There was a hint of glitter foundation in his eyebrows.

The welfare officer's eyes took in the sergeant in his entirety. 'And who do you think you are, Charlie Chaplin?'

'Certainly not, his marriage breeched a gap of thirty-five years! I am a mere sixteen years older than my wife.'

The welfare officer continued to the kitchen, looked at the pile of dinner plates and bowls, champagne, wine and liqueur glasses.

'I have a husband, a home and an income,' Tilly cried. 'Joe has loving grandparents, aunts, uncles –'

'Who are half the problem! There's a card on them – vagrancy and child neglect, truancy and illegal trading, tethering a horse illegally, the list goes on – and for five days a week, sometimes more, you've entrusted them your child! Your ruddy case file is six inches thick and goes back twenty years or more, which was when you committed your first crime, fratricide, and ends with an illegitimate child being raised by her vagrant grandparents living in a slum. Why wouldn't we keep an eye on you?'

The sergeant stepped between Tilly and the welfare officer. 'Your department has no inkling of what constitutes a good home and a loving family. I care for the boy too, his welfare is our utmost priority. He is not mistreated, abused or molested here.'

'You bohemians . . . you cannot guarantee that. You are morally repulsive, all of you.'

She almost laughed. 'You don't care about their welfare. What

I'd like to know is what happened to you to make you the way you are?'

His next words snatched her courage away.

'The salient point here is that we all know what happened to you, what you did as a child. The Head of Welfare might think you're reformed, but I do not.'

The welfare officer opened the fridge – there was food, and a couple of bottles of opened wine, which he poured down the sink. He listed the contents then checked the laundry and the rubbish bins.

'We celebrated the Queen's forthcoming coronation last night,' the sergeant lied, but the welfare officer was inspecting a neat line of the sergeant's hats on blocks: some fully realised, some works in progress. He continued back through the vacant shop and up the stairs. Tilly followed with Joe on her hip. His room was spotless and tidy, though the bed contained a tip truck and a sprinkling of sand, a crane, shovel, bucket and Joe's precious sticks. The officer announced the new bed was 'too high for a handicapped child. He should have a cot with a gate over the top, he'll fall out and hurt himself in the night then roll down the stairs. And he sleeps with dangerous objects.'

The officer upended a box of toys and, once the clattering mass had settled, he declared them inappropriate and Tilly neglectful. 'I see you want him to choke on small toys.' He picked up the McSwiney family teddy bear and chucked it at Tilly. 'It needs to be washed and disinfected, or burned.'

Next, he went to Tilly's workroom. He pulled back the eider-down on her big bed in the corner and looked at her sheets. 'Who sleeps here?'

'The odd cross-dresser and homosexual.'

The welfare officer said insolence wouldn't get her anywhere and Sergeant Farrat put his arm protectively around her, stead-ying her, for she was rattled, trembling beneath her defiant exterior. 'My wife sleeps there sometimes when our son's restless. This room's closer and she doesn't disturb me getting up to him.'

'I would suggest that so many sharp objects, needles, pins, quick unpicks, scissors, machinery, would be very fatal to a child.'

'Only if you let the child get near them.' Sergeant Farrat indicated the toddler fence that stopped Joe from getting into his mother's sewing room.

In Sergeant Farrat's room the double bed was made up neatly and the doors to the balcony ajar, the curtains lifting in the warm breeze. Feather boas wafted across the wardrobe door and Sergeant Farrat's red bar-strap wedge heels poked out from beneath the wardrobe. The welfare officer looked down at the very large ladies' shoes. He looked at Tilly's slippers, ancient, tartan, from a sale at the men's department at Myer. He sniffed and wandered across to the other wardrobe and found men's suits and shirts hanging. Finally, he sauntered down the stairs, sat at a table in the workroom and made notes, then opened the front door and walked out, leaving it wide open.

Tilly locked the door behind him and they sank into the nearest chairs, hearts racing, feeling queasy. Their greatest, unspoken fear was bigotry and ignorance, and the vilification it fostered. Both knew only too well that in society, those who were least understood were targeted, unfairly and incorrectly slurred, and one of the most common and slanderous labels was 'homosexual'. Neither the sergeant nor Tilly fitted that category, but it was mere months since the death penalty for sodomy had been abolished and homosexuality remained a criminal offence, and accused, even wrongly, they remained vulnerable to brutal judgement and the violence that accompanied it. To keep Joe, Tilly needed to stay, and the welfare officer's visit was their first reminder that in staying, Tilly's presence made them vulnerable, put at risk the sergeant's privacy, risked Joe, risked everything.

'It's all such a mess. I have to finish this collection because

Mrs Flock owes me so much money, even though I'm not being paid enough, and when she pays me I'll find a house . . .' Joe was frowning at her and offered her a wedge of squashed banana.

'Please, dear Tilly, stop. I am accustomed to fear and intimidation, as are you.' He caught sight of himself in the hall mirror opposite and went to look closely at the age lines around his eyes. 'Though it is wearing, I have to say.'

But Tilly was quietly weeping. 'I don't like my job, I don't like my boss, but if I leave I won't get paid . . . I'm sorry, Sergeant, truly I am.'

'Tsk! And what do you mean, "the odd cross-dresser and homosexual"? Don't give him ideas!'

'I'm getting more like my mother every day.'

'Aren't we all?'

There was another knock at the door, and the sergeant fled.

Through the small lens of the peephole Miss Peachy was holding zucchinis, an eggplant and a lettuce. Tilly opened the door, Joe still at her side.

'My dear,' she said, 'I don't want to intrude . . .'

Tilly sighed and reached down to Joe, who was clutching her leg.

Miss Peachy looked at her tired, irritated face. 'That man watches, and he has just stopped to talk to Mrs Rickett.' She leaned closer. 'He sits in his car across the park under that big elm. He has binoculars.' Miss Peachy produced a peach from her pocket and handed it to Joe, who smiled, studied the fruit and threw it on the ground.

'It won't bounce, but you can eat it.'

She reached out and wearily guided Miss Peachy into the shop. Miss Peachy handed her a clean handkerchief. Tilly wiped her cheeks.

'Next time I'll bang on the wall with my broom . . . if I see him in time.'

'If there's anything we can do, Miss Peachy, ever – anything – please let us know.'

'Well, there is something.' Miss Peachy had lived without nice neighbours for decades before Horatio returned. 'I'd like to come to your next party.'

'You are welcome in our home anytime, Miss Peachy.'

'And that lovely horse is welcome to trim my trees anytime he wants. I like his droppings for my vegetable garden, if that's all right.' She thrust the vegetables at Tilly.

'I'll speak to Edward, we can drop off a bag, I'm sure. And we can ask Barney to turn your soil for you?'

Miss Peachy clapped her hands. 'That would be so helpful.'

When Miss Peachy returned next door she climbed the stairs to her mother's bedroom and flung open the wardrobe door. She pulled out a fine pale silk and muslin gown that was her mother's. Perhaps Tilly would alter it for her, when she had time.


Gertrude drove to the railway station with her suitcase, left the keys in the ignition and waited on the platform, eyes to the west, the great silo behind her. Soon, the steam plume appeared and travelled thinly along the horizon. It grew, gradually, its engines winding down, becoming a slow train that turned at The Hill, its carriages tilting and the wheels squealing on the curved metal. Finally, the loud spurting thing was upon her. The boxes of tinned goods, bags of fresh foods and stack of newspapers tumbled from the guard's van, bouncing off the platform to roll into the thick Scotch thistles and Bathurst burrs that had consumed the absent stationmaster's pretty flowers. The train kept going, chuffing off into the horizon and leaving her covered in soot and gritty ash. She stamped her foot. 'It's not fair!'

She loaded her bus with her grocery supplies, drove back to her shop and made herself a cup of tea. She cut open the bundle of newspapers. Miss Post Office Picnic and Miss Nita Orland stared up at her. '*Actress Heralds New Talent*,' she read. '*No More Mystery at Salon Mystique*.'

And there were others, skinny women wearing superstar gowns and so-called 'Madame' Flock (more likely a *Madam)* looking stupid with her haughty grin. 'Madam' Flock wouldn't be smug if she knew her success was because of Gertrude. It was Gertrude who had handed Tilly Dunnage her first break. No one else in Dungatar had ever looked so good in a wedding gown . . . which is why she needed to get to Melbourne to Tilly Dunnage and get another dress! She stamped both feet several more times. Was it a conspiracy? Had someone – Elsbeth? – telephoned and told the train not to stop?

Gertrude gasped. There was more! A letter contributed to the 'Downtown Dungatar' section of the *Amalgamated Dungatar Winyerp Gazette Argus* said: 'Mrs Evan Pettyman and her companions Mr and Mrs Richard Hawker, and Miss Beula Harridene were guests at the Small Family Charity Coronation Ball.'

Directly below, in the 'In Itheca' section, a headline cried, 'Local Dressmaker Shines for the Queen.' The Itheca Dramatic Society sent their 'fondest congratulations' to their friend, Tilly Dunnage, a previous winner of the Best Costume Award . . .

It was a conspiracy. Gertrude marched through the shop to her room, bit her fist and flung herself onto her bed, sobbing like she hadn't since the asylum doctors had stopped her at the door and removed Felicity Joy from her suitcase.

When the sound of her sobbing reached the workers on the other side of the road, William Beaumont's hopes that Gertrude would allow them some petrol were dashed. The group returned to the surveyor's map.

\*

Marigold Pettyman was thinking about Friday night. No one at the Smalls Ball had noticed her at all; she did not get one compliment. She then started thinking about her money, and Mr Hawker, who would not give it to her, and the fact that it was money her father had earned, money he'd saved, nurtured and given to her. Using little Myrtle Dunnybum and her McSwiney sprog to get her hands on it hadn't worked, although, quite honestly, she didn't really want to hurt Tilly Dunnage, not before the winter collections anyway, and she didn't really want to hurt Tilly's innocent son. He was illegitimate, but he had the same blood coursing through his sweet little veins as her only-born child, Stewart. A vision came to her of Mr Hawker outside his Bourke Street office, a fat man in a striped suit sweating in the hot summer sunshine – a rotting walrus on the footpath, his feet loose at his ankles and a line of blood oozing towards the gutter. She had a good mind to sever all those neat little flexor tendons traversing his wrists, too. Even if she was returned to the asylum, at least she'd have her money, she could still buy nice frocks. Money meant she could pay for a private room. Her old urges were surfacing: she longed for the sterile floors and walls of the asylum, its antiseptic odours and sparkling hand basins. It was disgusting having to breathe Beula's air each night, to use the same hand soap, stand on the same bath mat. With money, she could build a house in Dungatar far better than anyone else's miserable, rudimentary kennel and just leave it there. Empty. Oh, how it would gall Elsbeth! She thought she was superior but Elsbeth's house was rotting and her fox fur had nits, she was sure. She searched through her handbag and found the card Arlen O'Connor had given her.

Next to her Beula was trying to focus on the black and white smudges in the murky newspaper. She knew it was that actress, and she could just make out that she was standing next to a man.

'He's handsome, isn't he, Beula?'

'I'll have to take your word for it.' Beula tried to remember what a handsome man looked like from her pre-handicapped life, the days when she saw everything, knew everyone and never missed a whisper. Some whispers came back to her quite different from how she'd started them and that was always amusing. She could cope being deaf because of the hearing aids, but not being able to see was just cruel, and disproportionally unfair. These days she was flat out just seeing her feet. It wasn't fair! The night she was injured she'd been trying to do the right thing. She'd witnessed, with her very own eyes, Tilly Dunnage and the town sergeant standing at Molly Dunnage's graveside, drenched, the sergeant wearing a frock for all to see. It was a black knee-length dress with a draped neck and a stylish, asymmetrical lampshade overskirt. Wool-crepe, very smart, completely ruined by the rain.

It had been her duty to find out more about the sergeant's debauchery, so that night, Beula had climbed up to Molly Dunnage's house on The Hill. Beula had found the town's only policeman and the murderess drunk, lurching all over that dirty little shack, half-dressed, singing and moaning, blathering on about how romantic songs portrayed false truths to innocent young women! Sheer drunken debauchery, and the deceased not cold in her grave. And then Tilly Dunnage opened the door and hurled the radiogram out into the darkness, and on that soft cloudy night, Beula had suddenly seen stars. Sergeant Farrat was not sympathetic at all; in fact, he just shoved her into the asylum, and didn't punish Tilly Dunnage. She'd always hoped her sight would return, but it hadn't.

She swung her legs over the side of the bed only to discover it was the wall side, so she swung her feet back to the other side of the bed, took one step and crashed into the side table. Marigold scolded her. 'Watch where you're going.'

'I can't bloody *watch* anything, can I?' Beula crashed her way to the bathroom.

Marigold reached for her disinfectant spray and pumped about half of the tiny bottle into the room. Then she removed the luggage tag – Beula Harridene, Toorak CWA – from Beula's cardigan, tore it up and threw it in the bin.

Beula returned, put on her cardigan and asked if she looked all right.

'You look perfectly all right,' said Marigold, not bothering to tell Beula her skirt was on inside out.

Marigold slid her feet out of her slippers and into her carefully placed shoes – other people had been walking on the floor in bare feet: warm, damp naked feet, the soft matter beneath their toenails leaking into the carpet fibres. She set off for the bathroom with her bottle of White King, some rubber gloves and clean underwear. When she was scrubbed and ready, they ate breakfast with the other ladies and then Marigold pressed a hanky over her mouth and nose and had the receptionist telephone Mr O'Connor. They waited at the tram stop, in the city grit and car fumes, the hanky still pressed to Marigold's nose and some spare gloves in her handbag in case she had to touch something.

# Chapter 18

JOE WAS CONFIDENT and comfortable in his new home and roamed through the house, up and down the stairs, from his room to his toys in the cubby over the sandpit where it was safe and sheltered. He had cardboard boxes to climb into and draw on, nurtured a healthy interest in anything with wheels and was able to watch motor vehicles passing from the sergeant's balcony. He didn't mind going to Mae's with his aunts and uncles but still quite enjoyed his own company. Tilly often found him in the cupboard under the sink with a toy screwdriver, or under his bed with his teddy bear and books. On this occasion, she found him in the sergeant's shoe cupboard with his truck. She put him in his high chair, an array of food in front of him. 'There's a lot to choose from here, Joe. So I want you to eat as much of it as you can.' She was handing him a spoonful of cereal when the doorbell rang.

She ignored it. The early visitor knocked but Tilly persisted with Joe and his spoon, which he had turned upside down.

The sergeant came down the stairs. 'I peeked from the balcony.'

'The welfare officer?'

'Worse, Beula and Marigold.'

'Right.' Tilly strode to the door and flung it open. 'It's seven o'clock in the morning.' She closed the door.

They knocked again, loudly, kept a finger on the doorbell, and Marigold cried, 'Let us in, it's a matter of life and death.'

She thought about the Ricketts down the street, the welfare

officer, Joe in his high chair trying to learn to eat. She wrenched the front door open and spoke pleasantly. 'You're like fox piss in a damp jumper, aren't you? Why don't you fart off back to the hellish cinders of Dungatar, where you belong?'

Marigold said, 'How very vulgar,' and stepped past her. Beula knocked her way to the staircase.

'How did you find me?'

'The telephone directory, Mrs Farrat's Hat Shop.'

Tilly was momentarily speechless. 'In that case you should have telephoned.'

'I want a dress for the Dungatar Coronation Ball. Please.'

'Go to Salon Mystique, now goodbye.'

'I'll just take that black dress I saw at Smalls Ball.'

'It's a one-off.'

Marigold burst into tears.

'Cry as much as you like,' Tilly said. 'I don't care.'

Tilly made her way through to the kitchen, Beula and Marigold following. Joe had upturned his cereal bowl onto his high chair tray, and Marigold recoiled at the milk and cereal dripping onto the floor. The longer she stayed in Melbourne, the grubbier she felt. The sergeant, these days accustomed to mess, placed shower caps over his lovely slippers and padded through the puddle to the stove to warm water for his morning cup.

'We know one of your secrets, we'll tell everyone.'

'You can tell anyone whatever you like, Beula, but if you do, Marigold will certainly not get any new dresses from me.' She ushered them back towards the front door.

Marigold snivelled and blew her nose, sobbing a little more. 'You are a cruel stepdaughter.'

'Like my father.' Tilly opened the front door. 'Please leave. Now.' She went back to Joe who was slapping his hand up and down in the milky puddle on his tray.

Marigold caught sight of a drawing on the workroom bench:

a pencil-line skirt with a floral detachable overskirt. There was a fuchsia fabric sample tacked to the bottom of the sketch. She stopped crying. Tears had never worked on Evan either; he'd just poured her more tonic and popped her into bed. She picked up the sketch and saw that the underskirt would have a striped fuchsia trim. 'How very unusual.'

'That's none of your concern,' said the sergeant.

'Leave now,' Tilly called, but they appeared in the kitchen again.

Joe pointed his spoon at Beula and said, 'Dortuss.'

'It's a BIG secret, Tilly Dunnage, one of your biggest.' Beula nodded, thrilled with herself but actually addressing a bowl of fruit on top of the fridge. 'A big secret from your past and we can tell everyone about your FRIEND, if we want to.'

Marigold warned, 'We said we'd save that until she agreed to my new gown, Beula!' She started pulling off her gloves. 'Your secret's parking the car, and he's going to help me get my money.'

And then Arlen O'Connor walked through Sergeant Farrat's front door and stood in front of her.

The well-dressed stalker, of course.

Tilly felt faint.

'You remember Mr O'Connor?'

Arlen O'Connor was running amok in Tilly's memory: Arlen arriving in the truck for the laundry, Arlen fighting the convent bully, Arlen saying, 'I'll be waiting for you.' And he had been waiting. When she'd walked through the big timber gates, a fourteen-year-old girl carrying all her possessions in a calico bag.

'I sent you forty pounds,' she said at last. 'You never came.'

'I sent you a letter.' He looked for somewhere to put his hat.

'I never got it.'

It was hard to gather her thoughts. A boy she hadn't seen since she was eighteen was standing in front of her, very much alive in a stylish suit. He looked strange to her, but very, very familiar.

She busied herself mopping up spilled milk. 'Forty quid was a lot of money, Arlen.'

'You can have it back, with interest.' He glanced at the sewing machines and milliner's blocks and general haberdashery detritus, his hat in his hand. 'That forty quid put me through university.'

'You always were wily.'

'And you were always "tell me that I can't and I'll show you I will". I must say, though, I didn't figure you'd go back to Shitty Shorty's to hide – that was smart.'

'Generally, I try not to collide with my past.'

'Your past is the foundation of your life – you have to keep referring to it so that you can grow from it.'

'I recall, Arlen, that whenever you try to sound profound, you're actually just stating the blindingly obvious.' It was getting far too familiar, and she started to feel quite unsettled. She scooped up some egg and held the spoon for Joe.

Joe looked at Beula. 'Dortuss.'

'Like us or not, Tilly, you need to come to terms with us.' Arlen put his business card on the table.

She pointed Joe's spoon at Arlen. 'See, there you go again. I have come to terms with you all, Arlen, and concluded I don't like any of you, and I'd prefer it if you disappeared again.'

Marigold suddenly blurted, 'No! Mr O'Connor has to get my money back.'

Joe yelled.

Beula said, 'We thought Mr O'Connor was a shyster but it turns out he's a trained lawyer.'

Joe yelled again.

'A lawyer?' She was elated, so pleased for him, and found it difficult not to throw her arms around him and cry, 'Hooray for you,' but she needed to be furious with him. It was the principle of it even though she knew it was silly given it was all so very long ago and she had thrived despite his abandonment.

He replaced a flowery straw hat on a hat block with his homburg and put the flowery hat on his head. 'We were best friends once. I'm hoping to be that friend to you again.'

Joe yelled, very loudly, and everyone looked at the small boy. He bore a startling resemblance to his father. The sergeant swished across the floor and took the spoon from Tilly and gave it to Joe, who plunged it into his boiled egg.

'What a bonny boy,' said Arlen.

Marigold pretended to smile at Joe. 'Hello, I'm your step-grandmother. You must never touch me unless I touch you first, do you understand?'

It occurred to Tilly that the fact that Teddy was not present, that Marigold and Beula had sent Joe's father to the silo on that fateful night, would never enter their minds.

'You just ignore them and get on with your breakfast, Joe,' she said. Which is what he did, pinching a cornflake in his tiny fingers and throwing it at Arlen's shiny shoes. It missed. 'Try the egg,' his mother said, and smiled at Arlen.

Marigold shuddered at the mess on the floor beneath Joe's chair. 'I always fed Stewart in the bath.'

'I still don't see why you're all here,' the sergeant demanded.

'Arlen's going to help us with the guardianship application. If we have Tilly and the boy we'll have a stronger case.'

Arlen said he thought the visit also had a lot to do with Marigold's need for a new frock.

'Have you seen the fashion and society pages? Every photo you see is because I mentioned to all the important people I met at the ball that you learned your trade in Dungatar, and that you were one of our better seamstresses.'

'I need a new dress too,' Beula said.

'I'd sleep in a vat of live leeches before I'd make you a dress, Beula.'

Beula said breezily, 'You know, Mr O'Connor, they said Teddy

McSwiney jumped into wheat but it turned out to be sorghum. Tilly was there, she's the only one who knows what really happened, whether he was pushed . . .'

The sergeant put his hand on Tilly's shoulder and said sweetly, 'Beula, why don't you go for a walk down Victoria Parade? It'll lead you straight into the deep murky river.'

Arlen removed his flowery hat, saying that William Beaumont had explained the events of the night Teddy McSwiney had fallen to his death.

The sergeant put his hand on his heart. 'You went to Dungatar? And got out unscathed?'

'The fact of the matter is, Evan Pettyman has left a lot of money, and Tilly and Joe are Mrs Pettyman's next of kin. I said I *could* help Mrs Pettyman get her money, but if she or Miss Harridene say anything I don't approve of –'

'Quite. Shut up, Beula.' Marigold handed her jacket to Beula and Beula hung it on Arlen's arm.

Joe started banging his spoon again.

Marigold put her arms out to be measured, and said she needed a nice suit for the hearing.

'What hearing?'

'The guardianship hearing,' Arlen said. 'If Mrs Pettyman is to get her money and return to Dungatar a happy woman, we could strengthen her case by showing she has a strong family unit supporting her. So, should you decide to attend the hearing you'll need to wear something conservative.' He put his homburg on.

'This is my *look*,' sniffed the sergeant. 'It's bohemian, as opposed to yours which is a little prime ministerial.'

'And bring the baby,' said Marigold.

'His name is Joel, and none of the Farrat family will be anyone's prop in any court drama.' Tilly went back to feeding her son his breakfast.

'Consider it a way of paying us back, making everything up to us.'

Tilly was almost astonished. 'Just leave.'

The sergeant hurried to the vestibule, and opened the front door to the early morning sunlight.

'Think of the future,' Arlen said. 'Joe's future.'

She knew what he was getting at but Tilly knew better than to entertain thoughts of any inheritance.

'Strictly speaking, Tilly, it's your father's money, so I'm happy to help Mrs Pettyman –'

'Good. You don't need me.'

Arlen stood perfectly still, and said, 'I've always needed you, Tilly.'

Everyone, including Joe, stopped while Tilly stared at Arlen, who held her gaze. Tilly knew that she too had needed him, all those years ago.

The three guests stepped out into the street. Marigold said she'd be back, and Beula headed off after a passing stranger.

As he walked away, Arlen turned. 'It was good to meet you, Sergeant.' He smiled warmly at Tilly and she waved before she could stop herself.

She rushed to her son. 'Joe, you spoke, you said a word – what was it? Remember the funny-looking lady with the dark glasses? You said her name, what was it?'

Joe threw his spoon onto the floor, smiled and clapped.

'I'm not sure I'm thrilled he called Beula a tortoise or miffed she was the first person he spoke to.'

'Actually,' said Tilly, scraping cereal from his hair, 'he talks to us all the time, don't you, Joe?' The boy looked at her and smiled, a wide, genuine smile aimed directly at her, for her, and it told her he loved her, his joyfulness spearing straight into her bursting heart.


Mr Hawker's wife served him porridge.

'What's this?'

'Be thankful I didn't give you grapefruit.' She put the cheque-book in front of him and a plate of poached eggs and toast in front of her son.

Mr Hawker muttered something about a bloody diet and crossed his arms. 'I'm not signing that until you give me a decent breakfast. I have to go out and work, for God's sake!'

'Your doctor said you have high blood pressure.'

'I'm perfectly all right.'

She returned with soft-boiled eggs, the tub of butter and jam toast. Mr Hawker signed the cheque and his wife tore it from the book.

'I tried,' she said, and Gladston said, 'You did.'

Mr Hawker swallowed three Aspros and poured sugar onto his porridge. 'Did you put salt in this?'

'A pinch.'

Gladston handed his father the salt and Mr Hawker added a few more pinches. Each went back to reading his Monday morning paper, and then it was time for the men to head off for the day. At the front door, Mrs Hawker handed her husband his hat and offered her cheek to her son.

'Thank you, Mother.'

'Gladston, dear, you know your father should walk from the bottom of the Bourke Street hill each day and take the stairs rather than the lift.'

'We both try to do what's best every day,' he replied, though they both knew neither of them ever tried very hard. Mrs Hawker cleared the dishes and attended to her gardening, shopping, lunch-eons, bridge and correspondence while her woman vacuumed her dustless carpets, polished her furniture and ironed her underwear.

As usual, Mr Hawker had Gladston stop outside the building while the traffic gathered behind him, like beetles encountering a rock, as Gladston levered his father from the back seat. Mr Hawker waddled across, applied his mass to the glass door and made for the lift. Gladston arrived, flung his father's discarded hat and coat aside, dropped the mail on the desk and sprayed the small leafy fern on his desk with a mist of water, one squeeze of the bottle.

They had barely settled when someone knocked. It was Marigold Pettyman and her friend, Miss Harridene. Gladston suggested his father would not see her at such short notice, but she pushed past him into Mr Hawker's office and found him at his safe. Mr Hawker slammed the metal door shut. 'What the hell?'

'Father, Mrs Pettyman –'

Mr Hawker hid his hands behind his back, icing sugar and crumbs littering his waistcoat. 'Get out, Gladston! You've failed at your job.'

Still, Gladston stayed. He knew his father would need him. To date, Gladston's entire career had been spent dreaming of another life. The study of law had given him his greatest gift, for it was in a university lecture on contracts that he realised what he really wanted, and when his father's heart or head finally exploded, he would start a new vocation: he would be a teacher. But teaching would not pay enough to support himself, possibly a wife and children, and his mother. He would need to keep the practice ticking over in some capacity.

For now, though, his father was still bellowing. 'Do you think, Mrs Pettyman, that you can just barge in anytime you like?'

'My money pays for this office.' She tried to peek behind him but he leaned back against the safe.

The safe was always locked, and Gladston was not permitted access.

'I've come to pay you the courtesy of informing you that I wish to annul the arrangement,' Marigold stated. Mr Hawker smiled. 'I have the letter from my new lawyer, Mr Arlen O'Connor. He will take over guardianship from you.'

Mr Hawker laughed, then coughed and reached for his chair, his merriment turning to pain. His fatty face turned red, tears rolled from his eyes and his tongue curled as he coughed and farted and drooled. Gladston swabbed his forehead with his hanky and, wiping custard and pastry from his tie, poured his father a tot of whisky.

'Crikey, you might get your new guardian by lunchtime,' said Beula.

Marigold said, 'I should have told him sooner.'

Gladston ushered the disgusted ladies to the reception room.

'You're not well, Father, you should take better care of your diet.'

'The doctor has been telling me I'm not well for years. YEARS. The point is that I'm still here and I feel perfectly well!'

Gladston read through the letter. Mr Arlen O'Connor, via the State Government, had applied to assume financial guardianship for Mrs Evan Pettyman. She was no longer confident in Mr Hawker's administration of her affairs and no longer needed guardianship care.

'I suggest,' he said, 'that since correspondence has arrived from Mr O'Connor, you should continue on with proceedings. You might not need guardianship of any kind, just someone to oversee financial affairs.'

He opened the door, saying that if there was anything she needed, to just telephone him. Beula walked into the door and Marigold apologised.

'No need to apologise. I understand that your friend is . . . handicapped.'

After they had left, Gladston placated his father with a cup of strong black coffee with cream and three sugars and a fresh cigar. Then he returned to his post and arranged meetings until noon, when, as ever, Mr Hawker emerged from his office, cigar smoke swirling. Gladston handed him his hat, helped him with his jacket and held the door open for him. He went to the window and watched his father emerge from the front door and head to his club. Then he spent the afternoon rifling through his father's desk, cupboards, drawers and files, searching for the code to the safe.

Every morning, when she turned the corner of Russell Street and rode down through the Paris end of Collins Street to the pretender salons closer to Elizabeth Street, Tilly saw the waiting women: Salon Mystique's new, almost 'decent', almost acceptable society ladies. And as she got closer to that factory of silk, pongee, shantung and satin, voile, crepe, organdie, netting and lace, gabardine, sharkskin, polka dots, plaids and florals, her eyes started to itch, her shoulders ached and her fingers stung. A restlessness swept through her, in anticipation of the hours of sitting and sewing. Once upon a time, when she followed the needle towards perfecting her craft, it had been wonderful. But no one seemed to see beyond their own reflection to elegant functionality anymore; no one saw the art or craft, the design, the structure, the idea of the garment they were hosting.

She stopped. 'I don't want to do this anymore.' A passing man gave her a sideways glance.

But there was just one more parade, with a fat pay packet, Joe and a future, freedom and independence, so she freewheeled down Collins Street, waved to Charles at his newspaper spot, leaned her bike against the lamppost and pushed through the women assembled at the door. Inside, it was chaos. Seamstresses and their Stockmans lined the salon, with some women forced to sit on the stairs, hand-stitching, while Clare sat rigid and wide-eyed at her desk.

Madame Flock came running at her. 'Thank God you're finally here! Nita Orland will be here any second and Miss Post Office is waiting and those women out there read in the newspaper that we're going on strike!'

'Not yet,' Tilly said. She needed Melbourne to see her designs.

Valda was nowhere to be seen.

Tilly slipped into her white coat, slung her tape measure around her neck, picked up her notebook and went to Miss Post Office Picnic, closing the fitting room curtain behind her. Miss Post Office shoved her hat at Tilly and started unbuttoning her dress. 'I need to win Miss Austraya, and Madam says I'm goin' in Gown of the Year. Can't wait to see what you come up with for that one. You up to it?'

Ambition had Miss Post Office Picnic by the throat, and only those desperate to be noticed entered Gown of the Year.

'No,' said Tilly, matter-of-factly. 'Valda will make you something unique, I'm sure.'

She thought about her forty pounds, and the business card on the telephone table at home.

# Chapter 19

WILLIAM STUDIED THE people of Dungatar as they queued for dinner at their temporary home: Lois, Septimus and Scotty, with his purple nose; Mrs Almanac, the crinoline covering her wheelchair; Miss Dimm, with her very thick glasses; Big Bobby Pickett, wearing his chain mail and breast plate; Muriel and Alvin Pratt; Faith, and Faith's boyfriend Reginald Blood the butcher, baroque attendant and murderer. These attendants, lords, officers, messengers, murderers and shield carriers were basically the only people who had not ventured elsewhere for a new life after the fire. Hamish had been posted to a bigger railway station, Ruth and Nancy had fled and lived happily in a cottage by the sea, but these malingerers in front of William remained, sad and discarded.

He was tired of them.

They had not made enough progress, had settled into their institutionalised lives. As mayor, he could assert authority, but to date, they had been unmanageable.

Bouncing on the balls of his feet, William declared, 'We'd better settle those town plans, get cracking on construction, don't you think?'

They glanced at him and turned their eyes to the luncheon spread.

That week, he had baled the hay and advertised, but it had not sold. William decided to appeal to his costumed guests over dinner, confident that they'd understand, cooperate, and offer solutions, and money.

'You chose to stay on after the fire,' he said. 'You said you all wanted to rebuild.'

'And that's what we're doing,' said Septimus. 'For free.'

Elsbeth pointed out that they had contributed *only* recalcitrant labour and bickering, and that she and William were providing the building material, 'Which cost actual money. Our money.'

They did not look at Elsbeth or William, or even Felicity Joy. They focused on their empty dinner plates, a torn lace cuff, a hole in some tights and a frayed velvet hem. William wanted to tell them that, apart from being just plain rude, they were also responsible for unravelling any harmony their community might have enjoyed, first during rehearsals for *Macbeth* three years prior, and then every year since, when they lost the eisteddfod and fought about it. Even after their homes had burned to the ground they still did not see why, see what had really caused that catastrophe. But William couldn't say these things, and usually that didn't matter because his mother would express such matters, but in this she couldn't see the truth of it either. What she did see, loud and clear, was that the Beaumont family could not contribute another penny until the people of Dungatar dug up their cashboxes or took the bus to Itheca or Winyerp and withdrew their secret savings to rebuild. 'You all know you've got a bit of money secreted and so does everybody else,' Elsbeth declared, stroking her motley fox fur.

'I haven't got a penny,' Irma Almanac said, dunking one of her special herb biscuits into her hot tea. 'Nancy and Ruth took our savings when they left after the fire.'

'Hamish took ours, too,' said Faith, but most of the Dungatar people thought that was fair enough since Faith had been having an affair with Reginald, and Faith always thought she was special because she sang in the band.

'Someone will have buried some,' said Elsbeth. 'You've got some, haven't you, Muriel?'

Muriel looked at her husband, who bent down to look at his ankle.

'Bobby Pickett's been paying cash for his watermelon fire-water.' No one said anything so Elsbeth turned her attention to the barmaid. 'And it has not gone unnoticed that Purl Bundle had new lingerie delivered last week.'

The people of New Dungatar sank a little in their chairs.

A small thin voice from up the back said, 'Can we leave it somewhere anonymous, so no one knows who's been holding back?'

'Bugger that,' said Purl, 'I want my money recorded, made official. I might get some back.'

'I doubt it. I'll get mine back first,' said Elsbeth.

'How're you going to get money back?'

'Rates?'

'No,' said William, 'rates are for sewerage, garbage collection, water and electricity infrastructure.'

'Well, how are you going to get your money back?'

There was an awkward silence and then Elsbeth said, 'Rent.'

The silence grew as the enormity of Elsbeth's proposal settled.

William said, 'Mother, we agreed they would pay us back as soon as they could.'

'Yes, and as agreed they will start paying us back in weekly rent until they have paid for their houses, but we paid for everything with our income, so they must pay back the capital plus the interest our savings would have earned had we been able to deposit it in the bank. We have gone without for these people, so they must pay the accrued interest on the money they have borrowed from us.'

Reginald Blood felt the hairs on his neck rise and he stood, his elbows crooked from years of accommodating his butcher's scabbard. 'What's the interest rate?'

'I would suggest fifty percent more than the banks charge, since

I have also provided years of accommodation here at Windswept Crest.'

The people of Dungatar stood with Reginald, as one.

'It's business,' said Elsbeth. 'You are all shopkeepers and trades-people, you understand that business must make profit to thrive, that you'll all benefit from the trickle-down effect . . .'

They surrounded her and she started shrinking in her chair.

'Well!' she cried. 'I am not some sort of charity. I am not rich!'

'Indeed not.' Alvin Pratt addressed the people around her. 'She was always just keeping up appearances, she never paid her bills. Pratts General Store basically supported her for years.'

Elsbeth threw her napkin on the table. 'You always charged too much, anyway.'

'She never paid us, either,' said Irma Almanac. 'I could do with that money.'

Bobby Pickett said that Elsbeth was a thief and his sister added, 'You're fired.'

'From what?'

'*King Lear*. You're just a talentless ham and a dullard and you keep telling us what we can and can't do.'

It was a scene from the ruin of the first eisteddfod, or rather, the competition and jealousy generated by Dungatar's produc-tion of *Macbeth*.

'You can't fire me, I am the director and the producer, and the lead role.'

'You're too old to play Cordelia.'

'I have makeup and a costume.'

'You're still too old,' said Irma.

'Anyway, there's no one left to play Cordelia.'

'I can,' said Irma Almanac.

Everyone in the room turned to look at Mrs Almanac smiling benignly in her wheelchair, her arthritic fingers like ginger bulbs and her tin of herb biscuits under her knee rug.

'"I love your Majesty according to my bond, no more nor less",' she recited, her rhythm and tone perfect.

Faith said, 'You can play Regan. I'll be Cordelia.'

'NO!' Elsbeth thumped the table and the cutlery jingled. 'I am Cordelia, and I am the producer so if I leave, so does the funding, FOR EVERYTHING.'

The entire cast of *King Lear* moved in on Elsbeth, who scuttled away towards her room.

Later, as her father lay in his narrow boyhood bed, the night noises evaporated and the house settled and perfectly still, Felicity Joy crept into William's room and he reached out to her, thinking she wanted a story read. 'They've locked Grandmother in the linen cupboard.'

He sighed and flung back the covers.

At lunchtime the next day, still smarting from her stint in the linen press the evening prior, Elsbeth Beaumont went to the kitchen and lifted the lid on the stockpot. She scraped around with the spoon until she'd found all four leg bones. 'I knew there were two missing. Do you think I can't count? I gave permission for *one* chook.'

'There weren't enough vegies to pad out the stew,' said Lois, who had chicken feathers in her hair and a spray of chicken blood across her apron.

'You could have used rice.'

'We don't like foreign food.'

'You're a greedy thief, Lois Pickett. You could live easily on half rations.'

'You're the fief, you never paid your bills and you're mean and nasty and you fink you're Hitler.'

The people in the kitchen ceased cooking, organising crockery and cutlery for lunch, and folded their arms.

'Oh, I see,' laughed Elsbeth. 'You're on strike, are you? Isn't that pointless? You'll just end up starving and homeless. There will be no chicken next week.' She looked at Felicity Joy. 'What are you doing?'

'Making a chicken sandwich.' She would take it to the safety of the roof, lean against the chimney with her book and search for messages from the red plains about anything out of the ordinary, leaving the adults to their endless squabbling.

'You'll end up as big as your mother. Have a carrot instead.' Elsbeth turned in her small worn shoes, marched back to her bedroom and resumed stitching the beaded hem of one ball gown onto another, the ruined faux-fur collar thrown deep into the corner of her infested wardrobe.

The following morning, William released her yet again from the top shelf of the linen press. It was the narrowest shelf, where the dust cloths and old jam jars were usually shoved, and was so confined that the tip of his mother's nose touched the ceiling and she was unable to move her arms in any meaningful way. They went to the kitchen for breakfast but found no one had washed the dinner or breakfast dishes and there was no scrambled eggs or milk left.

'Go and see if there are any eggs, that's if there are any chooks left.'

'You go,' said William. 'I'm not hungry.'

# Chapter 20

She was suspicious of Arlen O'Connor's true motives, and of his affiliation with Marigold, so Tilly was rattled when it dawned on her that she was, in truth, looking forward to seeing him. The quiet presence of the tall, attractive boy with straight black hair from her early teens had followed her for days. But, he had not come to her in Europe and he owed her forty quid.

At the Hotel Australia, she watched him walk up the stairs, check his wristwatch and saunter over to the bar. He ordered a drink and waited, one foot tapping to the soft jazz playing. Tilly noted that every girl in the lounge was watching him. Suddenly, she didn't want to be there, wondered why on earth she'd come. For God's sake, he was helping Marigold Pettyman. She stood up to leave, then he turned and smiled.

She was wearing a snug black and white striped shift, boat-necked and tied at the shoulders with polka-dot bows. It was made of a new fabric, a synthetic blend, and she was enjoying its flexibility if not the sensation against her skin. She was hatless, and her sandshoes were bright red.

He came across the bar towards her, all eyes in the room on him. 'That's an effective dress.'

She felt a little silly, as you do when you've been caught out. 'I whipped it up last night, it's an experiment.'

'How do you reckon it's going?'

'That depends.'

'Fair enough.' He grinned, looking at her for a little too long. 'You're still the same girl.'

'I'm thirsty, too.'

'So am I. What will you have, Mrs Farrat, gin or vodka?'

'Guess, since you know me so well.'

He went to the bar and ordered vodka martinis, the eyes in the room following him again. When he sat down with her, the room looked away.

'Now, what can I do for you, Mrs Farrat?'

'You can stop calling me that. I'd like my forty quid. Plus interest.'

'It's accumulated quite a bit since 1933. I bought shares in a cutlery company, postwar growth's building fast, trending towards scissors, anything that's stainless steel, for that matter.'

'I know about scissors.'

Arlen offered her a cigarette, which she accepted.

'She's worth quite a bit, your stepmother.' He held the lighter for her. 'Which is why Mr Hawker's stalling on the guardianship hearing.'

'There's not enough money in the world could make me feel anything other than horrible about anyone from Dungatar.'

'I'd like to see you doing what you want, being free.'

The drinks arrived and Tilly gulped, rather than sipped, and he watched her.

'All I want is my money to buy fabric and pay wages for three people for a month.'

'Four, including you. And you'll need a lawyer.'

She sighed.

Arlen shrugged. 'I know people, I can introduce you to fashion editors and photographers and I can help you set up a business. And I'm cheaper than any other lawyer you're ever going to get.'

He saw that he still had not won her.

'I can sort Marigold out, I'll get her off your back.'

'I need to lose those black Dungatar creatures. Because of them, my couture became a weapon. They used it to bolster the cruellest of impulses. It's sickening to think Marigold Pettyman is my next of kin.'

'It could be argued you are mine too, Mrs Farrat.'

Tilly put her hand to her mouth – she'd forgotten. She was fourteen, and Arlen had met her at the tram stop near the convent and taken her to the Shorts'. He introduced her as his wife and handed over a marriage certificate: Mr and Mrs Arlen Dunnage. They'd shared much – were for years all either of them had. Together they'd created a home in that so-called room behind the Shorts' and they'd revelled in their own place, in having a friend, someone to care for and look out for. Someone to come home to. The Shorts provided two camp stretchers, a small stove, a table and two chairs and they found discarded carpet to cover the brick floor. Arlen took great care building a wooden box which he put between their stretchers to support a kerosene lamp, his treasured harmonica and yoyo, and Tilly added a photograph of herself as a toddler with her mother. Arlen said they had the same cheek-bones, she and Molly. Tilly added her books on dressmaking and he stacked his books on his side – even then he dreamed of being a lawyer. Arlen kept the room prison-cell neat and they were able to keep themselves clean, almost warm, and mostly fed.

He looked at his wristwatch, and with a jolt, she understood he had somewhere else to go. 'Yes, I really should get going too,' she said, a little defensively.

'I'm sorry, I'd like to stay . . .' He stood up. 'I'll come and see you about the hearing and of course, your forty quid, if that's all right?'

'I'll cook dinner,' she offered, surprising herself.

'What'll you cook?'

She smiled. 'Your favourite, chicken.'

'That's not my favourite, chickens were just the easiest to steal.'

Tilly raised one eyebrow.

He feigned innocence. 'I only ever stole from very well stocked henhouses in salubrious suburbs.'

'We'll have vegetarian, then.'

Watching him walk away down Collins Street, she felt a pang of disappointment, but it was a beautiful April evening, balmy enough not to break a sweat, a perfect night for a bicycle ride. Arlen ran and jumped on a St Kilda tram and she decided she would cook him something wonderful for dinner, suddenly feeling confident and more secure than she had in years. Just then, as the tram rolled away, he glanced back at her from the open doorway and waved. He had caught her watching, again, but she didn't mind.

The next morning, Tilly found a note in the pocket of her white coat. All the seamstresses found notes in the pockets of their white coats. It was typed; some girls had carbon copies, but each note said the same thing.

> To the seamstresses and outworkers:
> According to the Clothing and Allied Trades Union the average pay for a seamstress or dressmaker is 59/- a week. You are getting paid 49/- and you are not rewarded or appreciated for the overtime. And you don't get time to look for better work and you can't take time off because your pay will be docked. If you want to fix it, meet at Young & Jackson after work on Friday.

She looked around the workroom, and the only person not reading the note or talking about it was Shirley, who was cutting around the edges of a piece of red-green moire, her tongue at the corner of her mouth and her brow creased.

She went to Shirley and whispered, 'We can't go on strike.'

'Dunno what you're talking about.'

'The winter coronation parade has to go ahead, we need our clothes to be seen.'

'I know,' said Shirley, and held the moire fabric up, blocking Tilly out.

Elizabeth McSwiney looked like a common girl, with her mother's unruly hair and thick shoes, but what people failed to see was that the shoes were vintage 1920s – Elizabeth's grandmother's – and her hair was merely natural: not dyed, not permed, just uncon-fined. Her aesthetic came from the space between her and the horizon across the plains of Dungatar, the natural world, where artifice was out of place. Elizabeth had grown up wondering what was beyond that horizon, imagining what adventure she might enjoy if she boarded the train and got off at the end. If she looked up, she saw the house on The Hill where a madwoman lived with a seamstress who had returned and transformed the town. The McSwineys had been the town recyclers and so Elizabeth and her sisters utilised Dungatar's discarded frocks, plucking them from the unruly montage of tip treasure and adjusting them to suit so that they graced the streets of Dungatar alongside Tilly Dunnage's finest.

'I've had three jobs since we left Dungatar,' she said, as Tilly prepared for their first customer. 'What I've learned is that I'm not cut out to eat when someone else tells me I can, I'm not happy if I can't have two sweet biscuits if I want and I'm buggered if I'll miss an important football match or a Saturday night dance just because some rich old bag suddenly decides she wants a different-coloured buckle on her fifty-pound belt.'

'Fair enough,' said Tilly, and looked at Barney. 'How do you feel about working with your sister, Barney?'

Barney shrugged. 'I'm not cut out to eat when she tells me to, and won't be happy if I can't have two sweet biscuits and I'm buggered if I'll miss football just because she's got to stay here putting a buckle on a belt.'

'Fair enough,' said Elizabeth.

The door to number 27 swung open and the porch light illuminated a proud but crooked young man wearing a new flannel three-piece suit, his mouth small and crowded with teeth, his face a rash of acne scars. His hair was shiny and parted badly, though it wasn't actually the part that was wrong but, rather, the shape of his head, and at the end of his withered leg his club foot was enormously booted. The Supreme Court judge removed his hat and was about to introduce himself when the crooked young man delivered a speech that sounded as if he'd learned it from a horse-race caller – 'Good evening my name is Barney McSwiney and I am very pleased to welcome you please come in and take a seat can I take your hat?'

'No.'

Barney said, 'Thank you,' and limped away, leaving the door wide open and the judge holding his felt hat, the night breeze shifting the hanging toiles and rattling paper and straw and ribbons in the millinery. For a moment he considered leaving but the sight of the hats, some finished, others not, kept him there.

There was fierce whispering from the next room and Barney limped back. He closed the front door and said, 'Please follow me,' and the judge was shown into the workroom between the hat shop and the kitchen, where Tilly and her new protégée, both wearing white dustcoats, waited.

After the initial instructions and pleasantries, Elizabeth set about measuring while Tilly asked questions.

'What is your primary consideration in clothing, fashion or couture?'

The judge looked puzzled, so Tilly prompted, 'Perhaps on your garments you like motif, colour, texture, or perhaps you like a garment that is inspired by architecture?'

'I've never been asked that before but, on the hop, I'd say there should be no such thing as clothing, it should be style at couture standard, or at least couture.'

'What do you prefer – juxtaposition or cohesion?'

'I'm a judge, so I need cohesion in the end, though juxtaposition is the source of most predicaments.'

'Colour?'

'Brown, grey, red, green, violet.'

Tilly wrote, *Boorishness, dullness, elegance, wealth, passion, nature, nobility.* 'Only one primary colour. Interesting. Concept?'

He rolled his eyes. 'Less is more. For pity's sake, is all this necessary?'

'It is for me,' Elizabeth said.

'Until she gets her eye in, and then she'll read everyone as they walk in the door. But, for now, you'll reap the benefits of Elizabeth's eager imagination and my learned one. Couture, for me, is the design of unique clothes, the best clothes for every single customer.'

Elizabeth nodded her agreement and turned an open sketchbook to him. The judge's eyebrows shot to the top of his forehead and he ran his hand over the sketch and then turned the page. Elizabeth arranged fabric swatches on the table in front of the judge and Tilly stepped back.

'Let's match the fabrics, see what we can come up with. Any particular fabric you prefer?' Elizabeth sounded as if she'd been asking that question for thirty years.

'Deary me, no, I'm not a fetishist.'

At the end of the evening, the judge withheld any verdict on the proceedings, saying simply, 'We will make one dress and I'll decide what will happen next once I've seen the outcome.'

Barney showed him to the door and tried to give him someone else's hat.

'We're on probation,' Elizabeth said.

'With hard labour and a suspended verdict,' Tilly said. But it had gone well, and Tilly felt a small surge of hope.

She telephoned Arlen.

# Chapter 21

Sensing that Marigold's institutionalised composure was slowly eroding out in the blaring world, Beula took advantage. She emerged from the bath pink and warm in her nightie and hopped into bed, leaving the bathroom door wide open. Marigold rushed to attack the steamy, wet room – incubator and home to ballooning clouds of moist body germs – with bleach and a scrubbing brush. When she emerged, she cried, 'You could have at least hung the bath mat up.'

'I can't see where to hang it!'

'It's simple courtesy,' Marigold continued, 'as well as hygienic, and I'm no one's servant.'

'No, you're not. In fact, you think you're someone special, with your nice frocks – you think Tilly Dunnage is your personal dressmaker.'

'Just because she won't make you a dress –'

Beula sat up in her bed. 'I've never been impressed by how things *look*.'

'That's fortunate, since you're blind. *Blind Beula, nar-nar na nar-na.*' Marigold danced at the end of Beula's bed while Beula jerked about trying to identify the source of the turbulence in the room.

'I'm concerned with what people are *like*.' She flung the covers back and stood up, arms sweeping through the air in search of Marigold.

'I'm beginning to see what *you're* like, Beula.' She tapped Beula on the arm, Beula swung and Marigold skipped to the other side of the room.

'You don't know the half of it,' Beula said, slumping back into bed and pulling the blankets up to her neck. 'At least I've never hidden who I am.'

'Well, you can't really, walking around with your name and address pinned to the back of your cardigan,' Marigold said, breathless from all the exertion.

'What I mean is I've never pretended to be anybody else. What would you do if you couldn't get a new Tilly Dunnage frock? Who would you be? Now, hop into bed with your tonic so you can forget you have to breathe the air I've farted into.'

Marigold gagged.

The next morning, Marigold did not assist Beula to dress and did not wait to lead her to the dining room. She rose, dressed, snipped the luggage tag from Beula's cardigan again and went to breakfast, where she joined Mrs Wrench on an entirely different table.

Beula woke to nothing; absolute silence, no smells and no movement. Not even the curtains swelled. She was alone, marooned in overcast helplessness. But Beula's fortitude had strengthened these past two years. She would show them.

On her way to the reception desk, Beula dislodged a pot from its stand and asked the portrait of Mary Jane Warnes, founder of the CWA, to phone Mr Hawker. The receptionist told her it was against the rules to wear a nightdress in the public areas, then looked up the number and made the call for her. Gladston put Beula through to Mr Hawker and held on to hear her report: Marigold Pettyman still took drugs every night and in fact had drugged and blackmailed her ex-lawyer into drafting a letter saying she was sane. She was also fearful of germs, which she claimed to be able to see. They were everywhere. Beula added that Tilly Dunnage had burned the town down, and that the arson department was looking for her. 'I've got more incriminating information if you want it. I can tell you things about Sergeant Farrat wearing dresses and Tilly Dunnage killing footballers that would make your teeth curl . . . but you'll have to pay me money for that information.'

There was a pause before Mr Hawker said, 'Goodbye,' and hung up.

The receptionist reached for the handpiece, somewhat traumatised.

'One more,' said Beula. 'I need to speak to the Welfare Department, Children's Services, actually.'

When she had finished telling her tales to the welfare officer, Beula placed the handpiece on the CWA Donations Box and left, the receptionist wide-eyed and speechless in her chair.

Beula stumbled behind her white cane to her room and sat on her bed, dabbing at the cavity where her nose had been and wondering why she didn't feel thrilled with herself, as she once would have. She decided to get changed, managing to remove her nightdress but failing to find her clothes, so she sat glumly on her bed in her full-brief cotton bloomers and singlet, her sense of fortitude evaporating. Everyone else had whatever they needed and wanted – Marigold, Children's Services, Mr Hawker, and that smug garment maker – but if Beula ever wanted to get dressed or eat again, she'd have to mollify her roommate.

Sergeant Farrat had curled his fringe flat against his forehead, his foundation spread carefully and evenly over his pale skin and his small moustache trimmed to a very thin line. Underneath the kimono he wore crisp linen underwear. His bed was made and the curtains drawn, and Joe stood at the sergeant's dressing table holding a storybook. 'Dortuss,' he said.

'You're right. Brown and green, not very vibrant.' He took off his dress and reached for the faille silk frock with the picture collar. Again, the sergeant scrutinised his reflection and considered simply wearing his police uniform. Navy suited him, and there was nothing like a suit with a good cut. Ex-policeman Horatio Farrat felt a momentary pang for his days in blue.

Tilly picked up Joe. 'You look like Louisa May Alcott.'

'Christ.'

'Kyse,' Joe repeated.

The sergeant tore off the flighty dress and reached for his blue velvet suit.

Joe said, 'Bardey.'

And Tilly said, 'Soon you'll see Barney.'

'Dortuss,' he said, and she decided they should read a different story. Perhaps *Little Red Riding Hood*, to prepare him for life, warn him of danger.

'Do you think Julie will like me in my suit?'

'I think Julie will like you in anything.'

The sergeant cleared his throat. 'I know you've been busy and would prefer an early night at home with our baby boy but . . .'

She shrugged. 'I'm very happy to stay with Joe at Mae's.' She was looking forward to waking up with Joe and his entire family, the family Teddy had woken to each day: a tight-knit, true family, held fast with love and loyalty, who would forever defend Joel, enfold and protect him, an entire army of them. 'We'll be out of your hair as soon as I can –'

'Don't,' he said. 'Don't ever say that. We are in this together and we always will be. We will do the best we can for each other.' The sergeant stared at her solemnly. 'You are my friend, and I love our little boy, though I preferred it when he couldn't speak, and he remains marginally incontinent –'

'He's trying!'

'I know.' He looked at Joe. 'I'm proud of you, son.'

'I hope you have the most wonderful night of your life.'

'Thank you,' he said, and put his hand over his eyes. 'I'm just so . . . so . . .'

'Full of longing?'

He nodded.

'Embrace and enjoy.' She gave him a hug. 'Your makeup is perfect and you smell divine.'

She rode away, waving up at Miss Peachy on her balcony as she passed.

At the McSwineys', Joe marched confidently up the front path, down the hall and into the arms of his grandfather sitting by the fire. He pointed at the flames and said, 'Pretty.'

Tilly felt a pang for Molly, who had nursed her grandson for only a few weeks. Edward, meanwhile, looked into Joe's eyes. Teddy was alive in the boy, but Joe was not reckless. Joe was a quiet, considered child, economic of movement and self-contained.

Half of Tilly wanted to stay, to sit with a cup of tea at the kitchen table, chatting to Edward by the hob, with the rest of the McSwineys washing through the house in their big family way: Mae at the helm, stern but fair, and Rex and Joe playing with the ferrets or the rabbit or the mice on the buffalo grass under the clothes line. It was safe there, mostly. She would rid them, one day, of the long shadow of the welfare officer.

Champagne waited in the ice bucket, the coupe glasses were in the fridge and thus chilled, the salad ready to be dressed and tossed. Candles warmed the room, incense burned, and the aroma of roasting lamb filled the house. A selection of cheeses, olives and savoury biscuits sat on the sideboard next to his mother's best napkins and her bone china plates. He moved the hors d'oeuvres to the coffee table and rearranged the lounge chairs, then rearranged the cushions on the couch and, dashing upstairs, looked at his reflection, undressed and then re-dressed before running back down the stairs and taking a long swig from the whisky decanter. He ran back upstairs to dress, again. 'You look awful,' he said, slumping on the bed, defeated. 'I'm a disaster!' Then he rallied, looked himself square in the mirror and said, 'Get a hold of yourself, man,' and dressed again in his blue suit.

Well before time he was waiting at the door, practising reaching for the handle, feigning a relaxed demeanour in the hall mirror. Outside, a car screeched to a halt, the gears juddered and the engine revved as it reversed. Immediately, the car door slammed and Julie's heavy, eager footfall led her to the stoop. A knock rang out and the sergeant pressed his hand to his heart. 'Be healed the scars which Cupid's arrows have left.' He took a deep breath. Julie knocked again, a little less confidently, so he straightened and fanned his damp face, pink with anticipation and nerves, and opened the door, smiling. 'Julie.'

Her Alice band featured a white bow which matched the one on the purse hanging primly from her arm. Her lovely eyes were looking straight at him and then she glanced down and the sergeant saw that she was twirling her foot. He gasped. 'Oh, my pretty hat! They're wonderful!'

'They're yours,' she said. They were a low stiletto, black velvet, and on the vamp sat a pert, fat, silky pompom made of shaved ostrich feathers. By far, they were the classiest shoes the sergeant had ever seen. He was breathless with greed and gratitude. She removed them and handed them – warm from her feet – to the sergeant. They felt deep and soft; the leather smelled like new leather, and the pompom was beating bee wings against his nose. He sank to the staircase, removed his brogues and slipped his feet into his new shoes. Emboldened, he stood and embraced Julie, who gasped and fell into him. Their lips found each other's and as they enjoyed a long soft kiss, Julie shed her coat. Somehow she managed also to shed her dress and, lips on lips, the sergeant removed his coat, and Julie raised her arms and her petticoat flew off and fell into a soft puddle, and in their urgency the sergeant found the glorious waves of Julie's warm, smooth, sumptuous hills, the slinky silk with lacy verges over her skin. Encountering no obvious boundaries to his exploration, he did as his wife had said: he embraced and enjoyed his new love with abandon.

It was much, much later, when they were exhausted, crumpled, damp and dishevelled, that Julie said, 'I'm so happy they fit.'

'Everything fits.'

'It does, but shoes are tricky.'

'The shoes are perfect.'

'Everything is perfect.'

They scrambled up from the floor, reorganised themselves and opened the champagne. They spent the rest of the evening trying on each other's clothes and shoes, and popping olives and cheese into each other's mouths, and entwining their arms and drinking from their champagne glasses and tearing moist lamb from the bone and tipping salt onto the crisp, hot potatoes and scoffing them and wiping their hands on the fine napkins. Eventually they retreated to bed with a stack of fashion magazines and when they tired of looking at shoes and frocks, they let lust take its pent-up course.


Nita and Tilly draped their coats over the backs of their chairs and settled with their drinks. 'The Razettes are performing,' Nita said.

'I've seen them.'

'We all have. A dozen times, but the thrill remains . . . will they spill anything?'

They drank and talked about their week; Nita had been

taken to square dancing at the Orama and decided it was not for her, though she quite liked her date, 'A base player, rhythm and timing.' They discussed the mannequin called Jane who had married the Earl of Dulkeith and had the word 'obey' struck from the wedding vows, and recalled that *South Pacific* had opened at Her Majesty's Theatre, to great acclaim.

'Yes,' said Tilly, 'all over the social pages. A lot of Arctic Fox fur and embroidered pigeon-grey satin. How are rehearsals for your play coming along?'

Nita rolled her eyes. It was an American play, *I Am a Camera*, and the American director entertained pretensions to conquer Melbourne. The production was pitched to an audience that didn't grasp the subtleties about the Nazi era, the actors were static and forced – Laurence Olivier rather than Montgomery Clift – her costume didn't suit what her character, Sally Bowles, was trying to convey, and her director was clueless. She lit a cigarette. 'You'll be relieved to know that I refused to sleep with him.'

While the Razettes performed, Tilly's thoughts took her all the way back to the Dungatar Social Committee's production of *Macbeth*, so atrociously executed. Her fingertips pinged remembering sewing all those ruffled bustles and dripping frills for those heedless Dungatar people, and, listening to Nita convey the plot of *I Am a Camera*, a sleeping suspicion stood up and waved to her. As she had done in Paris and Milan, was she nurturing people who had made money from war, people who saw only what they wanted and entertained only what was acceptable? Ultimately, that made Tilly one of them.

'We will come to see your play anyway, all of us.'

'I appreciate the support.'

'I've been doing some reckoning,' Tilly announced. 'I have a gift which I have used to great advantage for myself and others, but it's a gift that supports, primarily, the people who uphold morals I don't uphold. It's undermining me.'

Nita said, 'Well, you must choose a more satisfying denouement.'

There was silence as Tilly pondered the denouement that was slowly falling into place for her, then Nita abruptly raised the subject of gender bias and how the value of the gross domestic product was pitched against women. 'It's a conspiracy, you see, don't you?'

'I do see,' Tilly said, though her vision was becoming a little fuzzy around the edges. 'Goods and services favour males. Happily, my job is one that I can do even as I'm dying, but for you there should be more radio plays.'

'I might have another sidecar. Would you like another?'

'I think I might have ordered them, but we may as well have another since everything's against us.'

Elmer placed two cocktails in front of them. 'You are about to ingest your fourth drink, girls.'

'Thank you, we weren't sure.'

'Just remember, at any given moment you might be required to run, very fast.'

'We know,' said Nita, and Tilly added, 'Everyone's against us.' They toasted.

'Where will we run?'

'Out the door.'

They looked about to see where the door was located.

Back at Darling Street, Miss Peachy woke and went to her front door, but there was no one there. She wondered, for the first time that long, noisy night, what the knocking had been.

Sunday morning, Tilly turned in her cramped bed and her brain thudded dully towards the pillow, like a wet tennis ball. She wished someone would bring her a cup of warm sweet tea and several analgesics. Joe was standing by her bed, around him his aunts and uncles spread like resting alligators. Her son smiled at her. 'Mmmm.'

She whispered, 'Yes, I'm Mummy. And I'm happy to take third place after "tortoise" and "Christ".' She reached for her son, said the word again to him: 'Mummy. I am Mummy.' She quietly took him to the kitchen to make breakfast. He would not be put into his high chair, nor the floor, but clung to her like a koala to a branch and stayed on her hip while she made toast.

'Everything is all right, Joe. You are safe,' she whispered.

Mae arrived and put the kettle back on the stove.

'Something has happened, hasn't it?'

'Welfare. A brute of a man, that officer. Edward's put locks on the doors and the back gate, and he fixed the screen door and nailed barbed wire along the top of the back fence.'

'It's not fair, the last thing you need is the welfare –'

'We're used to it. But they'll take him one day, they don't approve of people like us.' Mae held her gaze: *Do something about it.*

'In a week or so, I'll resign. After the collection.' She would sew, night and day, she would get money together and hire a house or a shop. She would offer the sergeant accessories. Elizabeth would help and eventually, when she could pay a wage, she'd steal Shirley, if she would come. Businesses had started with less, and her reputation was growing.

Mae took her cup of tea to the back door.

'You can see him every day if you like,' Tilly said. 'Joe needs his family.'

'And we need him.' Just then, Mae stopped, ears pricked. Tilly could hear nothing, but Mae shot off down the hall. 'I hear you Mary Mae McSwiney! What's the idea coming home at this hour? And don't you think I don't know you've been in that car with that boy.'

Edward came to the kitchen and poured a cup of tea. 'I don't think we have to worry about Mary's chap. He doesn't look like much.'

'That's what my father thought when you showed up,' Mae said, returning, and Tilly's hopes rose a little. There would be more grandchildren for Mae and Edward.

On the ride home, Joe held tight to his little handlebars, and Tilly cried, the tears whipped away by the Sunday summer sunshine. She was fearful, guilty for causing the McSwineys heartache, and wishing with all her heart that she had Teddy. Everything would be all right if Teddy was with her. 'Stupid,' she wept, 'stupid, stupid, stupid.' She hated him for a while, as she sometimes did when she was alone, angry and pining, and then turned her pointless thoughts to the winter coronation parade – so close – and to her plan.

By the time she arrived in the Darling Street kitchen, she had applied her coping self, her fearless persona, and Joe was smiling on her hip. Her husband was beading a hat. She put Joe down and he scampered to his toy box. Tilly found that the remains of the bean and potato pie had been eaten. She slammed the fridge door, making the tonic bottles tink against the milk bottle, her coping, fearless persona replaced by frustration and hurt.

'Sorry,' the sergeant called, cheerfully. 'I suddenly felt famished.'

'Me too.'

The sergeant did not respond.

She wandered over and watched him test a spray of magpie feathers against the beads on the straw dome. 'Who is that for?'

'Miss Havisham, next door.'

'The Melbourne Cup won't have seen anything like that since 1915.'

The sergeant continued stitching, humming the love song 'I've Got a Feeling I'm Falling' a little too emphatically.

'I really do think you should move on from feathers.'

'And I think you've made enough Madame Vionnet impersonations and should move on to something original.'

'They are *compliments*, they're not reductive. I use the same principle of the bias cut. Do you know it was Molly who warned me about corsetry? When she gave up corsets she realised it's what's underneath that defines how a woman is, not her outward display.'

'Don't dare lecture me on the cruelty of corsetry or of accessory! And don't light that cigarette in my workroom! I don't sully your creative space.'

'But you steal things from it.'

'I do not!'

She pointed to the kimono he was wearing. 'And what about my net petticoats and my red sunglasses?'

He tore off the kimono, placed it on a coathanger and handed it to her. 'It seemed to me you were quite happy in men's dungarees these days.'

She turned her back on him and marched towards the backyard. The sergeant followed her, as did Joe, toddling along with his tip truck, calling, 'Cubby? Sannit? Cuddy, Sannit? Sannit?'

'Yes, dear boy, play in the sand, as you must. Myrtle Dunnage, you're being *very* mean. What happened, is it the signature pieces, are the seamstresses striking?'

'We seem to have avoided a strike.' She sighed. How was she to tell him there was more harassment? 'Welfare raided Mae.'

The sergeant's hand went to his mouth and his eyes widened.

Joe was saying all the new words he'd learned: 'Sannit, dortuss, toast, more, mick, peas, punkid, batado, gran, par, dad, mum and Bardy.'

'Joe was out with Barney and the kids. That welfare officer, really, why doesn't he just stay at home on weekends with his wife and family?'

'Bardy?'

'No more Barney today,' the sergeant told Joe. He turned to Tilly. 'The officer's not a marriage kind of person.'

'Unlike us,' Tilly said, and smiled. 'I'm sorry, I'm cross, and at least we like each other . . . most of the time.' She sat in the tipi with Joe, the sand and his truck. The sergeant dragged a garden chair over.

'Tell me all about it, dear.'

'Bardy?'

'No Barney today. Now shoosh, Joe.' Tilly continued, 'We have to get rid of welfare. I have a plan to make things better. After the preview show, I'll be home a lot more, I'm sorry, but I will start something new. I won't have much money but I will have customers – they will follow me from Salon Mystique – but I know I can't continue to risk your life, or lose Joe.'

'And I don't want to lose Julie.'

'Oh my God! Julie! How selfish of me. How was your evening?'

Her husband's cheeks blushed rosy and there came a faraway look in his eyes, and it was clear he was a man whose journey had taken him to bliss.

'I am the happiest man in Australia. They say that when you know, you know. And I know. She is perfect in every way and I can't see a future without her.'

'I will move out –'

'You can't move out, we're married.'

Joe pushed his truck across to the sergeant and upended the load of sand onto his Aladdin slippers. He sighed and emptied the sand from his shoe. 'I should have bought you a book, Joel, my boy.'

# Chapter 22

BEFORE SALON MYSTIQUE's *l'avant-première* of the winter coronation couture, Madame cast her proud eyes over the pastel bouquet of dresses, like a winner at a flower show: her collection of blossoming skirts, firm bodices with sleeves like petals, a couple of statement collars and one or two edged necklines, an angular train, lots of bows like butterflies and shiny coats with contrasting, mildly surprising details. The dresses were almost animated, as if they were poised for a gust of wind, and then Madame stopped at the masterpieces, the signatures, inspirations from Tilly's soul. They rested, unborn until anointed by a form, movement and daylight, until worshipped by mere mortals, like the Princess Elizabeth herself at her consecration. She inhaled, shakily, put her hand to her excited heart. Today the story of Salon Mystique would change forever.

Seating for the last season's summer parade had not been a problem, given only the usual habitués attended: about six potential customers, plus two chaps from the press and some curious spies from other houses. The spring show had not featured anything new, challenging or innovative by any stretch of anyone's imagination, but word of Salon Mystique's winter coronation collection had spread – apparently, it was to be startling – and Clare was again cowering behind her desk, the exhausted handset faintly beeping on her appointment book, the pages glaring darkly up at her. Before her, the hired chairs stretched like crosses at a memorial park and the dressers, a select number of mostly terrified seamstresses, buzzed and twitched in cubicles and nooks far from Madame Flock's unblinking eyes, checking they had the right accessories in the right places and the shoes in order of appearance.

Meanwhile, the young mannequins – newly minted from modelling school – chatted. The conversation was of Myer parades, the millinery parade at the Returned Nurses' Club, the Australian Institute of Radiology Ball, the Loveliest Night of the Year Parade – and, of course, the coronation. There was also the thrill of the latest rage, nylon fur coats. The younger models were to show Madame's designs, and while they waited they smoked, knitted or sipped tea, their bodies like concrete in corselets, girdles and step-ins. These girls also required the preferred foundation of the day, the Lana Turner–inspired brassiere – boned and wired, stiff-pointed with circular stitching – but those with more relaxed breasts and more seasoned waists who would normally need a *guêpière*, or waspie, were joyfully unconcerned about hourglass silhouettes, because these were the mannequins chosen especially for the Tilly Dunnage designs. They were experienced women who had reached their prime, and they simply draped themselves across the furniture in their white coats, and watched.

Today, Madame and Salon Mystique would give Melbourne something to talk about for decades to come, of that she was sure. She envisioned many seamstresses and potential customers gathered at her shopfront, peering in, tapping on the plate glass window, wanting a glimpse of Madame Flock.

Tilly was, at that moment, breakfasting at the Press Club with Arlen and Melbourne's most influential fashion editor, who happened to be a close acquaintance of Arlen's, that was to say, a client. Arlen placed a Bloody Mary in front of both Tilly and the editor, ordered Tilly's breakfast for her, and said, 'Tilly has designed and created the pieces you will see today.'

'In what way are they different from the usual Salon Mystique designs?'

'Mrs Flock is not a couturier,' Tilly said, 'she is a counterfeiter. The signature pieces display speculative thought and anticipate what people might want to wear, yet they still reflect the history of couture. My signature pieces sense the mood and alter the usual silhouette and they assume the entire retail sector has been, for far too long, conventional. It's an attempt at synthesis of the current political, cultural, societal and economic climates. My artistic inspiration comes from fashions that reflect what we would like Melbourne to be in 1953, 1954 or even 1965. But don't write any of that.'

Her breakfast arrived. The two men watched in awe as she piled a forkful of scrambled eggs onto a piece of toast, put a mushroom on top, stuffed it into her mouth and chewed.

She continued, 'But the bulk of the collection, and I use the word *bulk* indicatively, was designed by Mrs Flock and Valda. Together they have produced a collection that conveys a desperate attempt to cash in on the coronation year, its hierarchy and social celebrations – that is, mass-produced dresses for Princess Elizabeth doppelgangers, which means the collection is already defunct. You can write that.'

'I take it you won't be there for the next collection?' asked the editor.

She shook her head, her mouth still dealing with her delicious breakfast.

Arlen said, 'She will be dressing a select clientele to show a synthesis of hope and vision, but don't write that.' They didn't want the Welfare Department to know all her movements; they wanted the officer to sit in his car all night with his binoculars, trying to work everything out while pissing into a milk bottle.

'And under no circumstances will you mention my name in the same paragraph as the Miss Moomba pageant.'

'Ah,' said the editor, excited, 'I have an invitation to that. It's tonight.'

'What you can write,' said Tilly, mopping up the remains of her eggs with toast, 'is that the State Government and Clothing and Allied Trades Union should review pay and conditions for tailors and seamstresses if they want to avoid industrial action across the clothing manufacturing sector prior to the spring-summer collections.' She turned to Arlen, 'Are you going to eat that last piece of toast?'

Arlen handed over his uneaten toast.

'Can you pass me the jam, please?'

Arlen ordered her coffee. She could grow accustomed to being cared for.

When she arrived at work, finally, Tilly Dunnage brought the press clattering in after her. They found good vantage points on the stairs and sat holding pencils and notepads, cameras aimed. In the dressing rooms Tilly joined the seamstresses to watch, standing with Shirley as the long dark cars slid up to the kerb and feeling empathy with her co-workers, all of them fearful of losing their livelihoods in the lingering postwar economy.

Shirley said, 'Today, you just let things happen the way they happen, all right?' Tilly shrugged, and Shirley repeated, 'Just let things happen the way they do.'

'All right.' Around her, there was the usual air of suspense, but Tilly Dunnage also detected a thread of suppressed glee.

Madame Flock greeted the women as they came through the copper-edged door in their furs and diamonds. Beautiful women came with their lovely daughters, stylish ladies and their sisters, Mrs Drum arrived and announced she wanted a new frock for the Governor-General's swearing in, scheduled for May. 'We're sailing to Sydney on a ship just like the *Queen Mary*,' she said loudly, so that those close by could hear. 'I want you to bring my new dress to me in a nice box and hand it to me as I'm boarding.' This, so that she could be photographed like the wealthy establishment ladies sailing to London for the coronation season.

Mrs Piggot said she wanted Tilly Dunnage to design her a gown made entirely of mauve roses, and Mrs Theaver raised her wide nose and looked at Madame with her two close-set eyes. 'I hear your models are from June Dally-Watkins.'

'Yes,' said Madame, gleefully adding, 'but they all have the required *empoigner* and *enlever*.'

'Your French is very bad,' said Mrs Theaver, and lumbered off, her long arms dangling.

Clare tried to execute Madame Flock's carefully contrived seating plan but most ladies arrived in pairs and wanted to sit together, and one or two brought their husbands but had not booked them in. One woman brought her puppy, and a politician's wife brought two extra society ladies so Clare and Valda had to relinquish their desk chairs. A banker's wife demanded a better view – 'This is too close' – and was offered the stairs, which was doubly humiliating because an infamous mistress was shown to her vacated centre-front seat. The famous fashion editor sat with the jockeys' wives to the side. Mrs Churling announced loudly that she was only at Salon Mystique because she 'happened to be passing'. Outside, drivers leaned on their Bentleys and Jaguars, the north side of Collins Street static with a major traffic jam.

Mrs Budge didn't like her seat, so left. And then Nita Orland – the former Mrs Guston Small – arrived. She took her seat and the woman next to her hissed, '*Demimonde.*'

Nita replied, 'And you, madam, are a cushion on which too many warm bottoms have sat.'

Nita took her cushion from the chair and placed it beside a

journalist on the top step, who happened to be Arlen. His press card said, 'Guangming Daily'. When they both waved up to Tilly, they struck up a conversation.

A small skirmish at the door announced Marigold; Beula tapped along behind, a vase tumbling in her wake. They were given seats behind the jockeys' wives.

A celebrated pianist (and sister of a world-famous violinist) arrived ahead of an Honourable Minister's wife (who, it was well known, hadn't paid for anything since 1949), and a large lesbian from a local newspaper followed a smattering of establishment ladies looking gloriously bored. A pale gentleman arrived, wearing an immaculate grey three-piece suit and soft fur-felt hat with an unusually high crown, deep central crease and a red velvet band boasting several two-colour ostrich feather pompoms and quills. Clare showed him to a seat at the rear, and if she suspected he was actually the woman who'd ordered the sarong dress, she gave no hint. The mannequins agreed unanimously that he was the best-dressed man there. He brought a friend, a big-boned woman, sensibly dressed in a frock more suited to a six-year-old, but it matched her Alice band, and her suede pumps were startling. Elmer swept in next and sat down next to Sergeant Farrat and Julie; unimpressed with his view, he took a vase from its stand, marched across the runway to the front door and handed it to the cowering Clare, saying, 'Hay fever,' and sneezed to make the point.

The men nodded politely to the judge as he arrived with his wife, an ordinary woman with a sailor's complexion, reflecting that she spent most of her time at the beach house. The judge and his weathered wife sat with Mrs Caroline Hawker, who, Tilly noted, completely ignored Marigold and Beula.

Just as Clare moved to lock the salon door, two young women, cheaply but fashionably dressed (Margaret and Mary McSwiney), arrived, flustered. They were directed to the seating on the stairs with the journalists.

Shirley reached for Tilly's hand. The first dress was their signature piece – a day dress. Madame picked up an envelope and turned her back, fanning herself, then announced (badly), '*Aube robe.*' A hush fell over the crowd.

The curtain at the rear of the shop parted and a model glided out wearing a sky-blue day dress. It was obviously inspired by Dior's big-skirted, tight-waisted summer dresses, but this one was a little more *séduisant, effronté*. The neckline was V-shaped, low enough to expose just a peek, a seductive hint, of cleavage. The skirt was full, but not boldly so, accentuating the waist. Corsetry was not necessary. It was a dress that celebrated shape but didn't contort it. The skirt was two-tiered, the hem featuring deep ruffles. The top ruffle danced over the thighs and the tier beneath fell to midcalf. The trick was that the hemlines dipped at the back on each tier so that the mannequin's tanned, toned legs appeared amid a sweet, frothy mess of raw silk. The mannequin, Lisa, sold the dress to perfection, her gait short and free so that the skirts rustled gently and the dress was a song of captivating movement. Of course, it was sleeveless and an illusion of sorts: it appeared to be a sweet summery dress, yet there was a suggestion of feminine mystery under layers of dancing cloth. One felt the need to own this pretty garment, care for it. It was the dress every girl wanted, the dress they'd love and wear and wear and wear, and it floated through the room to gasps and even some enthusiastic clapping, which came from Elmer. And then Lisa turned and smiled, allowing space for Meredith, who arrived wearing a flamenco-inspired polka-dot dress, backless with an off-centre split that started at the waist. She deftly removed Lisa's belt and its large front bow buckle, and the dress became grown-up, sophisticated, suited to evening or cocktail wear. That was when the first flashbulb burst.

Tilly was alarmed when Natalie swept out wearing her second signature piece, an evening gown. The salon promptly exploded with a series of flashbulbs and crackling camera shutters. It was the black halter-neck, but with deep crimson silk satin, a cylinder of bias cut gathered between the shoulderblades by the crossed straps meeting at the top of the bodice. The front was high-necked, and a giant glittering brooch rested centre chest. The gathered fabric finished in a slight fishtail, which flicked at the heels.

Mrs Flock was panicked. Why had two signature pieces come out at once? Where were Madame's designs? But the ladies in the audience were absorbed, craning to see from the edge of their seats.

Shirley whispered into Tilly's ear, 'Tilly Dunnage, you've got to change things now, be fearless.'

Tilly was suddenly back at the silo with Teddy, and she saw his face, grinning, as he said, 'Fearless.'

Shirley held Tilly's arm, reassuringly, and then Suzanne sashayed in, wearing the cocktail dress – burgundy silk, a lithe dress based on a classic design. The bodice defined it and shouted, *couture*. It was constructed of one piece, seamed at the waist and shaped by graduated hexagons. Minuscule adjustments in the design of the tucking created the form but it was an illusion of detailed embellishment – ornament used for the composition of the dress. It was yet another must-have.

The seamstresses around Tilly smiled at her, touched her, congratulated her, said they had planned it all, that Mrs Flock and Valda knew nothing of it, that they would not lose their jobs, the union told them so. 'And besides,' said Shirley, 'she's going to need all the seamstresses she can get,' and turned again to the catwalk, for Annabel had arrived in the bridal gown. The crowd remained still, quiet, transfixed, but the cameras clattered for the wedding dress, which was a little too avant-garde for the ladies, and Madame Flock's least favourite gown; it was clear that Tilly was designing for a younger clientele, more for Miss Nita Orland than for Mrs Drum or Mmes Piggot, Churling or Theaver, but it was also adamantly clear that the audience loved what they had seen. What they loved even more was when Meredith arrived again and demonstrated how, in one deft action, the wedding gown could be whipped from Annabel's lithe body. Annabel was left standing almost naked in lingerie – chic, tactile night attire, lacy and silken. The ladies gasped, someone cried, 'Nudity, disgusting!'; others declared the pyjamas a guarantee to get any marriage off to a good start, but overall there was silence: a significant pause between the final dress and the eventual applause, large in its intensity, its tone deep and thoughtful, appreciative, the kind of applause couturiers dreamed of at the end of a show. Yet, only five dresses?

Mrs Flock went searching for Valda – What had happened? Where were her dresses? – but the crowd were on their feet, pushing forward while others sat silently, miffed that such fine clothing was available from a B-grade salon. And how to explain, extract themselves from their usual couturiers? Could they lie, say their new gown was from Paris? It was all very inconvenient. As the seamstresses watched, Madame Flock appeared on the runway, distressed, searching. Where was the remainder of the collection? Mercy and the Victor Stiebel centrepiece?

Someone in the audience called, 'Bravo!'

The crowd on the stairs parted, and the seamstresses and cutters, apprentices and pin picker-uppers followed Tilly and Shirley down the stairs onto the catwalk, where they shuffled Mrs Flock aside and bowed.

Then Elizabeth McSwiney, flanked by sisters Mary and Margaret in their home-made frocks, appeared on the runway and declared, 'Tilly Dunnage is responsible for the dresses you have seen today.'

Madame Flock started swatting them with a program.

Elizabeth yelled, 'Tilly Dunnage designed and made everything you saw today. She trained in Europe.'

Mary McSwiney held Tilly's hand. 'Now, you can be at home with Joe.'

The photographers clicked on, bulbs exploding as the room fell into chaos, people calling that the show wasn't long enough, and where were the other dresses; some tried to leave, appalled; others tried to get to Clare's desk to order dresses.

The bedlam increased as women fought. 'I want number one, and number three!'

Mrs Drum shoved a handful of pound notes at the mannequin wearing the blue dress. 'Give me that dress!' She called to Tilly, 'I'm having that dress, I'll make sure you get free meat for a year.'

'I want the burgundy cocktail dress,' someone cried and others called, 'Number two, I want number two,' and 'The wool crepe afternoon frock . . . the wedding dress, size extra small.'

Tilly removed her white coat. She made her way through the grasping crowd towards the door, women lunging at her, tugging her arms – someone even grabbed a handful of her short hair – but she ploughed on through the throng, shoving chairs aside and sending vases crashing to the floor. She caught Arlen's eye and felt someone take her hand. It was Nita, smiling at her, saying, 'Marvellous, Tilly, you are clever.'

Marigold appeared. 'You won't have a job now, dear *daughter*. You could come home, I'll build you a shop,' and Tilly leaned close to her.

'The only reason I'd ever go back to Dungatar would be to burn it down.'

Tilly and Nita made their escape from the salon straight into the fatty chest of the welfare officer. He pointed at Julie, behind them. 'That woman has stayed the night at your marital home, once when you failed to return to it. You are adulterers.'

'Tilly!' It was Arlen, standing on the footpath next to the welfare officer. He planted a kiss on Tilly's cheek.

'Who are you?' asked the welfare officer.

Arlen joked, 'I'm from the arson squad.' He was holding a small bunch of myrtle flowers.

'He's a journalist,' Tilly snapped.

'He told me he was a lawyer,' Marigold said.

Nita, seeing panic in Tilly's eyes, said to the officer, 'He's *my* friend.' She slipped her arms through Arlen's.

The inspector looked at Nita Orland and saw a hovering angel.

Tilly turned to Arlen. 'I'd like you to meet my friends Elizabeth, Mary and Margaret McSwiney.'

'Ah,' he said, understanding everything.

The officer, oblivious to the crowd around him, continued to stare at Nita.

'Wonderful show, Tilly my dear,' called the sergeant, flinging open the door of the waiting car, which was stuffed with flowers. 'The club?'

'Yes,' said Nita, conscious of the leering welfare officer.

Tilly said to the welfare officer, 'Sorry, can't chat.' She plunged into the bush of flowers, as did her husband, Julie and the McSwiney sisters. She thanked the sergeant and told him the flowers were a wonderful thought.

'I know! She loved them, didn't you, Julie?'

'Loved them,' and they rubbed noses.

As they drove away, Nita said to Arlen, 'Well, new friend, would you like to come with us to the club?'

'I'd love to,' he said, handing her the myrtle bouquet.

'Club?' said the welfare officer.

'Bowling club,' Nita said. 'You'd need someone to sign you in and I'm quite sure no one here's got a pen.'

He watched the astonishingly lovely creature raise her slender, gloved arm. He waved in response, but she was looking at a long black car sliding noiselessly up to the kerb. She opened her own door and the handsome man called Arlen got into the car after her and the woman of his dreams was whisked away to a bowling club somewhere while all around him women babbled and squeaked about the new seamstress in town, Tilly Dunnage, and what a clever, talented woman she was.

The officer was quite frozen, sniffing at the air for a final trace of the most beautiful woman he'd ever seen. 'Who was that, in the blue velvet?'

'Nita Orland,' said someone, 'she's an actress.'

Actresses were not respectable at all. He headed straight to the office to see if there was a file on her.

Inside, Clare was on her knees behind her quaint, spindly reception desk, a crowd of women heckling her, some cancelling appointments, others begging for one of the five dresses they'd seen.

Valda turned to Madame. 'Don't worry about all those women cancelling appointments, they'll be back when we win Miss Moomba.'

'How will we do that?'

'Tilly Dunnage left her sketchbook.' Valda held it aloft, triumphant.

But Madame still felt wretched. There was no way Valda could translate anything in that sketchbook.


Tilly did not go to the Hippocampus Club with her husband and his girlfriend, with Shirley, Elizabeth, Mary, Margaret, Nita, Arlen and Elmer. Tilly rode straight to Collingwood and sat at the dining table with Joe. 'Peeze,' he said, picking up the small round vegetable and putting it into his mouth. Then he again named all the new words he'd learned: 'Dortuss, toast, more, mick, peas, punkid, batado, Gran, Par, Dad, Mum and Bardy.'

'All right, son,' Edward said, 'that's enough.'

'More, Dortuss, toast, mick, peas —'

'Shoosh!' Mae pointed to his dinner.

He looked at his mother, bewildered, and she said, 'You can talk again later, it's our turn now. Eat up, there's a good boy.'

It's what Joe did these days, talked from dawn until he slept, wandering through the house with a trail of cotton or fabric scraps, shoes, utensils or twigs, happy in his busy life and secure in his home, talking, asking and asking and asking for things until someone gave them to him, pointing at things and naming them over and over until someone agreed or corrected him.

'He's like a wireless,' said Mae, and Edward shot, 'The gift of the gab, like his father,' and they thought of Teddy and that stupid, reckless gesture on that starry, lusty night. He was spared the fate of so many amid the ravages of war, because of his flat feet, instead staying home to trap rabbits and catch fish to sell to the locals, and he used those great, flat wedges to kick a football, making a hero of himself in Dungatar, but he was missing his greatest achievement.

Victoria, who was one of the least vocal members of the McSwiney family, broke the silence. 'What was the fashion parade like?'

Tilly described the preview parade, the mannequins and the clientele, the lovely dresses and the flashbulbs, and finally the bridal gown and the eruption of chaos caused by some 'well-meaning members of the public in the audience' that ended the ruinous event.

'Vanity . . . it will destroy,' said Edward.

Mae looked at Tilly. 'You've just got a few loose threads to tie off and the world's a whole new fabric factory.'


At the Hippocampus Club, while the sergeant and Julie canoodled in a dim corner, and Elizabeth, Mary and Margaret drank cocktails with Shirley, Nita chose Arlen O'Connor. It was very soon evident that he was not the sort to respond to flirtatiousness, so she lectured him instead on the inequality of women, especially when it came to divorce: 'I cited adultery as a reason for divorce then was humiliated, made to feel responsible for my husband's indiscretions. I received a pittance, which I handed to the lawyers I was forced to employ because my ex-husband chose to challenge my accusations. I've not recovered financially or emotionally.'

'I'll see if I can do something about those laws,' Arlen said, and she thought that he would, one day. Meanwhile, the Razettes – standing on their heads with cream cakes balanced on their shoes – went largely ignored by the Saturday night revellers.

Elizabeth turned to Arlen. 'And who are you, then, Mr O'Connor? How do you fit into Tilly's colourful life?'

'I took her on when Dungatar shafted her thirty-odd years ago.' He looked away, ending the conversation, which was fortunate because that's when Mary announced, 'I don't feel very well,' and vomited into her handbag. She was taken to the ladies' room and questioned closely by her sisters. It was established that Mary had been unwell and tired for several weeks and their advice was to 'ask Tilly if you can borrow one of her nice dresses, the sarge'll organise things – he did a good job with his own wedding.'

At that point, the Razettes left the stage, cream cakes intact, to mild applause as an octopus, a flounder and a gem fish took to the stage and began to play 'Fat Fanny Stomp'. At once, the entire club rose (apart from Mary) and started to dance, including Elizabeth, Margaret and Shirley, made exuberant by several Singapore Slings.

At that same time, Salon Mystique's quest for Miss Moomba – and then Miss Victoria and Miss Australia and onwards to overall Gown of the Year – was quashed after one soaring, breathless hour. Miss Post Office Picnic's lovely dress was a splendid smoky creation that featured Shirley's exceptional cutting and embroidery and some precise and delicate beading. All the fashion photographers and journalists admired it and photographed it. During score-counting deliberations, while the Miss Moomba guests were encouraged to dance and enjoy another drink, special guest General Wilfred Gonard asked Miss Post Office Picnic for a dance. The general's hold was vice-like as he steered her towards the gloomy area behind the tall floral decorations beside the band pit. As they moved into the darkness, General Gonard drew Miss Post Office even closer. She struggled, her bottom shot away from his hardening thrust and she pushed her fingernails deep into his palm. Excited, General Gonard sucked on the tiny girl's bird-like neck, and that's when his military medals punctured her inflated, padded breasts, which exploded, a camera flash lighting the desiccated tissue-paper spray across the general's glinting metal chest.

The Miss Moomba crown went to Miss Port Melbourne, but the photo of General Gonard and Miss Post Office Picnic stayed pinned to the journalists' tearoom noticeboard for years.

# Chapter 23

GERTRUDE BEAUMONT, NÉE Pratt, disembowelled the generator again, secured her shop against thieves again and set off with her small suitcase to the railway platform, again. While she waited under the burnt Dungatar sign, she took the newspaper photographs of the Salon Mystique winter coronation collection from her handbag to study, and was tearful. What Tilly Dunnage might create for her! But what bothered Gertrude most was the accompanying article announcing that the government would investigate the clothing and manufacturing sector for chronic underpayment. The textile, clothing, footwear and associated industry sector would be subject to close scrutiny, with a view to abolishing underpayment of its staff. The investigation would kick off with an examination of seamstresses' and tailors' wages. It wasn't fair. It would most likely impact the price of a gown.

The train driver saw the 'HELP' sign. Some miles passed before he saw 'Slow Down', then 'Stop at Dungatar', and finally, 'Collect passenger next stop'. A rope hung with rags intended to halt the train stretched from the water tower to the signal pole, but he was stopping anyway to uncouple the truck full of building supplies.

The buxom woman with the furious countenance, who carried a large white sheet pinned to a broom, stepped carefully along the sleepers towards him with her bag. He climbed up and opened the passenger compartment for her. 'Why didn't you just use the telephone?'

'Do you see a telephone pole behind me?' Walking out to Windswept Crest to beg to use the telephone was unthinkable.

The driver looked at the blonde puzzle on the vast plain and the occasional slice of shiny corrugated roofs, and pointed to the truck waiting on the siding, 'Be a whole town by the time you get back.'


The New Dungatarians had finally come good with their hidden savings when Elsbeth discontinued Sunday morning scones and some days passed quietly, not so much as a nail being hammered. The ongoing argument about life under feudal rule was set aside, temporarily, and William had telephoned and ordered stage two of the rebuild. Alvin Pratt perfected an account system, typing up Elsbeth's expenditure, using two carbon pages, and those who had contributed money and goods. He issued copies to Elsbeth and Purl Bundle and kept the master copy to himself.

And now the locals were drawing straws to see who would go to the shop for petrol, flour, butter and cheese. Muriel drew the short straw. 'I went last time.'

Elsbeth said, 'She's your daughter.'

When she'd left the asylum, William had welcomed Gertrude back to Windswept Crest, but Elsbeth and Gertrude had come to blows over the seat at the head of the table. Elsbeth had retained her prime position and Gertrude was dispatched back to Pratts Store. Three days later Muriel and Alvin showed up at Windswept Crest seeking asylum from their daughter.

Muriel looked to her husband. 'Alvin, you can go this time.'

Alvin said he'd sooner help Reginald kill the sheep.

'Reg is killing a sheep?' Fred stood up. 'I'd better help too.' All the men went to follow when all the women started bawling on about the men always getting the easy jobs.

'We have spent all week cooking, scrubbing the house and

repairing our costumes for *King Lear* while you men picked a couple of lettuces and did some drawing.'

'We were drawing plans for the fire station.'

'And you've never, not once, cleaned the toilet.'

Felicity Joy came in, her binoculars hanging from her small neck, and said, 'Mum's gone, she took a suitcase.'

Elsbeth beamed. 'How big was the suitcase? Did she take a trunk? Has she gone forever?'

'I'd say she'll be back in a week or two.'

William hung his head.

'I'd love some cheese,' Purl said.

Faith wondered if Gertrude had left any tinned peaches, and Felicity said, 'The train driver left a truck on the siding.'

They turned as one and ran, like rags blowing across the red dirt.

They parked opposite Pratts Store and disembarked warily. Around them New Dungatar had risen, the tongue-and-groove walls tall and pale. They checked for cars then crossed the road and found that Gertrude had bound the shop like a hostage. The tinned peaches, petrol, flour, butter and cheese were unattainable behind padlocked loops of chain holding the building tight. The six padlocked barrel bolts crisscrossed the front door, which also supported a drop bar screwed firmly into two thick brackets. Gertrude had also nailed an extra layer of wire netting to the windows and the locals were dismayed to see that the bowser hose was missing.

'Right,' said William, 'I think the men should –'

'No,' said Alvin. 'You can be feudal lord out at Fart Hill, but this is my store.'

William looked at his shoes and the men turned to Alvin, who declared, 'We'll enter via the floor. I need a volunteer, a small man.'

William thought to himself that Mr Pratt was a small man, seizing his daughter's empire while she was two hundred miles away, and he'd most likely make everyone pay cash for cheese and tinned fruit, denied and depleted as the people were.

Scotty Pullit and Fred Bundle, both small in stature, backed away. 'Spiders,' said Scotty, fearfully, and Fred said the arthritis in his legs meant he couldn't crawl.

Felicity Joy said, 'I'll go,' and Scotty was ashamed, so took another swig of his grog and crawled under with a drill and a saw.

Once they had gorged on Gertrude's larder – Alvin tallying up who ate what – they turned their attention to the truck loaded with building supplies on the siding. Felicity Joy watched the men struggle to load the contents onto the tractor cart, then watched them follow the tractor as it made its way towards the smooth black centre of Dungatar and the general store.

After much argument about placement, a neat pile of plaster-board, house paint, nails, windows and the corrugated iron for the verandah roofs sat on the ruined asphalt. In the distance, the roar of the approaching daily bus grew, so they parted and took refuge behind some new walls, letting the bus tear past, swerving rudely to avoid building materials stacked in the centre of the road.

'Right,' said Reginald, butcher and drummer in the Faithful O'Brien's Band, 'let's get on with this hall.' And they did, despite someone suggesting they start with a medical centre and William's protest over the need to build the fire station – 'Or at least install a pump of some sort!' Finally, the sharp crack of hammers nailing weatherboards swelled in the air of New Dungatar, and the odd cry of pain. The walls for the hall rose, and Mrs Almanac parked her chair in their shadow, with her box of bandaids and her needle ready to burst the blood blisters.

The welfare officer attended Nita's play. He made notes – Mr and Mrs Horatio Farrat attended, as did their so-called friend, the shoemaker, and the dark-haired glamour boy, Arlen O'Connor. He followed them all back to 27 Darling Street and noted that Nita left the premises with Arlen – at 3 am! The shoemaker did not leave.

The next day, the officer purchased every newspaper, cut out each (bad) review and photograph of the play, and placed them in the file titled 'Miss Nita Orland, Actress'. He then telephoned the newspapers demanding original prints of any photographs they had of Miss Nita Orland.

Each evening, the welfare officer checked his hair and brushed the shoulders of his coat and left the Children's Services wing and made his way to the Princess Theatre to watch *I Am a Camera*. He purchased flowers and had them sent to Nita's dressing room with a card, and after each performance he waited until the audience had filed out before going to the stage door. While Nita signed autographs and chatted with the handful of fans, the officer made notes – gender, age, height and what they said: 'Write "to Theodore and Maureen, love from Nita"' – until he was at last alone with her.

She smiled at him, accepted his flowers and signed his black-and-white original photograph. On the fifth night, he offered to escort her home.

She agreed, saying, 'Since you'll follow me anyway.'

'I only follow you because it's not safe to walk home alone at night, there are all sorts of odd people out and about.'

'All sorts,' she said, though this man obviously didn't think he was one of them. 'I like to walk,' she said. 'It's a way of unwinding.' She declined his offered arm but allowed the officer to accompany her all the way to her apartment block, where she left him at the front gate, certain he already knew which door was hers. Inside, she sighed and lit a cigarette, poured herself a nightcap and reached for her cat. Then she pulled the blinds down.

\*

As an unemployed woman, Tilly Dunnage slept late. She found her son at the kitchen table, conversing with his new father over a boiled egg and toast. The sergeant showed him how to spread a napkin on his lap, pick up the slice of toast and dunk it into the egg. 'Egg soldiers,' he said.

And Joe said, 'Igg dolder,' and plunged his fingers into the soft-boiled egg. Then Joe pointed his sticky yellow hand at the sergeant and said, 'Dar.'

'"Thank you" is the correct word, but you can say "ta" until you are three, then we will use appropriate language.'

Joe pointed his finger again, and said, 'Dar.' Then he looked behind the sergeant and said, 'Mummy.'

'Oh, thank goodness,' said the sergeant. 'I've used three napkins and he hasn't really swallowed a thing yet.' He secured the shower caps on his satin high-heeled slip-ons and made his way to the coffee pot.

Tilly put a bib around Joe's neck and spread newspaper under his high chair and left the boy to coordinate the egg and the toast with his mouth. The sergeant sat opposite them to cover his toast with Miss Peachy's peach jam, making sure it spread evenly all the way to the crusts. He mentioned it was time Joel learned the purpose of a knife and fork. Tilly wished him luck with that task, and suggested he stick with a spoon until the boy was four.

'I see in the newspapers that the Tailoresses' Association and Clothing and Allied Trades Union of Australia are lobbying for an inquiry into working conditions for the seamstresses and tailors of Victoria?'

'Yes, just about every seamstress in Australia has written to ask for better pay and conditions, including child care for working women.'

'Well,' he said. 'I wish you luck with that task.'

'I'm done with battles,' she said, and sipped her coffee.

The sergeant gave his wife his full attention. Tilly did not look weary anymore. She looked lovely. Her hair had grown and of late she had taken to wearing a dress and she was more content than he'd ever seen her, especially in the sandpit with Joe and his tip truck.

'Sergeant, I no longer want to make couture.'

'Coor,' said Joe, and dipped his bread soldier into some spilled yolk.

The sergeant glanced at last Sunday's papers. He had saved them because all five garments from Salon Mystique's winter coronation collection featured across the social pages. 'Really?'

'I'm pretty sure if I ask Arlen, he'll help me get my back pay, and I've got a plan.'

'Pan,' Joe said.

'I imagined I would just recruit a couple of capable *petites mains* – for example, Shirley, who has the hands of both a cutter and a lace maker.'

The sergeant was alarmed. 'Shirley?'

'Surely you can't doubt Shirley?'

Joe said, 'Shuree.'

'She sang "I Want to Be Loved by You" to the octopus at the 'Campus Club Saturday night.'

'And was she loved?'

'Not by the octopus.' Shirley had disappeared behind the canvas sea with the gem fish.

'I thought that we would make couture for that very exclusive group of wealthy patrons and make enough to survive on. But I can't, in all good conscience, continue doing that. I want to move forward, and I think the modern women will lead me.' She would somehow rid them of the tenacious welfare officer, they would get through the looming guardianship hearing and they would be free. She didn't seem to be able to do anything unless she asked for help from the McSwineys or the sergeant and now Arlen too and it was unsettling. To Tilly, it seemed that a life without burden wasn't too far away, she just needed to run a little faster to catch it.

The sergeant chewed his toast and looked thoughtfully at the workroom door. 'I will support you as much as I can in every way, but how much can you earn? How many hours in the day must you sew?'

'Fashion is a lie, a marketing tool that's all about the designer, the couturier's vision, not the individual. One should make dresses that announce true character, show someone at their best.' And she had done that. Over and over. A yearning in her for something different had arisen. 'Now I want to make attire that is accessible, unique, new. Madame Vionnet was organic. Original. Trailblazing, but exclusive.' She stood and started walking in circles around the sergeant.

'Balenciaga had four ateliers – tailoring and dressmaking – five hundred staff plus milliners and shoemakers, and each of his designers had a designated atelier. The seamstresses were lost in all of that but I knew he made his money by licensing his designs. To do that I need an individual style, something truly ground-breaking, *really* good clothes, well tailored, structurally simple and eternal, clever, fantastic creations, discreet and subtle. It's the cut, the drape, the fall, the movement, and it must be functional, fit for its purpose.'

She stood looking at him as he chewed his toast. His wife's plans meant a lot of people in one workroom . . . for a long time. And a lot of visitors to the house.

'This is an animated thought process and I'm very pleased to finally witness such enthusiasm, some joie de vivre, but where are you taking us, dear?'

Joe showed his last piece of yolk-sodden toast to the sergeant and said, 'Dar.'

'Yes,' said Tilly, 'that is Dad.'

'Dar,' he said, and while Tilly scraped the rest of the egg from its shell and fed it to Joe, the sergeant gathered himself by making a great fuss of nothing on his lap. He was very moved; he'd never imagined he'd be called 'Dar'.

Tilly released Joe. He turned at the back door, waved to them and ran to the tipi, where he picked up one of the sergeant's best silver spoons to shovel sand into his mother's espadrilles.

'You can be the *première* of the *tailleur*, "Dar", what do you think?'

The sergeant went to the back porch, still feeling great fondness, where he briefly contemplated retrieving his spoon. He concluded that he'd rather have the spoon re-silvered than ruin Joe's project or risk his satin high-heels. They matched his new dressing-gown. He came back inside and sat down. 'I'd rather do *flou*, soft fabrics, and I'd have my own special *espace de travail*. Julie can do the shoes?'

'Of course.'

'But I want to retain some creativity. Can't we make costumes for Nita, for the Razettes and the showgirls and boys at the Hippocampus Club? I can do embroidery, lovely beading and lace. My ability suits theatre costumes.'

Designing for theatre required a quality of improvisation, of sacrifice of craftsmanship to the effect, and it was leaning towards couture as costume. Tilly went and poured herself more coffee. Sergeant Farrat crossed his knees, and stared disapprovingly at her.

'You're pouting.'

'Am not.' He uncrossed and crossed his knees and studied his beautifully manicured fingernails while Tilly rethought her pitch. It was a partnership she was enjoying, after all.

'Very well, we'll do costumes as well. And some couture because it is about the craftsmanship, the details, what the garment is saying, which is mostly about tailoring, dressmaking, then follows the skills of ornament. We will not – absolutely will not – smother anything in artifice. I want my conceptual artistry happy, I want it married to my technical skills. Actually, what I really want to do is change the world.'

'I thought Dior changed the world in 1947.'

'He did, he put women back in corsets, a subconscious symbol of suffocation. We will be women designing for working women.'

'And theatre.'

'For our joyous, creative impulses. But we need to make money.' She was circling the room again, throwing her grand idea at his feet like a gauntlet. 'I need to license my designs. So here's my plan –'

'You are doing all of this from my front room?' he asked, sniffily.

'Oh God,' she sat down again. 'I'm being bossy. I sincerely apologise, I'm being careless and intrusive.'

There was a pause. They contemplated Joe, who was now filling his mother's espadrilles with water from his bucket.

'It's my turn to speak.' The sergeant took her hands and looked into her eyes, which he saw were burning with hope. 'I know exactly how we can frame our new venture. We will only take clients who pay, and who will not be offended by our doorman.'

'That is absolutely it, Sergeant Farrat. So, we are "seamsters" together?'

'Totally stitched up.' He walked to the shop and workroom. 'We will have our first show here, we will set it up properly. I'll pawn Mother's diamond. Again.'

'No, never – that ring is Julie's. I have money or, rather, Arlen has my money.' Tilly took the huge diamond from her finger and handed it to the sergeant.

Joe came back and said, 'Food.' Tilly cut him some apple and they stood in the workroom between the kitchen and the shop, Joe and his truck loaded with muddy wet slippers between them. They smiled at each other, and reached out over Joe's head and shook hands.

# Chapter 24

MR AND MRS Farrat enjoyed a delicious meal at number 9 Collins Street with Miss Nita Orland. The little shop was loud and busy with theatrical types and the odd brooding, thoughtful artist focusing on a notepad, pen in hand, a glass of wine close by. Tilly, Nita and the sergeant each had an especially good French onion soup and a delectable berry galette – compliments of the short dark proprietress – and discussed ideas for their bright futures. Five days had passed since the coronation parade and Tilly had recovered and felt more conviction for a new life than she'd ever felt.

Nita eyed the sketch for her fuchsia dress and felt the fabric sample. 'This will make me very happy.' She'd struggled to be happy of late, she said, though her unhappy story would be over the second the curtain fell on the closing performance of *I Am a Camera*. The sergeant announced to her that he had a request, a favour to ask. Would she model his centrepiece, his debut signature piece for their forthcoming couture venture?

'Try and stop me,' she replied.

Then Tilly expanded on her plan to move away from conceited customers.

'My ideal customer has an appointment later tonight,' Tilly said, the thought of the tenacious welfare officer watching across the park at the back of her mind, which brought with it a reminder that the guardianship hearing loomed.

'I'm excited for you both,' said Nita.

'I don't seem to be able to do anything unless I ask for help from the McSwineys or Arlen.'

Nita rolled her eyes. 'My dear Tilly, friends make life navigable. I must say, though, he's a good-looking friend, very handsome, your Arlen, but somewhat evasive.'

'He's always been self-contained.'

'Elusive. I've asked around – spreads himself wide, but thin.'

Tilly was a little taken aback; why was she asking around?

'Does Arlen have any vices?' Nita asked for coffee, please.

'Everyone has vices,' said the sergeant, and ordered a second helping of galette.

'Yes, but he kept us from starving.' Tilly explained that as young teenagers, Arlen was an unnervingly efficient thief and murderer of chooks. Back then, they'd started a journey together to somewhere better, a future. Some days, she felt she might as well get on the bus and go straight back to Dungatar. 'When I think about Arlen back when we were kids, I realise I felt quite safe. Now I'm terrified half the time but soon I will be independent, happy and free.'

'Me too,' said Nita. 'No one's coming to see the play, it's a flop. My career is dented, but the good news is the costume designer's pregnant . . . There'll be a job at the end of this run if you want to work in the theatre.'

Her mistress, Madame Vionnet, would say, 'I am a *couturier*, not a *costumier*.'

'Tilly Dunnage isn't sure about costumes,' sniffed the sergeant.

'Don't be a snob, Tilly! Clothes make a statement, costumes tell a story. You would like costumes – the process is about finding truth in fiction, and it's collaborative. But you do have to find the character in yourself so that you can make a genuine costume so that the actor can then find the character and be genuine so the audience can see the truth that the play conveys.'

'How very complex,' said the sergeant.

'It's good for us to go trawling around inside ourselves. And you, Tilly Dunnage from Dungatar, can read people, and, I dare say, a character. My costume designer can do neither.'

'I once made brocade pantaloons for *Macbeth*.'

'I'm certain it wasn't your idea.'

'Think of the Razettes,' said the sergeant, swirling his wine in its glass. 'Under their costumes they are nurses.'

She thought about the Razettes, blithely ironic in their averageness, their costumes allowing them to be performers. Though for Elmer, a satin strapless fishtail, a wig and false eyelashes meant he could be himself, or herself. His day costume allowed him to present as a conventional man.

'For me, wearing a costume is more of a hobby, some deep psychological scar from being raised fatherless, or perhaps I just liked dress-ups.' The sergeant looked at Tilly. 'But I fear for you, my dear, if you have to rummage around in yourself.'

But Tilly was at that moment processing the fact that she was already a costumier, that in effect she had been a costumier to those pretenders the entire time she had lived in Dungatar. It hadn't been necessary to 'trawl inside' to make disguises for those Dungatar clowns and Hop-Frogs in order that they could appear to be someone they were not. And she'd done enough trawling to know what she really wanted to make. She was working towards finding out who she really was, and she was beginning to realise it had something to do with the way she had been using costume.

'How's the time going?' asked Nita.

The sergeant looked at his watch. 'Very quickly.'

They stepped out into the dimly lit street and, with a sickening jolt, Tilly saw the welfare officer emerge into the lamplight and just stand there, watching.

'That's my stalker,' Nita said.

'He's my stalker too,' Tilly said.

'He's the welfare officer.' The sergeant put his arm around his wife.

'Well, he's consistent about my welfare: he's always somewhere,' Nita said. 'He follows me. He's not the first. And I have to say, I enjoy the flowers.'

'He sends you flowers?'

'They're delivered to my dressing room every night. The card always says he wants to save me, that I'm being corrupted, that it's not too late.'

'Does he follow you home?'

Nita shrugged. 'Yes, and he's here now to walk me to the theatre.'

'Be careful of him,' the sergeant warned. 'He has a great deal of power and he is a threat to us. You should report him.'

'He'll just say he's looking after my welfare.'

It was clear Nita should talk to Arlen about their mutual pursuer, yet she hesitated, pondered her reluctance and in the end, altruism won. 'Tell Arlen, he'll know what to do.'

On their tram ride home, sitting with the sergeant like a real husband and wife, Tilly decided that if anything were to happen between Nita and Arlen, then it must happen, and she must live her life with Arlen as a friend. He would be a good friend, though, and her lawyer.

In the meantime, opportunity awaited at 27 Darling Street.

Sunset painted the western walls bright red and the east walls black, and the street appeared devoid of pedestrians. There was no sign of the judge, so Tilly let the curtain fall and Elizabeth checked her wristwatch. Next door, Miss Peachy noted there was no sign of the welfare officer again. He had been absent these past nights.

When the judge finally arrived at East Melbourne a new sign

on the door said: 'Dressmaker and Milliner, by appointment. Telephone 1231.'

He pressed the bell, and waited. A woman dressed in something from 1850 stepped from her front door. 'Good evening, are you from the welfare too?'

'Certainly not!'

Miss Peachy stared back at the park. 'There's usually an officer over there, he watches.'

He rang the doorbell again and again the crooked young man in the flannel three-piece suit, grinning proudly, showed him inside. 'Good evening my name is Barney McSwiney and I am very pleased to welcome you to our new shop please come in and take a seat can I take your hat?'

'I don't have a hat.'

The young man said, 'Thank you,' and limped away, leaving the front door wide open. The judge shut the door. The hattery had been converted to a working salon, the parked bicycle replaced by a resurrected workbench along the back wall and, above it, shelves displayed Horatio's millinery skills as well as some beautiful old hats from the twenties and thirties. Framed photographs of remarkable European mannequins modelling haute couture hung proudly on the wall and a glass-topped cabinet protected some fine needlework and a pair of enormous cotton bloomers, beautifully made. A table for hand stitching was placed in the window light and on it a frothy coral silk chiffon gown was spread, some unfinished, precise and delicate beading creeping across its skirt.

A grey curtain cordoned off the area under the stairs, forming a change room. Opposite, a wardrobe-sized, gilt-edged mirror leaned against the wall. A dress hung limply on a plain hanger between a nude Stockman and a sewing machine. The colour was ordinary, the judge decided, and even though there were yards and yards of the stuff all in one garment, it looked very plain. It was not appealing at all.

Tilly Dunnage and her assistant appeared, showed the judge to the change room and left him to change into the plain, lifeless dress. He stripped down to his girdle and stockings and carefully hung his suit on the hanger provided. Next, he installed his rubber breasts in his brassiere and slipped the gown over his head, wriggling until it fell about him like a perfectly fitted sleeve. He fastened the pearl buttons at the side, slipped into the heels provided and stood back to look at herself. The dress was high-necked, waistless, with elbow-length sleeves, and was very sea-coloured. Yet it was luxurious. It really did fit very nicely. She sensed the tense silence in the salon, but turned again, just once more to look, and drew back the curtain to see herself from across the room, her reflection looking back. She looked as beautiful as she felt.

Esmeralda walked towards herself, the hem kicking out. The discreet pleat that fell from navel level burst open, and little surprises of sun-spray pleats the colour of sky frothed like small white caps on busy little waves. She was a choppy shore of azure satin, and scattered all over her ocean-coloured gown were sea horses, brocaded in rainbow colours, and tiny explosions of swimming sea creatures. Esmeralda stopped and saw that the fitted bodice was insouciantly interrupted by the inverted pleat, which piqued the eye's curiosity and drew it down to the seabed, where seaweed swayed around the hem. She twirled and the pleat danced out like turbulent sea. Delightful, playful but respectful, cheeky but sublimely so. Elizabeth handed Esmeralda a cap, which gave a nod to the American sailors' caps floating around the city from time to time, though this one was pert and sophisticated.

A voice from the kitchen asked, 'May I come in?'

'Please!' cried Esmeralda, and the sergeant arrived with a tray of champagne.

'Elizabeth will now introduce her dress,' Tilly said, and Elizabeth took her place beside the mirror, a deep blush washing over her throat. 'It's meant to be the sea.'

'I can see!' said Esmeralda, gleefully.

'The pleat?' said the sergeant.

Elizabeth explained that it was under the waves.

Esmeralda nodded but Elizabeth had been stalled by nerves, so Tilly expanded. 'The pleat is meant to evoke the rougher sea, the waves, and the hidden surprises beneath the surface. So, when you start to walk and the gown is disturbed there's a tiny tsunami. When you dance it's a sea storm.'

'It's incredible,' the sergeant said.

Esmeralda said, 'I have never been so happy. I never imagined I'd wear couture, let alone couture that is art and metaphor. My dear, you are marvellous.'

Elizabeth smiled. 'Tilly did most of it.'

'We went to the beach,' Barney said.

Elizabeth explained, 'My fiancé and I took Barney to St Kilda pier and when I came home I did some drawings.'

From there Tilly had articulated the vision and translated it into words.

'Well,' announced the sergeant. 'If you make me anything, just don't go to the zoo beforehand, will you?'

The judge sat down in his new dress. 'I want a complete wardrobe, all the basics. The garments must fit the essence of the real me, my true self.'

'What is the name of your true self?'

'Esmeralda.'

'Esmeralda, what is your basic day?'

The judge crossed his knees, watching the fabric tumble about his ankles. 'Initially, I want a morning costume, some general daywear.'

'That depends on what you do with your day –'

'Obviously not much outside of Esmeralda's home. But I would like a luncheon ensemble and some blouses and slacks for the evening.'

'Afternoon wear, a little black dress?'

'Cocktail, definitely. And I want two evening gowns.'

'Two?'

'All right, three . . . there are seven days in a week, after all. But they must match my evening chignon so I will show you my collection of wigs.'

'That will help.'

'Right. That's settled.'

Tilly ripped her measuring tape from her neck and flicked it like a whip. 'I'll wrap your dress for transport.'

Astonishingly, the judge said he would wear it home.

'Beware,' she said, 'the welfare officer might be watching.'

The judge sighed. 'If I see him I'll say that I will telephone the police and report him for lingering at a public toilet.'

Esmeralda went straight to the Hippocampus Club. It was classical night and Esmeralda chose to watch the string quartet from a stool at the bar. Every other patron, snuggled into their wooden kitchen chair or club chair, chaise longue or couch to enjoy Shostakovich, had to look past her to the stage, and if anyone wanted anything from Elmer, they had to stand next to her. On one occasion, between movements, someone gestured for an ashtray and Esmeralda said, 'Let me!' She stood up, smoothed her gown, grabbed the ashtray from Elmer and turned rather extravagantly so that the discreet pleat burst and the sky-coloured sun-sprays frothed. She grandly walked the long way past the stage and around the outside of the room to deliver the ashtray, her brocade seahorses and rainbow-coloured creatures swimming. She placed the ashtray on the table, turned and twirled twice, and skipped back to her stool, where she twirled again before sitting down and crossing her legs so that little white-capped surprises danced on choppy waves and the green grassy hem swayed.

*

The phone woke everyone very early in the morning, but stopped when no one answered. It was still dark outside, so Tilly drifted back to sleep. When the phone cut the air again she went downstairs. It was someone from the Hippocampus Club needing an appointment. The phone rang again. And again. It was very difficult to get Joe dressed and fed, and her thoughts went to Clare.

Joe's joy at launching empty cotton reels down the stairs was interrupted by Sergeant Farrat who emerged from the bathroom, put his palm to his forehead and said, 'Joel, dear. It is far too early.'

The sergeant said he'd need a cup of hot water before he could go near an appointment book so Tilly removed the handpiece from its cradle and left it upturned, smiling and beeping, on the telephone table.

'We haven't even opened up yet and we've got five enquiries for couture. I will not make clothing that worships at the altar of fashion.'

The sergeant used his policeman's voice. 'You can be picky when you can afford to be picky. At least they're not enquiries from Lois Pickett or Gertrude Pratt.'

Gertrude Pratt, wild-haired and glassy-eyed, her floral buttonthrough gaping to reveal her brassiere and its side zipper held with safety pins, showed up at the Toorak CWA hostel at dinnertime. She pulled out a chair and sat down. 'Hello. Long time no see.'

Around them, the diners stared.

'Not long enough,' Marigold said.

Beula said, 'Mrs Wrench always sits there.'

'Not *always*,' Gertrude said. 'Mrs Wrench isn't here now, is she? Anyway, she can sit next to Marigold.'

Marigold said that Mrs McNickle always sat next to her.

'She's not here either.' Gertrude flicked her napkin and lay it across her grubby lap, pushing her wiry hair out of her face. 'What did you pick, the beef or the omelette?'

'She's not with us,' Beula said and asked the waitress for the omelette. 'Charge it to room seven.'

'Seven?' said Gertrude. 'Good to know,' and Marigold knew she would haunt them now, follow them wherever they went.

Gertrude looked at Marigold's lovely frock. 'You've been to Tilly, I see.'

It wasn't a Tilly Dunnage dress at all; it was a plain sundress from Foy's. 'She was very pleased to see us,' Marigold lied.

'Most obliging,' Beula chimed.

'But you missed her coronation parade completely,' Marigold continued. 'It was wonderful, wasn't it, Beula?'

'Wonderful.'

'We have several dresses on order, don't we, Beula?'

Beula nodded. 'Several.'

'Well, I'll get something for the Dungatar Coronation Ball.'

Marigold beamed. 'Yes, I heard there is to be a ball.'

'Invitation only,' Gertrude lied.

'My invitation's most likely gone to the rest home at Winyerp,' Marigold said, brushing something from her skirt.

'There's no hall for a ball,' said Beula.

'William's building one.'

'Are they rehearsing for the eisteddfod again?'

'*King Lear*,' said Gertrude. 'But they argued so rehearsals were suspended, last I heard.'

'We'll take you to Salon Mystique first thing,' Marigold said, pleasantly.

Later, Beula was sitting on her bed watching the vague shape of Marigold who was preening in front of the mirror, all pretty in her newest Buckley & Nunn dress, her suitcase full of lovely frocks from Myer and Miss Brown at the Block Arcade and Nathan's and Curtis's and Salon Mystique. What she really wanted was at least one frock from Tilly Dunnage, and she absolutely needed something for the hearing regarding her financial administration, and it was only a matter of time before the cheques she'd left all over town started bouncing.

Though Beula didn't care for pretty dresses, she was disturbed that everyone else was getting what they wanted while she remained bereft of everything. 'Tilly Dunnage is treating you very badly, Marigold.'

'I don't care, I'll have my money soon.'

'Her baby is the only grandchild you'll ever have. If it wasn't for us she wouldn't have her son, yet you don't have yours because of her.'

'Which is why she'll have to make me that black dress.' She put her finger to her chin. 'Or perhaps I prefer the one with the fuchsia trim?'

'There were two people involved that day in the school-yard . . . your son died. You would have had real grandchildren by now, someone of your own to care for you. She's not going to care for you.'

'As I said, soon I'll have money and someone who will look after it and deposit it into my cheque account whenever I ask.'

Beula moved up the bed, closer to Marigold. 'We remain homeless because of her. And she said she was going back to Dungatar to burn it down, again.'

Marigold's vague shape leaned back from her, but Beula knew her words were seeping into Marigold's small impressionable thoughts. 'All we've ever known is suffering.' She sniffed and Marigold started going through her bag, searching for her tonic. Beula handed her the small brown bottle.

*

Gertrude was a little unsettled by the city noises – trams rattling and dinging, vehicles roaring past, and people! So many people. They wandered all over the footpath. 'Keep left!' she snapped to a wandering window shopper. The three women stopped outside Salon Mystique and Marigold said, 'Goodbye, Gertrude, we don't need to see Tilly Dunnage again, we have enough dresses.'

'Well, I want to see her,' Gertrude said, 'even if she did tell you she's going to burn the town down. I doubt she will, she'd know perfectly well we'd hang her from the water tower by her toes.'

Marigold shifted nervously. 'We need to go to the Myer ladies' lounge, don't we, Beula?'

'We do, I'm busting,' Beula said, and grabbed her pubic bone.

They fled down the Collins Street hill towards the ladies' rest rooms and Gertrude stepped into the salon. There was no one there, just a serene receptionist, very lovely, her dress perfect. Gertrude forwent any formalities. 'Have the prices of your frocks gone up because you're paying the seamstresses their award rates?'

Clare smiled tightly. 'A new Salon Mystique dress costs what it's worth.'

'Did Tilly make your dress?'

'She did, it's from the last collection.'

'Can you tell her Trudy Beaumont is here to see her, please. We're old friends.'

'She's not here.'

'We're friends,' Gertrude insisted. 'We went to school together.'

Clare looked at the frump before her, large and soft and misshapen around the midriff, and couldn't think of a single seamstress skilled enough to take her on. 'I'm sorry, the seam-stresses are on . . . are unavailable today.'

'I'll make an appointment for my old friend, Tilly. When will she be in?'

'Well, you might as well go back to the country and we'll write to you when she comes back.'

'How did you know I was from the country?'

The receptionist said nothing, just stood there, open-mouthed, looking at Gertrude's dry hair, her sunspots, freckled hands and badly fitting frock. 'Dust,' she said, finally. 'The dust on your shoes.'

Gertrude looked down. Her shoes were not dusty. She was conscious of her broken zipper, her flouncy coat from Winyerp and her Itheca haircut, as well as the effect on her midriff of the lack of fresh vegetables and salads.

'I'll see whoever you've got. As soon as possible. Please.'

'As I said, they've taken leave.'

Outside, Gertrude sighed. 'You will be Lady Macbeth again, or Gondril or whatever she's called. You will win best actress.' She headed for Myer.

At that moment, Gertrude Pratt was dangerously close to Tilly Dunnage. Half a block away.

'Some people call it swindlers lane, but Flinders Lane was very generous to me,' Tilly explained. 'I started out making what I was told to make for a manufacturer who bought fabric and designed, made and sold to retailers. Some manufacturers simply bought material and got someone else to design and make the garments and then they sold them but I wanted to design and make. We even had a house model, not just a Stockman or a girl off the factory floor. It used to be very exciting when the season shows were looming and the buyers from all over the country were here.'

Elizabeth pushed her messy hair away from her blue eyes, seeing the lane for what it was.

'This is a paradise of skilled seamstresses, talented bead workers and embroiderers. Mind you, there are some girls who've been happily making pockets and sleeves since they started.'

Elizabeth followed Tilly into the lane, and Tilly talked, a

woman remembering her happiest time. 'There are rodents in the walls and floors, the lifts can kill you, and the toilets are pretty grim in some places. But I worked with the best people and the best silks from Asia, corduroys from Czechoslovakia and cones of wool so soft they floated. You can find a supplier for anything here, furs, accessories, even models – any kind of button, lace, elastic and all types of haberdashery, and the most exclusive fabrics from anywhere on the planet.'

She stepped into a building where a man was leaning on a tall crude bench. He looked up from his newspaper and pointed to the tenants' directory on the wall. Then his face changed and he said, 'I'll be a monkey's uncle, if it isn't young Tilly.'

She shook his hand. 'Hello, Sid.'

He just kept looking at her. 'Well, I'll be a monkey's uncle.'

'This is my friend, Elizabeth.'

'Delighted to meet you, Elizabeth.'

'You too.'

'Tilly from the country. I remember, you made dresses for Mr Belman.'

'And bought most of the fabric from Mr Zeimer. Is he still here?'

Sid shook his head. 'They've all gone now, but Zelma's here. You go on up, she'll talk to you.'

Mr Zeimer's daughter, Zelma, was a diminutive, misshaped young woman who wheeled between the fabric bolts, tree trunk–sized and stacked ceiling-high, by turning a bicycle pedal attached to a chain that propelled her chair. Tilly remembered Zelma as a tiny, misshaped figure coddled in a deeply padded bassinette. She was like a crumbled cupcake, dressed in pink, her thin white hair tied in a topknot. Like her father, Zelma would have rare, luxurious and exotic fabric hidden and she would know how many yards of each she had. And like her father, Zelma knew to sell it only to those who knew best how to use it. Elizabeth had spied a bolt of doupioni on a bench and was running her fingertips gently across its edge.

'Some individual's going to get a special dress,' Zelma said. 'But I sell mostly to the opera and theatres these days, depending on the costumier, of course.'

She looked at Elizabeth, then Tilly. 'What did you say your name was?'

'Myrtle Dunnage, or Tilly. I used to buy fabrics for Mr Belman, but that was way back in 1930.'

Zelma rotated to face her. 'You went to Europe.'

'Yes.'

'What are you after?'

'I'm starting a small business, couture and casual wear.'

'Most salons are shut today. Outworkers are upset, every seamstress downed tools, meetings in every salon up Collins Street, I'm told.'

'Good to hear,' said Elizabeth, and Zelma wound her way to her desk. 'Nowadays people go for synthetics.'

'We're just starting our business, so I'm not after your best merchandise, yet. But I'll come back when we're on our feet and –' She blushed crimson when she looked down at Zelma's feet, tucked away and not functional.

Zelma laughed. 'Put your foot in it then, didn't you?' She turned her handle and faced her vast storeroom, the stacked blocks and rolls of treasure diminishing her fragile presence even more, and yelled, 'FRANK!'

Up in the rafters, someone said, 'Righto.'

'Frank will show you around,' Zelma said.

Elizabeth and Tilly jumped with fright as Frank, in a harness attached to the rafters, dropped from a great height, his hat jaunty and his moustache exuberant.

'After anything in particular?'

'I'm not sure, but I'd like to see what's possible.'

'Anything is possible,' Zelma said.

Forty-five minutes later, they left Frank hanging from the rafters in his rock-climbing harness, rewinding and reorganising bolts, dusting the eaves and killing a few rats. They followed the smell of roasting nuts and fried fish to the Manchester House Noshery.

'The coffee's good and the food's delicious.' Tilly pointed into the noisy cafe. 'European.'

Elizabeth looked confused by the food in front of her.

'Frankfurters and sauerkraut?' Tilly offered. 'Matzo ball soup?'

Elizabeth chose a cheese bagel.

They settled with their food and packages from Zeimer's and Elizabeth said, 'That mate of yours, Arlen, what's he hiding?'

Tilly shrugged. 'I've never found out.'

'He says you met at the convent. You lived close to each other when you left the convent, you were good friends.'

'We were,' Tilly said, putting down her knife and fork. She looked Elizabeth dead in the eye and said, 'It was a long time ago. We were kids, all we had was each other, and that stands for something. It's got to do with loyalty, friendship and shared adversity. He is no threat to anyone.' She picked up her cutlery.

'He's in love with you.'

'I don't think he's in love with me, Elizabeth, I think he's pleased that I'm back in his life. Now that you bring it up, I have to say that I'm quite pleased he's around. Nothing more.'

Elizabeth sat back, her expression sad. 'You're free to do as you choose now.'

'I am, and I choose to be free.' They turned their conversation to the future, but it was as if Teddy McSwiney was there again, watching from the table in the corner by the counter.

# Chapter 25

Miss Peachy noted that the welfare officer was back the next evening. He was in his car watching, and when Arlen O'Connor arrived for dinner, he started his car and drove away.

Arlen sat Joe on his knee and they read *Little Red Riding Hood* while Tilly basted the roast lamb and turned the vegetables. Julie and the sergeant joined them for dinner, Julie wearing a very pretty floral Alice band the sergeant had made for her. The flowers were raw silk and velvet with sprigs of dried Golden Guinea and the sergeant wore a caftan-inspired shift with polka-dot trims. Joe sat in his high chair chewing on a rib bone while they talked about the Korean War and *Captain Thunderbolt*, a film made but unseen because the protagonist's wife was Aboriginal. After orange cake, Arlen washed and dried the dishes, the sergeant and Julie ascended to their boudoir and closed the door, and Tilly put Joe to sleep. Then she sat with her friend at the kitchen table, drinking wine and smoking, the occasional silence between them easy and familiar. Tilly explained what she had in mind for her new venture, animated and exuberant, she stood and strode through the rooms in her sailor pants and tartan slippers describing how the dressing room would work, where the machines would sit, the cutting table, the Stockmans . . . 'And,' she cried, 'we have appointments already!'

'It looks like it will all come right for you,' he said.

'As it has for you.'

She plopped down next to him and picked up her wine, and

found herself staring at him, again. She decided that Arlen was the same, yet also different. 'You were always handsome, Arlen, but now you're almost dignified.'

'Comes with the job and the university education.'

'It's attractive.'

She reached into her shirt pocket for her tobacco and rolled a smoke of her own. Arlen went to the radio and found a station playing music – a swing band, Artie Shaw – and she recalled he'd taught her how to dance. They were quite good in the end, but Arlen a natural, Tilly just an enthusiast.

'Do you still go dancing?'

He came back to the table and poured them both more wine. 'Depending on my mood I'll go to the Palais, or a jazz club.'

'Who with?'

'A friend, Melanie. Her husband can't dance.' His tone was friendly but he was starting to feel interrogated.

'Have you got a girlfriend?'

'I wouldn't call them girlfriends.'

She leaned over and ground the cigarette stub into the ashtray. 'Do you break hearts?'

Then he was amused. 'The girls who pick me do so because I won't go anywhere near their heart.'

'And do you like Nita?'

He leaned back on his chair and clasped his hands behind his head, grinning at her. 'She's a wonderful girl, a stunner, but hard work, I'd imagine.'

She was about to ask him where he was headed in such a hurry the evening they had drinks at Hotel Australia, but he said, 'So? How was Europe?'

'Europe was where the fashion was. It was my future and I went and claimed it.' Tilly realised how her questions sounded, but she felt she had a right to pry. 'Why didn't you come?'

'I sat for the scholarship, I got it, and I wrote and told you.'

'And I never got the letter.'

'And that was bad luck.' He reached into his inside coat pocket and dropped a fat envelope in front of her. 'Have this instead.'

She opened the envelope, looked at the notes and was shocked. 'That's too much. Are you sure this is all mine? I mean, this includes the interest, does it, you're not giving me your entire life savings?'

'Your forty pounds got me set up for university, and that's the truth of it.'

'And look at us now.'

'We've come a long way, Dunnybum.'

She laughed. 'Haven't heard that for a long time.' There were other names – 'Poohead', 'Dungface', 'Dunnycan' or just plain 'Dunny', but Arlen had put a stop to the names the day he repelled the convent bully, a girl who resembled a silverback ape. Arlen was just the boy who came with the truck to pick up and deliver laundry, but one day he confronted the ape, saying, 'Her name is Tilly.'

'She's a murderer.'

But Arlen knew Tilly only as a terrified girl, her face red from the hot washing machines, who kept saying, 'I didn't mean it.'

He told the bully that since Myrtle was a murderer it'd be wise to call her what she wanted to be called, and then he made her say a hundred times, 'Myrtle's name is Tilly.'

He befriended Tilly, visiting her of a Saturday. Arlen, she sensed, was also from a fractured place, and he was her first ever real friendship – as was she for him – so she hated him for abandoning her. But here he was again, helping her fight the bullies and sitting at the kitchen table as they had when he was eighteen and she was fourteen, poor and hungry, but surviving.

She was about to broach the subject of Nita again when Joe appeared in the doorway, his bear in his arms. He was wearing Tilly's half-slip, the elastic waist pulled up under his arms, and a string of Sergeant Farrat's beads hung down as far as his pretty pink socks.

'You look very smart, Joe,' was all Tilly could manage.

Arlen said he might take him to the footy when he was a bit older. 'I don't mind what people wear but there's a world out there that does.'

'He'll grow up and be who he's going to be, just like Barney.'

'Or Sergeant Farrat.'

'Everyone has a secret.'

'I always wanted to know,' Arlen asked, 'did you murder your brother?'

'Oh, for God's sake, Arlen, I was ten years old!'

'I'm serious, I want to know.'

'Look . . . it was an accidental thing, a case of me or him, and I took a step that meant it was him. But what you really want to know is what happened to Teddy.'

'And also what happened in Europe to drive you home, and what did they do to your mother?'

'We'll explain everything one day.' She gathered Joe in her arms and stood to take him back to bed. 'There's a lot to explain and it's all painful.'

When he turned at the gate to wave goodnight, she was standing in the doorway with Joe on her hip. It occurred to him that he'd always loved her. And in the past few weeks she'd relaxed around him, was more like the friend he'd shared the Shorts' wood shed with.

To William's ears, the wind thrumming through the gaps left for doors and windows in the new walls was music. The hall, the school and most of the houses were being plastered, but the unhappy cast rehearsing Act 1, Scene 1, found the noise just plain narking and an argument began. Goneril (Faith) and

Regan (Purl) argued over line 300, 'He hath ever but slenderly known himself.'

'You're having a go at me, aren't you? You think I'm fat.'

'No,' said Regan, 'I'm speaking about our father, King Lear.'

'But you're really thinking about *me* when you say it. I am not silly, I am a performer. I know about method acting.' Faith put her hand to her ample breast and assumed a hurt posture.

'You won't be performing at the ball. Elsbeth says we'll use the wireless. Can't say I blame her.'

Faith's method-acting pose broke. 'Now you're being a bitch.'

Edmund (Reginald) and Edgar (Fred) came towards them over the brand-new floor, drawing their swords to rise in defence of their mistress and wife respectively.

William asked that they go outside to fight – he could take the opportunity to get the skirting boards in – so they relocated to the parched grass beneath the withered garden trees.

Fred waved his sword. 'You're on my land now, this is where the pub stood.'

'Not quite,' said Reginald, 'it's too close to the general store.'

'I'm the legitimate prince and I declare that you stole a foot of our kingdom.'

Opposite, Lear, the Dukes of Burgundy and Albany, Oswald, the Fool, a couple of ladies, and some flagbearers and courtesans advanced like the British Forces.

Their enemies on the other side of the road stilled.

'Actually,' said William, pausing, 'you've had an extra foot of land all these years, Fred, according to the survey map.' He pointed to the map, ending the matter.

Alvin Pratt said, 'That means I've been paying too much for my rates.'

Septimus said there was a slight crest in the centre of Alvin's land, 'Which means you've probably got an overall greater area of surface, so you've probably been charged accurately . . .'

Lois pointed at The Hill. 'Molly Dunnage should have paid top rates for her extra surface.'

The cast of *King Lear* looked around to see if there were any more slight inclines on the terrain.

William suggested that they should all pay the same rates since they were essentially all living on a hill, because the earth was round.

Septimus threw down his hard hat. 'The earth is flat! There are mountains on it and deep oceans but it is flat in that it is not round.' He put his hard hat back on and everyone let the conversation lapse because Septimus, as a baby, had been dropped on his head by his father, who was unusually tall.

'You're a fewdle lawd, William, you should relinquish the map, I don't fink you should be in charge of allocatin' land.'

'Lois, I am not a feudal lord, I'm just here to prod things along. We're nearly finished building a whole town! Why are you all picking on me?'

''Cos Molly Dunnage isn't here anymore.'

Scotty Pullit cried, 'STOP IT,' raising his arms like a referee, his sword slicing off the tip of William's long, straight Beaumont nose.

'See,' said Mrs Almanac, standing up out of her wheelchair, 'we need medical rooms first and foremost!'

# Chapter 26

On Sunday, Tilly sat with Joe at Mae's kitchen table, going through the farm animals in a picture book for the third time in a row, Joe repeating everything she said before turning back to the start. 'More?'

Mae thumped away at her ironing and Edward sat by the stove with his feet on the woodbox. She was wondering how to approach the subject of Arlen when Mae said, 'Where's your diamond?'

'I gave it back.'

'Why? Found someone else?'

She thought it was a joke, and laughed. 'The sergeant will give it to Julie.'

Mae nodded. 'You seem preoccupied by something, or someone.'

'Just thinking about the new business.'

'I guess you'll be heading back to Europe?'

'Just the odd trip to look at collections and buy fabrics, if we make enough money.'

'Catch up with old friends?'

Tilly realised Mae's questions weren't polite chitchat. She gave Mae her full attention, let her know she would be back. 'Elizabeth's proving to be a very good asset to the business – she has a feel for tailoring, though she's not very good with the flyaway fabrics.'

Mae's voice was hard. 'She's like me, hasn't got the patience for anything flighty or insubstantial.'

'Right.' Tilly prepared herself for whatever it was that was coming.

'Likes people to be upfront.'

Edward warned, 'Now. Mae.'

Tilly was a little afraid. 'What's wrong, Mae?'

'Elizabeth tells me you have another young man, that he's given you money.' She dipped her fingers into the bowl of water and flicked at the white cotton shirt she was ironing; some cold drops landed on Tilly.

'I have a friend, yes.' She brushed the drops from her blouse.

'That's not what Elizabeth says.'

'Elizabeth might have quite naturally made some assumptions.' Edward took his feet from the woodbox.

'Joe talks about him.'

'Joe *talks* about him?'

'He pointed at some rat with a gold tooth the other day and said, "Arlen".'

Edward stood up. 'Mae!'

'City boy, is he?' Mae dunked her fingers again and slapped them against the heat of the iron, her fingertips fizzing.

'Yes.' Tilly put her cup and saucer in the sink and when she turned both Edward and Mae were looking at her. 'He's my oldest friend, my first ever real friend.'

Mae put her iron down, the pillowcase in front of her flat, white and hot. 'We would have let our kids play with you when you were all youngsters, but you were trouble – still are – and we had Barney to think of and the welfare ready to swoop like we were dinner and they were starving.'

'I understand that.'

'I know you're going to start a new life –'

'I would never take Joe away from you. Neither Arlen nor I nor anyone will ever take Joe from you. I promise that on the memory of my first ever true love, the second person to show me true friendship, Joe's father.'

Mae got back to her ironing and Edward sat down.

At the door she stopped. 'And if it means anything at all, the best lover I ever had.'

Mae wet her fingers on the water bowl and patted her face and neck and Tilly knew Edward was grinning behind his newspaper.

The sergeant and Julie settled at the kitchen table with their tea and the weekend newspapers, the sergeant mindful of the diamond ring, polished and sparkling in its satin-lined velvet box, waiting in the biscuit tin for the right moment . . . for today Sergeant Farrat was going to tell Julie everything. He was going to start with his childhood as a misfit, his lifelong love of dressing, starting with hats, then his mother's frocks. And then he would tell her that he joined the police force for the colour blue, and because he had enormous respect for a tailored suit – so becoming on him. What was also appealing was the idea of order, being accepted, upholding the law, breaking the law in the safety of plain sight . . . *being* the law.

It would be difficult to communicate to Julie the tragedy of Stewart Pettyman, but not as humiliating as admitting his cowardly need for self-preservation in the face of Evan Pettyman's tyranny. He would start with the lies and secrets surrounding the circumstances of Tilly Dunnage's birth and end at the denoue-ment of the entire saga, the profound tragedy. The sergeant would slowly extrapolate the events leading to the needless death of Teddy McSwiney because of his love for Tilly, the love local society would not bear. He wondered if it was absolutely neces-sary to mention the official report about the Dungatar fire, but then realised it would be cowardly not to tell Julie. More lies and secrets.

He would tell her everything this evening, over dinner.

'I think by the time we get to the flower show it will be ruined by the crowds,' he said, and Julie added that the boggy grass underfoot would be bad for shoes.

'We could go to the Hippocampus Club?'

'No,' she said, turning a page of the newspaper, 'I'll just run into clients. Let's go to the pictures.'

'Oh my! *Roman Holiday*!'

Julie screwed up her face. 'I'd rather like to see *Shane*. It's on at the Capitol.'

'The Capitol's always nice.' The sergeant stood and cleared his throat. 'Julie, my love, I was wondering, if . . . though if you'd rather not, I won't, of course, but I wondered if at some point I might . . . dress for the day.'

'Of course, my dear. You must be who you are. Let's go and pick something out.' They went to the sergeant's room and selected a few frocks and shoes.

'We will look so fine together,' the sergeant said, and they ran down to the salon and the huge gilt-edged mirror. He removed his moire pantaloons and polka-dot shirt.

'I like the blue crepe,' Julie said and the sergeant held it up against himself.

'We'd both be wearing blue.'

'I don't mind,' Julie said, and it was at this point that the welfare officer strolled in and dropped his hat on the kitchen table. 'I let myself in the back gate.'

Sergeant Farrat almost threw the dress aside but remembered he was wearing a girdle so vanished behind the change-room curtain.

The welfare officer strolled around the workshop. He sniffed some feathers, poked his finger into a bead tin and raised his eyebrows at the semi-naked Stockman. He stopped at the sergeant's pile of frocks and held one up. It was a large brown satin slip with an embroidered lace overdress. The belt was gold.

'That's mine,' Julie said. 'I'm having it altered.'

'You're lying.'

Julie blushed deep red, tears filling her eyes.

The welfare officer put his face up close to hers. 'And you, cobbler, don't think I don't know what type most of your customers are.'

'Leave her out of this, she's an innocent bystander.' The sergeant stepped from behind the curtain, wearing his pantaloons and a white dustcoat which was way too small. He stepped in front of Julie, shielding her. 'What do you want?'

'I know all about you, Farrat. You're a pervert, a homosexual. You'll go to jail for what you get up to. I know that you're a police impersonator and I know the reason you were thrown out of the force.'

Julie gasped. She was under the impression Horatio had honourably retired from the police force. She turned away, holding the bench for support, and found herself gazing down into the biscuit tin at a velvet-covered ring case.

'It's not like it sounds,' the sergeant said, but Julie was staring at the small velvet box.

'And, Farrat, I know all about your so-called wife, but really she's your accomplice: Miss Myrtle Dunnage, murderess.'

Julie shut the biscuit tin. 'Murderess?'

He turned to Julie. 'I was going to tell you everything but I just didn't want to . . .' He could not speak; he couldn't say he didn't want to lose her in front of the welfare officer.

Julie would not meet his eyes. She wondered about the velvet ring case and if she had narrowly missed an enormous deceit.

'You're married, yet you've seduced this accomplice, this woman here – that is, if she is a woman.'

The shop door burst open and Tilly came rushing in with her bicycle, Joe in the baby seat. 'Julie!' she cried. 'How nice to see you.' Then she saw the welfare officer and her smile fell and shoulders slumped. 'Oh.'

She grabbed Joe, who was staring at the officer. 'Wolf.' They'd been reading *Red Riding Hood*.

The welfare officer spat, 'And an innocent child caught up in all of this . . . adultery and masquerading as an enforcer of the law to take the child, God knows what for. And this woman makes you and your sort cheap frocks. I have seen enough. You, "Mrs Farrat", simply spread evil wherever you go. You will lose that child.' He stepped into the change room and took a photograph of the blue crepe dress.

Tilly grabbed Julie's arm. 'It's nothing like he says it is, truly, he's not speaking the truth.'

Julie gently removed her arm from Tilly's grip and looked at Sergeant Farrat. 'You know I don't like secrets.'

'Please, I'll explain, I was going to tell you tonight, please, I love you, truly I do, please stay, let me explain.'

'I love you too, Julie,' Tilly added, wary of the officer. 'You are our dearest friend.'

Julie said, 'I'll just get my things.'

She had been lied to, deceived, played with and fooled, and she felt wretched. She found her coat and put it on and buttoned it all the way to the neck and put her handbag over her arm.

The sergeant watched Julie open the front door, step out into the dark and shut the door lightly behind her. He wanted to run to her, but just then the officer reached for Joe, who recoiled. Tilly reeled back, 'Don't touch my child!'

The officer grinned and circled the room. 'You are making a dress for the actress Miss Nita Orland?'

'Leave now.'

'Let me see the dress.'

'I don't know where it is.'

The sergeant fetched the fuchsia dress and brought it out to the officer. He rested the hook of the hanger on his middle finger and held the dress up, looking at it as someone would a lit chandelier in a black forest. The skirt was pencil line with a striped fuchsia trim and it featured a floral overskirt. The officer became almost human. 'This is what she wants?'

'Yes.'

'There is so little material. How much does a dress like this cost?'

'I won't know that until I know how long it takes to make it perfect,' said Tilly.

The sergeant reached to take the dress from him but the officer snatched it away.

'I will take this dress, and I will give you a little money for it.' He searched for his wallet in his coat pocket.

'It's not finished.' She pulled the overskirt off. 'See? The skirt isn't sewn on properly.'

The welfare officer studied the skirt, and then at the dress. 'I will come back when you have sewn it together properly,' he said, happily, and moved to the front door. 'But I will not tell you exactly when!'

His large frame in the doorway momentarily darkening their vestibule, Tilly closed and locked the door behind him.

'We're ruined,' the sergeant said, sinking into the nearest chair. 'I've completely ruined all of us.'

'We will never be ruined, my friend. We will just go on fighting every battle that comes our way.'

'But what about Julie, she thinks –'

'The truth will out, Sergeant.'

'I know, that's the problem . . .'

'We have Arlen, he will help us.'

'If they are suspicious you'll have to hide, run away with Joe.'

'You're upset, Sergeant. It won't come to that. The welfare officer has no case. He can't prove who owns the dresses in this establishment.'

The sergeant sobbed, 'Oh, my Julie . . .'

'You and Julie are perfect for each other. She loves you, Sergeant, she'll be back.'

Joe looked at the sergeant's tears and reached for him. Tilly relinquished her son and Joe settled into the sergeant's arms.

Tilly phoned Arlen.

Arlen came via the back lane. She watched him as he inspected the gate. He was dressed in Sunday casual clothes, his sports jacket plain and his trousers a subtle striped light wool, slim-legged. On his way to her he paused at Joe's sandpit and picked up the sergeant's silver spoon, brushing it off, then stepped into the kitchen. The sergeant was sitting at the kitchen table with his head in his hands, and Joe was standing at his knees, patting him.

'Thank you for coming,' Tilly said.

Arlen put his hat on Joe's head, opened the cupboard under the sink and found the sergeant's inadequate toolbox. He took a lock from his pocket and fixed it to the back gate, Joe standing at his side, watching and pointing, then repeating, 'Screw, screwdriver, lock.'

He returned to the kitchen table and said, 'He can't prove anything, he's just a bully.'

'But Julie . . .'

'True love conquers all, Sarge.' He stood at the kitchen window and looked out at Miss Peachy's side wall. 'I can see that you're both already unhappy, but I have to tell you that the board has ordered a hearing regarding Marigold's application for a new financial administrator.'

'I don't care about Marigold,' Tilly said.

The sergeant shook his head, saying that she was a danger, as was Beula. 'It's best to give them what they want and send them home.'

Arlen sat back down at the table. 'This is just a hunch, but the hearing might have something to do with the Children's Services

Officer, and Mr Hawker. They'll try to prove she has no capacity to manage her affairs, that is, that she's insane.'

'They would, wouldn't they?'

'Since there's money at stake, I'd say Mr Hawker would have thoroughly researched you, Tilly. I think together they probably know everything about all of us as well.'

The sergeant dissolved again, his face in his hands.

'We'll appeal the guardianship matter, if necessary, and I have a plan. There's that nasty welfare officer lurking, stalking Nita.'

'You know about that?' Tilly asked.

'Nita's explained everything to me, and I'm seeing her later.'

So . . . Nita had captivated her friend. Tilly put her hand on the sergeant's shoulder, feeling a little of his pain.

Arlen sat down next to Sergeant Farrat. 'Write to Julie, explain everything, she'll understand once she knows the truth.'

'She thinks I am a deceitful liar.'

'Take the letter to her and put it in her hand.'

Tilly made them all lunch, though the sergeant had no appetite, then Arlen put locks on all of the doors and windows, and barbed wire along the top of the fences.

Mid-afternoon, Miss Peachy arrived with scones and tea. 'I didn't see that officer arrive, I only saw him leave.'

'He's ruined everything,' said the sergeant.

Arlen said he couldn't stay, and asked for a towel, and while Tilly and Miss Peachy drank tea and ate scones, Arlen hummed, washing up and combing his hair in the bathroom. Then he stood on the back porch and dusted off his jacket before he left to meet Miss Nita Orland. Tilly was sure she could smell cologne.

At the table, the sergeant sniffed and blew his nose.

Miss Peachy sighed. 'Love is like a mutton chop: sometimes cold and sometimes hot.'

\*

For Gertrude, home beckoned; her responsibilities to her life and produce business in Dungatar pulled at her. Those unnatural hags in Dungatar could destroy anything. She could drink no more tea at the Myer cafeteria and was unsettled by the loud city and its multistorey walls; there wasn't enough sunshine and there were no stars at night. She was having little success finding Tilly Dunnage and her suspicions about a conspiracy were being confirmed at every turn. Salon Mystique was part of it now, obviously encouraged by Marigold and Beula. Together, they were denying her a new frock for the Dungatar Ball. She wanted to go home. At least there she could watch William through her shop window. She telephoned Winyerp and asked them to put her through to Windswept Crest. Elsbeth answered and said the mayor was 'unavailable'. Then she denied Gertrude the sound of her daughter's voice, as well. 'Felicity is busy,' she said, and hung up. Gertrude chucked the handset on the desk in front of the CWA receptionist and went shopping.

'The people from Dungatar are dreadful,' said the receptionist.

At Mark Foy's, Gertrude scowled at her reflection. She looked like a floral fridge, but they wouldn't notice in Dungatar. It was a new dress and she would alight the train and march triumphantly down the main street in front of all those sad people who spent their days hammering nails and mending their torn hems and lace trims.

'I could make a dress better than this,' she scoffed.

And the sales assistant replied, 'Well, why don't you?'

'I will.' It occurred to Gertrude that she could buy a sewing machine and never go without pretty dresses again. She'd make one dress for each day of the year. How hard could it be? All she needed was a pattern. Gertrude thought about her shop, sitting there all alone, vulnerable to the pilferers of Dungatar. Her new sign would read:

Gertrude Beaumont,
General Store and Dressmaking,
by appointment

'I want to try that one too,' she said, pointing at a smart brown velvet suit, a fetching pleated slit at the back of the skirt.

'And I'll take the green evening gown with the diamantes, thank you.' It was imperative she look stunning at the Dungatar Coronation Ball, reclaim William as she'd done the first time. And she needed to intimidate all those frumps when they came to her shop asking for Epsom salts or toilet paper. They would be envious; they would need her and her sewing machine. She might even make the *King Lear* costumes. That would irk her bloody awful mother-in-law, the cow.

'As you wish,' said the assistant, thinking the green gown was just the thing for this rude woman to prance about in, looking like a Christmas tree on a windy day. Gertrude left a deposit and organised to collect everything on Saturday, when alterations were complete.

She arrived at dinner wearing her brown velvet suit. The entire CWA dining room turned to stare, and Marigold told her loudly that she looked like a full set of stacked luggage. Gertrude turned pale and felt herself slipping into that detached state where everything was fast and she burned inside, but she reined it in. If she was going to become unhinged again, then she would do so in her own good time, in her own home town. Trudy Beaumont smiled. 'You're wrong. I look lovely, and if my husband was here he would tell me that I look lovely because, unlike your husband, mine would never abuse me, he loves and respects me.'

'His mother doesn't,' Beula snapped.

'You know nothing of love, Beula, and you'll never feel love.'

'I've been loved,' she cried.

'No, you haven't,' said Gertrude, 'you were used by your friend Marigold's husband and cast aside.'

Marigold rolled her eyes. There didn't seem to be anyone in Dungatar who hadn't been approached, insulted or violated by her dead husband.

Gertrude left, skipping dessert, and went straight to Marigold's room.

A lifetime working at Pratts General Store had taught Gertrude much, and so the next morning, when she signed Marigold's name on the cheque torn from Marigold's chequebook to pay her CWA account, she did so with a flourish. She caught a taxi to the city, booked in for one night at the Menzies, signed another cheque to collect her new frocks, then went shopping again. She purchased some makeup and stockings, a nightie and some underwear, a nice vanity set for her dressing table and a new pair of slippers. Then she bought a few pretty things for Felicity Joy and headed for the haberdashery department at Myer, where she purchased a nice Singer sewing machine and overlocker. She gave her address as Windswept Crest, Dungatar, and signed another cheque for the freight. Then she selected dressmaking patterns, thinking in particular of Felicity, Faith, Lois, Miss Dimm, Purl and Muriel. And something big and loose for poor Irma Almanac.

On Sunday, the taxi dropped her at the railway station, where she paid for her ticket home and bought lunch, using her final cheque for some extra cash. Before she found her first-class seat on the train, she purchased every glossy fashion magazine she could find.

# Chapter 27

THE SERGEANT HAD been weeping for days, was disinterested in the new dresses being created in his front room, would not eat, sleep or speak or, alarmingly, bathe. Everything upset him – nice things, ugly things, kindness, sternness – and he could not bear anyone smiling.

Elizabeth and Shirley heard a thin, distant sound, like a sad kitten, from upstairs. They looked at Tilly.

'I've tried – Julie will not answer her telephone nor would she speak to me when I visited her shop. She says I lied to her, too.'

'It's too sad,' Shirley said.

Elizabeth said, 'Try again.'

Julie's shop was in an arcade that ran between Flinders Lane and Collins Street. The shopfront was tiny, and windows either side of the central door were neatly cluttered with belts, shoes, handbags and hats. Inside, Julie sat at her counter, staring off into space, a half-made shoe cradled in the womb of her leather apron. She looked up when the bell clanged. Her hair was not brushed. 'Oh, it's you.'

Arlen said he wanted a new pair of shoes and thrust her a page he'd torn from some fashion magazine.

'You can buy those at Myer,' she said, and handed him back the page.

'I know,' he said, 'but I want a yellow pair.'

'You don't, you're just here because you were sent.'

'That's true, but I will have the shoes, but perhaps in green rather than yellow.'

'That's better.' Julie opened the counter door to her workshop. 'Take off your shoes, please.'

Her cheeks were damp and pruned like fingertips too long in water, and she was weeping the quiet, slow tears of the completely annihilated. 'Stand up, please.'

He stood, and she measured his foot on her pleasantly cold Brannock Device and asked him to stand on some brown paper. She traced his foot, the pencil tickling his soles like small, circumnavigating ants, and studied the heft of his arch. Her sadness was beginning to eke into his happy morning mood when Tilly stepped into the shop.

'This is entrapment,' Julie said, retreating behind her counter.

'I'm sorry, but it's a misunderstanding and you and the sergeant are suffering for no reason.'

Arlen said, 'It *is* a misunderstanding, you need to hear the story.'

'More lies and secrets.'

'Sergeant Farrat doesn't lie.'

'Your marriage is a lie.'

'Theirs is a marriage that is not a matter of the heart,' Arlen said. 'Though it is for love . . . of Joe.'

Sister Patricia had caught them in the laundry once, when he and Tilly were kids. They were just talking, but Sister Patricia said that love was dangerous, that they did not understand matters of the heart. But they did; they understood because of the absence of love, of having once had it from their mothers, and then not. To avoid misunderstandings, Arlen had decided it was best not to let people know what was in his heart, but he'd come to learn over the years that this just led to further misunderstanding.

'I thought he was someone else,' Julie sobbed. Arlen gave her his handkerchief.

'You have not seen all of him yet, and he is sorry for that, but I have a lot to do with the way he was forced to live his life. Can I tell you now, will you listen?'

Arlen moved her work stool closer to her and she perched on its edge, her eyes averted.

Tilly started at the beginning, when her father took advantage of her mother, a sweet, naive girl in an isolated town. Tilly was born, Evan denied them, and they were cast out. Tilly described her childhood, of being teased and bullied for being a bastard, how that had led to the death of Stewart Pettyman.

She was sent to the convent, she explained, where she met Arlen. Sister Maria told her that Molly had abandoned her, and so off Tilly went to Europe, only to learn of Molly's plight, her descent into madness. She spoke of her return to her mother, her intentions to ease her grief, to settle her past.

Here, Arlen moved to look out of the shop window, his distress turned away from Tilly.

The sergeant, feeling responsible and guilty for not caring for Mad Molly better, for not standing by little Myrtle and the truth he knew so well, stepped up, but by doing so he was made vulnerable and, eventually, discharged from the police force.

'Secrets are a weapon,' Tilly said. 'And the sergeant had many secrets. The sergeant and I went to Dungatar because we thought the town would offer us peace and freedom. We found evil. They did not accept me, they used the art and beauty of my dresses against each other and against me, and the outcomes were ruinous, to say the least. I fled, revenge burning in my wake, and again the sergeant helped me. The District Inspector's report stated it was a spark from the burning tip.'

Tilly paused, and Arlen came and lay his hands gently on her shoulders, and continued the story. 'To allow Tilly to have Joe with her, the sergeant again offered to help, and it grieves them both sorely that you, Julie, are a victim of those tragic circumstances.'

'Please accept my apology,' Tilly beseeched. 'The sergeant has not lied, Julie. He just hadn't got around to telling you about the terrible events.'

Julie was rolling Arlen's sodden handkerchief around her thumb, the tears dripping onto her leather apron.

'I should have told you,' Tilly said. 'You should know that the sergeant saved me.'

'But he didn't tell me, and I have been hurt before, very badly.'

'Our lives are meant to be truthful and finally, you have heard the truth. Just think about it, please.'

'I do nothing else but think about it.'

The builders were paused outside Pratts Store. William – a great wad of cotton wool taped to his nose – had been able to get Septimus, Scotty and Alvin to agree on the best trees to plant for the streetscape, the distance between the gutter and the paving, but now they were arguing over the size of the windows on the town hall.

'I am advocating for standard regulations,' he pleaded. 'We don't want some inspector to come along and tell us to start again, do we?'

Someone called, 'Yoo-hoo.'

They all turned to see. It was Gertrude Pratt, picking her way through the tufts of sooty grass towards the bedraggled workers. She was wearing a new dress and shoes, hat and gloves, the flowers on her full skirt moving like lily pads on a choppy pond.

'I've got a trunk and a couple of sewing machines on the railway platform,' she said. 'Someone will need to fetch them for me. Daddy, you could do that, couldn't you?'

Alvin said Elsbeth wouldn't let anyone borrow the bus.

'Hasn't someone got a horse?'

'We used to have one . . .' It had belonged to Edward McSwiney, and he was gone.

'Well, William can drive the tractor, surely?'

Lois threw down her level. 'William's helping us. What is it wif you people that you fink you can just get what you want, whenever you want?'

'The magic word,' William said, captivated by the sight of his wife in her pretty dress.

'What?'

'The magic word, Gert, I mean, Trudy. Please.'

'Please?'

'That's it. I'll get your luggage.' He handed the tape measure to the nearest person. 'You look very pretty, Trudy.'

'No, she doesn't,' said Lois. 'She looks like a hot air balloon.'

Gertrude ignored her, fluttering her eyelashes at her estranged husband. 'I see you're building the hall, William . . . dear?'

'Yes, for Mother's coronation ball.'

He watched her unbolt the shop door, the chains rattling, and then step inside and start bellowing, 'Mutiny! Who lives here now?'

'We do,' said Alvin.

Gertrude was appalled, gobsmacked. 'I'm homeless!'

'You made them homeless,' said Lois. 'You drove them out of their own home. They had to move out there with Elsbef and it was already crowded.'

'We don't want to live there anymore,' said Muriel. 'So we moved back to our shop.'

Gertrude turned to her parents, their cuffs grubby, the feathers in their hats crumpled. 'Well, I couldn't live with Elsbeth either, but I had to live somewhere.'

'You've got nice new clothes,' said Muriel, sadly.

Something gave way in Gertrude and she became the woman she had been three years prior, on the precipice of the premiere performance of the Scottish play at the Winyerp and Itheca Dramatic Society Eisteddfod. Her face contorted and turned puce and she began to burn inside; everything was very fast and she felt like she was watching herself. She started sweating, spitting as she screamed, 'But you've stolen my home from me. And I've lost my daughter as well . . . I hope you develop dysentery and I hope you all get the pox and die of dehydration because the enormous sores all over your body ooze so much and I hope your bits turn shiny black and drop off and I hope you women melt and smell like a hot rotted fishing boat.'

William moved to his estranged wife and spoke softly into her blotchy, sweaty face. 'Come and stay at Windswept Crest, with me and Felicity.'

'NEVER,' screamed Gertrude. 'I will never live with your mother again! It's either her or me, William.'

Gertrude turned and ran towards the creek and William said, 'Blast!'

Gertrude thrashed the living daylights out of a small tree with a branch and lobbed a few clods into the creek and eventually, after a ramble along the creek bank, her emotions were restored. She felt calm as she approached The Hill, kindling in her arms, a pocketful of Mrs Almanac's herbs and Molly Dunnage's hip flask filled with Scotty Pullit's watermelon firewater. She dropped the kindling by the fireplace and sat down, looking around the ruined site. The chimney was intact, the green leafy arms of the vine clinging to it. She would have William build some walls and she'd put her sewing machine and overlocker next to the fireplace. And she would stick the sign to the letterbox at the base of The Hill:

Trudy Beaumont,
Qualified Dressmaker and Costume Maker,
by appointment

She smoothed her new Melbourne dress. It wasn't a Tilly Dunnage original but she looked better than anyone else in the town. The sound of an engine travelled up to her and she saw him coming on his big strong tractor. William did not have their daughter with him, but he had all her luggage and her sewing machines and was in shirtsleeves and braces, his serge work trousers clean and loose on his thin frame – working far too hard, sending him grey at the temples. She thought he looked more handsome than she'd ever seen him. Gertrude took another swig of the flask, reached in and boosted her breasts in her bra.

He looked down at his lovely wife sitting on a hearth near the shell of the burnt wheelchair. 'I'm sorry, Mother won't let me bring Flick on the tractor.'

Gertrude shrugged. 'She's old.'

'Yes, I suppose she can't be blamed.'

'I meant she's *old*, she'll be *dead soon*, then we can do what we like.' She would resume her role as leading actress and director. 'Close your mouth, William, and sit down. You forgot wine glasses, didn't you? We'll just drink from the bottle.'

'Trudy, you can't stay here.'

'I can do whatever I want.'

'It could get cold or windy and what if it rains?'

'It could be worse, I could be out there at Fart Hill with all those stewed prunes. All I need is a table; I'm going to be a seamstress.'

'You have no electric power for your sewing machines.'

'Shit.'

'Let me build you a room, you must have some shelter.' The town didn't need a church, no one was about to get married or christened, and graveside services were both cheaper and quite acceptable, so he would use the timber allocated for that.

'That would help,' she said, and smiled at him. 'What happened to your nose?'

'Oh, it's nothing. If you want anything, Gert, um, Trudy, just ask. Please.'

'I will. But it's quite lovely up here, wonderful view, you can see everything.'

William glanced around for somewhere to sit, then leaned on the chimney. 'Apparently Evan Pettyman put Molly up here so he could watch her.'

'You'd better get home, your mother will see you up here with me and she'll be apoplectic.'

'I don't care.'

'And give Felicity Joy a kiss for me and tell her I have some new dresses for her.'

'I will, though she'd prefer shorts.'

'It's a phase,' she said, and patted the seat beside her. He sat down on the melted sewing machine. 'Our daughter needs me. We should reunite, William.'

He took her hand. 'Oh, Gert, I mean, Trudy. I'd do anything to have you back.'

'Good. Send your mother to Melbourne to her cousin Una and let me move back out to the farm.'

'I'll work something out. You need to be with me and Flick.' He gestured at Dungatar. 'I've built a town!'

'I'm glad you've built the hall, I have a new pretty frock for the ball.'

'Of course you do.' They looked out over pale yellow timber frames, constructed in neat lines across the black, razed nothing-ness to the vast wheat crops, turning golden, and the red roof at Fart Hill. 'Look,' he said. 'I can see Flick.' At the base of the chimney a small figure leaned; above her a thin curl of smoke escaped.

'Felicity Joy,' she said, and they waved.

Later, when it was dark and Felicity Joy was gone, Gertrude allowed William to pleasure her against the chimney. William's marriage was recovered and he knew that with a woman like Gert, or rather *Trudy*, on his arm, he could do anything, possibly even evict his mother from his life.

'It would be better if I had a bed,' Gertrude said, and they looked across to Molly Dunnage's blackened, buckled bedframe. Next time he would bring a few new springs and some wire to mend the holes in the base.

She watched William drive away on his loud tractor and looked up at the great Milky Way, sighed and slept the sleep of a loved woman, confident Elsbeth Beaumont would soon be banished to wait on the railway platform.

She awoke to someone prodding her and opened her eyes to the end of a piece of four-by-two timber. She pushed it away. It appeared again and she saw, from within the sag in the wire base of her bed, William's withered mother staring down at her, the stars in the purple sky around her not quite extinguished.

'I'm told these days you're a dressmaker.'

'I'm having a nightmare about you, aren't I?'

Elsbeth smiled. 'No, you're wide awake.' She drew herself up to her full height. 'I'm holding a coronation ball, it's all planned. We're going to listen to the crowning ceremony on the radio while having drinks and canapés, and we might even dance. If anyone comes to you for a new dress, they'll find themselves homeless.'

'They're already homeless.'

'On that subject, Marigold Pettyman is on her way back. This is her land. She's going to live here, so you have to go.'

'This is Tilly Dunnage's land and she's coming home too, except she's coming to burn the town down again.'

'Rubbish. Tilly Dunnage wouldn't dare come back here – we'd stick a white-hot poker in her armpit and make her apologise as we sawed her head off.'

'If either Tilly or Marigold comes home I'll just have to move out to Fart Hill with my husband and daughter.'

'Over my dead body.'

'If you like.' Gertrude scrambled up and stared her scrawny mother-in-law down, all the while knowing she looked very pretty in her new pink lacy nightie with its pink ribbon trims.

'You're to be gone by sunset.'

'You'd better be gone by the time I count to five.'

Gertrude counted to five. Elsbeth remained, nose to nose, her right hand pointing to Gertrude's suitcase. Gertrude put one foot behind her mother-in-law's ankles and pushed her so that she fell back onto the ground. She nudged her and watched Elsbeth roll down The Hill, her moth-eaten fox fur flapping, ash and grass seeds sticking to her like coconut to a lamington. She came to rest at the base of the burnt-out railway carriage that Mae McSwiney had once used as a dining room.

Out at Fart Hill, Felicity Joy lowered her binoculars. She thought for a minute or two and then went and told her father that his mother lay lifeless at the edge of the tip.

William rescued Elsbeth, who was mute and traumatised, placed her neatly on the cart behind the tractor, and tucked a blanket around her. Then he admonished his wife, 'She's frail, Gertrude, you could have killed her.'

'She started it,' Gertrude said. 'They all hate me, all those people, they're jealous. I know how poor Molly and Tilly Dunnage felt.'

Later, when his mother was safely in bed, still unable to communicate, William joined the breakfast queue, whistling while he waited for eggs and toast in the Fart Hill kitchen.

# Chapter 28

As USUAL, THE welfare officer attended the Princess Theatre to watch *I Am a Camera*, then waited at the stage door until the small crowd departed. She smiled at him, as she always did, and he escorted her to the front door of her St Kilda Road apartment, where she said goodnight and thanked him for his advice on the privileges of marriage and family. On this night, though, when Nita switched on the lights she did not close her curtains. She removed her coat, hat and hair clip, letting her dark hair fall around her shoulders. She smiled her beautiful smile to her own reflection in the black window glass and sat by the window with her cat, sipping a glass of beer – so refreshing after a night projecting her voice to the heavens. It was at this point that Arlen called from her spare bedroom that he had 'many shots' and slipped outside, his camera safely in his pocket.

Nita waited, and about fifteen minutes later, there was a scuffle outside her flat. She was not at all shocked when the policeman informed her that a passing man had phoned and reported a peeping Tom. 'He saw the offender in the light from your window . . . peeping in.'

'Oh,' said Nita, 'that would be the pervert who follows me from the theatre. He's deluded and a menace, says he's some sort of policeman, but no one believes him. Ask the doorman.'

'We'll take care of him, lock him up straight away.'

'That would be most convenient.'

A little later, Arlen telephoned to thank her and to say goodnight.

Given the guardianship appeal was to take place on a Friday, only Gladston was available to attend. As they ate breakfast, Mr Hawker said, 'Here's a chance for you to show your best, son.'

'Always,' said Gladston, for his father had not yet noticed that he always showed his best.

His father turned the page. 'Foregone conclusion, of course . . . once they hear all the evidence.'

Mrs Hawker put more French toast in front of her husband. Gladston dug into his grapefruit.

Tilly opened the sergeant's bedroom curtains, just a little, put a cup of hot water next to him and sat on the end of his bed, Joe on her lap. 'It's the hearing today, Marigold's future will be decided. We have to front up and make her look relatively normal for the magistrate.'

He pulled the sheet over his head, and Tilly said the outing would do him good. She reminded him that she and Arlen had been to see Julie, that Julie understood and that things would be all right.

'Even a mended heart stays a little bit cracked.'

'Depends how well it's mended.'

She left to prepare his breakfast. The ABC News jingle warbled up the stairs, and then the firm, modulated tones of the newsreader. Sergeant Farrat rolled over, opened his eyes and looked into the concerned blue eyes of Joe, who stood very close to his bed, his teddy bear under his arm, his nappy low. 'Good morning, Joe.'

'Dar,' he said, and ran a few garbled words together which his stepfather was able to interpret.

'No, son.' He sipped his hot water. 'I did not wet the bed last night. I'm upset because of something else.'

Joe stayed to listen.

The sergeant stroked the boy's fair curls. 'Son, sometimes life is hard, but you'll get the hang of the potty, most people do.'

A little while later, the sergeant emerged from his room and quietly descended the stairs but only made it as far as the telephone table, where he sat chewing his thumbnail and looking vacantly at the wall opposite. Tilly offered egg on toast but he declined so she suggested he wear his grey suit. 'Would you like me to run you a bath?'

He nodded, and whispered, 'If you like.'


Over at the CWA hostel, Arlen escorted Miss Beula Harridene and Marigold to the taxi, one lady on each arm. He sat Beula and her cane in the front seat.

'Give you a better view,' said Marigold, sliding a little closer to Arlen in the back seat.

The ladies – well, Marigold – took in the sights of the wealthy houses and Toorak Road shops, and when the Yarra River came into sight from the top of the Punt Road hill, Arlen turned to Marigold and asked how she felt.

'A little nervous, thank you.' Her hand went to her rash.

'Once, when I was very young, I got caught stealing a chicken. I was very hungry.'

'Of course you were,' said Beula.

'The owner of the chicken locked me in the chook pen and called the police, but while we waited, I managed to convince him I was putting the chook back.'

'That's got nothing to do with Marigold's money,' Beula pointed out.

'I know that I can walk into that room and say things that will convince the magistrate that you are more than capable of taking care of yourself despite Mr Hawker's evidence. All you do is put yourself in the place of the magistrate and imagine what he wants to see, show it to him, and say what they want to hear. I looked at those coppers when I was a kid and I knew they wanted me to be afraid, a snivelling coward and a thief, so I was. I took an egg out of my pocket and put it on the desk and convinced the police I was actually only stealing an egg. They believed me *and* my fib. So, you might not like what you hear me say today, but I'll just be the man they want to see, I'll be saying what they want to hear. They'll end up believing they're your saviours.'

Beula and Mr and Mrs Horatio Farrat supported the applicant, Marigold Pettyman, as well as Arlen O'Connor, her lawyer, who sat opposite the tribunal members, three stern men in suits – a specialist lawyer, a member of a rural Freemasons Society and the superintendent from the Winyerp Asylum. All were friendly acquaintances of Mrs Pettyman's lawyer and current guardian, Mr Hawker, who was unable to attend but had sent along his son. Mr Hawker had also organised an additional witness, a Children's Services officer, to provide evidence against the applicants.

It was apparent the Children's Services officer was running late.

Gladston Hawker sat alone, relevant documentation sitting boldly on the desk in front of him. It didn't look as if he'd even opened the envelope let alone read what was inside. His father's brief was to discredit the image of the 'strong family unit' and the financial guardianship applicant entirely. Further to this, Myrtle Dunnage, and therefore her friend Arlen O'Connor, were adulterers and conniving opportunists trying to usurp Mr Hawker. Myrtle Dunnage was also a single mother and a criminal. And, the letter Marigold presented stating that she had recovered her sanity was a hoax. Mrs Pettyman was manipulative, dishonest and mentally unstable (she believed she was able to see microorganisms) and therefore did not possess the mental capacity to control her financial affairs.

Fifteen minutes passed. The experts became twitchy and the tension in the hearing room thickened. The magistrate looked at Arlen and directed him with his eyes to the clock. At the twenty-five-minute mark, the experts started to murmur and the specialist lawyer suggested they begin proceedings without the welfare officer.

Up until this point Tilly had seen only Arlen's back. She noted that Arlen, unlike everyone else in the room, did not wear a hat, and so his hair did not feature a circumnavigating dent. She had also pondered his shoulders under the very fine wool of his dark navy suit jacket. Then he stood up. Casual and commanding, he unbuttoned his fine suit. The jacket was single-breasted, only two buttons, designed to wear open, exposing a contrasting pale blue, double-breasted vest. The jacket lapels were slim, notched, and his slender burgundy-coloured tie had almost indiscernible black polka dots. The pocket square, coy in its precise pouch, matched, and though she couldn't see down to his shoes, she imagined his socks were entirely in accordance, and that his shoes were possibly slip-ons. The cuffs of his cream-coloured silk shirt were French clasped with unimposing lapis lazuli cufflinks. Everyone else in the room was dressed in soggy, double-breasted wool.

To present his argument, Arlen O'Connor used a voice that bore no likeness to the young man Tilly had met at the convent, yet it was authentically Arlen. 'Mrs Pettyman has lived a troubled past but has recovered capacity, and whilst she is on parole, pursuant to the *Lunacy Act 1956*, she accepts that she still might require a guardian.'

He paused to make eye contact with each of the expert witnesses, who, like everyone else in the room, were galvanised by the man. Everyone felt he was speaking to them, and only them.

'Mrs Pettyman does not seek to abandon the good counsel and protection of having her financial affairs administered, which shows a great level of insight from this woman.'

He was playing to the paternalistic values in the room, Tilly saw, and was guiding them to the conclusion he wanted them to come to.

'It is nonetheless perverse that a woman with her remorse and heartbreak should be hindered in her recovery by the constant reminder of her deceased husband, which will surely be the case should her affairs continue to be administered through her deceased husband's close acquaintance and confidant, Mr Hawker. Mrs Pettyman, however, does not seek release from the safety and protection of a man who knows what is best for her; on the contrary, m'lord, this widow, this vilomah, accepts that she will be alone, so wants to ensure that she has a guardian who will be readily available as her years advance, preferably without the constant reminders of her dead husband and deceased son.'

The hearing room was silent, and Tilly had to stop herself from applauding, her heart growing a little bigger in her proud breast. The experts blinked and shifted in their chairs and the magistrate became aware that he was gawping.

'Yes, yes . . .' He turned abruptly to Marigold. 'Mrs Pettyman, what do you want?'

'I want my money.'

The magistrate shook his head, disappointed, and looked again to Arlen.

Arlen put his hand lightly between Marigold's shoulders and leaned down to her.

'Will you explain to us, Mrs Pettyman, in your own words, why you should take control of your finances at this time in your life?'

Arlen then stepped away, offering Marigold the spotlight. She looked into his very dark eyes and stood up. The woman before the magistrate was calm, verging on elderly, well dressed and immaculately groomed.

'Mr Hawker was a very good friend of my husband,' she said, pleasantly. 'And he has nurtured our financial affairs successfully and profitably for many, many decades, and I appreciate that. But we are getting older, Mr Hawker and I, and I wish to live my remaining years enjoying some of the benefits of Mr Hawker's diligence, knowing that someone young, fit and healthy can go on overseeing my security and happiness should anything unpleasant occur to either Mr Hawker or myself. The lawyer representing me today, Mr O'Connor, will oversee payment for the building of my new home and set up a fund for me so that a sum enters my account each month, thus ensuring I live as I please, but within my means. And he's young enough to guide me into my dotage and eventually, administer my estate.'

Marigold took a moment and then proceeded, her voice hurt. 'My late husband, Evan Pettyman, had some flaws, as some people do, and I have long known that he is the natural father of Myrtle Dunnage. It has been . . . traumatic, but what it means is that I have a grandchild.' She smiled at Tilly, whose amazement at how this was all unfolding was not easy to disguise.

'I'd like to make my grandson, Joel Edward, the sole bene-ficiary of our estate and, of course, that will occur well after Mr Hawker has retired, or died.'

And in this way, Marigold could maintain contact with Tilly for the many dresses she intended to purchase, leaving nothing to anyone.

'Thank you,' said Marigold, smoothing the back of her skirt with her gloved arm before primly sitting on her hardwood chair.

The superintendent stood, preparing to speak, but was told to sit down. He'd wanted to confirm that he was entirely happy with Marigold's mental health and her proven ability to survive in larger society. This was not entirely true, it was just that his asylum had proved much more peaceful without Marigold and her dangerous friend, Miss Harridene.

The magistrate looked at Gladston. 'Well?'

The applicants and their supporters braced themselves for the evidence against them. They expected Gladston would cite Marigold's insanity, her drug and alcohol abuse, depression, trauma, stress, hysteria. Tilly, Arlen and the sergeant were fearful of anything that Mr Hawker might have dredged up, accusations from their combined pasts . . . for example, geronticide (Molly), siblicide (Stewart), amicicide (Teddy) and arson (Dungatar).

The applicants and supporters went so far as to speculate that Gladston might call Mr and Mrs Short, perhaps a representative from Winyerp Asylum or the nurse Marigold had drugged on the train – or even Elsbeth Beaumont could show up, or Gertrude, or anyone from Dungatar or Salon Mystique.

Instead, Gladston stood and put his thumbs in his waistcoat pockets and considered Tilly's fat file in front of him, and the one beside it – equally fat – on Marigold Pettyman. Then he looked at the ceiling, an unhurried man, handsome in a genteel sort of way, but there was something cagey about him. Tilly felt a tiny quiver of fear, and looked at her sensible shoes. She should have rubbed them once more with the polishing rag but otherwise she had presented as expected, all the while distracting herself from what Mr Hawker's son was about to do with Marigold's future. She just wanted the two plague-scarred gorgons to get their money and fly on their brooms home to Hades.

'I'm sure,' Gladston said, quite suddenly, 'that after the previous testimonies, some of us feel this is all very straight-forward. The reasons presented for changing Mrs Pettyman's arrangements outwardly demonstrate that she has . . . capacity. So, if Mrs Pettyman wants her own money and prefers a new financial administrator she likes and trusts, then I am satisfied with her new nominated arrangements. The applicants' case is valid and sound and it is only right that Mrs Pettyman have someone professional and capable who would guide her and make sure her future years are far better than those to date. Further to that, it is the law.'

Gladston Hawker merely *presented* as quiet and unassuming.

The people in the room looked to Arlen, who was busy buttoning his jacket. The magistrate started packing away his files and the specialist lawyer looked at his watch, moved his eyebrows in the direction of the club and his companions nodded, affirming they could retire for the day. The panel rose, but Gladston stepped forward. 'Just one thing, if you would, gentlemen.' He slid all the necessary papers across the desk and reached into his jacket pocket for a pen.

'It's the end of a busy day after a busy week, after all, and Mrs Pettyman wishes to return home as soon as possible.'

Outside, Tilly and Arlen thanked Gladston and shook his hand. Marigold announced that she'd like to catch the train home Sunday which only left the next day for shopping, so could someone deposit some money in her account within the hour. Gladston signed a blank cheque for her. Beula said, a little too gleefully, 'What you just did could kill your father.'

Gladston replied simply, 'It could,' then turned to Arlen, saying, 'Good job,' and Arlen agreed, 'I'll be in touch.' Gladston said he looked forward to his call, they shook hands and Gladston walked off down Collins Street, a spring in his step. Marigold and Beula, meanwhile, headed for Georges and the three o'clock fashion parades at Myer.

Left standing on a busy city street with Arlen and Sergeant Farrat after such a momentous morning, Tilly was lost for words, but thrilled. She didn't want to thank Arlen, again; she'd been thanking him since she was ten years old. So she smiled up at him, and he grinned back at her. She managed, 'Well, my word . . .' but could say no more because she was fighting the impulse to slide her arms around his waist between the lining of his fine wool jacket and his vest, press her cheek to his silk shirt, and squeeze.

The sergeant coughed, breaking the gaze between them, and they turned to him.

'You go ahead,' Arlen said, 'I'll meet you soon,' and Tilly handed him the car keys. She was looking forward to a glass of wine, perhaps several.

Mr Hawker spent the morning stark naked on his back in the middle of Una Pleasance's bed. These days, it often took Una a little longer to coax him to ecstasy, but on this day, he felt more like his old self, even a little light-headed, though it had taken him quite some time to regain his strength. He bathed, and while Una telephoned for a taxi, Mr Hawker scribbled off a cheque for ten quid. Then he crossed it out and made it for fifteen.

He had the taxi drop him at his club and when his colleagues arrived, smiling, Mr Hawker's heart lurched a little.

'All very straightforward,' said the specialist lawyer, and the superintendent and Freemason agreed.

'A very well-prepared case.'

Mr Hawker ordered a round of drinks and offered the men cigars, which they accepted.

'Yes,' said the lawyer, from beneath the swell of thick, curling smoke, 'all very uncomplicated. We appreciate the case.'

'If there's anything we can ever do for you . . .'

The specialist lawyer affirmed that Gladston was 'a fine boy, very fair and righteous. He'll have an entirely satisfactory career, though possibly not as lucrative as it could be.'

The Freemason added that there was 'always a place for good honest lawyers like him and that O'Connor fellow.'

Mr Hawker was beginning to feel a little unsettled.

The superintendent nodded. 'Quite an impressive chap.'

The Freemason continued, 'And you won't miss the administration of it all either. Woman are so tricky to deal with.' He knocked back his whisky in one.

'I don't have much to do with it all,' Mr Hawker said weakly, 'Gladston sees to all the administration.'

That's when Mr Hawker felt suddenly unwell, as though his digestive system had turned to hot cheese and his heart needed to get out of his chest as fast as it could.

Gladston drove towards home, tapping the steering wheel to a tune in his head (Beethoven's Symphony No. 9). He found his mother sitting in his father's chair, painting her fingernails by the light of her husband's special reading lamp, a glass of sherry beside her.

'Dear,' she said, 'your father's had another turn. He's in the hospital again – just for the weekend, the doctor says.'

'In good hands, then.'

'Yes. You up to anything tonight?'

'Yes, dining with Jeanette.' He retrieved the key to his father's liquor cupboard.

'Did you speak to her about the way she holds her knife?'

Gladston poured himself a large Scotch. 'Yes, she says she only changes her grip when the meat's tough.'

Mrs Hawker blew on her nails. Surely Jeanette wasn't implying the meat Mrs Hawker served was tough?

Arlen parked the sergeant's red Balilla outside Hotel Australia and led poor, sad Julie by the hand through the foyer, her hair still unbrushed but, as always, her shoes wonderful. The sergeant waited with Tilly behind the monstera plant. They looked like a couple from 1943 in their sensible two-piece grey suits, the jackets double-breasted with wide lapels. The sergeant was saved by a crisp white shirt and subtle blue silk tie. His black leather gloves sat on the table beside the ice bucket. Tilly looked like a politician's wife, but then she took her hat off and her hair sprang up and she looked a little more like Tilly. Next to her, Tilly's husband trembled.

Julie appeared, hesitated, but succumbed and came slowly with Arlen to sit at the table. She kept her eyes on her big folded hands in her lap. To the sergeant, she seemed pale and weak, and his heart ached with the burden of fifty years of deception, frustration, longing, loss and distress that had manifested in this person, the one person in his life he was prepared to die for. 'Hello,' he said, and Tilly asked Julie if she'd like a drink.

She shook her head. 'I don't want anything.'

The sergeant gasped. 'Anything?'

She shook her head. 'I'm not thirsty.'

Tilly said, 'We are glad and grateful Arlen was able to persuade you to come, Julie, but Sergeant Farrat is my true friend, one of just a few, and he has been sorely misunderstood and so I thought –'

The sergeant blurted, 'I cannot tell you how sorry I am for even being born. If I could –'

'No,' Julie cried, reaching across Tilly for the sergeant's hand. 'I'm sorry. I'm sorry for little Myrtle and Teddy McSwiney, the hate and hypocrisy of that dreadful town, the intolerance of society towards individualism.'

A waiter arrived, bearing wine and savoury tarts and bite-sized sandwiches, but the sergeant and Julie were reaching for each other across Tilly, Julie saying that she understood, now, and could he ever forgive her?

'I thought I'd lose you. I've never felt like this before.' They clutched each other as if they were drowning, and Tilly removed herself from between them as they continued to apologise. Tilly offered them savouries. They took two each and then another, still holding each other.

Arlen poured wine, they drank, and he refilled their glasses as they ate more savouries and ordered a bowl of hot chips. Tilly and Arlen sat, like parents attending their son's first date, so Arlen said, 'Gosh, is that the time? We'd better get going.'

As he and Tilly stood on the steps to the hotel, she felt awe and a kind of yearning for what the sergeant and Julie had. She felt grounded living with Horatio, anchored by her delightful housemate, and adored the security of family. But she would have to move on now, for his sake. She wondered if Nita had found the same oneness with Arlen and suddenly felt panicked, a little breathless. She was about to lose everything again, except Joe. She must hold on to Joe.

'You want a lift, Tilly?'

'No, thanks. I'm going to Collingwood, I'll catch a tram.'

'I'll drop you.'

'No. You go, I'm sure you have to be somewhere, with someone.'

He turned her to look at him. 'I think the McSwineys need to let you go.'

'They're Joe's family.' And she could even rely on them.

'Yes, but it's also a way of being with him.'

'I suppose.' But she didn't go there to be with Teddy.

He held her hands in his. 'I won't ever let your private thoughts, or your affections, get between you and me. You can have yours, and I'll have mine, I'd just like you to be around, if you will.'

She knew it was some sort of proposal, an offer similar to the one he'd made when she was fourteen, and thought to tell him of her curse, but she was not cursed. 'All right,' she said. She knew little of his last twenty years, except that he'd worked as a truck driver and put himself through university, and found it hard to get a job because he hadn't gone to the right school. She was also reminded that, even though she'd known him better than anyone for almost ten years of her early life, he remained an enigma.

'Are you hungry?'

'Starving,' she said, and they headed down to The Society to eat, her arm looped through his.

They were waiting for their steak and salad when she put down her glass of Cabernet. 'So, Arlen, old friend, under that beautiful suit you're wearing, what are your precious thoughts and affections?'

'You've heard it before; born in Fitzroy, mother shot through, the old man did his best, died when I was twelve, I got a job delivering laundry.' He was always the boy alone on the edge of the gang, he always heard the nuns coming before anyone, knew which nun slept in what cell and what time the fresh fruit arrived of a Monday morning. Someone once told her he slept with his eyes open, but he didn't.

'Do you still sleep facing the door?'

'I have a system for doing life, it works.'

'What do you want, what propels you?'

He thought for a moment. 'Now that you've asked, I am genuinely happy that I have you and Joe in my life.'

Whatever it was that she'd tried not to recognise grew to a warm sense of anticipation. 'I don't want you to have to keep rescuing me.'

He put down his knife and fork and poured more wine for them both. 'You're my girl, Tilly, always were. That's just the way it is for me.'

Wordless for the second time that day, she smiled, raised her glass, feeling wonderful, lovely, pleased and everything else, or perhaps it was the wine, or the suit?

'I'll get your business set up properly, and you and I and Joe will sort something out. I won't be a threat to the McSwineys; the welfare will get tired of us.'

'What about Nita?'

'What about her?'

'You seem to be very friendly with her.'

He smiled. 'She's a good actress.' And he told her why the welfare officer was absent from the hearing.

It wasn't the wine. Something had definitely changed.


Back at Darling Street, in a nest of crumpled sheets and pillows, the sergeant reached across Julie to his suit and took out a small velvet box. He sat up in the bed, looked down at his love, her fine strong arms, her lovely blue eyes and blonde hair and her perfectly defined chin. 'Julie Hunnyman, you are the blood in my veins and the air I breathe. Will you do me the honour of being my permanent true love and friend for eternity?'

Julie said, 'You are all of those things for me too, Horatio, and you give me more pleasure than I've ever known, such excruciating peaks of love that I almost burst. I trust you and believe you, you are my soul mate, and my *sole* mate.' She smiled and offered him her left hand. It didn't fit, so he placed the diamond on her pinky finger and said, 'I'll have it stretched.'

'No, it's better there, it won't scratch the shoe leather.'

She was so clever, his Julie.

# Chapter 29

SOME WEEKS AFTER Tilly Dunnage and her husband set up shop in the old millinery, Miss Peachy, Shirley, Elizabeth, Mae, Barney, Joe, the Supreme Court judge, Edward and Julie assembled to view Tilly's sketches of the first collection. It was all on butcher's paper, fabric samples pinned to the corners and clipped to an artist's easel in the middle of the shopfront room. What most excited those assembled was the sergeant's secret signature piece, his *aperçu*, *l'avant-première*, for the creative arm of the enterprise.

Upstairs, Sergeant Farrat was helping Nita dress, while the others waited for Arlen. At least once a week Arlen would arrive with his briefcase and contracts and questions and over breakfast or lunch or dinner they would discuss living budgets, their mission and financial and non-financial drivers, and sometimes Arlen would stay after hours drinking wine and smoking. One night, Julie had suggested they go dancing. The sergeant had Miss Peachy take a photograph of the four of them and Arlen put his arm around Tilly's shoulder and she leaned in to him. The following week, it was Tilly who suggested they go dancing. It was about moving intuitively and considerately, music and a union of bodies, the strength in Arlen's arms, and Tilly enjoying being guided, and when the tune ended Arlen held her until the next tune started, and they looked at each other and knew what to do.

He sometimes stayed, sleeping on the couch, and in the night when she woke, she was alert to his long body folded there. Over the weeks, agreements were thrashed out, documents signed, insurance paid, powers of attorney established and last will and testament written, witnessed and placed in a safe in Arlen's office and, finally, their business – Molly and Friends – was established. Elizabeth came daily, and sometimes Margaret and occasionally Mary, who was to marry when the baby was born. Though they implored her not to, Miss Peachy provided a solid supply of fresh vegetables and advice on the durability and practicality of 1900 fashions: 'Why don't you put a hem lifter on that coat so it can become a jacket?', 'Serge is always durable, they used it for ride-astride skirts and it always looked well riding or walking.'

Barney and Mae arrived early each day. Barney occupied Joe, and Nita was often there working with the sergeant on his signature piece.

No one had seen the welfare officer for a very long time.

When Arlen finally arrived for the viewing, Mae shot at him, 'We've been waiting for you.'

Mae was often curt, but Arlen accepted it as part of life within this particular community. He dumped his briefcase on the stairs and his hat on a millinery block.

'I'm sorry, Mae,' he said, and Tilly addressed the gathered friends and employees. 'What you will see in my sketches are luxury clothes for ordinary women and girls, prêt à porter, as they say in France. We propose a show twice a year, summer and winter, of good affordable clothes that are elegant and fashionable. The range will be limited so that not every second factory girl or typist in an office or out dancing will be wearing the same dress. We hope, in time, to sell to Myer, Georges and the like.'

To approving nods all around, Tilly pointed to the silk top-stitched mikado dress she'd created.

'We might design uniforms too!' the sergeant cried, coming down the stairs, very excited. 'My ambition is to design for an entire airline.'

Tilly continued, 'I haven't sat with this collection long enough . . . but by the time it's made, I'll feel better. My themes are of work and fashion but often collections don't achieve everything. Form is the design emphasis, and the fabric fits the form and the function, but the motifs – pockets and practicality – could vary more from garment to garment. We'll do that as we go. The motif needs to be rich to give depth to the theme. And texture must complement the motif, the colours must emit the emotion so –'

'Oh, stop it!' cried the sergeant. 'It'll be better than anything Melbourne's ever seen, and generally I think the silhouette looks pleasing – loose yet structured, full yet sleek, lively where appropriate.'

'And now, we will see the sergeant's closing signature piece.'

'Good.' The sergeant took his place before them. 'I will command the creative costume arm of Molly and Friends, so you will not die from being sensible, girls.' He gestured to the stairs.

The mannequin did not appear, and so the sergeant ascended the stairs. After a brief moment he called down, 'We've momentarily lost the egg.'

'An egg?' the judge said. 'I didn't realise breakfast was involved,' and chuckled.

Tilly said she was starting to feel nervous, and Mae declared that the best thing for nerves was vacuuming.

'I think I'll make a drink instead,' Arlen suggested. 'Would anyone like one?'

Arlen prepared many sidecars.

Finally, Nita Orland appeared at the top of the stairs . . . as a bird. Her hair was swept up and sprouted an ebony crest above her beautiful face. She wore black lipstick and kohl rimmed her brown eyes. Her body was covered entirely in feathers, shiny black feathers sweeping down from her neck, along her arms to her black-tipped fingernails and down to her knees, as smooth and close as a raven's breast. The feathery pelt gave way to a mess of black and grey sprays and small nests of busy ostrich feathers that trailed to a wedged tail. But it was the startling shoulder ornaments that captured everyone. Wing mantles at Nita's breasts were the launching place for a fell of brilliantly coloured feathers that crept upwards and over her shoulders, flat like wings at rest. These avian arms grew from tiny feathers, red and green and pink, and as the fell slithered up and dropped over her shoulders, the feathers gradually increased in size and length – crimson, grey, blue, pale pink and green – growing longer and thicker and reaching down to the bird's tail, where the fringe of long primary feathers spiked, shards of vivid colour against the dark floating tail. In one claw rested a luminous ostrich egg, her talons black against the pale shell.

As the startling cockatoo descended, the judge reached for a chair, overcome, and the rest of the small audience stood, applauding until their hands hurt. The glorious creature placed the ostrich egg in the 'Best Costume, Winyerp Drama Association, 1950' cup, and Tilly declared, 'I think that is the most glorious thing I've ever seen.'

Miss Peachy rushed to Horatio and embraced him, her high grey bun under his chin. 'Your mother would have loved this costume!'

Arlen made another round of sidecars.

'The Bird Dress is for Julie,' said the sergeant, reaching for his girlfriend's hand. 'This creation represents the *Ave* family, the avians who have existed for sixty million years, and that is what I hope for my partnerships, my art, my creations and specialised customers. The bird is a perfect metaphor, given they are beautiful, they sing, dance and fly, are free travellers, sharp observers, and they are most often monogamous.' Julie blushed, and the group were silent, in awe of the glory of every perfectly placed plume, quill and feather.

'I can't see you selling many of them, though,' said Mae.

*

Later, as they discussed the logistics of the night, the judge said, 'Look, it's coronation night, a cold June night, and I am not concerned. Let's just go.'

So Miss Peachy, Tilly, Nita, Arlen, Horatio, Julie, Barney, Margaret, Elizabeth and her fiancé, and Mary and her beau happily headed off to the Hippocampus Club for the festivities.

Margaret and Elizabeth McSwiney went as maids of honour and Miss Peachy as Queen Victoria, veiled from head to toe in mourning black. Julie was Queen Elizabeth I, her neck ruffle so broad she had to lift it up at the sides to get through the door, and Nita was Anne Boleyn. The handbag that hung from her shoulder on a pearl necklace was her decapitated head.

Julie said, 'Mummy, was your grandfather really a hatter?'

'Oh, yes,' said Nita. 'A very successful one.'

'That explains why I make shoes, I suppose.'

Tilly looked particularly lovely in a blue silk crepe suit, her waistband sporting covered buttons specially designed by Mainbocher, because Wallis Simpson was meagre and formless. The belt and buttons gave the illusion that she at least had a curve at the waist.

Barney appeared as an American Indian chief, complete with feathered headdress and horse – bareback, naturally. Several scalps hung from his shoulders. When the Sultan of Brunei arrived, Serenity directed him towards Augustus Gaius Octavius, also known as Elmer, who had the drinks lined up along the bar. Next, Prince Eugène of Ligne arrived, then a sheikh from Kuwait. Augustus also welcomed the footmen, a minor bishop and the Queen Mother. Members of the Household Brigade, in red coats and oversized busbies, brought up the rear of Queen Sālote Tupou III of Tonga, who was admonished by the judge, dressed as a corgi, for looking more regally imposing than Princess Elizabeth. An aide-de-camp arrived with a friend dressed as little Prince Charles, in shorts and a school cap, his nanny (carrying a cane) in tow. There were kings and queens of Europe, Kaiser Wilhelm I and Edward VIII. Julius Caesar and Dwight D. Eisenhower spent the evening talking to Nikita Khrushchev and a fellow who explained that he carried a guitar because he was BB King. His friend came as King Freddie of Uganda, and insisted on being called by his full title, Sir Edward Frederick William David Walugembe Mutebi Luwangula Mutesa II.

As per the custom, all clients were reminded that Serenity was a judo black belt, and also of the location of the escape routes. Easiest was to bolt up the stairs to the roof and escape via the attic dormer window, but only if you were prepared to jump across to next door's tree. Given that the doors were reinforced with steel plates and the windows barred, those afraid of heights could use the stage trapdoor and crawl out to the laneway. Feeling safe, the partygoers proceeded to celebrate the Queen's coronation, yet Tilly was reluctant to dance despite the launch of Molly and Friends. She couldn't help but keep one eye on the two most attractive people in the room – Arlen, dressed as Richard III, and Nita, as Anne Boleyn. It was undeniable the two monarchs were flirting, and Tilly finally admitted to herself that she was feeling jealous.

Midway through the party God himself arrived and declared he had descended from heaven to oversee. Richard III took God to task for awarding him a spinal curve.

The judge cross-examined Him for creating, then condemning, homosexuality, cross-dressing and other ambiguities, and questioned why the Bible stipulated that adulterers must be killed. As for virgins who lie about their virginity, must they really be stoned to death? Or, thus, should those who kill deflowered women be excused? And what of victims having to marry their rapists? In the end, God gave up and cried, 'All right, all right! Yes, I should have included a foreword explaining that the story wasn't to be taken literally, but people should consider how out of date the story is. Mind you, it was a bestseller in its day.'

'And,' said the Queen Mother's minor bishop, 'it's very badly written.'

It did not go unnoticed that Tilly Dunnage was somewhat flat when, by all reports, her first collection on paper was very impressive. Was she envious of the sergeant's avian creation? Nita sidled up to her, congratulated her again and declared BB King handsome.

'Not rich enough for you, I fear.'

'No. But he has a guitar.' She put her finger to her cheek, the eyes of the sparkling skull deep and black. 'His hands will make me sing.'

Tilly laughed, and they headed to the bar because BB King was talking to Elmer and Nita needed more champagne.

'So,' Nita asked, ashing her cigarette into her spare head, 'will you speak the other language, the language of costume?'

Tilly curtsied. 'We'd be delighted, Your Majesty.'

'We're doing The Scottish Play.'

Tilly looked crestfallen and Nita said she was joking. 'We're actually doing *The Crucible*. I am playing Elizabeth Proctor, but I know you will make me look warm and good.'

Nita proceeded to flirt with BB King, and then it was time for the coronation.

The sergeant stood importantly in his cream satin, beaded Norman Hartnell lookalike gown, Julie beside him, her pancake white and red curls towering and laced with plastic pearls and gemstones, flowers, stuffed birds and a nest of mice. A footman mentioned that the new monarch looked a little frumpish, so Julie retorted, 'Only because we were aiming for authenticity.'

The royal guests fell quiet and the sergeant began the slow bridal march towards the throne, Elizabeth I behind her, and then came Anne Boleyn, carrying her decapitated head and its cardboard St Edward's Crown. The Archbishop of Canterbury brought up the rear, with his orb and sceptre, and a few bridesmaids.

Elizabeth I looked lovingly at Sergeant Farrat as he took his place on the throne and was crowned Queen Elizabeth II, and as the new Queen set about knighting everyone and handing out chunks of Wales, Ireland and Scotland, the music played and the floor quaked with dancing subjects and royals.

Richard III arrived and asked what the serious discussion was about, and Tilly declared she couldn't really take him seriously after having seen him wearing stockings and pantaloons.

'Whereas you, Wallis Simpson, could make me as happy as Edward VIII by dancing with me,' he said.

Nita turned to BB King and cried, 'And YOU can make me happy.' BB King cast aside his guitar and carried Anne Boleyn to the dance floor.

Tilly Dunnage decided to seize the missing bit of the brilliant future she had launched with help from her friends. As Wallis Simpson, she would completely disarm Arlen, at least for the night. She grabbed him and dragged him to the dance floor, laughing when he lifted and spun her, happy knowing that, back at Mae's, Joe slept in his cot, his grandparents asleep beside him, his young aunts and uncles spread around, and the gates and doors locked and barred.

The police raided 27 Darling Street at 6.30 am. They forced the front door, broke down the locked gate and tumbled over Miss Peachy's fence, trampling her vegetable garden and filling their shoes with Graham's manure. They found a man and a guitar entwined in calico and sequined offcuts on the upturned kitchen table. Miss Nita Orland was curled beside him. Two young chaps slept on some fabric bolts under the workroom table, and upstairs Mary and Elizabeth were asleep in Tilly's bed. All were fully clothed. They could not locate Wallis Simpson or the hunchback in balloon pants, but marched the other lewd offenders to the kitchen, where a wall of uniformed police held them.

Tilly Dunnage woke in the tipi. She was encased in a bedspread, her hip settled in a dent in the sand. Arlen's arm held her, snug as gumnuts, and all around them was the sound of yelling. 'Police, stop, now!'

Miss Peachy was apparently hosing down a young constable standing on her artichoke bush, accusing him of trespassing and, inside, men called and doors slammed.

'Joe,' Arlen said.

They bolted out through the back gate and ran, as fast as they could, to Victoria Street, where Arlen jumped in front of a car, stopping it by waving a five-pound note. He put Tilly in the car, gave the driver the address, and ran towards the tram stop.

Senior Sergeant Cutter, a short-waisted man with skin like bouclé, entered Sergeant Farrat's bedroom with four policemen in tow, all perfectly in step, hands behind their backs. They looked disapprovingly at the large woman and her pale companion clinging to each other against the elaborate, cushioned bedhead. Senior Sergeant Cutter gestured to the wardrobe. A constable stepped forward and opened the door.

Senior Sergeant Cutter selected the gold swing coat, held it as though it was covered in ants. 'This is a very large coat.'

'It's mine,' said Julie.

'Experience in these matters tells me it's more likely to belong to Mr Farrat.'

'Oh? You've experience wearing women's clothing?' It was Arlen, standing at the door in his torn tights and pantaloons.

Senior Sergeant Cutter looked at Arlen with cold hatred. 'We were informed, reliably, that we'd find extra-large women's clothing in this house.'

Julie jumped out of bed in her sixteenth-century petticoat, pushed her shoulders back and stretched to her full height, taking a step towards Senior Sergeant Cutter. 'Who told you that?'

'None of your fucking business. Who are you, anyway?'

'She's Her Majesty Queen Elizabeth the first.' Arlen pointed to his hump. 'Just call me Your Highness.'

'Horatio Farrat's police history and various reports have told us why he was posted to Dungatar. We have witnesses who will testify that he wears women's clothing.'

'Gossip isn't evidence. Even if women's clothing did hang on his line it doesn't mean he wears it, or that he's perverted. You're in a dressmaker's atelier, you can't prove who owns what. You have no case.'

'We'll make one. This coat is too big for a woman.'

And that was when Julie took the coat and put it on. It was a little short but fitted across the shoulders.

The sergeant said, 'My wife, as you will have seen during your surveillance, wears men's coveralls because they are convenient.'

Julie agreed. 'And sometimes I purchase men's work shoes because they fit.'

Senior Sergeant Cutter turned his back on them. 'You can explain everything down at the station.' A constable dragged Sergeant Farrat from his bed and down the stairs by the arm.

'Do not rough-handle that man, he has done nothing wrong!' cried Julie, and Senior Sergeant Cutter squared up to her. She stepped up, placing her bare foot on Cutter's shoe, pressing with the full weight of her magnificence, bearing down on him. There was a faint 'click' as the metal eye of Senior Sergeant Cutter's lace-ups pressed into his flesh and, beneath it, his cuneiform bone. His face did not change but Julie saw in his oyster-grey eyes that she had caused pain. 'That's assault,' he whispered.

'And you have *in*sulted us. Slanderer.'

'You people aren't fit to move in decent society.'

'I'm familiar with men like you. You're corrupt and a bully, that's far from decent.'

'Handcuff her.'

'There's no need,' she said, and allowed herself to be led away, managing to bump a blue minion into the arms of a naked Stockman, triggering another constable to stumble sideways and plop down the stairs. Senior Sergeant Cutter dismissed the remaining police officers, then walked in circles, screaming silently, unable to bear weight on his broken foot.

On her way to the kitchen, Mae checked on Rex and Joe, curled in their cot and fortified by the sleeping relatives around them. She went to the window and looked out to the galah, preening in the new sunny day. The faint roar of kettle-simmering filled the silence. She went to the outhouse, opened the door and found Edward sitting there reading the paper, so she went to the small patch of bare earth in the yard and emptied her bladder.

Joe woke, stood in his cot and took in his surrounds. Rex was sitting up at the other end of the cot, and the window to the world outside showed a weatherboard wall. He could see no lemon gum, which meant that Grandma or Pa, his Uncle Barney or even his mother would come. He could hear them shouting, so he stood with Rex, holding the bars of the cot, watching the door. Then someone he'd never seen before arrived, but he recognised the type, and shrank, though he knew those arms were long.

Mae's panties were still at her ankles when the loud banging started and the house erupted in shouts and crying children. The back gate cracked and pushed open; a blue wall of men marched through the house. By the time she got to the kitchen, the welfare officer's assistant had Joe and was heading out the door. The welfare officer held Rex by the leg, but he clung to Charlotte, screaming. Mae picked up the fire poker and ran at the welfare officer, but was intercepted by the driver, who whacked Mae's forearm with a truncheon. She gasped and bent in pain, mute with agony.

The stranger stopped at the corner and Tilly burst from the car. The welfare officer's car waited, the door open and ready, and a woman headed towards it carrying a child. It was Joe. Tilly ran, screaming. Joe saw her and held out one small, round arm, his face creasing in misery. A policeman emerged from the house and then the cyclopean form of the officer, carrying Rex like he was a log under his arm, and finally Edward, who was attached to the welfare officer's leg and being dragged along the ground. The policeman smashed the truncheon into Edward's head and shoulders, again and again, and Tilly screamed, running as fast as her legs would go, but the car roared away, leaving a plume of blue smoke and Edward, curled on the road. All along the street, women came out in night attire and stood with their hands over their mouths as the slim girl with the short brown hair ran all the way up the street, bellowing like a cow being burned alive.

Mae was sitting at the table, keening quietly, her head in her arms, the little girls, Charlotte and Victoria, and her boys around her. The strength drained from Tilly and she folded onto the floor, rubbing her poor, burning leg muscles, trying to get air into her heaving lungs. Out on the street, someone's mother called down the hall, 'Anything we can do?'

'Thanks,' said Edward, who limped in, blood soaking his face.

'They took our babies,' Mae said.

'Why?' Tilly gasped.

'They said we have vermin,' Charlotte cried, 'but it's just George's pet mice and the rabbit, and they said the horse manure Barney's collecting to sell was dangerous, that it could explode, that it made flies.'

'They said Mum's uncivilised,' Victoria said, 'and that we live in a slum.'

'Apparently under the Children's Charter we're classified as "socially inadequate",' said Mae, angrily, and Tilly rolled onto her side on the floor and drew her knees up, the image of Joel with his arm reaching playing over and over, and with it came Teddy's face, grinning at her from the edge of the silo.

Edward stepped forward, his broken family around him, and said, 'We'll fix this.'

And Mae said, 'My word we will.'

Miss Peachy, wearing a dressing-gown, her hair coiled in rags, was shoved into the Black Maria in front of the entire neighbourhood. She was driven to police headquarters, fingerprinted, photographed and placed in holding rooms with Elizabeth and her fiancé, Mary and her young man, Margaret, Nita, BB King, Barney, Julie and the sergeant.

Thinking the task easy, the police officers started with Barney. They sat opposite him and glared, until he pointed to the scalps around his neck and said cheerfully, 'These aren't real. I'm not a real Indian Chief. I've been to a royal dress-up party. The Queen got crowned.'

'Did you see anything unusual in the behaviour of the people at the gathering last night?'

Barney thought for a long moment, clutching his feathered headdress, and said, 'No.'

'What about . . . suggestive or lewd?'

'I don't know those people and if I did I wouldn't have recognised them because it was a royal dress-up party for the Queen.'

They asked him if he'd seen men kissing each other, or embracing, and he said again, 'No, that happens at New Year's Eve parties, people kiss and hug on New Year's Eve because they're happy.'

'Everyone was happy last night, weren't they?'

'Yes, because of the new queen,' Barney said, emphatically. 'It wasn't New Year's Eve last night.'

As they returned him to the cell, he called back, 'New Year's Eve is in January.'

The people in the holding cells were shown photographs of the events of the previous night – men dancing together, men dressed as women, women dressed as kings, page boys and footmen and Henry VIII, women dancing and holding hands, someone throwing toilet paper at the Queen, the Queen Mother standing on her hands with her panties exposed, the crown being used as an ashtray, the Archbishop of Canterbury using the sceptre to hit the orb between someone else's legs.

'We wanted to play polo but we didn't have enough horses so we played croquet,' Nita explained, and BB King said photographs did not show the truth, they showed only what the photographer wanted seen.

The policeman turned to Miss Peachy. 'And what have you got to say for yourself, madam?'

Miss Peachy replied, 'The young constable who encountered my pitchfork will need a tetanus injection, because of the horse manure.'

The photos were taken by King John, a redhead wearing a paper crown who slipped in when Augustus Gaius Octavius opened the door to admit the Empress Julia Agrippina of Rome. He had a camera, but no one noticed it. And now the holding cells and interview rooms were filled with royalty in crushed costumes and the warm, sleepy smell of stale champagne and cigarettes. The group had anticipated the large sable and white fur coat of the Queen's corgi, but the judge did not appear. They snuggled against each other and slept.

It was Arlen O'Connor who came to their rescue, wearing a fine dark navy suit and carrying a briefcase. 'There exists no law against fancy dress,' he argued, and there was no way of proving that the people in the photographs were doing anything unusual, except attending a costume party. The Hippocampus Club was licensed, paid its taxes and was in accordance with all health regulations, so the charge of lèse-majesté, sedition and blasphemy would not stand. In fact, Arlen continued, the actions of the police constituted brutality and harassment, intimidation, false arrest, false imprisonment, police perjury, police corruption, unwarranted surveillance and unwarranted searches.

After some agonising hours, bored to death, starving and thirsty, hungover and sticky, the impersonators and pornographers found all the violence and trauma amounted to nothing. Suddenly, miraculously, they were released from prison into the prim streets of Melbourne on a Wednesday afternoon, still seditiously bedraggled, blasphemously half drunk, in tattered, treasonously laughable royal costume to stand beneath the bunting and swinging royal flags adorning the lampposts. Except for Sergeant Farrat.

Senior Sergeant Cutter declared, 'There is an accusation of bigamy. Our officers are scouring the records as we stand here. So, until "Mrs Farrat" shows up, Mr Farrat will be held in custody.'

Arlen put his arm around Julie, who heaved with rage and worry in her royal petticoat. 'They cannot hold him, and they know perfectly well that Mrs Farrat is in a state of torpor from anguish, and they will find no evidence of bigamy.'

Eventually, Sergeant Farrat was released, because Arlen pointed out that they had no evidence, only accusations, and he suspected the Queen's corgi might have intervened.

# Chapter 30

ARLEN ARRIVED EARLY the next morning and Mae gathered herself. She drew her family, her army, around her. 'We'll go to the department and retrieve what's ours. Girls, get Tilly organised.'

Mae's three big girls dragged Tilly to a sitting position and pulled her to her feet. They led her to the bathroom, stripped her clothes off and put her in the bath. Then they dressed her, weaved their arms through hers and made her walk with them, all of them, traipsing up the hill towards the Welfare Department, a glut of irritated office workers caught behind the line of McSwineys spread across the footpath: Edward and Mae, Barney, George, Victoria, Charles, Henry and Charlotte, neat as pins, looking fresh as the shine after rain, while Elizabeth, Margaret and Mary enfolded the staggering girl, all following Arlen.

It took all of Tilly's strength to remind herself that it was not she who had caused this. She had done nothing malicious or bad, it was other people. Dragging her along the footpath, Elizabeth murmured, 'Nearly there, Til,' and Tilly whispered, 'Just one more battle.' One day, soon, she would be rid of all her extraneous cargo, sailing free.

They were left on a long bench in a cold room with small, high windows and their personal visions of their terrified babies whimpering in icy dormitories. An adolescent, wearing a suit that would not fit him for many years to come, handed Edward an envelope. 'Saved me a walk to the letterbox.' It was a letter from the National Society for the Prevention of Cruelty to Children, stipulating, 'The 1889 charter, the *Prevention of Cruelty to Children Act*, enables the intervention of society and authorities to protect children from cruelty or neglect perpetrated by their parents. Parents or caregivers can no longer assume ownership of a child and therefore the right to treat their child in any way they see fit.' The neglect, apparently, was ill treatment, insufficient food provided, insufficient clothing, medical aid and lodging, taking part in a public exhibition or performance where life or limbs are endangered (riding the horse and cart), and truancy.

Arlen requested an appointment with the head of the Children's Department, their most senior officer, and was denied. He requested an appeal hearing, to no avail. And so, he was forced to point out that he knew the welfare officer concerned with the case was currently suspended due to accusations of perversion, and thus hardly the man to make sound judgements. He then produced a photograph of the welfare officer outside Nita Orland's window, and another flash photo taken from inside the house.

Eventually, word came that an appeal was granted 'given the family had sufficient means to employ a lawyer – two lawyers, in fact, Mr Gladston Hawker and Mr Arlen O'Connor, from the firm of Earl and Dowdle – who could prove that appropriate circumstances to care for the children existed, in keeping with the children's welfare department criteria.'

The McSwineys went home, a defeated family carrying defiance in their bearing. 'We'll go and see Rex on Sunday,' Edward said.

Tilly didn't want to go back to her home, where Joe's tip trucks waited, his teddy bear, his wooden tools and little chest of drawers spilling shorts and shirts and small trousers with braces and tiny socks and singlets, the potty he'd worked hard to make a perfunctory part of his day, and she didn't want her grief compounding the McSwineys' sadness, their disappointment that she was merely 'trouble', so she followed Arlen to the pub and drank Scotch, and then to an Italian restaurant for spaghetti and red wine, and then back to the pub to a room above the bar. She woke in his arms, his tummy against her back, his knees tucked in behind hers and his breath on her shoulder. In the night, Teddy had come to her, and again smiled and winked. As he walked away, he turned and waved. And so here she was, in the after-glow of rage spent, and in her heart, she felt Arlen had always been softly holding her.

'I fear for my baby boy,' she whispered.

'Sister Patricia's there, and he knows the place – his mother and family came for him once, they'll be back, he believes that.'

'Mae says I shouldn't visit, that it will just make him sad when I leave, but what will they say if I don't go?'

'We'll go and see him, explain it to him, but remember, we survived, he'll survive, and we have the judge on our side.'

'I'm either being saved by some man or ruining his life.'

'I'm saving you because I'm a lawyer and a friend.'

'I am cursed, after all,' she half grinned.

Arlen smiled. 'I used to think I was bad too, but I just didn't fit with the usual drongos.'

'My life is Molly's.'

'Molly didn't have forty quid or a lawyer and she got her baby girl back in the end. It's the drongos.' He pulled her a little closer. 'We will have your boy back.'

He made a boiled egg in his electric kettle and waited while she ate. Like their abode at Shorty's, Arlen's room was a space for someone possessed by no one and nothing. There was a double bed, a desk, reading lamp and radio, and beside the lounge chair and standard lamp, a stack of books: *The Adventures of Augie March*, *The Old Man and the Sea*, *Legal History in Australia*. Arlen's wardrobe showed clearly what was biggest in his life. Crisp, ironed business shirts – colour matched – hung with bespoke suits, brown, grey, black and the dark navy blue one. Parked neatly beneath were polished shoes.

She handed him her breakfast plate. 'What sort of lawyer are you?'

'A good one.'

'You stand up for what's right.'

'As do you.'

'I've stood up in many places appearing as someone I am not,' she mused. 'Actually, I've always dressed according to how people needed me to appear, though I confess I dressed badly to annoy Mrs Flock. But most of the time I wear appropriate costumes to be what people need to see. But that's because I've believed myself inadequate. My true self is actually a strong tree in a cyclone, I know that now. And I've seen enough of the learned, decent folk of authority to know that sometimes the costumes they wear are a lie. The hierarchy works only for the people who maintain it. Yet there are some magistrates and judges that are true, human. So, I'll present as a strong woman, honest and truthful and the good mother that I am, and I'll trust that the magistrate will see that and treat me accordingly.'

'"Know thyself and you'll understand the nature of humans," or something like that, as Aristotle said.'

Arlen took over the plate and spoon and ate his eggs, then he put her in a taxi and sent her home to the soft and constant presence of her odd husband and his girlfriend.

Still filled with resentment at Tilly Dunnage for denying her new frocks, and making up for the years spent sequestered in her dismal house in Dungatar, Marigold continued shopping. Another trail of signed cheques followed her through every arcade frock shop and respectable salon all the way up Collins Street. Beula took the opportunity to purchase a new outfit, and on Sunday, they left the CWA Ladies Hostel early. At the station, the taxi driver loaded Marigold's many suitcases onto a luggage trolley. Beula pushed the trolley all the way to the platform, feeling marvellous in her new bordered, button-through, seersucker peasant frock. It had a scooped, flounce-collared neckline and small puffed sleeves, and she had also purchased smart Mexican vinyl huar-aches to match her small straw bonnet. It was an outfit straight from Rockmans of Bourke Street, which dressed the 'not-so-slim' figure, but Marigold hadn't mentioned that to Beula.

Marigold was desperate to get home to build the best house in Dungatar and buy a new bed that housed only her very own germs but, more importantly, she wanted to get off the train looking marvellous. She wanted Elsbeth Beaumont to turn green and Gertrude to stamp her feet and scream; she wanted to feel lovely in that desolate, razed landscape. Marigold needed satin lining against her skin and the heft of a substantial cloth to protect her from the harsh, bacteria-infected elements, and the air, infused with other people's droplets.

In the chilly morning air, a man, slight and nimble and dressed in dark clothing, approached. 'Ladies,' he said.

'What?'

'Allow me to wheel your suitcases down to the luggage truck, load 'em up for you?'

'Certainly not,' said Marigold. They needed to start throwing suitcases out of the carriage as soon as Mad Molly's house came into view.

The man said, 'No worries,' and left, and Marigold looked around for the ticket box. 'I've had to pay for everything, Beula, even the cotton wool for your seeping wounds. Just look after the suitcases, I'll be back soon.' She went searching for the ticket box, leaving Beula sitting on the bench, her head cocked at faraway sounds and her hands resting on her white cane.

When Marigold returned, the luggage was gone.

'It's there,' said Beula, pointing at nothing.

Marigold seized Beula's white cane and struck her, smashing her dark glasses. She tore the luggage tag from Beula's cardigan, again. 'I never get anything I want, ever. Someone always ruins everything!'

She rushed off to find the nearest police station, tears wetting her cheeks, her rash rising like rhodoid embroidery, and Beula behind her, arms reaching like a demented sleepwalker.

In the middle of Spencer Street, Beula lost sight of Marigold's blurry form and stayed circling, her broken cane swooping through the air. The last thing Beula saw was a big green square thing bearing down on her, brakes screeching, metal on metal, and a furious *ding ding ding DINGDINGDING* . . .

Marigold ran back and looked down at the lower half of Beula poking out from under the tram. 'Beula,' she said, and kicked her ankle. Beula's leg rolled away, and blood trickled into the tram track.

She headed back to the ticket office to have Beula's ticket reimbursed.


It was a cold day, but the McSwiney family, Arlen, Tilly and the sergeant sat in the convent garden with Rex and Joe and ate a picnic lunch, huddled in their coats, warming their hands around hot thermos tea. They had patty cakes for the children and a new Matchbox toy each and spoke of when the boys would come home again. Rex was quiet, but Joe did not speak at all.

From the belltower, Sister Maria watched, but Tilly ignored her, focusing instead on the good and true things in life – the people around her and the future waiting.

They stayed until it was far too cold for everyone and promised they would see each other soon. 'We will come back for you,' Tilly said. Joe clung to his mother and reached for Mae, but stuck close to Rex when it was clear that all those nice people were abandoning them.

Marigold Pettyman pulled the emergency chain and the train came to a screaming halt, almost dead centre at the Dungatar platform. She alighted, ignored the furious, gesticulating train driver and, in her one remaining new outfit, walked towards the worn grey track that was the main street, her handbag over her arm and her gait comfortable in her new flared skirt. She noted that the burnt and buckled asphalt had been steamrolled flat and, startlingly, the town was erected. It was bald and raw but it had risen again, brand-new. On string strung between buildings, dozens of Union Jack flags flapped, whipping around in the breeze like cockatoos with caught claws. Where the chemist once stood, there was a new hall. But they had rebuilt everything else exactly where it had been before.

Pratts Store was shut so she leaned on the wall, sheltering from the dust stinging her calves. On the noticeboard – adorned with a bejewelled crown cut from gold paper – a note announced the coming Coronation Ball. 'June 2' had been crossed out and the date for the coming Saturday added. There was also an advertisement, 'Trudy Beaumont, Qualified Dressmaker, The Hill, by appointment'.

Brand-new Dungatar was deserted. There was no one to see Marigold's new dress.

'I see you have a new outfit?'

Marigold squealed. Such a fright!

Gertrude Pratt was behind her, appraising Marigold's lovely blue suit, its pinched waist and hip-length jacket and flared skirt. Marigold looked shapely.

'Don't miss a trick, do you?' She moved so that her new skirt shifted prettily.

'I'm the Dungatar seamstress now.'

'No point, Tilly Dunnage is coming back to burn the town down again.'

'So I hear, but I doubt she'll bother.'

Marigold waved away a fly. 'Where is everyone?'

'They're on strike again, something about William stealing timber flooring from Mrs Almanac.'

'She can have Beula's timber.'

Gertrude walked to the end of the small verandah so that Marigold could see her new dress. 'Your house isn't built because you weren't here to help.'

'I'll go to The Hill. My husband purchased that land. It's mine.'

Gertrude marched back, declaring, 'I live there now. William's built me a little place. He's the shire president, we elected him last year, don't you remember?'

'How could I forget? He was the sole candidate. Just because he's mayor doesn't mean he's above the law. He's building on my land.'

'The hut was built long ago by a man whose job was to spot advancing Aborigines and bushrangers. He dropped dead, the council acquired it and dug the tip at the base.'

'And then my husband bought it for Mad Molly.'

Gertrude squinted into the sun. 'Yes, but did he ever actually pay for it?'

'You are squatting on land that isn't yours.' Marigold shrugged. 'You belong in the shop with your parents.'

'No chance,' called Muriel from inside, and the shop door opened. Muriel and Alvin Pratt shook their heads.

'We're not Gert's type anymore,' Alvin said. 'She's accustomed to fine things, isn't that right, Gert?'

'Trudy. Call me Trudy.' She smiled at Marigold, smoothed her new skirt over her thighs. 'Anyway, I'll be moving back to Windswept Crest soon.'

'Make it tonight.' Marigold turned and feigned a dignified exit across the razed landscape in her new outfit, luggageless, miserable and heading towards nothing, nowhere. Then she remembered Scotty Pullit's still on the creek bank. She filled her tonic bottle and took a few fronds of Irma Almanac's fat sticky herbs for a soothing cup of tea.

Felicity Joy saw her mother walking towards Fart Hill. She lowered her binoculars, climbed down from the roof and went to find her father. 'Can we discuss something, Dad?'

William sat in the cab of the Triumph Gloria, which he was mining for spare parts, and faced his small, earnest daughter. 'I'm listening.'

Felicity Joy and her father reached an agreement regarding pretty dresses, sensible shoes and the practicality of dungarees and shorts, then William coupled the trailer to the tractor and set off to retrieve his evicted wife and all her possessions.

He drove her triumphantly back through the main street, past the leftover plasterboard, plumbing pipes and adaptors, elbows and nipples, couplings and unions, paint tins and floor polish, a dark grey curl of dust behind him. He pulled up at the front steps of the Windswept Crest homestead and helped his wife down just as Elsbeth came trotting around the side of the house with the garden hose, the stream aimed at the grocer's daughter. Elsbeth was scooped up by her own son and placed on the top shelf of the linen press again.

That evening, Gertrude swept into the dining room late, looking like a painted doll and smelling like a garden, and was told by Septimus that she wasn't on the roster for head table. 'You have to wait your turn, Gertrude.'

'Call me Trudy.'

Elsbeth said, 'You'll have to put your name down on the roster, and you'll be allocated jobs as well, like cooking, laundry, cleaning, gardening, mucking out the stables . . .'

There was a small thud as Felicity Joy landed on the floor.

'Sorry, Felicity,' said her mother. 'I really didn't mean to bump you off, I just wanted some of your chair.' Felicity went to sit on her father's knee.

Elsbeth tapped the side of her glass with a fork. The diners turned to her.

'Admission to the coronation celebration will be a shilling. Refreshments will be included.'

Lois objected, 'But we'll be supplying them!'

Sensing an argument building, William started thinking about bed, and his wife in her petticoat reaching for her pretty nightie. He checked his watch, but it was only seven o'clock.

Gertrude said, 'The coronation has come and gone, Elsbeth, you've missed it.'

'For such an occasion, celebrations will continue for months, Gertrude *Pratt*.'

'It won't be much fun without the band.' Faith shrugged. 'And no one's got anything decent to wear.'

'I have lots of new things to wear,' said Gertrude, smugly stroking her pretty new frock.

Elsbeth said she looked like a gout-ravaged toe.

'Oh, that reminds me . . .' Gertrude handed her husband an invoice. William turned pale. His mother snatched it and turned crimson. It was an invoice for the most expensive dress Gertrude had purchased, and she'd bought it before she'd torn out a wad of cheques from the back of Marigold's chequebook.

Elsbeth slammed her fork down. 'How dare you!'

Gertrude sprinkled more salt onto her potato. 'It's just one dress.'

'That we know of!' Elsbeth looked to her son, furious. 'William?'

William carefully put down his cutlery, placing his fork one inch from the table edge and half an inch from his plate. 'Well, Mother, you're spending our capital on a ball.'

Elsbeth's chin moved, preparing to speak, but her son had challenged her in public and this had momentarily cast her adrift in a desert of blustery miscomprehension. 'It's for the community, and the Queen!'

Gertrude slammed the salt shaker down. 'Raise your hands if you care about the Queen's coronation?'

No one raised their hands, but Faith said they all cared about the ball, that she'd be happy to get the band back together, they could still have a dance even if it was dark and there was no electricity.

William pointed out that it was June, and freezing cold.

'See?' said Elsbeth. 'Everyone wants a ball.'

'Get out,' said Gertrude.

William put his head in his hands.

'You can't throw me out, you silly girl. You're in my house.'

Gertrude rolled her eyes. 'I live here now, I'll live here long after you're dead. Now get out.'

'If I go, so does everyone else. You will have no labour force to complete the town plumbing!'

William groaned. It was a repeat of the same argument they'd had the day of the eisteddfod three years prior – every year, for that matter.

His mother continued, 'And I'll forbid anyone from using the bus.'

'Oh . . . f . . . fiddlesticks,' said Gertrude, and clenched her fists at her temples.

'You started this, RUDE-Y the Terrible.'

Faith started bawling, and William cried, 'Mother, you're ruining it for everyone –'

'Me? It's not me that's ruining it, it's Gert-RUDE!'

Purl stood. 'You're ruining it, Els-BAG, you think you're the Queen and you're the one that's rude.'

'How dare you, you're just a –'

'We've had this argument,' said William. 'What I need to say is –'

'Marigold's back. She's got *lots* of money, so we don't need you, ELS-BAG. You can just leave.'

'I will not go. Get out, all of you.'

'Not going. I am married to William.'

'You are a chunky seductress and an impostor.'

Felicity put her fingers in her ears, and her father yelled, 'STOP!'

They stopped. No one had ever heard William raise his voice.

'Enough!' William stood up. 'Mother, you will now pack your bags and go.'

'Don't be ridiculous, William. Pass me the wine.'

'You can go and stay with your cousin Una in Melbourne, I'll drop you at the train station on Sunday.'

'Una won't have me,' Elsbeth said. 'We owe her money.' She stood up, trembling, and stamped her foot. 'You're just a bunch of hams, dullards, shopkeepers and halfwits; you're uncouth, grotesque and common – loathsome, all of you.' Then Elsbeth picked up a handful of mashed potato and started chucking it at everyone around the table.

William scooped her up and carried her out.


Marigold had spent the day in her new house on The Hill scraping dirt from the chimney bricks and digging sawdust from between the new floorboards. She settled by the fire, relishing the peaceful solitude, and while she waited for the can of beans to warm she contained the ash so that it didn't spill onto her newly polished hearth. She had polished the stoop as well. It had been a wonderful day.

After dinner, she wearily brushed her teeth and washed her face and hands and hopped into bed, surveying the stars through the gaps in her new, unfinished roof. It was all very crude but nothing a bit of paint, a couple of gallons of disinfectant and some more polish couldn't fix. And the garden, established and tended by Tilly Dunnage, was emerging. She remembered seeing Tilly's red tomatoes, her crop of squeaky silverbeet, pumpkins as big as Cinderella's carriage and carrots the size of rabbits. If only one of the McSwineys were available to trap a few bunnies for her, catch a fish or two, she could eat a balanced, nutritious, clean diet. She sighed, the Milky Way putting on a show for her. 'This is perfect,' she said, and snuggled down in her bed.

William carried his mother to the bus, Elsbeth screaming, 'I hope I never set eyes on any of you ever again! You are all common dolts, oafs and imbeciles.'

For the entire trip to Dungatar she hissed and growled at him, like a trussed possum, and when they got to the small dwelling on top of The Hill, Marigold sat up in bed, clutching her handbag, and told them they'd regret it if they came any closer.

'I'll take off my shoes,' William said.

'I don't want her, I don't want to live with anyone. I'm free for the first time in my life. I have my own germs, I don't have to worry about other people drinking from my cups or sucking on my forks, I can see people approaching and stop them. Up here, I'm above everyone.' Including Elsbeth.

In his arms, Elsbeth wriggled. 'Where will I go?'

'Frankly, you can go to the tip as far as I'm concerned.' Marigold lay down and pulled the blanket up over her head.

William looked down at the McSwineys' camp beside the tip, smiled, and set off down The Hill, his mother in his arms. 'No! This is all very wrong, the tip is for people of poverty.'

'You have a great poverty of character, Mother,' said William, and settled her into Mae McSwiney's burnt-out dining room. He put her balding fox fur around her shoulders and left her there, lamplight from the dwelling up on The Hill blinking across the plains.

It was a beautiful evening and he paused to gaze up at the embers of the stellar swoop, before setting off home to his wife, who had resumed her seat at the head of the table as Trudy Beaumont, and her role as leading lady, theatre producer and director.

# Chapter 31

ON THE MORNING of the hearing, Tilly applied her costume and said to her reflection, 'Find the character in yourself so that you can convey the truth and the audience will see that truth conveyed.' And, though inside she was sick with anticipation and failure, she reminded herself that she was a tree that had survived many cyclones. 'I know who I am.' She combed her hair neatly, raised her chin and set off with her sensible handbag on her arm, her inner truth and worthiness shining.

Again, they traipsed up the Collins Street hill towards the department. Again, they were left on a long bench in a cold room with small, high windows. The Welfare Department's primary children's officer, though suspended, sat at the back of the pompous brown room, his tiny head propped on his big shoulders.

Mr Hawker, red-faced and murky-eyed, wearing what the sergeant deemed slub, informed the assembled nuns, the affable Head of the Welfare Department, the magistrate and disinterested officials that Tilly was under investigation for arson, that she had murdered her brother and the father of her baby.

Barney leaned over to Tilly and whispered loudly, 'People say things about me too, Tilly!'

'And,' the welfare officer called, 'she's a bigamist, she's been married before.'

He turned and pointed, and there was Mr Short, leaning on a walking stick, his chest like a copper pipe and his chin so long it hid his tie-knot. Mr Hawker held up a marriage certificate.

'You can search Births, Deaths and Marriages for the last forty years and you won't find a record of a marriage of either me or Tilly,' Arlen said. 'The certificate is fake, I paid a bloke in a pub a quid for it.'

'They told me they were married,' cried Mr Short.

The welfare officer's face contorted. 'You lived in sin!'

'We shared quarters,' Arlen said, calmly. 'Mr Short made us live in the shed. He provided us with a canvas stretcher each.'

The assembled nuns, Head of the Welfare Department, Children's Services officers and the magistrate found the lawyer, Mr O'Connor, compelling, but disgust was consuming the welfare officer. 'She was underage.'

'You can ask Myrtle Dunnage, but you'll find we were just brother and sister in that room, and Mr and Mrs Short were accessories; they harboured us and took our money for three years and the convent let them do it. But what we are asking you to grant is custody of Joe to his mother, who can provide for him. Children fare better with their mothers, as good men with good mothers will attest. Joe can equally be placed with his grandparents and aunts and uncles, the McSwiney family.' He gestured to them, sitting upright and respectable behind him, and went on to detail that Rex was well cared for in a loving, responsible family.

Arlen continued, 'Your honour, I have a witness present who will guarantee the child Joel Edward Dunnage's future both financially and legally. The child has a wealthy benefactor who will also act as a godfather, or guardian.'

Gladston Hawker stood and agreed that he would pay for both children's schooling if necessary and act as a probationary guide and support to the Farrat and McSwiney families.

'He's no longer employed,' Mr Hawker called across the court, and Arlen said Mr Gladston Hawker was employed by Earl and Dowdle. He then offered a letter of support from a Supreme

Court judge, and Tilly was pleased she and Elizabeth had put so much time and energy into his blue sea gown.

The magistrate, who did not appear to be listening, suddenly remembered where he was and shuffled the inch-high stack of well-thumbed papers before him.

Then Arlen produced some magazines – *People*, *The Land Girl*, *Women's Weekly*, *Woman's Day*, and *Vogue* – and was about to exhibit photos of Tilly's couture, to explain that Tilly Dunnage was a leading fashion designer set for a secure future, that she had references from magazine photographers, fashion editors and businesspeople in the clothing industry, but the magistrate again appeared to be thinking about something else.

The Head of the Welfare Department yawned.

The magistrate glanced at Tilly and the McSwiney ensemble, and mumbled, 'Yes, yes, enough, enough.' He rubbed his thick eyebrows and looked at the papers in his long, soft hands, adjusted his spectacles, licked his thumb and found the page he wanted and began to read, the court deadly quiet save for one of his courtroom offsiders snoring softly beside him.

Eventually, the magistrate sat back and threw his glasses onto the pile of papers. 'These hearings are always a complete waste of time.' He rubbed his forehead again and blustered that no one had presented any sound evidence to hold either of the children in custody, that the state felt the child was better with, at the very least, a foster mother, or a relative, but preferably its own mother, provided that mother had sufficient means to support the child, which she obviously had. He became exasperated when he said the state could not afford to keep every child 'with a dubious interpretation of a mother'.

Again, he fell silent and seemed to lose track. 'However' – the people in the room jolted to attention – 'until his mother is cleared of the accusations of bigamy, trauma, geronticide, fratricide, amicicide and arson, the child Joel Edward Dunnage will be released into . . .' He stopped, sifted through his papers again. 'I read somewhere that there is a grandmother.'

Mae sat forward; Edward squared his shoulders.

The magistrate found the page he wanted. 'Yes. A woman with sound financial arrangements who had earlier applied for custody of Joel Edward Dunnage? Mrs Pettyman? Is Mrs Evan Pettyman in the court today?'

'No, Your Honour,' said Mr Hawker, weakly.

The welfare officer stood and boomed, 'She has inherited a great deal of money and returned to her home.'

The magistrate continued, 'Insinuation and murk surround the circumstances of the child's home life and the type of people he lives with and, given the implied extended family circumstances and the unexplored qualifications of the so-called "guardians", and until all of these matters are deemed satisfactory by the Welfare Department, the child will reside with Mrs Pettyman, of Dungatar.'

'But Mrs Pettyman is no longer in Melbourne,' Arlen reminded him.

The welfare officer raised himself to his full height and declared that he would take the child to Dungatar, 'in the rural countryside, a quaint, safe town, a mere train ride away.'

'The child will be accompanied to its grandmother by a qualified children's nurse.'

'The matter of Rex McSwiney –'

'That child is released,' the magistrate said impatiently. 'We can't save every urchin with a grubby nose in the state.'


Mae walked in circles, hands on her hips, her eyes open and staring. Edward nursed Rex, who curled against him, and Tilly sat at the kitchen table, smoking, while Arlen talked on the telephone in the hall. The sergeant made tea and the rest of the McSwineys sat on the stools at the sewing machines and seamstress tables, or the stairs, any clear surface they could find.

Then Arlen came in and Edward said, 'We'll fix this, won't we?'

And Arlen replied, 'We will.'

'We'll go there,' said Mae.

Edward asked, 'How will you get there?'

'There's a daily bus,' Tilly suggested, but Arlen said the bus hadn't stopped there since the fire and rubbed the back of his head, remembering the pain of the flying suitcase.

'I can't believe I'm going back to Dungatar,' Tilly said. 'It's a fetid cauldron of bubbling venom.' But she wasn't afraid.

The sergeant stood up, announcing, 'We'll need to get Joe and flee quickly. We'll go in my car.'

Julie put her hand to her heart. 'Oh!' The sergeant said he'd be careful, and everyone looked at something else as they kissed.

'We'll leave at five o'clock in the morning,' declared Mae, and the sergeant winced. He was not a morning person.

'If we don't stop, we'll get there by teatime.'

'When was the last time you had the car serviced, Sarge?'

The sergeant looked thoughtful. Edward and Arlen nodded faintly across the room. Edward went for his toolbox and Arlen removed his jacket. They spent a great many hours tinkering under the bonnet, tightening wheel nuts, pumping up the spare tyre, changing the oil and checking the radiator.


Julie was modelling clay over a last – a woman's size ten – trying to get it to a shape that would accommodate the client's blistered bunion. 'She told me that if her bunion doesn't hurt then she won't drink as much.'

'Sounds reasonable.'

'I'll make the vamp leather mesh, wide, cover the painful bunion with a bow.'

Oh, so clever, his Julie. The sergeant was mesmerised by her hands smoothing another last, which was covered in a stiff, dry chamois.

The sergeant's every move was equally absorbing for Julie. She loved the way he moved across a room to make a cup of hot water; she loved to watch him shave.

'These are Nita's,' she said, and drew – very deftly – the outline of the shoe. 'A standard stiletto but I'll make the counter of the quarter high because I'm making the top line of the vamp quite low. You'll just see where her toes begin. A little toe cleavage. You will come back from Dungatar, won't you?'

'Even if I lose my arms and legs and have to drag myself back by my chin.'

Julie placed the last and scissors down gently beside her tools – the very sharp hook knives and tacks, the little hammer and needles, the leather threads – the heady glue smell and aroma of boot polish swelling – and looked into the sergeant's eyes. 'Oh, Horatio.'

Later, as they lounged against the wainscoting, their clothes askew, the sergeant said, 'So, what do you think we should do next?'

'I could eat, let's go to the Ritz.'

'No, I mean, in life.'

She sat up. 'Travel! I'd love to go to Venice. The shoes! The history! The Calegheri, or shoemakers' guild, started in 1278 and even today there remain buildings with bas reliefs representing shoes.'

The sergeant picked up a shoe, and was studying it. 'We will go on a business trip with my wife to purchase fabrics, see a few fashion shows. And you will research shoes.'

'Apparently, near Padua there is a grand villa that is a museum of the best models of shoes in the world, but . . . would that be boring for you?'

'Never,' said the sergeant.

# Chapter 32

THE NEXT MORNING, Mrs Caroline Hawker placed a warm plate of steaming poached eggs and bacon, buttery fried mushrooms and thick pancakes with fresh cream and jam in front of her husband, who sat at one side of the table reading the newspaper. Mrs Hawker sat opposite, opened her broadsheet newspaper and skewered a wedge of grapefruit, which she washed down with a sip of black tea and honey.

'Oh dear,' she said suddenly, dumping her cup back in its saucer. 'This is very interesting . . . on page three.'

Her husband found the same photo and accompanying article on page two of his tabloid. It was a large black-and-white photograph of the welfare officer. He appeared to have been caught peeping into a window, and the snap was taken at night so the flash exacerbated his startled, terrified expression; it was quite apparent his fly was unzipped.

'A set-up,' said Mr Hawker. 'Obviously just got caught short.'

'Read on,' said Mrs Hawker. The actress concerned had kept a diary; the welfare officer had been following her, so she had employed a photographer, a witness, who possessed plenty of photographic evidence taken from both inside and outside her apartment. Mrs Hawker shook her head, adding that she hoped whoever took over the welfare officer's cases was a caring person who worked to resurrect and repair impoverished children and their families rather than tear them apart.

Mr Hawker's morning got worse. He pulled up at the kerb,

struggled from his car and walked to the lift, then found his office door wide open and the premises in disarray. He slumped in his chair, red-faced and sweating, his hand on his chest. 'I've been burgled.'

The police arrived an hour or so later, and so did Gladston.

'You did this!' he cried, but Gladston said it was a coincidence, that he'd just dropped in to clean out his desk and retrieve his pot plant.

The constable listed the missing contents of the safe as his father recited: the titles to the family home, birth certificates, certificates of stocks, bonds and investments had not been stolen, but a brown paper bag containing five vanilla slices and five thousand pounds in cash was gone, along with some blue film reels, and Mrs Hawker's 'trinkets'.

'Nothing very valuable,' he told the policeman. 'She doesn't come from money. Strangely, my last will and testament is also missing, but that's not a problem.' He smirked at Gladston. 'I was about to write a new one anyway.'

When the police had gone, Gladston volunteered to summon a handyman to secure the place.

'I don't need you to do that, Gladston. I have a new secretary, she'll do all of that when she gets here tomorrow.'

Gladston helped his father into his coat, saw him to the elevator and waved away the lingering pipe smoke. He went to his own desk, sprayed his pot plant once, and unlocked the top drawer. Hands shaking, he took out a shoebox marked 'used pen nibs' and dug beneath the dulled nibs and empty ink bottles to find the manila envelope. His mother's heirlooms were there, and only fifty quid was missing from the cash, but four thousand, nine hundred and fifty pounds would do for the time being. Most important was the will . . . which he had written himself, according to his father's instructions. Handy to have a copy, just in case.

He dialled Earl and Dowdle and asked for Arlen O'Connor again. 'It seems to have gone well, thank you.'

'Indeed, and thank you again, Mr Hawker.'

'It's been a pleasure, Mr O'Connor.'

There was a pause in the conversation, just the sound of wind passing over wires, and finally Gladston said, 'You mentioned at the pub the other night you had ideas regarding sound investments?'

'I did mention that, yes. Let me get back to you on that.'

'Much obliged.'


As he shuffled down the hill, flushed, a man in shock, a breeze lifted Mr Hawker's hat from his head and it tumbled and rolled to the gutter. A young man picked it up and called, 'Oi,' but Mr Hawker was oblivious. The young man raced after him, put his hand on his shoulder and his hat on his head at the same time, and that's when Mr Hawker gasped and fell, face first, onto the footpath, snapping his incisors off at the gums. His hat rolled back into the gutter and his teeth, a semicircle of filthy little brown stumps, rested in the slimy pool of saliva and blood on the concrete.

'Myocardial infarction, I'd say,' a passing doctor declared. 'Dead before he hit the concrete.' He leaned a little closer then looked up at the terrified young man. 'Infective endocarditis, a fatal systemic disease associated with dental diseases. Always look after your teeth, son.'

Una Pleasance waited until lunchtime before she phoned his club. The receptionist asked if she was a close relative of Mr Hawker.

'I'm his secretary, and a very close friend.'

'I see,' said the receptionist, a little cattily. 'You should telephone his wife. Mrs Hawker will explain why her husband will no longer be attending the club.'

\*

The sergeant loaded his one small suitcase, sleeping bag, folded stretcher and his mother's small pink leather vanity box (her gold-embossed initials matching the gold locks and hinges) into the Fiat Balilla. He placed the picnic basket containing wine, some nice cheeses, olives and crusty bread on the passenger seat. He took a cleaning sponge from one of his pockets and polished the windscreen. Mae looked at his Brixton cap, matching gloves, scarf and tweed driving suit, her face a question: *Why?*

The sergeant pointed at his pockets. 'Maps, sunglasses and binoculars, a plastic-lined pocket for a rag to wipe the oil dipstick, and a sponge. Barney, be a champ and fetch the card table, will you? Arlen can put it in the boot for us.'

Barney hurried away, and Mae put the picnic basket on the back seat and made herself comfortable in the front with her school case. Mrs Peachy brought them fresh fruit and a spinach pie and Tilly arrived carrying a bag for Joe and a small canvas bag for herself.

'Got everything you need?'

'I'll need to stop to pick up the dynamite and the Winchester .44-40s,' Tilly said, flinging her bags onto the back seat.

Mae raised her eyebrows. 'Or you could just sort it out with a box of matches.'

Edward came with sleeping bags, another food basket and a thermos. Tilly settled into the small space on the back seat next to the food, *The Crucible* on her lap to read, but was ejected while Arlen and Edward rearranged the luggage in a way that suited them. She settled in behind Mae again and tied a magenta scarf around her head, a flag symbolising their war with Dungatar. Be fearless, she told herself, steeling herself with the memory of that warm night after the pre-season kick-off ball.

The sergeant had said to her, 'You'll be safe with Teddy,' and she had looked forward to dancing to the Faithful O'Briens, while all around her people wore dresses she'd made. Tilly had anticipated a nice walk home with her new boyfriend in her lovely new dress, the magenta silk organza creation conceived as a sarong – a copy – but a compliment.

'Dangerous,' Teddy had said when he arrived to collect her, and they kissed, their first, a warm, soft, delicious kiss that made her toes curl. Teddy helped her into his car as though she were crystal and she smiled. He drove down The Hill holding her hand.

Mae reached back for Tilly's hand. It was the first time Mae had ever touched her. 'You know, I had this dream . . . it sounds silly, but Teddy stood at the end of my bed, alive as a sunny day, and said, "If thou wake, he cannot sleep." We'll get our baby back, then we'll all sleep.'

'Yes,' was all Tilly could say, and she squeezed Mae's hand.

Barney arrived with the card table but there was no room for it anywhere. Edward leaned over to give Mae a peck on the cheek and reminded everyone that he'd have gone but someone had to stay with the children. 'The welfare and all.'

Arlen, wary of Mae's feelings, blew Tilly a kiss. It was Barney who leaned over and gave her an actual kiss, passing Joe's teddy bear carefully into her arms.

She checked her watch. It was only a matter of hours before she would hold her son again. She put her sunglasses on.

Mae put her hand on her hat. 'Plant it, Sarge.'

Miss Peachy, Arlen, Edward and Barney waved until the Fiat turned the corner.

The nurse lied. She told Joel Edward Dunnage that they were on their way to meet his grandmother, so Joe thought about Mae and turned his attention to the pictures flashing past the window. The landscape was varied – suburban, rural, flat, undulating, hilly, then a series of country towns – and there were trees and houses, people and animals, all sorts of farm machinery, and humans doing things he'd never seen before, like collecting and checking tickets and buying lunch from the dining car, and Joe asked about them all, several times, and repeated everything the nurse replied. He spoke fondly of the sandwiches he ate and the banana he squashed in his fingers, and thrilled at how the milk he'd poured onto the leather seat vanished into the folds. But the nurse was nice and he was a happy child and accustomed to being passed around to strangers, most of whom were gentle. Because language was a new and wondrous thing, he learned all the names of the animals, the features of the landscape and vegetation, every fixture in the cabin and every accessory the nurse wore or carried. He learned the contents of her purse and her pockets and commented on and queried every person who walked past the door. And so, when the train slowed, he said, 'Stop?'

The nurse said, 'Yes, stop.'

Joe repeated the word, 'Stop,' and the nurse repeated the word, and from the next cubicle the welfare officer cried, 'Yes, stop! You've been talking for *nine hours*.'

'Seven,' called the nurse. 'He slept for two hours.'

She kissed the boy's apple cheek and told him he was a very good boy, and he said, 'Very good boy?'

'Yes, very good boy.'

And Joe repeated, 'Very good boy.'

The welfare officer, irritated, called, 'Make him stop, woman!'

Joe said, 'Woman?'

And the nurse said, 'Me, I'm a woman and you're a boy.' And the officer stormed out of the passenger car, down to the dining car, and asked for a cup of very strong tea.

But all the while the land got flatter and more desolate, there were no towns and only farm vehicles, the odd farmer, and many animals, and the train moved further and further away from the city and the nurse became anxious. She felt exposed in all the space. Finally, the passengers felt the carriage warp around the slow southward curve, glanced up and, through their carriage window, saw the ruins of an old house, Mad Molly's house.

The nurse stood on the Dungatar platform with the toddler, watching the train draw away, the child captivated by the steam engine. As the goods van went past, the welfare officer was felled by a stack of newspapers thrown by the guard.

When he woke, ants were biting his eyelids and crawling through his hair and down his neck, under his collar to his armpits, and the baby and nurse were nowhere in sight. He smelled soot and burnt timber, and when he stood up he took in his surrounds. So, it was true. That adulteress and murderess had burned the town down, though the black trees spurted green frothy fronds and new buildings sat brightly on the dark, dusty ground. The weatherboards needed painting, the corrugated iron roofs and water tanks shone. A very large grain silo loomed by the railway line and one structure, incomplete, watched over the town from the top of a hill, an aberration on the airstrip-flat plains. It was silent and very, very still. His head ached and he'd scraped the skin from his knees when he'd fallen. At his feet was a burst pile of newspapers, pages blowing across the plains and rising in eddies. He limped towards the main street, but could see no living human anywhere. Big puddles of pink, blue, green and grey sat vividly on the burnt ground. He dipped a finger in one puddle and smelled it. As he suspected, it was house paint.

Outside Pratts, he stopped to read the noticeboard, and was hit in the middle of his back by a clod of dried clay. He turned, and saw a head jutting up from the floor joists of a house under construction. The man was small, an alcoholic by the look of him, and he demanded to know why the officer was there.

'I'm looking for Mrs Marigold Pettyman,' he said, his hands raised in surrender.

'You're the second person to ask after her today.' Scotty Pullit studied the hulking stranger and decided he'd be a good man to have onside.

'Did you see a nurse, she's got a toddler with her?' the stranger asked.

'She's gone, she stopped the bus.' He shook his head in disbelief.

The nurse had gone to The Hill, found no one there, and staggered back down, still carrying the child. She'd flopped down on Pratts Store steps, exhausted and panicky. 'I don't know how you live in this place. There's nothing here.'

Septimus gestured at the buildings around him. 'We've rebuilt a whole bloody town!'

The nurse asked about transport out of Dungatar. As they explained that the train was due in seven days, and the daily bus didn't stop, they watched the nurse wilt.

The nurse said, 'I was told to bring the child here and deliver him to Marigold Pettyman, but she's not home.'

'She'll be at the creek,' said Irma Almanac, pointing in the direction of Scotty's still, and asked if she'd care to stay and help them since Dungatar had no medical service.

Then a faint roar came to them from far away and they all looked to where the road vanished into the horizon. The nurse perked up. 'I'm sorry, I have to go.'

'We'll build you a house.'

The nurse shook her head; the bus grew louder. 'You need to deliver the child to Mrs Pettyman. If a big man in a dark coat comes asking, don't let him anywhere near the child, I'm certain his mother will come and collect him as soon as she can.'

The locals scattered as the passenger bus came hurtling out of the nothingness. The nurse stood in the middle of the road in her nice white uniform. She removed her red cape and waved it, like a matador, and the vehicle came to a skidding, juddering halt three feet in front of her, sooty dust, burning rubber and the smell of hot oil filling the air. The driver opened the door and yelled impatiently, 'Quick, hop in.' So she did.

'So, where's the child now?' asked the stranger.

Scotty Pullit replied, 'You can be on our side.'

'He should be on our side,' said a voice from behind him. 'You've got more numbers.'

The officer lowered his arms. 'Tell me where the child is.'

'Fart Hill.' The small man pointed to a house just beyond the edge of town, and beckoned for the welfare officer to join his team.

Rocks and stones came flying from behind the raw timber wall, then the door to the store opened and tinned fruit and beans flew out. The welfare officer covered his head with his arms and dropped to his skun knees, yelping in pain. Several men and women came running from both sides, wielding swords. They were dressed in dated costumes, ripped and stained, and some were paint-splattered – great splashes of pink, grey and white in their hair and stiffening their costumes – and as a new tin of paint came cartwheeling, great arcs of pink curling though the air, the officer crawled to a stack of clear varnish tins. All fell silent while the armies gathered the tins and rocks and retreated. The officer asked the small alcoholic man if he could find accommodation, '. . . and I need medical attention,' he said, the knees of his trousers wet with blood, but a frail woman in a wheelchair said there were no medical facilities.

'What are you fighting about?'

'This battle is about paint,' called Alvin Pratt. 'Most people want white houses, but there's not enough white paint, so some have to settle for white trims, but no one will agree on who gets the pink houses.'

The officer suggested they draw straws.

'We did,' said the woman who featured dried green paint.

'It was rigged.'

'It wasn't.'

'Was.'

'Wasn't.'

'Was.'

The tins and rocks started flying again so the officer crawled in under the joists with Scotty Pullit, Lois and Bobby Pickett and their comrades.

As daylight dimmed, dinnertime was declared and the new man in town boarded the bus out to Fart Hill with some of the locals. The opposing side stayed in town, huddling in one of the new houses near the general store.

On the short drive out to Fart Hill, newspaper pages blowing around in the breezy air, the welfare officer asked why everyone was dressed as medieval serfs, but had his head almost bitten off. 'We're not serfs!'

They could not get the boy to speak, so Felicity Joy and Irma Almanac fed Joe, showed him his bed, next to Flick's, and when his little chin started to pucker and his eyes filled with tears, they told him he would see his mother again 'soon'. The wide-open spaces, the lack of streetlights and trams worried him a little, so Felicity took him to the shed and William started up the tractor for him. He clapped his little hands and jumped up and down in his bib and brace shorts, laughing. William sat him in the tractor seat and he remained there, happily, until the bus from town arrived. Young Joe turned his big blue eyes to the bus, his face a mask of anticipation. William and Felicity assumed he was looking for his mother. When instead the officer alighted, Joe flinched and climbed back to Felicity, digging his soft little fingernails into her. William suggested she keep the boy out of sight.

Before dinner, the officer approached Irma Almanac, who was chopping vegetables. 'I need to see Marigold Pettyman,' he said.

Irma pointed the knife at him. 'You leave that child alone. And you leave Marigold alone, she's had enough of you men, child-stealers and bullies . . . we all have.'

At dinner, the child still did not appear and the welfare officer observed that most of the men were injured, their thumbnails blackened and fingers scabbed by small building mishaps. Clearly incompetent. He looked aghast at his slimy grey pork chop and asked if there was anything else to eat.

'Off you go to the kitchen and ask,' said a common woman called Faith.

The welfare officer took his meal back to Irma Almanac and asked for an egg on toast. His meal was tipped into the pig food bucket and he was told the kitchen was closed. He returned and complained but was told no one had any say unless they'd lived in Dungatar for over twenty-five years. He sat forlornly while everyone else sawed away at their pork chop and mashed potato.

At the head of head table, Gertrude rang her little bell and the dining room fell silent. 'Who owns the child?'

William said, 'A nurse dropped him off. He's a relative of Marigold's, and his name's Joe.'

Lois pointed to the welfare officer. 'The kid's got something to do with him but the nurse said he was a horrible man and that we should give him back to his mother when she comes.'

'OVER MY DEAD BODY,' howled the welfare officer, but was reminded he was not permitted to speak.

'Who is his mother?'

'You told me I wasn't allowed to speak.'

'If you tell us who his mother is we will allow you to eat breakfast.'

'His mother and her friend, an actress, are bad people. They ruined my reputation. Her name is Myrtle Dunnage.'

Some rolled their eyes and nodded, others looked shocked, most looked at their paint-splattered costumes.

'You're not the only thing she's ruined,' said Faith.

'She really is coming back?' Gertrude asked, breathlessly, and looked to the mantelpiece and visualised gleaming new trophy cups – Best Actress, Best Production, Best Costume.

'You from the arson department?' Purl asked. 'Well, you're in luck, apparently she's going to burn the town down again.'

'We'll shackle her to my sewing machines,' Gertrude said.

William said smugly, 'I said we should have built the fire station, didn't I?'

The next morning, the locals rose early. It was a cold June morning with frost on the grass and thin clouds above. The ladies on breakfast duty, Irma, Purl and Faith, sat the small boy on the potty by the warm stove and dressed him snugly and fed him porridge and egg, and he said, 'Wed toes, pees,' and so they gave him strawberry jam toast. Irma helped Felicity fill her satchel with a brown paper bag of biscuits and dried fruit, some extra warm clothes, sandwiches, a bottle of milk, four boiled eggs, some pencils and a drawing book, and sent them off for a day of hide and seek.

'Your mother knows you're here,' they consoled, but they saw the child as bait.

The people queued for breakfast and then boarded the bus to town. William noted the new man had not fronted and decided he could not stay at Windswept Crest again. He wasn't pulling his weight, and Tilly Dunnage's toddler clearly didn't like the man. Felicity dragged her new best friend in a billy cart to the henhouse to collect eggs, then to the vegetable patch, where they ate gritty carrots, and when the officer emerged from his bunk in the old meat safe, Felicity Joy climbed with the boy to the top of the spindly ladder and vanished across the bright red verandah roof of Fart Hill homestead with the fat satchel and her binoculars. They watched the locals shoot off in all directions when the daily bus roared through, and as it vanished into the horizon, the New Dungatarians resumed lobbing missiles at each other.

The welfare officer found he was last to breakfast. All that remained was cereal. While Mrs Almanac sliced a dead piglet apart on the kitchen table, the officer scooped his meagre breakfast greedily. When he got to the shallow milky pond at the bottom of his bowl, small black grains of mice shit appeared with the undissolved sugar.

The closer the red car got to Dungatar, the more intensely the three people in the Fiat felt. The sergeant was fearful, yet excited. Mae's anger grew, but she kept her eyes firmly on the road ahead and the speedometer, and calmed herself. Tilly had long ago cast aside *The Crucible*, for she knew the story already. She was quietly resolved. She had survived these Dungatar creatures before; this was her chance to overcome. Three miles out, blurry buildings came into focus – The Hill, the tall round water tower and the silo, a solid dark testament to Teddy McSwiney.

'This place . . . the pain,' Mae muttered, and Tilly replied, 'Pain will no longer be our curse. It is our revenge and our reason.'

'Seems fair,' said Mae, but the sergeant cautioned, 'Softly . . . we are here only to get our boy.'

At the edge of the town they passed a small mountain of charred timber, charcoal furniture, springs and metal frames, naked couches, beds and gutted refrigerators. Apart from the yellow maze of creamy new timber structures, the landscape remained darkened. One or two houses boasted neat earth-coloured chimneys, and there were green blooms bursting from the trees and along the creek.

The sergeant drove straight up to Tilly's old home and parked beside her chimney, tall and strong, its long thin shadow reaching across the brand-new township to the silo. As the sun lowered in the sky a chill settled between the new walls of Molly's ruined dwelling. It was apparent that someone was living there. The contents of a makeshift cupboard were militarily precise, the walls immaculate and the floor scrubbed. A kettle sat by the hob and Molly's charred hip flask rested on a crossbeam. They scrutinised the town below. It was perfectly static save for newspaper pages swirling. There was no sign of a small child.

Mae pointed. 'I'd say he'd be out there.'

'Yes,' said Tilly. The three people ignored the silo and focused beyond the new buildings to the red roof of Fart Hill, the afternoon sun a spotlight on the house in wheat stubble, the purpling sky around it endless.

Tilly was actually a little moved by the familiar view that she and Molly shared and a sadness washed through her, and then a familiar inner fire ignited and she wanted to run, scream, smash the place down. She picked up a burned and rusted golf club (a seven wood) lying in the vegetable garden, which she noted had been weeded.

'There's someone living there, too,' said Mae, and pointed to the smoke wafting from a campfire in the remnants of Mae's happy family camp, now just roly-poly metal knots from caravans and sheds, and the skeletal remains of Teddy's caravan.

They drove down The Hill and Mae kicked through the scraps of her old patch, her face set with disgust. An empty tin of vegetables sat with an open tin of spam on the stone beside the camp pot, and in the burnt-out railway carriage a figure was curled in the mesh base of what was once Mae and Edward's bed.

She looked down at Elsbeth Beaumont, an old woman, sleeping open-mouthed and reeking of alcohol, clutching a piece of four-by-two.

'You're not Goldilocks, are you?'

Mae crept away.

The sergeant and Tilly had folded down the roof of the Balilla and were settled and waiting.

They drove straight down the main street, past the gawping locals gathered on Pratts' verandah waiting for the bus to take them to Fart Hill. The sergeant kept his eyes on the road ahead and Mae waved like the new Queen Elizabeth. Tilly sat, her fighting bandana loud and her dark glasses huge, her lipstick perfect and her arm draped casually along the edge of the convertible. In her free hand, she held the golf club.

Joe was first to spot the red Fiat coming. He pointed his chubby finger and said, 'Mummm,' and Felicity Joy gathered him to her and waited to see this evil woman Myrtle Dunnage, murderess, arsoness and bastard. What was clear was that, like Felicity Joy, this baby boy liked his mother, though no one else seemed to.

'Here she comes.'

The boy sitting between her knees stayed very still, his eyes on the little red car. 'Dar,' he said, and smiled at Felicity.

'They're coming,' Irma Almanac cried, and turned her wheelchair to the actors and gardeners and chicken stranglers and kindling collectors and cleaners, all running to see the people in the red car. They stood guard before the house. Gertrude arrived and stood front and centre. She was wearing a new frock from Myer that she felt reflected her station as mayor's wife and respected thespian.

It was like a re-run of an old film, the sergeant getting out of a car, meekly authoritative, but his policeman blue was gone and he was dressed in a driving suit, tweed calf-length pants and matching jacket with many pockets. Mae was attired in the flounced muu-muu she always wore. But it was evil Tilly Dunnage they wanted to see, and there she was, confronting, very present, beautiful and exotic. Without even glancing at them, she tightened the red scarf around her head, strode off towards the machinery shed in her cuffed men's trousers, swinging a golf club, to search for her boy.

'Hello,' said William, loudly, 'what can we do for you?' He ushered the sergeant back towards the car, and whispered, 'It's not safe here.'

Mae barged through the crowd into the house and Gertrude circled the Balilla, hoping to see a sewing machine, perhaps some cloth bolts or packages. She asked the sergeant, 'Why are you back?'

'We missed you?' he suggested.

Tilly combed through the outbuildings and though she did not find the boy, she found a small excavation site in the rose garden and an ancient toy tip truck loaded and ready to go. She wandered towards the back door, and then she heard him – 'Mummy,' – and looked up. Felicity pointed to the insubstantial timber ladder leaning against the house.

Tilly climbed and tiptoed across the flimsy verandah roof, following a beam.

The sergeant followed the locals and found Mae in the kitchen, where, wielding a bloodied kitchen knife, she had the welfare officer backed against the wall. The decapitated head of a piglet rested on the table.

'They won't give me Joe.'

'He's with his mother,' said the sergeant, and pointed to the ceiling.

For one moment, Mae saw Teddy and Tilly, two silhouettes on a corrugated silver roof under a velvet black sky shot with starshine, and a cold, white moon. Mae sliced the air with the knife, and the locals moved back a little.

High above them, Joe was in his mother's arms leaning against the chimney, warmed by the wood stove. Tilly studied her son. He was perfectly sound, his fat little feet warm in his boots and his soft arms firmly around her neck. He listened to the conversation Tilly was having with Felicity Joy about her adventures with Joe over the last couple of days.

The welfare officer, his arms raised in surrender again, said to those gathered in the kitchen, 'The innocent boy belongs to the murderess who burned this town down and she's also a bigamist – I am here to rescue him.'

'So you keep saying,' said Gertrude, 'but we'll keep Tilly Dunnage captive until she pays us back for burning down our town. We need costumes for *King Lear*.'

'And a new outfit each would go some way to repairing the damage and loss,' added Faith.

Gertrude assured the officer, 'She won't be allowed matches or flames of any kind.'

'I'll go fetch them,' said Bobby Pickett, and lumbered outside.

'Don't frighten her,' Mae called, but the sergeant said, 'Softly, Mae . . .'

He then told the people in the kitchen that no matter what Tilly Dunnage supposedly owed the people of Dungatar, they had no right to kidnap her child. 'And anyway, if you'd paid your house insurance you'd have your lives back.'

'Have we paid this time?' Faith asked, and they looked at each other.

'Elsbeth said she'd paid,' Purl offered, a little doubtfully.

'Anyway,' Faith sniped, 'Tilly Dunnage killed your son, Mae McSwiney!'

The hair on the back of Mae's neck stood on end. 'You killed my son, you people here in this room. Ask yourselves the reason you're bereft and destitute and standing in Elsbeth Beaumont's kitchen dressed in eighteenth-century rags.'

The people in the kitchen were self-conscious and perplexed. Finally, Lois ventured, 'Because they're the only clothes we've got?'

The welfare officer whispered, 'I am surrounded by murdering women,' and Mae turned the blade to him. He raised his arms higher.

Outside, Bobby Pickett started to climb, cautiously, for he was a big man and Felicity's ladder was flimsy. When he was almost at the top, he paused, careful not to look down.

At the sight of him, Tilly passed Joe to Felicity and picked up the golf club, but Felicity Joy said, 'Just wait,' and the top ladder rung gave way and Bobby sank from sight, the rungs snapping under his thin leather slippers and his hands gathering splinters on the slide down.

In the kitchen, Mae tapped the welfare officer's coat with the knife. 'You have no right to claim my grandson. I was in the courtroom, I heard what the magistrate said.'

The welfare officer relented a little and confessed the baby had been awarded to his step-grandmother, but it was a temporary arrangement and he was merely there to oversee the child's care.

Mae cried, 'You can't let Marigold have our baby, she'll drug him. I'm his real grandmother.'

All around the room, pennies dropped.

'That Teddy's boy?'

'He's the son of a star full-forward?'

'That baby's got potential,' Fred said.

'An athlete.' Reginald gathered the men to him. 'Let Marigold keep the kid, we'll start training him up when he's five, what do you say?'

Gertrude stamped her foot. 'No one can have the child until Tilly Dunnage has paid!'

'I will see he is placed safely, as intended, otherwise I will alert the authorities,' said the welfare officer.

The locals saw that this interloper was a threat to their standing in the football world, and therefore their general contentment, and they pressed towards him, furious.

The sergeant saw his opportunity and announced, 'The welfare officer is a peeping Tom.'

'That's a lie.' He lowered his arms.

'It's true,' said Mae, boiling with rage. 'You are no better than these people in this room, you hypocrite. But you can't keep anything secret here. Everybody knows everything about everyone but no one ever tells because then someone else'll tell their secret to the world, or the AUTHORITIES. You don't matter, officer, it's open slather on outcasts.'

The sergeant smoothed the newspaper clippings all over the kitchen table and everyone saw the welfare officer at Nita Orland's window, his eyes lit red in the glare of the camera flash, his hands clawed.

'That's not me,' cried the officer. 'That's my brother.'

Sergeant Farrat reached into the bundle of photographs that Arlen had supplied and started distributing them to everyone in the kitchen, one shiny pornographic print each, of the officer looking into a window where a very beautiful woman sat in a skimpy dress holding a cat and a glass of beer.

'That woman is just an actress!' he snarled, and Gertrude reached up and slapped his face.

'HOW DARE YOU!'

The welfare officer was shocked, and even more so when Faith grabbed the pig knife from Mae and ran at him, 'I'm with Lady Macbeth! Out, damned pervert!'

'This place is a cult! You're growing marijuana and running an illegal still on the creek bank.'

'The marijuana is medicinal,' said Irma, and slammed her biscuit tin against the welfare officer's grazed knee.

'I will report you all to the necessary authorities. This is no place for those children.'

The appalled Shakespearean actors took up kitchen implements and ushered the welfare officer towards the door.

'Do not threaten us,' said Reginald, and Mae warned, 'People in this town have died for less.'

Up on the roof, Joe and his mother clung to each other, Felicity pressed against them, Tilly's eyes on the cemetery beyond New Dungatar. She recalled Pablo coming to her, and as he'd moved back into the light, he'd said, 'Mother.' She yearned to see Molly and tell her what she had failed to say, and what she now knew, and she felt that at some point, Molly had probably felt the same about her own dead father, and that Molly probably knew Tilly would feel as she had. If she could just burrow down through the dirt to her mother and say, 'Because of you, because we had time together here in Dungatar, I am all right.'

From below, the welfare officer, called, 'Do not think you will be free of me, Myrtle Dunnage. I will ruin you and your smutty friends, I know you're not what you appear to be.'

'You're wrong,' she called, watching the officer limp across the orange plains turning bleak at dusk as the newly installed sunset-lit windows of Dungatar vanished in the darkness.

'What have you got in your satchel, Flick?'

'Two sandwiches, two hard-boiled eggs, some dried fruit, some water, lead pencils and a colouring book.'

'Can I have a pencil and some paper, please?'

'What colour?'

'Black, if you've got it, or brown.'

Felicity found her pencil and book.

'If I write a letter, will you ask your father to take it to the cemetery and read it out to my mother?'

'Mad Molly?'

'Yes.'

'Just tell me, I'll remember.'

'Please tell her that I came back, again, and that Joe is here too.

Tell her what he looks like, that he is like his father.' She cried a little and waited, Felicity Joy writing across the page, her letters big, some back to front or upside down.

'Say that Joe is observant and curious and interested, but he's also like his grandfather, Edward, a quiet little boy, a bit solitary . . . actually, I'll write all that, your dad will read it out.'

She wrote that they were happy and secure, and knew what she wanted to do and she understood what had happened to them both, and that she could now proceed, '. . . and because of you, my dear mother, I have true friends and I can live freely, and truthfully.'

Felicity put the drawing book in her satchel and buckled it shut and put her arms through the shoulder straps and leaned against the chimney.

Around the Fart Hill house, the Dungatarians milled, strange in their costumes, mad men and women, strong in their group.

'You burned our town down, Dunnybum, so we're going to take your son. We might even torture and starve you if we feel like it.'

Tilly raised an eyebrow at Lois's strong words. She had assumed Lois Pickett would remain benign and laughable her entire life, but she was truly one of them now. They had not changed from school days, the group had always bayed up at her, cornered her, chased her, but they were just bullies who had been bullied.

Gertrude called, 'We think we can come to an arrangement. You can make everything up to us if you stay a while.'

'I have done nothing wrong. You did it to yourselves.'

'You caused the death of our star full-forward,' said Fred. 'So just give us the boy, and through him we'll honour Teddy.'

'My son was far more, far better than your ruddy football game,' shot back Mae. 'And my grandson isn't going to play any of your games. You people always treated us badly.'

'We didn't do nuffink,' said Lois.

'But you could have,' said the sergeant. 'You could have stopped it.'

'What?'

'Your hypocrisy, prejudices and lies, and you can't see what you are . . . that's the biggest tragedy.'

'We can easily get you down,' said Reginald, his hand wavering around where his scabbard had once hung from his butcher's belt.

Faith said, 'You can't have that child back, we'll give him to the arson man or welfare officer or whoever he is. You're not a fit mother.'

And Purl added, 'Like Molly, she wasn't either.'

But Irma Almanac said, 'What would you two faithless strumpets know about being mothers, or being good *people*, for that matter?'

Tilly whispered, 'I will not let anyone hurt you, Felicity, and I will not hurt you.' She pulled the girl to her and called down, 'Shall I prove to you that I am not a cursed murderess?'

The locals mingled, consulting each other; what if she did, what if she dived off with the children? They argued, but ultimately declared it cold, dark, and that tomorrow was another day. 'Let her stay up there all night.'

Sergeant Farrat called, as menacingly as he could, 'I want you all to know that I'll patrol tonight and no one will go anywhere near Tilly Dunnage nor will anyone try to goad her down.' He could not let them up there, he would not relive that terrible night, another fall, another tragedy.

'I will stay with the sergeant,' said William, using his deepest voice. 'Are you warm enough, Felicity Joy?'

Felicity said, 'I'm good, Dad. It's pretty up here.' She pointed to the sparkling night sky.

The men stayed, but the women moved inside, grumbling. Tilly snuggled against the chimney with Felicity Joy and Joe.

She told stories as the house below ceased to thrum and everything fell silent.

Felicity whispered, 'If they come up in the night they'll fall through the roof, it's all rusty.'

As the life of night creatures commenced, the men below snored and Tilly dozed, her sleeping charges close.

While Marigold had been out collecting wood, she came to a decision. She would paint her house entirely white; white walls, inside and out, white floorboards, white roof. She spent time scraping the dirt out of each nail hole, then dusted every wall inside and out, and wiped them down. Then she swept and scrubbed the floor, and it was while she was spreading a newspaper pathway across her immaculate floor that she saw the article about the welfare officer. And that's why, when the perverted peeping Tom appeared from behind the chimney, the firelight flickering across his tall presence, Marigold had a fearful sense of déjà vu. Uninvited, the welfare officer walked across Marigold's floor in his dusty shoes. Then he plonked his great bottom on her polished hearth.

'Good evening, Mrs Pettyman.'

Marigold sat on her haunches, the newspaper article very much on her mind.

'Your step-grandson is in danger, he needs your help. I can take you to him.'

'You can't be here,' she said, quietly.

'There's no accommodation in this town. In the morning we'll go and get your grandson. I'll just stay by the fire, you can sleep, you won't even know I'm here.'

'This is my house.' She was alone in it, on her knees on the floor with just a dust brush for protection. The fellow leaned his filthy elbow on the new table.

'You can sleep, I won't wake you.'

Evan used to give her tonic: she would wake in the morning as if from death, feeling something irksome had happened to her, Evan snoring, his pink hairy back to her.

'I see,' she said. 'Would you mind passing me my handbag?'

'Don't run away. Myrtle Dunnage has done something evil to me too, so you and I will take the boy from her. You will come with me tomorrow to get him, or I'll have you committed again. I can do that. Everyone knows you're unstable, drug dependent and neurotic, the doctor knows all about you!'

'Certifiable . . .' she said, fondly, and he gave her the handbag.

It was exactly how she remembered it: Evan sneering, 'Why don't you fall down, Marigold, faint, have one of your headache fits – you're insane.' She felt ambushed, like she had when her husband's sprog suddenly ran at her, his head down like a bull charging, and knocked her to the floor. He had learned much from his father. Little Myrtle had decided not to die; she stepped to the side and the boy ran head first into the hard brick wall and crumpled onto the hot dry grass. It occurred to Marigold that Evan had sent poor Molly Dunnage mad too, said the same things to her, but Molly could not save herself, she had to wait for her little girl to come home.

Kneeling before the welfare officer, Marigold opened her handbag. The officer saw something catch the firelight as she reached behind him, then he felt the razor-sharp carving knife slice his calcaneal tendons. As they snapped, they made a sound like a wooden lid slamming shut, and the officer landed on Marigold's clean timber floor, trumpeting like a tortured elephant, his Achilles tendons coiling behind his knee joints.

'This is very wrong,' he bellowed. 'Please, I'll bleed to death.'

Marigold looked at him twitching, smearing a red puddle across her lovely new floor, his shins like loose thread at the ends of his knees. She wiped the knife on her dress, then dropped it back into her handbag.

'Please,' he cried again. 'I'll bleed to death.'

'Eventually,' she said, and poured herself a glass of Scotty Pullit's watermelon firewater.

Mae drove to the cemetery by the banks of the beautiful creek, where she and her children had enjoyed so many playful, happy times, where they'd fished and canoed and caught yabbies and baked spuds and damper, and scraped their first leech from their soft little bodies. She built a fire and put the billy on to boil, rolled out her sleeping bag, then took her pannikin of hot water and sat on Teddy's grave. 'My beautiful boy,' she said, wiping the dust from his headstone with her hem. 'I'll tell you a story,' and she told the story of Joel Edward Dunnage, 'bright sprite, and greatest gift since you,' and she explained why Tilly was here, back in Dungatar, and that this would be her final battle. 'She has us now, and Joe, our angel boy with a considered temperament, and he will live a life of love and truth, we'll make sure of that, my son, even if it kills us.' She told him that Edward was still Edward, though a little further removed from everyone since he'd lost his first-born son, and that Elizabeth had a fiancé and Mary was pregnant and that Margaret looked set to be a spinster and that Barney had a job as a doorman and Charlie sold papers and the kids hated school but she was sure Charlotte would go to university and Victoria wanted to be a doctor. And then she cried that she missed him. 'It's like being thirsty all the time.'

As the sergeant slept soundly on the narrow canvas in his sleeping bag, his few remaining locks of hair taped in place, Gertrude dragged out a director's chair and joined her husband. 'I'm not like them, am I, William.'

It was a statement rather than a question.

'Gert, I mean, Trudy, you've adapted to your new role, you've battled these Dungatar people at their own game but you haven't won the war. People end up good only if they learn to be better. To rise, or perhaps to win, you need to know both yourself and the enemy.' He looked to the house and all the people in it and said, 'Some people don't have the capacity.'

She wasn't entirely sure what he meant but thanked him for his honesty, almost adding that she didn't deserve him, but she actually did deserve to be Trudy Beaumont. 'I will try to be better, for you. More like a mayor's wife.'

He would have preferred it if she'd said she'd like to be a better person, but for the time being it was the house and taunting his mother she liked best. They would have more children, hopefully, and they would be as wise and kind as Flick, and she would live the life she wanted and be happier, and he would run the farm, all by himself. Trudy, unlike his mother, had no opinion whatsoever on anything to do with farming. He smiled, and put his arm around his sumptuous wife.

At some point in the night, Tilly Dunnage woke to possums thumping around in the attic, and looked across the plains to Dungatar, invisible in the pitch black. A faint glow burned on the top of The Hill. She was born in that house; Mae McSwiney had helped deliver her. Dungatar was the place of firsts, for little Myrtle. But now there was Arlen, a new business, friends and family life waiting for her. When she'd first come back from Europe she'd run into Mae at the library corner. 'It's better to keep to yourself around here,' said Mae. 'Nothing ever really changes, *Myrtle*.'

# Chapter 33

THE COCKATOOS AND corellas and galahs, loud and rude, woke Mae. She stoked her little fire and boiled the billy and this time, it was to Molly's mound of dried, cracked earth that she went with her pannikin. She considered the thriving Scotch thistle and wild oats sheltering the graves, and plugged a few dandelions and grass fronds around the headstone – Molly Dunnage, Dearly Loved. She addressed her speech to Molly and all the spirits around, taking up the story where Molly left off. 'So, your daughter is married to Sergeant Farrat, happily; it is a *mariage blanc*, for convenience, and they are starting a small business to make practical, sensible clothes, naturally they're stylish, but they're designed to make people more who they are, better at what they do. They are "clothes that don't disguise or lie, clothes that reflect the truth about the wearer", according to the sarge.'

She turned and said to the residents, 'It'll work, they'll sell. Tilly is getting more like you, but your daughter and our grandson are able to make good the life you gave them, Molly. They will live lives that honour you, lives that confound and defy the tragedies heaped upon you. They have all manner of love in their life now.'

She chucked the tepid dregs of her gritty creek water away and continued, speaking up, 'Our boy Joe might want to come back here one day, and he can, because those hookworms who are alive now will be out here. Sorry to point that out to you. But, I must also point out, and you won't be surprised to hear this, Molly, that the people of Dungatar have not learned their lesson. So we'll take them on one last time, and end the pain.'

In the mesh base of Mae and Edward McSwiney's marital bed, Elsbeth Beaumont stirred. She sat up, gingerly, peeling away the eiderdown, taking in the ruin around her. How had it all come to this? Had she been too harsh on William as a boy, was she being punished for sending him to the linen cupboard? Whatever had occurred, it can't have been her fault. She had been a sound example to him, and everyone agreed everything was the fault of Molly Dunnage.

There was no smoke from a fire up on The Hill, so no point going up there to ask for a cup of tea. Elsbeth set out to wash, and with her cup in her hand, she headed towards the bend in the creek where the still waited.

Her back and legs stiff and hurting, Tilly watched the stars fade and the sky turn grey above the frosty black earth, her magenta scarf low over her ears and the children huddled in the curve of her body, as if in her womb, their blanket stiff with cold. She wondered if she should just flee. She could climb down with Joe, wake her husband and run to Mae, yet there was the matter of the sour people of Dungatar. And though she was fearful for her boy and the small girl stirring against her, in light of what the people of Dungatar had done, what they had not done, they mustn't be abandoned, yet.

The house stirred and the tattered people emerged and surrounded the building, their faces angled up to her: Fred, Purl, Lois and Bobby, his feet swollen and his hands bandaged. Septimus in his hard hat, Miss Dimm behind her thick glasses, and Reginald and flashy Faith, William and Gertrude in their pyjamas and dressing-gowns. The opposing faction – Scotty, Marigold, Muriel, Alvin and others – dribbled in from the town across the crop stubble to unite with their foes against the common enemy. They all carried weapons – pitchforks and shovels and chains, padlocks and ropes, swords and medieval axes and machetes, and in their grubby costumes looked like people who had stood too close at a witch's pyre.

Gertrude cried up to Tilly, 'I want my child.'

Tilly perched at the edge of the roof, mindful of the flimsy verandah, an infant either side of her. 'I want mine too.'

'You made us all homeless and penniless,' said Faith.

She shrugged. 'Sometimes things just don't *seem* fair.'

Fred stepped forward and spoke on behalf of the people. 'We at the Dungatar Football Club would like to offer your boy a good future, a healthy sporting life. So, you can either choose to stay here and make dresses, or we will come up there and drag you down. We're united in this cause.'

They nodded, agreed, and Marigold said, 'What cause?'

The people noted that she had spilled red paint all over her nice new Melbourne outfit.

'Revenge,' someone said, while someone else disagreed, 'We want nice new clothes.' Others said the cause was football, some said winning the eisteddfod.

Purl asked if anyone had thought about how they would keep Tilly Dunnage there, and what to do with the sergeant and Mae.

'We'll discuss that over breakfast,' said Lois, and William called, 'No you won't, you'll argue and nothing will happen.'

Muriel Pratt said, 'We are united in Hell, because of her.'

'No,' said the sergeant. 'Your lives are hell because of the lies Evan Pettyman told. But the lies are dead, they died when Marigold killed Evan – he's gone, so there's nothing to fear, you're free to embrace truthful futures. You've all learned what it's like to be cast out. I don't see you tyrannising Marigold for defending herself, so why is her self-defence any different from Tilly's?'

They looked to Marigold again, perplexed by the red paint. It had completely ruined her nice new suit.

William tried a different tactic, appealing to their true natures. 'If it weren't for Tilly you'd all still be the same as you were five years ago. Stuck. Passive. Wearing drab clothes, no balls or concerts, no drama club or social club. You wouldn't be getting new homes!'

'We were on top of the ladder, then we lost our star full-forward.'

William's voice was full of despair. 'But *you* drove them to the top of the silo, don't you see? It was you!'

'Well,' said Gertrude, as if she'd found the perfect solution for everything, 'now we want Tilly to come down.'

'But only to make new bloody frocks!' The sergeant circled in front of them, his arms wide. 'And for what?'

William looked at his wife. 'Surely you see, Trudy, that we're trying to free you from yourselves?'

Gertrude pouted. 'But don't *you* see, William, dear, that if she comes down we can also retrieve our child.'

'And I really do need a new dress,' said Marigold, picking up her stiff skirt and letting it flap against her small thighs.

'That one looks like it's got blood all over it,' observed Muriel Pratt. 'Cut your finger, did you?'

'No,' she said, showing everyone her fingers, 'I fell and accidentally hurt the welfare officer.'

The sergeant looked aghast.

'As you say, it was self-defence,' said Marigold. 'He was a pervert.'

The crowd nodded in agreement. 'Child stealer, Peeping Tom,' they cried.

'Was?' The sergeant's hand went to his heart.

Then Gertrude said, 'By the way, where is Blind Beula?'

'She fell too.'

Tilly put her arm around Felicity Joy. 'Not everyone's like these people.'

Felicity Joy said, 'I'm not,' and handed Joe a boiled egg.

'Beckfast,' he said, and held his egg out to show the watching people.

Tilly had been like these children once, pure and malleable and innocent, and here she was, trapped again, the same old bloodthirsty crowd below. And she was still innocent.

The sergeant sighed. 'Marigold, I can't help you this time, I'm not a policeman anymore.'

'She's got lots of money,' said Gertrude. 'She can hire a lawyer.'

'I've got a new lawyer,' said Marigold, thrilled with herself. 'He's very good. Because of him I've got enough money to build a lovely new home, a whole town, if I want to.'

'You can also buy everyone new clothes,' said Tilly. 'None of us are coming down until you all apologise to me, admit you've been wrong and tell me why you've been wrong and why you ruined so many lives, including your own.'

'Fat chance,' said Lois, and Irma said, 'They'll never do that because then they'd have to agree with you.'

'"We are betrayed by what is false within",' Tilly cried.

Gertrude put her hand out to Felicity Joy. 'Come, child, come to Mummy.'

Felicity shook her head, 'You haven't learned your lesson.'

William smiled at his daughter, sitting up there on the roof swinging her legs and peeling herself a hard-boiled egg.

'We're not getting anywhere arguing,' said Septimus, and William cried, 'Hallelujah!' but the crowd, eager for action, rumbled and waved their weapons, and Alvin Pratt and Reginald placed a table beside the house and went for chairs to build a way to capture Tilly Dunnage.


Mae parked the Fiat outside Pratts and stood in the middle of the road, the sun still climbing in the east. The air smelled of dew on grass and cold and the buildings around her were brand-new and creamy. There was no sign of life anywhere. She wandered to the new hall which smelled of timber and sawdust. A box of coronation decorations waited by the stage, and as she walked across the new floor it gave under her feet. They had taken the care to build a sprung floor. The rejection and scorn from the past filled her. Disgusted, she bellowed, 'Think you're all going to do some dancing? Have another belle of the ball competition, you soulless ghouls?'

In anger, she kicked a bottle of linseed oil sitting by a newly hewn table and watched it spread across the special new dance floor towards the stacked tins of polish and paint. She danced over to them and opened one more, pouring it in big circles as she twirled around the hall, and as she went she kicked over more tins. Then she wandered outside and into Lois and Bobby Pickett's new house, where she opened a tin of paint and dribbled it out the door and across the dry grass to the crisp new building next door. Mae started to enjoy herself. She found a hammer and bashed a few tins open. All over brand-new Dungatar she went, bashing at paint tins and splashing colours up and down the fence lines and in and out of front doors, pink, green, white, blue and grey. She approached a tin of varnish as if it were the welfare officer, smashed it until it was a flat, crumpled thing in a pond of slime. She picked a half-gallon tin of furniture stain for Elsbeth Beaumont, and for Beula a bottle of turpentine, and as she hammered and smashed she called their names, 'Marigold, you are just shellac!' She raised her hammer high and brought it down again and again, calling the cans of paint thinner and floor varnish Muriel and Elsbeth and Lois and Faith and Purl and Fred, battering away at the tins until they caved and bled, and then she walked away, toxic fluids soaking into driveways and seeping across lounge-room floors.

Wet with paint, her shoes soaked with spirits and thinners, she went to the car, raised the rainbow-coloured hammer, and swore, words a grandmother should never say – but they were words for the cruelty, discriminations and injustices heaped on her, for her lost son, and on Teddy's girlfriend and only child. To Mae, Joel Edward represented Teddy's future, and Mary's baby deserved a cousin.

Mae lit a match and chucked it into Pratts Store, revved the little Fiat and fishtailed off, its red nose arrowed towards the last building, the faded posh house on the rise. As she bumped over the grate under the grand Windswept Crest sign, the paint inside Pratts Store boiled and spat, flames eating it. Mae saw Tilly, Joe and Felicity Joy sitting together along the roof, below them, the townsfolk rattling their pitchforks and shovels, sabres, swords and medieval axes and machetes.

Reginald Blood, standing on a chair on top of a table, saw the red car coming and reached to haul himself up to the roof. The crowd scattered, the car plunged into the table beneath Reginald and he cartwheeled through space, landing beside the defunct water feature. Tilly, Joe and Felicity looked down into the soft interior of the car. Joe waved at his multicoloured grandma. She waved back and sprang out of the car, holding the hammer high, the air around her shimmering with accelerant fumes. Fred stepped forward, so she whacked his knee with the hammer and he folded. She stood with the sergeant, Tilly above her.

'Right, you lot,' Mae cried. 'You tried to take Barney, and you took Teddy. You will not take Joe. And you will not have Tilly Dunnage. You people have not admitted anything, so there's nothing for it but to try one more time to make you see what you are.'

The people of Dungatar rattled their chains and raised their weapons, calling, 'She cursed us, she is responsible for what happened.'

'No,' said Tilly, 'you are responsible for what I did.'

Mae stepped closer to the car, glancing towards the town, and Tilly followed her gaze. Across the heads of the Dungatarians, smoke, speckled with embers, billowed. Soon ash would start falling and the smell of their burning town would envelop them. She smiled, joyous.

The sergeant, too, saw the flames licking above the town and began to panic. He'd promised Julie he'd return safely. He side-stepped discreetly to the car.

In the distance, unopened paint tins started to explode, a faint *phutt* coming to them from far away. The locals, waving smoke away, squabbled about what to do next and who would traverse the flimsy roof to seize Dunnybum and her bastard kid. Ash started feathering down and black smoke closed out the day.

Joe turned his eyes to the town, a look of wonderment on his face. He pointed – 'Pretty,' – and the locals turned to see. Great red flames shot high, black smoke and embers ballooned. Dumbfounded, the locals started to move towards the fire. Then they started bawling, crying out and running through the stubble.

William climbed to the bonnet of the car and Felicity fell into his arms. He took Joe, and held a hand out for Tilly.

Gertrude studied the approaching fire, then the house, and looked down at her new pretty dressing-gown. William said, 'We're fully insured,' and walked towards the creek, his arm around her, his daughter on his shoulders. Then he remembered his mother, but his mother would survive, she would make sure of it.

The sergeant started the car, Mae beside him and Tilly in the back with their boy. He despaired, 'Are we destined to spend our lives as fugitives?'

Mae shrugged. 'The mayor's on our side.'

'We'll tell the authorities about the welfare officer, where to search for his remains,' said Tilly.

The fire, a mile wide, swallowed the town, and the people charged towards it, as one. The little red car overtook the running people, and Tilly called, 'Don't! Don't run into the fire!' But they ran on, and just as the flames reached the edge of William's wheat stubble, they grew tired, faltered, and petered out, breathless and bent, holding their aching sides. The petrol bowsers at Pratts exploded, sending bright sparkling missiles into the smoky sky, and Joe smiled and clapped.

Mae called, 'We'll pop back in a couple of years, see how the rebuild's coming along.'

The fire found fresh fuel in the dry straw and it raced. The locals turned and blundered back, but the fire was faster than the people of Dungatar and flames licked their coat hems and burned the soles of their eighteenth-century slippers. Some tripped and fell.

The sergeant steered the little Fiat off over the plains. 'Surely they won't rebuild?'

William and Gertrude stood under a lovely river red gum and watched the great Dungatar bonfire, awestruck at how rapidly it chewed through the stubble towards the homestead, aghast when the frantic locals started to disappear into the wall of flames and smoke, their cries cut short as their lungs filled with scorching air.

Above the inferno, on top of The Hill, the chimney stood triumphant, a victory finger casting a long dark arrow across the burning landscape.

THE END

# Acknowledgements

I greatly appreciate the faith and careful guidance of Mathilda Imlah, Emma Schwarcz, Clare Keighery, Brianne Collins, and the support shown by all at Pan Macmillan.

Also, thanks to my readers Morgan McLay, Terry, Sue Maslin and Myfanwy Jones.

I am grateful for invaluable conversations I had many years ago with two excellent seamstresses, both experts from the Paris end of Collins Street, Mrs Marjorie 'Midge' Ross and Heather Lavender.

Special thanks to Billy Charles Horneman and Imogen McLay.

*The Dressmaker* and all that followed is because of my lovely mum, Dorothy, also an excellent seamstress.